ONE BIG
HAPPY
FAMILY

ALSO BY JAMIE DAY

The Block Party

ONE BIG HAPPY FAMILY

JAMIE DAY

ST. MARTIN'S PRESS

New York

First published in the United States by St. Martin's Press, an imprint of St. Martin's Publishing Group

ONE BIG HAPPY FAMILY. Copyright © 2024 by J.D. Publications LLC. All rights reserved. Printed in the United States of America. For information, address St. Martin's Publishing Group, 120 Broadway, New York, NY 10271.

Designed by Donna Sinisgalli Noetzel

www.stmartins.com

The Library of Congress Cataloging-in-Publication Data is available upon request.

ISBN 978-1-250-28320-7 (hardcover)
ISBN 978-1-250-36105-9 (Canadian Edition)
ISBN 978-1-250-28327-6 (ebook)

Our books may be purchased in bulk for promotional, educational, or business use. Please contact your local bookseller or the Macmillan Corporate and Premium Sales Department at 1-800-221-7945, extension 5442, or by email at MacmillanSpecialMarkets@macmillan.com.

First Edition: 2024

10 9 8 7 6 5 4 3 2 1

For Erik and Val,

here's to your happily ever after

Part 1

THE PRECIPICE

Chapter 1

The power flickers on and off, as if the hotel is taking a dying gasp. I draw in a breath and hold it, but thankfully the lights come on as the wind dies down. It's cold comfort. In a matter of time, they'll go out again, and eventually they'll stay out. I'm standing in the alcove directly off our Great Room with my hands clenched into fists. The anticipation is killing me.

Driving rain pelts the exterior like thousands of fingers tapping against the roof and walls. A monster is knocking to get in. This particular monster has a name. The meteorologists call him Larry, the most powerful hurricane to ravage the coast of Maine since Gerda made landfall back in 1969. A large tree is blocking the steep road leading up to the Precipice Hotel. The road itself is a rolling river of mud, impassable on foot or by car. There is no way out. No place for me to go. But I can't stay here.

I scope out my surroundings, planning my escape route before the lights go out again. Sure enough, a fresh gust gradually crescendos into a loud roar. The hotel shakes, and just as I feared, everything goes dark. My breath catches in my throat as a band of fear pulls tight across my chest.

I turn around, taking a tentative step forward, trying to orient myself in this void. Memory is my guide. I've worked as a housekeeper here for the last two years. "Chambermaid" is my official title, which is super outdated, misogynistic, and way uncool, but so was my boss. I should know this place like the back of my hand, but anxiety seems to have short-circuited my brain.

My biggest problem is that this hotel is full of *stuff.* It's like an antique shop of countless treasures and curiosities, transformed into a funky travel destination in Nowhere, Maine.

If I have my bearings, the grand staircase in our Great Room is to the left, but that goes to the second floor, and I want to go out, not up. There's an exit through the foyer, and I inch my way toward it. I don't have much time.

I take several small, cautious steps, keeping both hands in front of me, using them like antennae to sense my surroundings. Outside, the wind continues to wail. In my whole life—all nineteen years of it— I've never heard such a terrible, bone-rattling sound. The gusts shake the walls of this sturdy structure in an unending shudder.

My breath sputters no matter how I try to calm myself. Just when I think I'm nearing the foyer, my foot connects hard with what I'm sure is a table leg. The contact makes a loud thud and I hear the sound of breaking glass when something (a tall vase, perhaps?) tumbles to the floor.

The crash reverberates, no doubt giving away my position. I go completely still, eyes pointlessly probing the inky gloom, ears fighting to pick up any noise other than the wind. Another fierce gust shakes the windows—and my nerves, with equal measure. Terrified, I can't move from where I stand.

Somewhere behind me, the three Bishop sisters are cloaked in this impenetrable darkness. Only one question remains: Which sister is coming to kill me?

Chapter 2

Wednesday, three days earlier

This room looks like a war zone. *My god. What the hell happened here?*

Beer and wine bottles litter the floor. A chair has toppled over, probably due to the weight of wet towels someone thoughtlessly draped across the back.

Every food group from the gas station convenience store is well represented. We've got your basic snack cakes—Twinkies and Devil Dogs. There's the chip family of snacks, several packages of Cheetos, Doritos, and Who-Would-Eat-Those. Crumbs are scattered across the bedspread as if put there to feed the birds.

Clothes carpet the floor, making it impossible to tell what's clean and dirty. I see a few half-empty Gatorade bottles, likely mixed with vodka. And that's the stuff that's *easy* to clean.

When I took this job, George Bishop, the former owner (former because he's dead), didn't explain that I'd have to deal with the worst waste humanity had to offer. But here I am. Ready to deal.

I go to my cart, which I've parked in the hallway. It's packed with all the stuff you'd expect to find on a maid's cart—sheets, towels, sanitizer, window cleaner, toilet bowl cleaner, your basic dusting and polishing cloths, etc., etc. But what I need for this room is a hazmat suit. I text Rodrigo. He's the front desk manager and my only friend at work— really one of my only friends in town.

OMG the Magnolia Room. Come. You won't believe your eyes.

I can't believe my nose, either. I've been to bus stations that smelled better.

I should be used to it by now. I've done this job long enough. In my time working at the Precipice Hotel (so named for its precarious perch at the edge of Gull Hill, overlooking the ocean in Jonesport, Maine), I've learned to deal with the indignities that come with being a hotel maid.

The guests, like any animal, always leave a trail, but some are worse than others. I've cleaned up blood, puke, spit . . . and yeah, semen. We call condoms swimming in the toilet bowl "whitefish," and I've seen my fair share.

I'm good at my job. I make rooms look like they've never been touched. I'm like a CSI investigator in reverse. I'm the one you pay to make the crime scene disappear.

Best part of my job is the short commute to work. I actually live at the hotel, in a little room off the kitchen that was once a utility closet or pantry. There's about as much privacy as there is space, but I can't beat the rent, which is free. I don't love sleeping under a cloud of bacon grease and sautéed onions, but you get what you pay for.

It's not all bad. My room is large enough to hold a bed, a few boxes, a bookcase, and a hissing, spitting old radiator.

At least I don't have to cook. That's not my thing. As long as I like what Olga, our chef, makes for the guests, I'm always well fed. I have everything I need to live a comfortable life here. I guess you could say I'm the only permanent guest of the Precipice Hotel.

George Bishop offered me these accommodations as part of my employment package. I was seventeen. I should have been more cautious, but I was naïve and desperate. Bad combo. I figured George was desperate as well. It's not easy getting reliable help, especially up here in Maine where the population is older and young people drop from the state census like leaves in autumn. It took me about six months to realize that George's offer of free room and board, plus my wages and tips, was little more than a trap.

This shouldn't be my life.

That's often my first thought as the workday begins. I'm not even twenty yet. My back shouldn't feel like a mule kicked it. My knees shouldn't creak like rusty hinges. My skin shouldn't look vampire white. My long brown hair and brown eyes should have a little shine. I should have moved away from this town by now, built a life where I could go to parties, meet a boy, maybe enroll in college. But my Nana Kelley needs me and I need her, so I'm stuck here cleaning up other people's messes—or in this case, disasters.

Rodrigo shows up a minute after getting my text. I haven't touched anything yet. I need to gather my resolve first.

"Oh my god, Charley . . . I'm so sorry."

Rodrigo places an arm around me like we're at the wake of a beloved relative. "I thought Larry wasn't coming until this weekend."

I roll my eyes at his lame attempt at humor. "Not funny, and besides, the weatherman keeps saying that Larry's gonna miss us."

"Tell that to our guests. Pretty much everyone has canceled."

"I sure wish *these* folks had," I say, shaking my head with disgust. "What do you know about them, anyway?" I can't mask my loathing.

"A couple from New York. I guess it's their twentieth wedding anniversary."

"That's about how long it's going to take me to clean this room."

I'm exaggerating, of course. It'll take no more than forty minutes from top to bottom, spick-and-span. I'm *that* good.

"Where are they now?"

There's a reason for my question, but Rodrigo doesn't know that.

"Downstairs, having breakfast," he says. "Olga is grumbling about them, too. Evidently, their eggs were *runny.*"

"Olga grumbles about everyone," I say, depositing a dustpan full of trash I've collected off the floor into the wastebasket on my cart.

"Do you want help?" Rodrigo asks.

"Yeah, call in the National Guard," I say.

Instead, Rodrigo sends me a dimpled smile. He's as swarthy and good-looking as his name sounds—dark hair, dark eyes, with a jawline chiseled from granite. *Well-groomed* doesn't do him justice. Even with a scattering of scruff, he looks aristocratic, as if he were a prince masquerading as a front desk manager. He's a few years older, and I definitely would have hooked up with him, or at least tried to, but I'm not really his type.

Too female.

Rodrigo has a big heart. He would have left this town ages ago if it weren't for his mother, whom he helps support financially because it's hard to earn a living at minimum wage—trust me, I know. Guess we have more in common than our place of employment.

After clearing away the wrappers and crumbs, I strip the bed, while Rodrigo sneers with contempt. "We should charge these guests with cruel and unusual punishment." He offers this assessment from the doorway, refusing to set foot inside. His work uniform is stain-free, not so much as a wrinkle. In a few hours, my button-down blue scrub dress will look like someone used it as a napkin.

"It's not the worst I've dealt with," I say. Sadly, I'm not lying.

We have a total of fourteen guest rooms at the hotel: three on the first floor, eight on the second, and three more on the third floor. Each room is uniquely named based on a design theme. Occupancy is lower now that it's September and the summer season is winding down. From May until Labor Day there are three maids on staff, but I'm the only year-round help.

While we're situated off the beaten path, we have regular guests who return each season. Winter's always a bit of a ghost town, but we get a few cross-country skiers and packs of snowmobilers making their way to Canada. Neither activity is my idea of fun, but to each their own.

Summer is when I make the bulk of my money, because tips and occupancy rates go hand in hand. There's nothing quite like the promise of the white tip envelope we put in every room. My heart patters with hope at each encounter, though more often than not it's anticlimactic. But still, there's a definite thrill. Will it be a twenty inside, or will someone forgo the recommended three to five dollars per day of stay to slip me a forty for the week? Each time, it's like Christmas morning wrapped up in 2-D packaging. Ironically, the messier a room, the lower the tips, or at least that's been my experience. I'm sure the only thing these guests will leave me is more trash.

I'm not about to half-ass it just because I know my efforts won't be appreciated. I'm a professional, and this job means everything to me because it means everything to my Nana Kelley. She's all I have left in this world.

Well, Nana *and* Rodrigo, and he understands my situation. He knows what an evil prick George Bishop was, too. Not that I had anything to do with the man's death, but good riddance to him. Nana would probably smack me upside the head if she heard me speak ill of the dead, but if I told her all the stuff George did (or tried to do) to me while he was alive, she'd probably pull him out of his icebox at the morgue and give his cold, dead cheek a hard backhand.

Even with Larry on the move, George's three daughters are coming to Jonesport to bury their dad. I suppose they'll get details on their inheritance as well, which I assume includes the Precipice. Nobody is telling me to have the hotel spotless for their arrival, but I don't need reminders. I can't make a bad first impression. I'm assuming Victoria, Iris, and Faith Bishop are going to be my new bosses. Lord knows, they can't be worse than my last.

"I would stay and help you clean," Rodrigo says, "but I'm super trying to avoid MRSA. You understand, right?"

He waves goodbye to me from the doorway. I give him the finger.

Truth is, I'm glad he's gone. I've got work to do. With the bed stripped, I inspect the mattress for stains. That's usually good for a bribe because the hotel charges a substantial fee for damages, but this one is surprisingly clean. I make the bed, which I could do blindfolded. After folding the clothes, bagging the dirty laundry (gloves on, of course), I wipe all visible surfaces using my cleaning cloths.

I need to be efficient cleaning the bathroom. I enter wielding my Clorox bottle like an Old West sheriff stepping into a showdown. After I've finished, the chrome is so shiny there's not a single watermark to be found. Next, I hurriedly replace the towels, soaps, and water glasses, restock the tea and coffee, and make sure the DO NOT DISTURB sign is hung on the inside doorknob.

When that's done, I fluff the pillows, adjust the curtains so they look straight, and reset the temp to our standard 68 degrees. Last is vacuuming. I always vacuum last to collect the dust particles I kick up while cleaning.

I step back to assess my efforts, pleased with the results. That's the crazy part. Even though the job is backbreaking, aging me at an accelerated rate, I still take pride in my work.

The room looks pristine, but there's one more thing I have to do.

I check the time. Good. Very good.

Then I say my mantra, like always: *I'm doing this for her . . . I don't have a choice.*

I steal a quick peek into the hallway. The coast is clear, but it might not be for long. Then I check the dresser drawers. In the bottom one, I find what I'm hoping to see—a brown wallet resting atop a pile of underwear.

My heart is pounding. I shouldn't do this. I know better. It's at this point I hate myself the most. But I'm not doing this to go on a shopping spree.

I listen for footsteps in the hall as I retrieve the wallet from the drawer. All is quiet. I pry the billfold open. There's a lot of cash inside. I add it up quickly, counting one hundred seventy-five dollars.

I won't take it all, that would raise a red flag, but I can take forty—two tens and a twenty—that I doubt will be missed. Somehow the guests leave just enough cash lying around for me to nab fives, tens, and twenties that usually make up for my monthly shortfall.

I put the wallet back in the dresser where I found it, close the drawer, and rise to go. The guilt is already pecking at my skull like a woodpecker trying to break into my brain. When I turn for the door, I gasp aloud at the sight of the room's occupants looming in the doorway. They're eyeing me with grave suspicion. My throat closes like a crimped straw, making it difficult to swallow.

"You startled me," I say nervously.

The man enters first. He's exactly as I imagined—big and beefy with beady eyes and close-cropped hair, the kind of guest I know all too well. Perpetually pissed off. He looks like just the sort who'd complain about runny eggs. His wife is equally intimidating. She could take me down one-handed.

They're clearly annoyed that I'm still in their room, but do they know? Did they see?

I say a silent prayer: *Oh, God, please, please. Never again. Never again. I promise. I'll stop. I'll find another way. Just let me be safe!*

The man glares at me. My knees begin to buckle.

"I'm sorry," I exhale in a shaky whisper. "I was just finishing."

"Well, hurry up," growls the man. "We're ready to lie down after the overpriced crappy breakfast we had."

"I'm done, it's all yours," I say softly, bowing like a servant.

There's no *Thank you for the cleanup*. No kind smile or friendly gesture, either. Just more glowering looks from these entitled guests.

I slide past them into the hallway, clutching my cart like it's a life raft. I hear them mutter something unpleasant about me under their breath before slamming the door behind them.

I wheel my cart down the hall, body shaking. I've never come that close to getting caught before. Gingerly, I brush my fingers against the pocket of my dress where I stashed the forty bucks.

Regret hits me, but not for what I've done. I'm still forty short.

I know what I promised God, but there are six more rooms to clean. And that means six more chances to get lucky.

Chapter 3

I'm standing in front of Janice's desk at Guiding Way, rubbing my hands nervously as she opens the envelope. I don't know why I'm so anxious. It's all there, thanks to Nana's Social Security, my wages, tips, and, well . . . a little extra help. I scored more cash in the last few rooms I cleaned, barely reaching the amount I needed. I'm no saint. Honestly, I disgust myself most days, but I do what has to be done.

After she's finished counting the money, I finally get the smile I've been waiting for. Janice records the transaction in her laptop computer. Her kind eyes wash over me as she places the envelope inside a metal cash box.

She prints out a receipt showing a zero balance. My elation is short-lived. Every payment starts the clock again. Now I've got less than a month to make rent.

Ironically, while I'm the one responsible for making up the shortfall, it's Janice who manages Nana's bank account. She has power of attorney, not me. I was a minor when my grandmother moved to Guiding Way and someone had to manage her finances. The court was more interested in getting me into foster care than in signing a petition to declare me an adult.

Having Janice in charge of Nana's money is a bit like the fox guarding the henhouse, but I trust her with my life. She's on the up-and-up, not a thief like me.

"Thanks for this, Charley," says Janice. "I know it's not easy for you."

"I'm sorry I'm a few days late."

Actually, it's more like a week.

"Not to worry, hon. I know you do your best. Are you gearing up for the storm?"

Janice peers out her office window at the gray and overcast sky. Of course she's talking about Larry. It's all anybody's been talking about.

"I don't know. The weather report keeps saying it's going to miss us by miles."

"And do you believe that? We rely too much on computers these days to tell us what the animals know."

I raise my eyebrows. "The animals?"

"Sure. We always see deer nibbling at the sedge grass growing on the property, but they haven't been around. And the birds aren't chirping like they normally do. They know. Larry *is* coming. I suggest you and Rodrigo take precautions. We are."

"Yeah, I suppose you're right. Almost all our bookings were canceled."

"Just another form of birdsong," says Janice. "You've got to look and listen for the signs. You ask me, we put too much faith in systems, and not enough in common sense."

I nod as if in vigorous agreement.

"I'll mention it to Rodrigo," I say. "We can get some plywood at True Value."

"If there's any left," Janice says, making me feel bad for being too relaxed, especially with the Bishop sisters coming. Maybe they'll think I'm lazy and not worth keeping on, which would be a disaster for Nana.

As if to drive home my concern, I hear loud banging outside the office window. A moment later, Janice's office goes dark. There's more hammering before Janice yells, "Steve, darling, can that please wait? I'm with Charley."

Down comes the plywood, allowing light back in. Steve's bearded face appears in the window.

"Sorry," he says sweetly, his voice muted through the windowpane.

I love this couple, but seeing their affection for each other always makes me a bit sad. I've often wished Janice were my mom, but that feels like a betrayal of my dead mother, so I can't win.

"There are so many vintage keepsakes in that hotel," continues Janice. "I'd hate to see any of it get damaged. It's a real treasure trove."

I know what she means. According to all the travel blogs, the Precipice is considered eclectic, eccentric, unique, unusual, that sort of thing. George's collecting habit was well known up and down the coast of Maine.

Imagine taking everything at an antique store—all the glass lampshades, knickknacks, rugs, pictures, all the odds and ends—and throwing it all up in the air, and somehow it lands artfully in place, magically unbroken. That's essentially the design aesthetic of the hotel.

"Rodrigo and I will get on it," I assure her. "The Bishop sisters are still coming. It's their stuff now, so I guess we *should* take precautions . . . you know, just in case."

I'm thinking of the quiet birds and the absent deer.

"I'm sure they're inheriting the hotel," says Janice, as though stating a fact.

"I suppose. George's lawyer is coming to stay as well. I think they're doing a reading of the will or something. Do you know the Bishops?" I ask. "I'm worried. I mean, I really need to keep my job, my living situation, all of it."

"Well, I *knew* them . . . we all did, but I haven't seen those three in ages. It's a small town, though, so we get news here and there."

"What are they like? I don't know a thing about them," I say.

Janice scratches her head like she's trying to unearth a memory. Her hair is the color mine will be soon if I stay on this job.

"Let's see, there's Victoria—she goes by Vicki. She's the oldest. Then there's Iris, and the youngest is Faith, who was a pretty successful model at one time. Vicki is the business-minded one, if I remember correctly. She and her husband own a chain of jewelry stores in and around Boston. I'd say she's the one you need to impress most."

"Is she nice?"

Janice makes a slight grimace. "Eh. She was a young woman when I saw her last, so it's tricky to say. But I hear she's more like her father than the others, so I wonder if she'll be a little, um, *eccentric*."

I suspect she's talking about George's obsession with conspiracy theories, not his octopus arms. I've never confided in Janice about that. Didn't want her pressuring me into quitting or confronting my boss on my behalf and getting me fired. That would have been a disaster for Nana.

"Hopefully, she doesn't think the world is flat," I say. "At least George didn't take it *that* far."

"I don't know . . . I also heard that Iris Bishop's had some drug troubles." Janice's expression turns somber. "And I don't know much about Faith aside from her modeling career. Word is she married a woman named Hope, but that's about it."

"Hope and Faith," I say. "That's cute."

"Maybe so, but don't let the sweet names fool you. The Bishops don't have the best reputation in town."

"What do you mean?" I ask.

"Let's just say there haven't been a lot of tears shed for George—or his wife, when she passed. And apparently the sisters were their own special brand of trouble back in the day, if you believe town talk."

Janice's warning gaze bores into me. But it's only a moment before her affable smile returns. Janice is like a lot of Mainers I know—a salt-of-the-earth type. She's a bit weathered and calls it like she sees it. Tough as she is, you'll never meet a more compassionate person. It's on display in the framed inspirational quotes she's hung in the halls of Guiding Way:

> *Wrinkles go only where the smiles have been.*
> *Growing old is mandatory, but growing up is optional!*
> *Aging is just another word for living.*

While I'm naturally curious, I resist the urge to press for more de-tails. She's not one to spread rumors. I trust she'd tell me if there was something I needed to know. For now, I take it as friendly advice to proceed with caution.

Janice clears her throat. "Sweetie . . . I'm sorry about this, but there's something I have to tell you, and it's not about the Bishops."

Anxiety grips me. *Is Nana okay?* "What is it?"

"I've got to raise the rent," she says, sighing with regret.

My stomach takes a roller-coaster plunge. "What? Why? You know I can barely make ends meet as it is!"

"I know, but we're struggling here. I've cut you as much of a break as I can, but if I can't keep the lights on, everyone suffers. I'm sorry to do this, kiddo, I really am, but it's going to be an extra hundred a month. That's as low as I can go."

"A hundred dollars?" I can barely get out the words. "That's twelve hundred more a year. I can't afford that!"

"Heating costs are sinking us, and the almanac's predicting a brutal winter."

Brutal winter means fewer guests at the hotel and fewer opportunities to skim a little extra.

"I get your struggles, honey," Janice says. "But you know we count dimes. Talk to the Bishops. Ask about a raise. I'm sure they'll want to help if they can."

"Right," I say. I can't bear to look her in the eyes. This isn't her fault. She's always done her best by me. But this hit is brutal.

Janice shuffles papers on her desk from one pile to another. I get the message. She's always moving things around to try and make this place work. I mean, she didn't start Guiding Way to get rich.

The grounds aren't much—a flat patch of scraggly grass growing on the side of a busy one-lane highway—but it's the only elder care around these parts. Ideally, I'd still be living with Nana in her old house on Feeney Street. But we had to sell it after she almost burned the place down. She thought the stove was the washing machine and put a pile of clothes inside before turning it on. Thankfully, Jonesport has a responsive fire department. They came almost as soon as the smoke alarm went off.

I knew her memory was going. All the signs were there.

Confusion.

Forgetting words.

Losing things.

Sometimes she thought I was someone else. Then she'd catch herself and get embarrassed.

After the fire, Nana couldn't be left alone. It was for her own safety. In stepped Janice. Jonesport is a small town where everyone knows your name and problems. She agreed to help and became my business partner of sorts. With a little encouragement from me, Janice took on the role of Nana's official guardian. Together, we organized the yard sales, picked the broker, and managed all the details of selling the house and moving her to Guiding Way.

Unfortunately, the sale didn't give me much of a financial cushion. What I learned through that difficult process was that life isn't cheap and reverse mortgages are for suckers. One day I'll find the guy who roped Nana into signing away her life and shove a stick up his (or her) butt. My mom should have been the one watching out for her mother, but she was too busy getting high to care.

Janice let me live with her for a time, but her daughter had to move in after a messy divorce and she came with newborn twins, so those arrangements were cramped and chaotic. Not only was my housing situation a nightmare, I also needed more money and high school was getting in the way. I dropped out and started waitressing at the local diner while working toward my GED. That's when I met George Bishop.

He ordered waffles and fries, I remember that clearly. Then while I was clearing his table and he was leaving a ridiculously generous tip, George made me an offer I couldn't refuse.

"Obviously, I don't want anything to change," says Janice.

"Obviously," I repeat morosely.

"And if there's anything I can do . . ."

"Yeah, please don't raise the rent," I plead.

"Anything else."

"I'll figure something out," I say with confidence I don't feel.

Janice steps out from behind her cluttered desk to give me a hug. We embrace warmly. I don't hold a grudge or any ill will toward her. She's just doing her job. I know she cares deeply for me. Loves me like a daughter, or so she says.

I head toward Nana's apartment for our daily visit, lost in a sea of worries. I peer up at the dark clouds gathered overhead. A blustery wind picks up, whipping my hair in front of my eyes, plastering my light jacket tight against my body. Cold dread seeps into my bones.

I pause and listen intently.

Janice is right.

The birds *aren't* singing.

Chapter 4

When I enter Nana's apartment, a familiar smell hits me hard: sort of a combination of old people potpourri and musty magazines. The apartment isn't much, one large space divided into a living room on one side and a bedroom on the other. There's a small but clean bathroom equipped with safety features—hand railings, emergency buttons, no-slip mats. Janice thought of it all.

I find Nana sitting in her favorite armchair knitting by the window. She's making a hat. She loves bright-colored yarn. I have a drawer full of clothes she's knitted for me over the years. I haven't tossed any of it, even the socks that no longer fit. Her newest creation has enough orange and red to make it good for hunting season. Somehow her brain remembers how to do this, even though she can't always remember how to dress herself, what year it is . . . or who I am.

"I already have fresh sheets, dear," Nana says without looking up from her knitting. Even from the doorway, I can see that she's using seed stitching. She taught me how to knit, and that's usually what we do together when I visit. But right now I'm housekeeping to her. In a few minutes, that will probably change and she'll think I'm someone else. Doubtful that someone will be me.

"Nana, it's me . . . it's Charley, I've come to knit with you."

I pull a half-finished scarf from my shoulder bag, hoping the bright green yarn might jog her memory. The distance in her gaze only deepens. Once a vibrant blue, Nana's eyes now appear gray, as if the color has dimmed with each memory lost. I watch her trying to puzzle it out—my face, my clothes, a scent perhaps, all little echoes of something familiar—but who am I if not the maid?

I slip the scarf back into my bag. I'll get to that later. There's a second chair I drag across the floor so I can sit close to her. I crack open the window to let in a strong breeze and let out the other stale odors. But loneliness has a smell, and sorrow does, too—odors that even the wind can't carry away.

Nana sets her knitting needles on her lap. Her expression shifts ever so slightly, little by little, until she looks frustrated and disapproving.

"You're late, Mary Beth," Nana says, her tone suddenly sharp.

I flinch. Nana might as well have plunged one of those needles directly into my heart.

"No, Nana, it's me," I say again. "It's Charley."

Why do I bother? Hope hurts. I should let it go. But I've always been stubborn—just like my mom, Mary Beth.

"You're supposed to come home right after school," Nana tells me, still scolding.

"Nana . . . I'm Charley, not Mary Beth."

"You know what time I expect you," she continues, ignoring me.

I might be stubborn, but I also know when it's a losing battle.

"Sorry I'm late, Mom," I say, slipping into character as if a director just shouted *action*.

Nana returns a tender smile. All is forgiven.

I wouldn't do this if Janice hadn't encouraged it. "Your nana's reality is as true to her as yours is to you," she had assured me. "Sometimes playing along can make her feel more comfortable."

For Nana to be comfortable, I had to become my mother before she started shooting up, a young woman I barely had the pleasure to know.

"How's school going? Have you been keeping up with your math homework? You don't want to fall behind. You remember what happened last time?"

Here's where I want to break down and shake her out of it. I don't want to play along anymore because I know this story, and it doesn't end well.

I want to tell Nana what happens. All of it. The whole sad tale whirls through my mind.

Mom does fine in math class, no worries there. She's actually a good student and graduates with plans to go to college. But all that changes the night she goes to the bowling alley in Belfast. Nana should have been worried about *that* night more than math class, because that's when my mom meets Frank Owens.

Frank is an aspiring NASCAR driver, of all things. Oh, he gets Mary Beth under his spell faster than you can shift from second to third. College plans go right out the window. Mom wants to go with Frank to Tennessee to watch him drive around a track at a crazy high speed. "Over my dead body" is Nana's threat, but obviously that doesn't happen. Mom goes and Nana can't stop her. Mom has high hopes for her future, but she doesn't know how hard it is to become a NASCAR driver.

Guess what? Neither does Frank.

Before long, she's living in a shithole trailer, in a shithole trailer park, while Frank gets drunk and pretends to go to his job as an auto mechanic. To make ends meet, Mom works as a waitress at a place that's a short step up from a Waffle House. She gets pinched on the butt and shorted on the tips.

Frank starts blaming Mom for his failed dreams, when he should be blaming his crappy driving skills and Budweiser. He was a pretty good amateur racer on the Maine circuit, but he had a cheap car that made him a lot less competitive. The real stock cars are something else entirely. The costs are huge, and Frank never has enough money for a good one. When he does scrape together a ride, he is so outmatched he finishes in the back of the pack, if he finishes at all.

The first black eye Mom blames on a fall. After the last one, she buys a bus ticket back to Jonesport, wishing she could get three years of her life back. But she returns home carrying more than just her luggage. I'm in her belly.

I'll never meet Frank Owens, and he'll never know about me.

Now she's back home, broke and broken. Her dreams are shattered, but I come into the world without complications. Easiest delivery that year, according to her ob-gyn. But being a single mother isn't easy—no, it's anything but. So what's next? More crappy jobs, no time for that degree, and she's got a kid to care for, too. Life becomes a grind. Or maybe the hamster wheel metaphor is better. Either way, Mom is feeling it. The emptiness. The loneliness. It's just her and Nana—and me.

The local bar becomes her escape pod. She goes there to forget who she is. It works. The men buy her drinks. They like her. She likes herself when she's there. Laughing. Dancing to the jukebox. She likes nineties music. Grunge. Prince. TLC. Goo Goo Dolls. I can't say which guy introduces her to the pills. Doesn't matter. All of them—and there are plenty—are basically one guy to me. Thanks to them, she learns to grind up her pills before snorting them. It's a faster high that way.

Little by little, it's less Mom and more Nana looking after me. There are lots of fights. Jewelry goes missing. There's a big blowout over it. I'm ten years old. This is when I become a reader. I get lost in my books. It's safer there. *Harry Potter*. *Diary of a Wimpy Kid*. And my favorite—*A Series of Unfortunate Events*.

My life story.

Mom can barely hold down a job. Getting her next high is full-time work. When the oxy supply gets tight, heroin is there. Cheap and easy to get—especially in a coastal town where there's not much to do.

Buddy is a junkie who pretends to be a truck driver. They meet at the bar Mom lives at—I mean, *frequents*. He has a source, he says. That's his pickup line, and sadly, it works. I'm fourteen when they meet. Mom moves in with him. I want to stay with Nana, but Mom wants me to go with her. There's another big fight. Mom insists. Nana tells her she'll go to court unless Mom gets clean.

Mom can't do it. Dying is easier. And Nana won't go to court.

Besides, her early signs of Alzheimer's are becoming more obvious, so I move in with Mom—and Buddy.

Since I'm not drugs, I only sort of matter to my mother for these years. As long as I'm not in the way, I'm fine. I become invisible. She and Buddy can't really see me. Nobody can. Nobody but Nana, who makes sure I get all my meals because the only thing junkies cook is heroin.

Eventually, everyone on drugs finds a bottom, and my mother is no exception. Nana bails her out of jail. I don't know what she did, and nobody will tell me. I know better than to ask. I bounce back to Nana's house.

Enter NA—Narcotics Anonymous. Mom stops using. She goes to meetings. She kicks Buddy out of the apartment. She's the one paying for it. He's still using and not working.

Things take a turn for the better. Mom wants me to move back in with her again. It's time, she says. She's done the hard work. Nana gets it, and she loves me enough to let me go.

Books are still my safe haven.

Now it's *If I Stay, Me Before You,* and *The Lovely Bones.*

Instead of cutting to feel, I read. If it can make me cry, I read it again . . . and again.

My mother tries to be a mom. She cooks dinner (sort of, but a lot of it comes frozen) and asks about my schoolwork. She doesn't beat me, doesn't yell. She's not crazy anymore. She's clean.

Part of me knows how it's going to end, even if for now it all seems good. I'll come home from school, and it will be over. I'll find her on her bed. She'll be blue. There will be a needle in her arm.

I don't know why she found Buddy again. Maybe she tried to help him get clean, and like a drowning person, he dragged his would-be savior down into the depths with him. Whatever the reason, Buddy comes back. He's living in the apartment with us again. He swears he's not using, but I don't believe him. Nana doesn't, either.

One winter day, I come home from school and it's quiet in the apartment. Buddy's not there, but I see my mother's navy wool coat draped over the kitchen chair. It's still wet from the snowfall. I call to her. No answer. I go down the hall to her bedroom. I open the door.

The story ends the way I knew it would, with a phone call to Nana, me barely able to get out the words, doubled over in pain, tears streaming down my face.

Nana's the one who calls 911.

Some hours later, the doctors will tell me there was nothing I could have done. I'll spend every day from that day forward coming up with reasons why they're wrong.

"I'm so proud of you, Mary Beth," Nana says, patting me on my knee. "Your grades have really improved."

"Thanks, Nana," I say, then catch myself. "I mean, Mom."

"Are you still going to the bowling alley tonight?" she asks tenderly. "You know I expect you home before midnight."

"Yeah, I'm still going," I say.

Because that's how it is with this story.

Nana always asks. And Mary Beth always goes.

Chapter 5

I drive my small Honda with a big dent in the right rear bumper and questionable tires up the winding road to the Precipice Hotel. Sharp turns and switchbacks make this an always-harrowing experience, even in good weather. The forecast still has the storm staying out at sea, but the ominous dark clouds say otherwise. If it does hit, this road will be a river of mud. No way my rickety little ride would make it from the bottom to the top. In fact, I'm not sure this car will even make it another day. There's always a new something clanking or clacking under the hood, as if my car's trying to tell me it's on its last wheels. If I end up needing another major repair, especially now with Nana's rent increase, I'll be going everywhere on foot—including the hardware store, where I just picked up the supplies Rodrigo needs to install plywood over the windows. Just in case.

At the top of the hill, I find plenty of parking. The threat of the storm has scared most of the guests away. That's good, on one hand, because it means less work for me, and my back certainly could use it. But it also means less money when I need it the most.

When I enter our welcoming foyer, I take one look at the plush chairs bracketing a tall bookshelf full of well-worn hardcovers and notice they need dusting. I always focus on what needs to be done, not what I've accomplished. I suspect that's some sort of life lesson, but I don't have time to dwell on it.

Farther inside, directly across from the entrance, is our old-timey reception area, complete with a brass bell that seems quaint until guests start slamming it. On the dark oak counter stands a working antique typewriter that never gets used but serves as a charming nostalgic decoration.

Rodrigo's not at the front desk. With so much cleaning to do, I don't have time to go looking for him. I set the bag of screws and nails he wanted next to the typewriter and text him to let him know it's there. I leave the foyer, taking a left that brings me into a large, open room.

I can always tell the first-timers to the Precipice—they're the ones who stop and gawk. The space is airy and large, like you've entered an old English church with vaulted arches and a post-and-beam ceiling. Across from me is our curved staircase, with a mahogany railing that ends in a large, rounded newel-post (Rodrigo taught me the word for that). A red carpet runner adds a touch of warmth and style to the wide stairs that connect the first floor to the upper levels.

As George would have wanted, we've got a fire burning brightly in the hearth. The stone fireplace looks like it could be centuries old, its individual stones large as hubcaps. The flames help illuminate our colorful stained-glass windows and the funky lamps scattered throughout the space.

It's sort of an assault on the eyes, to be honest, a kaleidoscope of colors created from a swirling array of trinkets large and small. There's hardly an inch of wall space that isn't covered with art of some type, paintings and faded prints that I've dusted more times than I can count.

Where there's no artwork, shelving units line the walls, stuffed with a mix of old books and an assortment of odd figurines and small sculptures. George was a nonstop collector of oddities. He didn't use much discretion when it came to which ones he displayed. I heard one guest describe the hotel as a burlesque theater that collided with a fortune-teller's den. I had to google *burlesque,* but yeah, that's kind of accurate.

Once again, all I can see is the work that lies ahead. The area rug, which occupies most of the floor and is handwoven with red, orange, and gold threads, needs vacuuming. The same could be said for the various pieces of old-fashioned furniture that adorn the rug—ornate couches and wingback chairs with upholstery fit for royalty.

For the sake of efficiency, I should clean the guest rooms first. I'll be sure to do an exceptional job, because if the Bishop sisters are anything like their father, they'll be on the hunt for things to critique.

I stroll into the curved alcove at the back of the room, where comfy sitting chairs line a bank of windows overlooking the bluff of Gull Hill. The cliff's steep drop-off is what gave the Precipice its name.

Before I begin cleaning, I always take a look at the sea. It reminds me that there's more to life than Windex and bleach. Sometimes I fantasize about sailing away to a magical land on a big boat where I can escape what feels like a dead-end life. But today the sea churns violently, its waves crowned with frothy whitecaps. I certainly wouldn't want to be out there on any vessel. Reluctantly, I retrace my steps back to the grand staircase. No time for daydreams.

My cart lives in a large closet at the end of the second-floor hallway. I spend so much time with it that it feels like an extension of myself. I should give her a name. Bessie? That seems fitting, suggesting an over-milked farm cow, which is often how I feel.

Pushing my cart, I make my way over to the Oak Room. I don't see a privacy sign on the door handle, so I knock. As expected, there's no response, since I think I saw the guests leaving. I reach for my master key to let myself inside.

Just before I can unlock the door, a woman approaches from the staircase. She's looking right at me.

"Excuse me," the woman says, her voice a little uncertain.

"Yes?" I squint my eyes, trying to match her face to a room. The hotel is small enough that I know all the guests and where they're staying. She looks vaguely familiar, but I can't seem to place her. She's got a large wheely bag, so she must be a guest, but we have no new reservations given the weather.

"We met before . . . at the Sunrise Stop, in line for coffee," the woman says. "I'm Bree."

Bree! Oh yes, that's right.

"I'm sorry," I say. "I remember now, a couple of days ago, you asked me what I recommended."

"And you told me the macchiato—which was awesome, by the way, thank you," says Bree. "I'm sorry, I didn't get your name that day."

"I'm Charley, Charley Kelley," I say. "And you're Bree, you said?"

"That's right. Bree Bradford."

Bree's at least ten years my senior, with wavy brown hair and stunning blue eyes reminiscent of a perfect summer day. At the coffee shop, she asked touristy questions about the area. We shared a few quick laughs about *not getting there from here, lobstah,* that sort of thing. She got her macchiato and went on her way.

Usually I don't store such fleeting encounters in my memory because my day-to-day is a constant stream of strangers breezing in and out. Yet she made me pause, earning more attention than usual. Her gaze had an intensity that resonated with me. She radiated a unique energy, a vibration I could almost feel, like I was meeting a kindred spirit—a fellow survivor of hardship and struggle.

"Are you, like, staying here?" I ask, gesturing to the rooms off the hallway.

She lowers her eyes. I'm guessing no, she's not.

"No, still at that Airbnb with my boyfriend," Bree tells me, which I remember from our conversation. His name is Jack or Jackson—something like that.

"Did you get up to Acadia?" I remember that plan as well.

"No, not yet . . . actually, not ever," Bree says, her expression forlorn. "This is kind of awkward, but you mentioned working here, and I've come to talk with you about something." She peers over my shoulder, insinuating that this something needs discretion. "Is there a place where we could do that? Talk, in private?"

I give her an appraising stare, conveying my suspicion. She meets my gaze, desperation evident in her eyes. While most customers treat me with an air of superiority, Bree doesn't, which is somewhat refreshing and works in her favor.

After hesitating a moment, I use the master key to open the door to the Wisteria Room. It's clean and we can talk privately. I lead Bree inside. It's one of my favorite rooms; it's bright and airy, yet cozy, covered with Victorian wallpaper. The room holds a king-size bed with a plush duvet and fringed velvet pillows that I've enjoyed for a few afternoon naps. The ceiling features beautiful exposed beams that evoke another era. Similar to the rest of the hotel, interesting collectibles are dispersed throughout.

Bree goes over to the door that opens to a second-story deck, offering stunning views of the lawn, gardens, and sea—certainly a place worthy of the high cost per night.

I stay in the center of the room, my arms folded across my chest. I'm not in the mood to take on anyone's problems, but I feel certain that's what's about to happen.

"I've got a problem, a big one," Bree begins, her voice tense.

Score one for my instincts.

"Okay," I respond warily.

"I'm in danger."

This sets me back on my heels. Trouble I can handle, but danger is a different story.

"It's my boyfriend—Jake. I mentioned him earlier," Bree continues, advancing toward me.

Jake, not Jackson. Nobody's perfect.

"I need a place to hide—from him—for a little while," she says.

I gape at her. "Um, well . . . why are you coming to me? Can't you, you know, go to the police or something?"

Bree has her phone out, as though she was anticipating my question. She keys her passcode before thrusting the device into my hand. "These are the last messages he sent me," she says, her voice shaking slightly.

I take my time scrolling through the text stream while Bree anxiously reads along over my shoulder.

Where are you?

Answer me OR ELSE.

Are you with someone?

Dammit, Bree. ANSWER ME!!

You really think you can do this?
You can't get away from me. I
won't let you.

You'll regret it, I swear. You will.

My skin is clammy as I hand Bree back her phone. I want to scrub the texts from my brain. It's triggered visceral memories of the men who tried to control my mother using drugs as a twisted form of love.

"It's not enough. For the police, I mean," Bree says. "There's nothing they can do with this. He didn't make any overt threats. Jake is smart like that. He just can't accept the fact that I broke up with him. And stupid me for doing so on this trip, because I know what he's capable of—and it's not good. But I can't undo it . . . And now he's a powder keg. I should have waited until I was home, but things got physical, and it just wasn't safe to stay . . ."

"Can't you take off? Leave him behind?"

"How? I don't have a car," Bree says. "I walked here. And I'm out of money. He's got all the cash. That's one of the ways he controls me. I can get some money for a bus ticket home, but it's going to take time."

She looks increasingly anxious.

"Where do you live?" I ask. She gives off city vibes.

"Boston—for now," she says, confirming my hunch. "But that's all up in the air. I may need to disappear for a while, just to get away from him. I haven't thought that far ahead. This is the best I could come up with on short notice."

My eyes grow wide. "You're saying you want to hide here? That's your best plan?" I blurt out in disbelief.

"I know it sounds crazy, but things got bad, the worst it's ever been. I read somewhere that if you want to disappear, it's best to stay right where you are. I'm sorry to do this to you, but I don't know anyone else in the area," says Bree. "I just need a few days, maybe ride out this storm if it hits. And I promise, I'll make it up to you somehow."

"What if he comes here looking for you?" I ask. "There's not a lot of hotels in the area to choose from. Like, *none.*"

"He knows I can't afford this place." Bree motions to the expensive decor. "If anything, he'll think I hitched a ride to a Motel 6, or that I hooked up with another guy. He *always* thinks there's another guy."

I go quiet, sinking into thought. I like Bree and want to help her. When I look in her eyes, I see someone I can relate to, which is rare. With most guests, I feel judged. Often people look at me like a curiosity. *What brought a young girl with so much promise to a dead-end job like hotel maid?* I always resist a lecture, but it dances on my tongue. *You should be grateful there are people like me to clean your room, wash your sheets, and make your bed.*

"You said you don't have any cash. How are you going to pay for the room? Do you have a credit card?" I say, narrowing my eyes, skeptical of her ability to pay.

Bree bites her bottom lip, which is answer enough.

"I can't use a credit card. He'll see the transaction and know where I am. I just need to hide out for a week or so."

"A week?" I gasp.

"I know I'm asking a lot, but I *really* need this. And I know Jake, how he gets when he feels threatened. Trust me, the police can't keep me safe from him. But you can."

Bree pauses, taking a moment to think something over.

"How about this," she says. "I can give you five hundred—not today, but in a few days—and then another five hundred as soon as I get back to work. Jake didn't like me bartending because he'd get jealous of the guys, but there are a bunch of places that would love to have me back. I make good money, great tips. I'll be able to pay you. I promise. All you have to do is let me stay here, help me hide for a week."

I'm sure bartenders get better tips than maids. Call me jealous. Also, call me practical. A thousand dollars is a lot of extra cash lying around, and it couldn't come at a better time.

"The Bishop sisters will be here soon," I say.

Bree's eyebrows knit together. "Who?"

"The daughters of George Bishop. He's the owner, or he was the owner . . . he's dead. And now his daughters are coming here with their families to read the will and settle the estate. Everyone is staying at this hotel, and I'm not sure which rooms they'll want to take."

"That's fine. I just need one."

"Well, you may have to move rooms, is what I'm saying. I can't let them know you're here. They'll expect a credit card on file, and if a customer is paying cash, we get it all up front. That's our policy."

Bree lets out a relieved breath. Basically, I've announced my intention to help.

"Okay, so we'll play frogger," she says. "I'll leap from one room to the other at your command. It's only for a little while, Charley, please. I need this. I wouldn't ask if I had a better option."

She gives me what may be her best pleading look. I'm worried she's about to fall to her knees and beg—how can I say no?

A lot can go wrong with this scheme, I think as I slip into a lengthy silence. Rodrigo's definitely not going to be happy with me, but what choice do I have? Nana means the world to me. I try to keep my face as inscrutable as a poker player's, but Bree's already smiling. She knows she's got me.

"Okay," I say, exhaling the word as if it pained me. "I'll do it. I'll help. But I need twelve hundred, not a thousand. That's still a bargain, and you can pay me later, but I need it in cash. And go where I say, keep out of sight. I'll make sure nobody knows you're here."

She extends her hand. "Deal," says Bree. "You won't regret it."

"I think I already do," I mutter. "You can stay in this room tonight. It's empty."

"Great!"

"And then I'll just move you around as needed."

"Whatever you say."

My expression turns somber.

"I have enough troubles of my own," I say, looking her in the eyes. "I can't handle any more. So please promise me, Bree, promise you're not putting me in any danger. I really need the money, and I need to take care of my nana."

"No, I'm not. I promise you, Charley, I promise," says Bree.

And I think: *She might be an even worse poker player than I am.*

Chapter 6

Thursday

I don't know anything about prepping for a hurricane. I've never been in one before—unless my entire life counts. Thankfully, I have Rodrigo to help. Janice was right about the lumberyard running low on supplies, even though the experts keep saying the storm is going to miss us.

The guests don't seem to believe the rosy weather reports. Three checked out early, and the ones who were coming canceled their reservations entirely. Unfortunately, the Bishop sisters haven't changed their plans. Perhaps they would postpone, but there is the matter of a funeral. According to the obituary in our local paper, George's burial is scheduled for this coming Monday.

Rodrigo and I can't board up every window—there are far too many and not enough plywood boards. The plan is to cover the first-floor windows facing the ocean, those in the alcove especially. It will give us a large, dry place to huddle together as we ride out the storm and protect some of the more expensive pieces of furniture.

Rodrigo hammers nails into the plywood from his precarious perch on a stepladder. Even from down below, I can see him grimacing in disapproval. He's not upset with the plywood; he's angry with me.

"You're being foolish," he scolds as he drives a nail into the board with a few well-placed strikes of his hammer.

My arms are shaking as I try to keep the heavy wood from falling backward onto my head. The wind isn't helping. It keeps trying to rip the plywood out of my hands. Behind me, the gusty breeze has flattened most of the tall grasses that line the bluff of Gull Hill. I'm losing faith in the meteorologists. Judging by Rodrigo's expression, he's losing faith in me.

"She's desperate, and so am I," I tell Rodrigo. "It's twelve hundred bucks—the entire cost of Nana's rent increase for the year."

"And how much of that twelve hundred is in your pocket right now?" he asks—*bam! bam!* —as he pounds another nail into place.

"She doesn't have it on her—I told you that already. She was running for her life."

"*Allegedly* running," Rodrigo reminds me. "You don't know a thing about this woman. Really."

Bam! Another nail. He does that one with extra force, as though putting an exclamation point on his decree.

"Whatever," I grumble up at him. "You're just assuming the worst. Honestly, you're more annoying than an ad you can't skip on YouTube."

Rodrigo shoots me a beady-eyed stare from above. He knows what I've just started, and I can almost see the gears churning in his head. "Oh, really?" he says. "Well . . . you're more annoying than a group text message at midnight."

I almost laugh at that one, but any trace of a smile quickly dims. This is serious business. We're trying to outduel each other.

It all began about a year ago, when out of sheer boredom, Rodrigo and I invented the game we now call "More Annoying Than . . ." The rules are simple: Make a comparison between the person and something annoying. The first one to laugh has to buy the other coffee at Sunrise Stop. We've played many rounds since the game's inception, and we're pretty much tied.

Now I need a good comeback, because those midnight group text messages *are* super annoying. Sadly my mind goes blank, until I recall something that happened to me at Guiding Way.

"You're more annoying than an automated faucet that won't turn back on—and your hands are all soapy."

Rodrigo starts to chuckle but holds it in. "Oh yeah? Well, you're more annoying than a million hashtags strung together . . . #charley# annoying#holdthedamnboardsteady#youregonnagetfired."

I get his true intent, and it's nothing to laugh at. The game is officially over. It's a draw.

He climbs down from the ladder. We both step back warily because neither of us is sure the board is going to stay put, but it does.

"Why do you do it?" he asks, his voice softening. "If there's a stray *anything,* you're taking it in. Remember the raccoon?"

"It was a *baby,*" I remind him.

"For a bit. Then it was a hissing monster that you kept in your room until George made you call animal control."

"I nursed that little creature back to health," I say proudly.

That was true. After scooping the poor fella into a box, I fed the wayward raccoon a diet of cat food, fresh fruit, and eggs. And Bandit—that's what I named him (unoriginal, I know)—got spunky in no time, and yeah, they really *are* nocturnal.

"I'm just saying that you're putting your job at risk helping out a person you don't know from a hole in the wall."

"But can you really know a hole?" asks a voice to my right.

Rodrigo and I turn at the same time to see Bree approaching. My jaw goes a little slack.

"I think of a hole as a dark place where things go and then disappear," says Bree. "I mean, I guess I *am* trying to disappear. But I'll be here for a while, so maybe we should get to know each other better."

"Okay," says Rodrigo, stepping forward, assessing Bree suspiciously. "Tell me about yourself."

I hear Bree take in a breath. "Well . . . I'm Bree Bradford from Boston. I work as a bartender."

"I know this game," Rodrigo says with mock delight. "I'm Rodrigo from Rockport, and I work as a radio repairman. Charley, your turn."

"Cute," says Bree, "but alliteration aside, it's all true—or at least it was. I'm not working right now. But I'll get a job as soon as I get back home." Bree glances over to me. "Like I said, I have plenty of places interested in hiring me." Turning to Rodrigo, she adds, "And I'm on the run from an abusive boyfriend named Jake, who didn't like me working as a bartender because he's got a jealous streak five miles wide, and shame on me that I let him control me. But no more. Thanks to Charley, I'm hanging out here until he gets tired of looking for me or has to leave Maine to get back to work, whichever comes first."

Bree extends her hand to Rodrigo, signaling the end of her lengthy introduction. He doesn't take it right away. His stony expression conveys that he's still not sold on our new guest. He tilts his head to one side, eyeing Bree like he's my protective father. Eventually, he shakes her hand.

"So you're our frogger," he says, drawing out the word. "Which room did she hide you in?"

"Wisteria, for now," I tell him.

Rodrigo makes a tsk-tsk sound. He knows, as do I, that it's one of the most expensive rooms we have. What can I say? I felt bad for her.

"Best sleep I've had in ages," Bree says.

"Well, it should be. That room is three-fifty a night. And that's the off-season rate."

"Like I said, I'm gonna make it up to Charley," Bree says.

Rodrigo's mouth slips into a frown. "She'll need more than your twelve hundred dollars if she loses her job."

"She won't lose anything," Bree promises. "I'll be extra careful once the Bishop sisters arrive. That was our deal."

Rodrigo still doesn't look convinced. He's eyeing her up and down, assessing her shrewdly. I have the sense he's checking out her wardrobe, and I am, too—a cashmere sweater and what could be designer jeans. Her ankle boots are vintage leather, very chic. She wears her style with elegant ease. I can't help but be a little skeptical. *How does she have these nice clothes, but not have the money to pay me?* Maybe Jake bought them for her. What do I know?

Rodrigo does the dad stance—arms folded, standing extra tall. "You both need to be hypervigilant starting right *now*," he warns, "because Vicki Bishop and her husband, Todd, are arriving in a few hours, and Todd already informed me that they'll be staying in the Wisteria Room."

"Shit," I grumble. "I'll move her to French Country."

"Taken. They're our only remaining guests, so I gave them a late checkout."

"Right," I say with a sigh.

Rodrigo's expression softens, but he won't take his eyes off Bree. "Put her in the Library Room," he says with a huff. "If you're going to hide, you may as well have something to read."

Bree smiles appreciatively.

"We can't board that room from the outside," Rodrigo continues. "But we can tape some plastic bags over the windows. That way, our little stowaway will stay nice and dry if Larry makes landfall. And if he doesn't, the plastic will keep you out of sight. The Cub Scouts weren't actively recruiting a lot of gay Hispanic boys from Maine who were on the run with a single mother hiding from ICE, but I do know how to be prepared."

Bree chuckles and so do I, but Rodrigo isn't smiling.

"That's a true story about me and my mother, for your information," he says, "and for the moment this is a no-levity zone, Ms. Bree—at least until you and I get to know each other better. You can stay here and help me board up windows while Charley gets your room ready. Plastic bags and tape are in the kitchen," he tells me. "I'm going to stay here with Ms. Bree and suss out our frogger like she's never been sussed before."

He sends her a tough-guy stare that isn't nearly as intimidating as he'd like to believe.

"Looking forward to it," Bree says with swagger that I admire.

Rodrigo sends me off with a wave of his hand, his nails buffed to a shine. The only polish I use is Pledge.

"Go," he instructs. "I've got this."

Chapter 7

I walk to the spacious kitchen, where Olga greets me with a grunt. She's standing near a well-stocked spice rack covering a portion of the floral-patterned wallpaper that gives the kitchen the quaint feel of an old English country home.

"He wants me to stay—says the storm is going to miss, but what if it doesn't? I've got to protect my house," she growls.

Reaching up, she grabs a copper pot, one of a dozen or so that dangle from the ceiling on wrought-iron hooks. I recoil slightly when she slams the pot onto the long wooden butcher-block counter that runs through the center of the room. I take a step back, bumping up against a shelving unit stocked with glass jars full of flour, sugar, and salt, among other cooking ingredients. Thankfully none fall off and break. I don't need Olga any angrier.

"Who? What?" I ask.

"Todd," snarls Olga, who's wearing her white cook's uniform.

Todd. Vicki's husband. Right.

"It's ridiculous. I'm not his property," Olga declares as she gets down another pot. "I have to look out for myself, too, you know. I put up with George for all these years, and it doesn't look like things are going to get any better with his replacements."

With so few guests remaining, she's not as busy as usual. Normally she's a whirlwind, going from burner to burner on the oversize stainless-steel stove, but instead of meal prep, she places the two pots she got down into a cardboard box set open on the counter. *What's going on?*

Olga doesn't suffer fools easily. She's a hardy Mainer now who's retained a Scandinavian accent since her immigration here from Sweden decades ago. She keeps her hair short and her face makeup-free because Olga has time in her day only for things that matter.

It's clear from her dour expression that looking after her house during a hurricane is one such thing. That house is all she has left. It's where she raised her only son, Samuel, who died many years ago. I don't know any of the details of Sam's death, but I believe the loss is the reason for her gruff exterior. Olga's a kind woman, but she keeps her heart hidden beneath a thick coat of armor to protect it from breaking again.

A picture of Sam hangs in the upstairs hallway. George framed photos of his favorite staff throughout the years and put them on display to give the impression that he treated his employees like family. In the photo of Sam, he's in the kitchen, standing next to a tall pile of freshly washed dishes. Olga is smiling beside him. I heard it was one of the last pictures ever taken of her beloved son.

It happens to be next to a photo that always catches my attention—it's of a beautiful young woman, leaning up against a sporty gleaming white car. She's dressed in an outfit similar to the scrub dress I have to wear, but she's so much prettier than me. She has a gorgeous smile, though it's hard to read. It feels melancholic, but maybe I'm projecting. That sad smile could be the reason I relate to her so much. Not sure how she could afford the fancy car on the stipend George paid, but I don't know her circumstances. I'm guessing she didn't have to cover her nana's ever-increasing rent.

Olga bangs her pots and pans together angrily while I get the trash bags and tape as fast as I can, departing in a hurry to prepare Bree's room. I don't need Olga's temper turning on me.

From a window in the upstairs Library Room, I peer into the backyard, where Bree and Rodrigo are putting up plywood. The chokeberry and gray dogwood bushes have long lost their flowers, but they still help beautify the landscape out back. From what I can see, they're getting along just fine. They appear to be talking amiably, and

I even see Bree crack up at something Rodrigo said. That's no surprise. Rodrigo keeps me laughing all the time.

I get started covering the windows, but all the books distract me. This room is full of them—hence the name—and it even has a cool wooden ladder that slides across the wall so you can reach the shelves way up high. Guests are always leaving new books behind, which I put away with care like I'm a librarian. That's a job I could see myself doing. I can't think of a better career than matching people with books.

This is my favorite room in the hotel, or at least it was. Now I hate cleaning it, and there's a reason I never considered hiding Bree in here.

I pull a random volume off the shelf. For me, books are magic. They transport me to a different world. Opening the cover of a new book never fails to fill with hope. It's as though it's whispering that I have the power to choose a different life, even if I never seem to leave the one I have.

I run my fingers along the binding as though I can absorb the text by touch alone. The faint scent of old leather and ink follows me as I carry the book to the bed. As I'm sitting down, my hand brushes the cottony bedspread, and the wood frame creaks under my weight. That sound triggers something within me. My heart jitters like it did that day. My skin prickles once again, as if my body is alerting me to danger.

Then it's as if I've stepped into the pages of a novel. Only it's my own story, my memory, transporting me back to the moment everything changed.

I see myself, or the shadow of me from a couple of years ago, dusting the windowsills in this very room. My back's to the door, so I don't see George enter. I imagine he stalks in like a panther on the prowl, but he could have been an elephant and I wouldn't have heard him. I'm hyperfocused on my work. I'm new on the job, but I've quickly discovered how particular George can be about the dusting—particular about everything, really.

Something makes me turn. I gasp when I see him.

"You scared me," I say.

He doesn't smile. Doesn't speak.

My stomach tightens. I'm in trouble. I've done something wrong. I can feel it.

He scans the room like a drill sergeant conducting a barracks inspection. Judgment radiates off him. He drags a plump finger across the windowsill I just dusted. While this makes no sound, it might as well be nails on a chalkboard. He lifts his hand to eye level, rubbing his fingers together as though something offensive coats the tips. He shakes his head in disapproval.

"Do you honestly think this is acceptable?" he asks, wheezing out the words like an asthmatic.

I know better than to answer.

"Learn how to clean properly or I'll toss you out on your ass. Find another job that will give you free room and board—good luck with that."

"I understand," I say, my head bowed. "I'm sorry. I'll do better."

"Damn straight you will," George says. "Or you'll be gone before you can say 'welfare.'"

He waddles out of the room without another word. George is about as fit as he is kind. I've heard from the staff that he's always on a diet, telling Olga to make him this or that depending on the current weight loss fad he's trying. The diets never work, and he's forever looking for someone to blame for the pounds not coming off.

He might be physically doughy, but there's nothing soft about George Bishop. He's an intimidating presence, and yet I can see there was once a handsome man under that fleshy exterior. He has luminous blue eyes and something of a kind smile when he decides to use it, like on the day he lured me away from the diner to work here. Many guests, including me, have mistaken his cheery disposition and rosy complexion for a jovial nature, when in fact it's nothing more than a bear trap designed to lure money out of wallets or pretty girls away from their dreadful waitressing gigs.

George finds me sometime later that day. He asks me to follow him back to the Library Room. I gasp when I enter. He's got a bottle of wine open on a table by the bed and two candles burning. To this day, the smell of beeswax and lavender makes me shiver. He invites me to sit down on the bed.

I know an order when I hear one.

The bedframe groans under his weight, as if in pain. He wants to know if I'm old enough to drink. He knows I'm not, but he seems to need to hear me say it, like it's a turn-on or something.

"I'm sorry I was so hard on you earlier," he says. "But I'm teaching you to have high standards."

"Thanks," I say, unsure how else to respond.

I feel incredibly nervous sitting on a bed next to this imposing individual who smells like old tobacco and sweat. Instinctively, my eyes dart about, searching for the nearest exit. Unfortunately, to get there, I have to go past George.

He pours two glasses of wine, and before I can say, *no thank you*, he has pressed one into my hand, as if insisting I drink. I take a small, tentative sip. My throat closes up from fear. I'm not sure I can swallow.

"What do you think?" He appraises my body up and down, as if he's savoring me instead of the wine. "It's from the year you were born. The grapes that year were sweet and ripe . . . just like you."

With that, I manage to suck down an extra big gulp of wine, hoping it will calm my nerves. No luck. My hands are so shaky I'm worried I'm going to drop the glass.

George places a hand on my knee. I freeze like his touch has turned me to stone. "You could put in a little more effort, though, and I'm not talking about your cleaning," he says.

"What do you mean?" I ask, surprised I could get out the words. My anxiety is rising. His probing gaze burns a hole into my skull.

"I'm saying with a little more care, you could really turn heads. I saw it immediately at the diner. You have an incredible body. I can help you, Charley—a little makeup, some new clothes that show you off . . ." He slides closer, his face intimately near mine, the smell of his stale breath overpowering me.

Instinctively, I push him away.

George acts amused, a condescending half-smile on his lips. "I like girls who play hard to get," he says. "But I always win in the end."

He slides his hand to my inner thigh, as though staking his claim.

Chapter 8

At one-fifteen, the bell over the front door announces the arrival of the first Bishop sister. She's dressed like most guests, her clothing practical and casual for the long car ride. Her floral-patterned crop pants, pearl-white trainers, and cute long-sleeved pink top are the perfect outfit for someone not ready to let go of summer. She enters like a warm breeze, her gleaming smile coming across as both affable and sincere. With a pair of designer sunglasses resting on her head like a glossy tiara, she exudes an aura of nonchalant perfection. Nestled in the crook of her arm, a taupe Fendi purse made of soft suede with a striped texture signals some level of status, its sleek design adding to her overall confident appearance.

She enters with a swagger like she owns the place, which technically she does. But I have a feeling she looks this in charge wherever she goes. Some people just have a commanding presence, and she's definitely one of them—polished and poised, with shimmering, healthy blond hair pulled back into a tight ponytail, calling attention to her pretty face and ageless skin.

As she approaches, my eyes are drawn to the sparkling pendant she's wearing. It's the largest diamond I've ever seen, surrounded by a cluster of smaller diamonds, hanging from a gleaming silver chain. Shiny silver hoop earrings complement her necklace to perfection. If pawned, her jewelry would probably keep Nana at Guiding Way for life.

Following close behind the woman is a middle-aged man I assume to be her husband. His attire is casual chic, with a sport coat over a crisp blue button-down. The shirt matches the color of his eyes, which dart about our Great Room, taking it all in as if it's his first viewing. I suspect that's not true, though none of the family has visited during my employment.

The man's reaction isn't unusual. Visitors are always in awe of the collection of crap (I mean art) that George has bought over the years.

I'm a little surprised that I find this man mildly attractive. He's tall and self-assured, with light brown hair that's slightly graying at the temples. He has the chiseled features of a classic Hollywood leading man and a lopsided grin that's impossible not to find endearing. There's something mischievous and playful in his eyes. When he looks at me, I catch a spark that I suspect can turn into an inferno without warning.

Rodrigo, who has emerged from behind the front desk to greet our new arrivals, jumps into action. His attention lingers on the man a beat too long. It's clear he's noticed his good looks as well. The man hands over the two suitcases he's carrying, giving Rodrigo an appreciative nod, but no tip. The woman, who smiles warmly at me, isn't carrying any luggage at all, unless her fancy Fendi bag counts.

She looks at her gold watch. "Six hours and fifteen minutes," she says to the man. "If we had left at seven like I told you we should, we would have been here at one o'clock on the dot. Now my eating schedule is going to be all wonky."

Great. A control freak. Just what I need.

The woman's focus shifts to me. "You must be Charley," she says with enthusiasm. Her voice is warm and inviting as she gives me a wide smile. I have to admit, I'm a little jealous of her perfectly straight, envelope-white teeth. I should have had braces when I was eleven, but my family prioritized groceries over dental work.

Before I can answer, the woman wraps her arms around me as if she's a beloved aunt. The embrace sparks an unexpected rush of good feelings. It's only when we break apart that I realize how much I've needed physical touch, any contact at all. I've been lonely, and now I'm missing my mother. In my imagination, I often cast guests into the role of my mother—or the woman I wish she had been, without drugs, alcohol, and awful men. This woman would certainly get a call-back audition for the part.

"I've heard so much about you," she says, peering deeply into my eyes. I feel like a snake being charmed by her bedazzling jewels and hypnotic stare. "I'm Victoria, but you must call me Vicki, deal? We're family, as far as I'm concerned. My father told me so much about you—raved, really."

Pawed, actually, I think. Already I like this woman too much to tarnish her memory of her beloved dad, so I keep my mouth shut.

Nana always tried to be the mother mine never could be, but she had the disadvantage of brittle bones and a fading memory. Over the years, I've encountered plenty of women like Vicki—put-together moms with a perfect wardrobe, a perfect husband, and perfect little kids that they somehow manage to control without yelling. If Vicki has children, I imagine they'd be around my age. Her skin looks spa-serviced, but up close I can spot the telltale signs of aging around her eyes and lips. Concealer can hide only so much.

"This is Todd, my husband."

She pulls Todd toward her as if he's some kind of stage prop. The decor seems to hold his attention more than our introduction.

"Forgive his manners," says Vicki. "Todd hasn't been to the Precipice in, what? Eight years, hon? More?"

Todd ponders. "Well, eight years ago I was in Africa, and after that it was the Amazon," he says, squinting his eyes as though peering into the past.

"Please, let's not bore Charley to death with stories of your exploits."

"I'm just trying to figure out when I was here last," Todd explains. "When was Everest?"

"In your dreams," says Vicki.

"Just because I didn't summit doesn't mean I didn't climb it."

"Let's just say it's been a while since you were last here," Vicki clarifies tersely.

I'm thinking, *Vicki hasn't been a frequent flier here, either.*

"Well, excuse me if I didn't visit your dad in the boonies very often,"

Todd retorts. "But we had our adventures together. Just last year, I took him to Vegas for his birthday."

"You took him to the *Bunny Ranch*," Vicki corrects in disgust. Turning to me, she says, "It's a whorehouse . . . and a legal one, at that."

Can't say I've had this level of candor with new guests before. I'm totally speechless and somewhat intrigued.

"*Brothel* is the preferred term," says Todd, who puffs up defensively. "Those women are professionals."

"Oh, I bet you know *all about* their professionalism," says Vicki, offering a tinged smile.

"I told you I abstained. It was a birthday gift for your father, and given his unexpected passing, a well-timed one at that."

"Believe me, Todd, you've made it quite clear you should be awarded a medal for your restraint and *generous* spirit."

"And your dad made it clear that the butter churner was a life-changing experience."

Rodrigo asks, "What's the butter—"

Vicki cuts him off. "Don't ask," she says. "Just look it up for yourself or use your imagination."

Todd sneers. "You don't appreciate a thing I do. And I'd have visited the hotel more often if it wasn't located in the sticks of Maine. No nightlife. No adventure. No excitement. There's nothing but nothing around here."

Vicki throws up her hands in exasperation. "People come from all over just to enjoy the views—and visit Acadia National Park, which you've never even seen, so you shouldn't comment."

"Oh, whatever," grumbles Todd. "It's too damn cold here. Even in the summer, you can't swim in the ocean, and I'm no fan of the moose. But I will say, perhaps I should have visited more." I watch him eye everything greedily, like he's ready to pack it up and take it all with him. "There's a lot here we could sell at our stores. George even told me there's at least one piece of art that collectors all over the world would envy. Poor fellow never got around to having it appraised. Never did tell us which painting it was."

"Well, we're not removing a thing," Vicki warns. "I told you, we're not shutting this place down. We'll figure out the logistics of running it later. And as for this mysterious painting—Daddy was full of tall tales, so I don't give his hidden treasure story much credence."

I feel slightly relieved to know I may still have a job, and more than a little curious about this painting.

Turning to me, Vicki says, "Todd is always concocting a new moneymaking scheme to fund his adventures ... only most of them are money-*losing*."

"Har-har," replies Todd.

Eyeing me, Vicki continues, "Todd and I have seven gift and jewelry stores in the Boston area."

"I think we might be opening store number eight," Todd says, rubbing his hands together as he continues his assessment of all the treasures surrounding us.

"We sell a wide mix of items at our stores," Vicki tells me. "A lot of it comes from estate sales, so this place is like a trip to the bank for my husband, who happens to want a trip to Antarctica. He's seeing dollar signs, not my father's beloved antiques."

"We've gone through a bit of a rough patch," Todd explains, turning to look at Vicki. "On account of your sister, no less."

Vicki grips Todd's arm, glaring at him. "This isn't the time or the place for that," she says. Almost immediately, her affable smile returns as if "Loose Lips Vicki" hadn't been upset at all. I may have initially offered Vicki a callback for the "mom role," but now I'm having second thoughts about her suitability for the part. Something tells me there's a lot more to Vicki Bishop than meets the eye.

Rodrigo and I seem to be on the same page as we exchange wary glances.

Redirecting her attention to Rodrigo, Vicki says, "I'll give my husband a pass. We're both utterly exhausted from our trip. I'm going to need to double my Pilates classes next week after sitting in the car so long. I desperately want to go to my room and freshen up. Rodrigo, can you unlock the Library Room for us, please?"

Panic floods my chest. I go perfectly still, trying not to look alarmed, but inside I'm completely freaking out.

The Library Room . . . oh, shit. Bree. Disaster.

"I've already requested the Wisteria Room," says Todd.

"Yes, we have that room prepped and ready for you," I say proudly.

Vicki eyes Todd with disdain. "You don't know a thing about these rooms, or me, for that matter," she says.

"I looked it up online." Todd's voice rises with exasperation. "The Wisteria Room is the best—well, the most expensive."

"Always the most expensive for you," says Vicki with a groan. "But when will you learn that the most expensive isn't always the best? Besides, if you paid any attention at all, you'd know that my mother *died* in the Wisteria Room. I'm not staying there. No thank you. The Library Room was always my favorite. It used to be full of children's books when we were kids. I can't tell you how many afternoons I spent getting lost in those stories. My sisters and I fought over that room like crazy, so I want to claim it before they do."

My anxiety goes through the roof. When we stashed Bree in there, we did so assuming the sisters wouldn't want one of the smaller rooms in the hotel. Now I'm finding out it holds special significance for them *all*. Can you say *nightmare*?

"You can't stay in there," I blurt out.

Vicki falls back on her heels, clearly not accustomed to hearing *no* for an answer, especially from an employee.

"I'm sorry, but . . . why the hell not?" she asks. "Are there guests staying in that room? Are there *any* guests at all in the hotel?"

My heart is doing a tap dance in my chest.

"No," I stammer. "All reservations were canceled because of the weather."

"For a fee, I hope," says Todd. "You didn't let them cancel for free, did you?"

"Oh, you and your dollar signs," Vicki complains. "It's all you care about."

Her smile is as icy as an arctic blast, but she quickly refocuses her attention on me, more interested in the room where Bree is hiding than in antagonizing her husband.

"So if it's empty," she continues, "I'll have my bags brought there."

Rodrigo, who is hovering nearby with the luggage, locks eyes with me. He knows I'm too anxious to speak up.

"Um, yeah—about the Library Room. It's not ready, not yet anyway," says Rodrigo, stumbling over the words. "We haven't secured it—for the storm, I mean. The weather reports now have Larry making a direct hit on Jonesport. And with the ocean winds picking up tonight, I'd hate for you to be in there if something was to happen. Charley can have it ready for you in the morning, no problem at all, if that's all right with you."

Vicki pats Rodrigo on his cheek with affection. "Do you actually listen to those weather people? Really? I'm guessing you devour the mainstream news as well," she says, putting *news* in air quotes. "These storms are never as bad as they predict. Everything is 'once in a generation' these days. The media hypes up the weather to get viewers glued to their televisions, when they're not out buying needless supplies to prop up the economy. Next you'll tell me you think that climate change is real. We'll be fine there. So Library Room, please."

"No!" I shout.

Vicki switches her focus from Rodrigo to me, completely puzzled. Rodrigo shoots me a desperate look and I know I've got to come up with something quick.

"The room is a mess," I spit out. "There's plywood to replace the plastic bags over the windows, and nails, all that kind of stuff, all over the place." I wave my arms in a big circle to emphasize the extent of the disaster. "It's a tetanus shot waiting to happen," I add for good measure. "I promise, I'll have it clean for you by morning."

"By morning?" says Vicki, who sounds rather annoyed.

"Let it go, honey," Todd implores, taking hold of his wife's arm. "Let the staff do their job."

"Fine," Vicki mutters. "Put me in the Italian Room next door. That way it'll be easy-peasy to move us when it's ready. And leave the windows uncovered, please. Even if this hurricane hits, it won't be nearly as bad as everyone is making it out to be."

Meanwhile, I'm thinking: *The Italian Room next door? Way too close for comfort. I'll have to warn Bree to be extra quiet.*

If Bree calls attention to herself, perfect Vicki and her financially motivated husband might want to see the credit card transaction or cash deposit. And I'll be utterly screwed.

Chapter 9

The coast is clear—all seems quiet. Vicki and Todd are huddled in George's office off the reception area, going over paperwork and whatnot. This gives me time to sneak some bread, cheese, and a bottle of Pellegrino up to Bree's room, feeding her like a stray cat. I'm relieved that Bree's conversation with Rodrigo earlier in the day had gone surprisingly well. Despite his initial reservations, he liked her enough to keep our secret.

Rodrigo had conveyed part of their backyard chat for my benefit. "I told her you've got a heart of gold and sometimes it overtakes your better judgment," he said. "I warned her, in no uncertain terms, that if she breaks it by breaking her promise to you, she'll have a hurricane on her hands that's a heck of a lot worse than Larry."

I hugged him in gratitude. I love his sweet and saucy sides equally. He may have doubts, but I feel confident I'll get my money.

When I arrive at Bree's room, I use a light knock to alert her. We didn't establish a secret code, so when she doesn't answer, I let myself in. I whisper, "It's me, Charley," as I open the door, taking a furtive glance down the hall before slipping inside. Bree leaps off the bed as if it's electrified and scurries to a corner of the room, trying to hide. I quietly shut the door behind me as Bree is catching her breath.

"Holy shit. I thought it was game over," says Bree, still breathing hard. Her whispered voice is ripe with relief. She steps forward into the light, a hand on her chest. I can almost feel her racing heart.

"I brought you something to eat," I say. "Thought you might be hungry. It's not much, but I'm sure I can sneak you some leftovers after dinner."

I set the silver tray down on a small table adjacent to one of the large covered windows. Bree grabs two glasses before taking a seat, inviting me to join her. She drinks and eats, being extra careful with the silverware, trying not to make any clatter.

"I heard people next door," Bree says with apprehension. "Really freaked me out. Is someone staying in that room?"

She points to the adjacent wall.

"That would be Vicki and Todd," I say.

A look of unease flickers across Bree's face. "She wants *this* room," I explain, "but we made up a story that it wasn't ready and put her off for a day. She settled on the Italian Room until she can move in here. You'll need to change rooms, most likely tonight, after they go to bed. But please stay put until I come get you—no late-night strolls allowed. And whatever you do, don't open the fire exit at the end of the hall; you can get outside that way, but it will set off the alarm. Guests make that mistake all the time."

"Got it, but why does Vicki want this room so bad?" Bree asks.

I shrug. "I guess the sisters had story time in here when they were kids. It's sentimental to them."

Bree sighs. "I get it, at least in theory. I was an only child, so I don't have those kinds of shared memories." She looks wistful as she impales a hunk of cheese with her fork. Then with genuine curiosity, she asks, "What about your family? Do you have brothers and sisters? And what about your parents, are you close to them?"

My eyes fill with sorrow and I can see that Bree regrets her question. This whole arrangement revolves around meeting our immediate needs—like safety and money, the basic stuff of survival. I had no intention of opening up to Bree beyond the bare minimum. This woman is still essentially a stranger. But when the person you love most in the world can't remember your name, it leaves you feeling adrift. I want so badly to be seen and heard, to feel like my story, small as it is, matters to somebody other than me. Which is why, when Bree inquires, I feel strangely compelled to open up. And like Rodrigo said, my heart and better judgment are sometimes at odds.

"I don't know my father, and my mom died a few years ago. My nana is all I have now. She lives at a place called Guiding Way."

"I'm sorry to hear about your mom," Bree says. "That must be tough, especially to lose her when you're still so young."

A pit opens in my stomach as Bree touches my hand. It's as if she knew I was about to cry. I appreciate that she's being careful with my emotions. It makes me trust her more.

"What's Guiding Way?" she asks.

"It's a senior living home. Nana has dementia, so she can't be on her own anymore."

Bree's face twists with empathy. "Oh, that's just terrible. Life is crazy unfair—and so incredibly fragile. My mom died, too, a long time ago. I guess we've got that sad story in common. That type of loss changes you."

"What happened to your mom, if you don't mind my asking?"

"It was cancer," says Bree darkly. She leaves it at that, but there's definitely more to the story than she's willing to share. It's like I can almost see the walls coming up around her. I'm smart enough to let it go. The flood of emotion seems to subside when she looks at me.

"After my mother died, I ended up in foster care," Bree continues. "It was, um . . . well, let's just say, *not* a good experience."

"You never knew your father, either?" I ask.

Bree's mouth tightens. "I found out who he was later on in life. But no, I didn't grow up knowing him. Unfortunately, most of the men in my life have really sucked. I almost had a stepfather—but, well, that didn't work out. Things would have been a whole lot different for me if it had, that's for sure." Bree momentarily averts her gaze. When she looks back at me, there's distance in her eyes. "What about you?" she asks. "You said you never met your father?"

Now I'm the one who briefly looks away. "I know his name, but that's about it. Never met him. He charmed my mom into following him to Tennessee so he could become a NASCAR driver. From the stories I heard, he got angry when he didn't win and then took it out on my mom. She left, he stayed, and that was the end of it. I don't think he even knows I exist."

I'm not sad telling Bree this. I often think of Frank, as I'm always role-playing my mother, Mary Beth, for Nana. I don't mind talking about Frank, I don't really care about him, but I'd give anything for Nana to remember my name.

"I know about guys like that—abusers. I have one for an ex-boyfriend."

Bree rolls up the sleeve of her shirt, revealing an ugly purple and black bruise marking a good portion of her right forearm.

"He did this to you? Jake? That's his name, right?"

Bree nods and I flinch, as if the physical violence she endured touched me as well.

"I hope you'll be safe here," I say. "I'll do my best to keep you out of sight. Have you heard from him again?"

"Funny you should ask. He sent me these messages just a little while ago." Taking out her phone, Bree does some navigating before passing it over to me. I read.

Where are you??!

I can't take this silence.

I know you're doing this to hurt
me. It's not fair. I barely touched
you and you act like I attacked
you. You're WAY overreacting—
like always.

You know how much I love you.
It would kill me to think you're
with someone else. I couldn't
stand it. You know that, Bree.

I can't let that happen . . . I
WON'T.

You know what I'm capable of.

My expression hardens as I hand Bree her phone.

"He *did* attack me," she says. "Gave me this parting gift before I ran." Again, she points to her bruised arm.

"What does he mean, 'You know what I'm capable of'?"

"He's threatening me," says Bree as if the answer should be obvious.

"Can you go to the police *now*?" I ask, hopeful.

Bree shakes her head. "I've been dealing with this abuse from Jake for a long time," she says. "There's not much the police can do. Restraining orders don't help when someone is determined to kill you."

I wince.

"Don't worry, I don't think he'll find me here," she says. "You just might be saving my life, Charley."

I feel the full weight of that responsibility. It's almost too much to bear.

I've had my fill of sadness for the day, so I get ready to go. Bree thanks me again as I make my way to the door. I promise to bring her more food after dinner, before we make the big move.

As I'm closing the door behind me, I hear a voice at my back. "Getting my room ready?"

Whirling, I come face-to-face with Vicki Bishop. She's changed outfits but looks no less put together in her fitted jeans and beige cardigan over a silky white blouse. In place of the diamond pendant, she's now wearing a pearl necklace that I'm sure isn't fake. She's even prettier with her blond hair out of its ponytail, falling loosely over her shoulders and softening her features. I don't have my work uniform on, and my cart is in the utility closet at the end of the hall, but at least I left the silver tray inside the room, so I don't have to explain that.

"I was just checking out the workload . . . shouldn't be too bad. I'll have it all set by the morning," I say.

I'm speaking extra loudly, hoping that Bree will hear and hide in a closet. Before I get a chance to fully close the door, Vicki places her hand on the doorknob. My heart rockets to my throat as she pushes it open a crack. I'm trying not to scream.

Vicki pauses, turning to me. "On second thought, let's you and I take a little stroll," she says, pulling the door closed. At least I can breathe again. "There are things we should discuss." Her blue eyes have frosted over.

A slight tremor passes through me. Something tells me Bree being discovered might actually be better than a walk-and-talk with Vicki Bishop.

Chapter 10

'm strolling the grounds with Vicki, bracing myself for what's to come. Is she letting the staff go? Or planning to hire some militant new manager who will make our lives miserable? Maybe she wants to cut our pay.

Even as my mind spins, I can't help but take in my surroundings. It's impossible to ignore the scenic beauty of this place. If I do lose my job, I'll miss these magnificent views, not to mention the paycheck. As we amble along the curved brick walkway abutting the sprawling gardens and lush green lawn, my gaze travels over the bluff of Gull Hill to the frothy, turbulent ocean beyond.

Second only to the awe of the sea is the Precipice itself. It is truly a sight to behold. The rambling four-story structure with curved walls and sloping roofs, fronted with charming weather-worn shingles, looks more like some rich dude's home than a hotel. It's a statement piece, that's for sure. I remember coming here as a kid with my nana. We didn't have the money for an overnight stay, but I got to weave in and out of the archways and gaze over the rickety wooden fence that provides a flimsy barrier between the hotel grounds and a hundred-foot plunge to the shoreline. This time of day, small groups of people usually gather outside, enjoying the vista from candy-colored Adirondack chairs sprinkled over the lawn or from under the cover of our large dome-topped gazebo. But not today.

At Vicki's request, I have a clipboard in hand to take notes. She marches at a purposeful pace, with me trailing behind. Her gaze darts about as she observes it all with an eye for detail.

"We have a lot to go over before the others arrive. My sister Faith should be here soon, and my son, Quinn, will arrive after dinner with my other sister, Iris. Quinn is such a sweetheart. He offered to come late and drive his aunt, who doesn't have her license."

Vicki's eye roll suggests that's a story for another day, so I don't pry. But great. I can only imagine what this lady did to lose her license. And if this rando guy, Quinn, is anything like his mom, he'll probably be overindulged and intolerable. But of course he's her little angel. Whatever.

"He's about your age," she tells me. "I'm sure you two will hit it off splendidly." She adds a playful wink, her perfectly applied cherry-red lipstick spreading into a crescent as she smiles. "I'd be surprised if he doesn't take an immediate interest in you, Charley. He's quite the charmer. And I think he's got a thing for the plain old girl-next-door types."

Plain old what?!

If this is intended to be a compliment, I'm not exactly feeling the love.

Vicki resumes her assessment. "We need to get a roofer here," she tells me while I'm still obsessing over my looks. "I can't even imagine how much that's going to cost. And the gutters? When were those last cleaned?"

"I don't know," I say, wondering why she isn't asking Rodrigo instead of the maid.

"Well, take down a note to have them serviced."

"Right," I say, jotting the note on the paper secured to my clipboard.

She runs her hand along a section of shingles.

"These feel rotted," she says, eyeing me expectantly.

Unsure what to do, I brush my hand along the same spots she touched. They feel like shingles to me.

"You want these looked at?" I ask.

She peers at me as though I'm dim. "Of course," she says, so I write *shingles* on the paper, unsure what to do or who to call. I quickly fall into step behind her as she walks the hotel's perimeter. She crouches down near the foundation.

"Ants," she says grimly.

I write down: *pest control.*

She's back up and walking. "Paint—all the railings and shutters."

"Yes, ma'am," I say like I'm addressing a drill sergeant.

"My father didn't care for *anything* very well."

I get the feeling her assessment applies to his children as well as to his possessions.

"We're just going to have to redo this whole place," she says, exasperated.

She makes her way to the colorful Adirondack chairs. After tugging on the back of some, she acts surprised that they don't come apart in her grasp.

"These are so rickety," she declares. "We'll need to replace them all."

I trail her back over to the hotel, glancing at the chairs, which seem perfectly fine to me.

"The wildflower garden has to go as well," she says. "It basically looks like a bunch of weeds."

"It's lovely when they're all in bloom," I tell her.

She lowers her sunglasses to the bridge of her nose. "What, for three weeks out of the year?"

"Right," I say, jotting down *Get rid of the garden.*

"And all these windows are nothing but drafty," she says. "They'll all have to go."

I nod before adding *new windows* to my ever-growing list.

Vicki comes to a complete stop. She faces the hotel like a boxer squaring off against a larger, more formidable opponent.

"It's *all* going to have to go," she says, heaving a big sigh.

"What is?" I ask.

"Everything . . . inside and out," she says. "We're going to need to redo it all."

"Redo it?" I ask.

"Yes," Vicki answers curtly. "I hate to admit that my husband is right, but in this case, I think he is. The outside is as bad as the interior. And all that *stuff*? You can't think clearly. There's so much clutter."

"But that's sort of what gives the hotel its charm," I say, knowing it's not my place to interject, but that doesn't stop me. I'm unsure how Vicki takes my assessment because she doesn't lower her glasses to let me see her eyes.

"There's simply too much stuff," she repeats, closing off any avenues for debate. "We need to standardize. The walls should all be beige. And we need more traditional art—more New England coastal scenes, ships, that sort of thing. There's no rhyme or reason to any of it. Figurines from Asia. Art Deco prints of God knows what. African masks. It's a global calamity in there, that's what it is."

"What would you like to do differently?" I ask.

"Streamline, make it all uniform," Vicki says. "Couches and chairs that look like they actually go together. Something like this."

She shows me a picture on her phone of a hotel that could be a showroom at a Pottery Barn. It's so boring I want to yawn.

"That looks nice," I lie.

"We should probably just tear the place down and turn it into condos. We'd make a killing," she says.

I gulp, knowing that also means I'd have no place to live. Vicki takes a step back as if the added distance allows her to assess things more properly.

"We used to live up there," she tells me, pointing to the third floor. "That was our bedroom, in fact—Faith, Iris, and me, we slept there." She directs my attention to what I know is the Tiger Lily Room, so named for the stunning wallpaper decorated with that namesake flower. It surprises me, but my heart breaks a little at the thought that all these rooms will lose their uniqueness. They'll be no different than a Hilton, or worse . . . condos. Most of my memories of this place are of me on my hands and knees scrubbing around toilets, ignoring rude guests, or fending off George's advances. Yet somehow news of this grand makeover leaves me feeling empty inside. But last I checked, nobody was asking for my opinion.

"Mom and Dad's room was over there," Vicki says, directing my

attention to what we call the Mayflower Room. The walls are decorated with unique astronomy prints that George rescued from somebody's attic in Portland, but I'm sure Vicki's well aware of the room's
history. "Those were good old days, that's for sure . . . at least for a
time," Vicki says, her voice falling flat.

She turns to look at me, her eyes still concealed behind her designer sunglasses. "So, tell me, did you and my father ever spend time
together in that room?"

I swallow hard.

"Excuse me?" I stammer.

"You heard me, Charley. It's a simple question. Did you and he
ever spend time up *there*—in the room where my parents slept, in
their bed?"

"Um . . . no," I say, still stumbling for the words, which makes me
sound untruthful. She removes her glasses, and immediately, I want
her to put them back on. She's seeing me differently now. Like I'm
a tempting ripe red apple dangling from the tree. I'm what she used
to be, young and glowing. Nothing drooping. No parts sagging. Skin
shimmering like sunlight off the waves. My jeans are full. My breasts
are perky. It's as if I have *temptress* emblazoned on my wrinkle-free
forehead.

"I'm not an idiot," she tells me. "I know who he is—who he was.
Just level with me, Charley. Did you or didn't you?"

A breeze pushes hair in front of my eyes. I brush the strands away
with the back of my hand. I want Vicki to break into a smile, let me
in on the joke, but she still looks accusatory.

"Honestly, Charley, I'd have more respect for you if you'd just come
clean."

I glance at the notes scribbled on my paper. Now I get why she
wanted this one-on-one time. She's trying to pry something out of me
that didn't happen. I try to keep my expression neutral when I answer
because it feels like I'm facing a human lie detector. Even a twitch
might fill her with doubt.

"He, um—well, he made some advances, if that's what you're
asking."

"That's not what I'm asking, Charley. I'm asking if you slept with my father. Not sure how I can make that any clearer."

Reading her expression, the verdict is already in. I'm guilty as charged. Now, how to convince her of the truth? I've never had an adult speak to me this way before, so direct and forward. It's jarring. I don't know what Vicki would be like if she lost her temper, flipped her lid, went off the rails, so to speak, but I'm fairly certain it wouldn't be pretty.

I spit out three words: "No, I didn't." I'm hoping that by holding her hard stare, I'm essentially holding my ground.

Vicki takes her time forming an opinion. I'm trying not to blink. She gazes longingly up to the third floor. I can almost see the memories dropping down into her head. When she looks back at me, there's a tinge of a smile.

"I believe you," she says. "And I'm sorry. For what he must have put you through."

"It's okay, I handled it," I say.

"But you're so young to be living in the lion's den."

"No bites," I say, realizing too late that my comment might come across as insensitive.

"You're lucky," Vicki tells me, a no-nonsense edge to her voice. "You look like her. You're his type."

"Like who?" I ask.

"Christine," she says.

I ask the next logical question: "Who is Christine?"

"She was a maid, just like you," Vicki says, her expression as inscrutable as the sphinx.

With that, she turns from me. She walks along the garden path, past the walls that need refurbishing, the gutters that need fixing, and the flowers she thinks need pulling.

Chapter 11

Here's what I've learned about Vicki Bishop in our short time together: she's nuts. Okay, that's a bit harsh. Let's go with *neurotic*.
The Library Room suddenly isn't her biggest priority. Getting the rest
of the hotel in shape for the next batch of arrivals is top of her mind.
I thought I had done a good job, but evidently, I'm not up to her high
standards. She wants the whole downstairs redone. The Great Room,
the dining room, the foyer, our alcove, all of it cleaned again.

For the past forty-five minutes, she's trailed me from room to
room like I'm under surveillance. I fluff a pillow this way, and she fluffs
it that way. I open a curtain an inch, and she opens it an inch more.

Her eyes must function like a carpenter's level, because she keeps
making imperceptible adjustments to almost every picture in sight.
She uses her fingers to check for dust the same way her father used to,
so this apple didn't land too far from the daddy tree. At least she hasn't
rested her hand on my inner thigh. But even if George was a freak
about the dust, not to mention other things, he never rearranged the
cleaning items on my cart the way Vicki's done. Really, Vic. I know
where the trash bags belong—now, leave my Bessie alone!

Bottom line: I can't help but feel silently judged in this woman's
presence.

"We're going to get this place put together, Charley," she says as if
the hotel is the setting for a disaster movie.

Is nothing good enough for her? Judging by the depth of Vicki's
frown lines, I'd say no.

I do pick up on the word *we*, as though we're in this together, but clearly, that's not how it's going to be. There might not be an *I* in "team," but there's no *we*, either. She'll say, and I'll do, and that's fine—it's life on the bottom rung. I'm accustomed to it.

For the entire time she trails me, all she talks about is *the stuff, the stuff, the stuff,* and *the stuff.* So much of it. Too much of it. Dust-collecting, mold-growing, allergy-spreading *stuff.* As if it were my fault that her father was an eclectic hoarder.

"But the guests like it," I remind her, and she just waves me off as though I need to have my head examined. It's artfully displayed and very tastefully organized. It's why we get so many reviews. But Vicki seems to have her mind made up, and I get the sense she's not easily dissuaded, so I don't say anything more.

When Todd shows up in the Great Room following his afternoon nap, Vicki makes a big show of how she—the Amazing Vicki Bishop—has set everything right.

Todd sits on a chair by the fire. He gives the room a cursory once-over before turning his attention back to his phone, not seeming very impressed. "Looks about the same," he says with a profound lack of interest. "But if we sell it all, you won't have nearly as much to fuss with."

Vicki harrumphs. "I told you we're not selling a thing," she says, and then looks at me with warning eyes. She's saying one thing to me and something else to Todd. *Very interesting.*

And this is when I think I understand Vicki Bishop slightly better. She has a profound need for order and control. Everything about her fits together like a jigsaw puzzle, all pieces having a purpose and a place. *So what's Todd's place in Vicki's world?* That's one puzzle piece that hasn't clicked yet.

In all the cleaning chaos, I didn't hear the bell chime, signaling a new arrival. Vicki whirls around, her face lighting up like a Christmas tree.

"Faith," she calls out, beaming. Arms wide, Vicki approaches the two women who just entered the Great Room. She hugs a strikingly beautiful brunette, who towers at least four inches over her sister.

The presence of this remarkable-looking individual momentarily takes my breath away. There are a lot of attractive people in the world, and I see plenty at the hotel, but this woman is on another level. She's not young, so I imagine what a head-turner she'd have been at my age. She'd be social media royalty, that's for sure.

On closer inspection, there's not so much as a wrinkle on her unblemished face. And her eyebrows seem frozen in place. I immediately get the sense that she has one expression and it's always camera ready. I've no doubt this is a woman who wants to hold on to her youthful beauty the way Vicki clings to control.

So this is Faith Bishop—the former model turned who knows what? But something suddenly strikes me as odd. For someone who made her living via the camera, there's not a single picture of her in the hotel. Not one. There are staff photos dating back over thirty years, but George couldn't bother framing one of his daughter's glamour shots? Call me curious about that as well.

"Look at you. You look utterly amazing," says Vicki to her sister, hints of jealousy slipping into her voice.

"Oh, you can thank Hope for that. She's making these amazing organic face creams that are top-notch. I'm trying to convince her to market them. My skin's never looked so good."

"You'll have to get me a sample," says Vicki. "And, Hope, so good to see you . . . these terrible circumstances aside, of course."

Hmmm. I'm not sure I believe these sentiments from Vicki. I've yet to see any genuine grief. After my mom died, I could feel Nana's pain as if it was a presence in the room. But there hasn't been a single tear shed for George.

There are more hugs as Todd does his meet and greet with Faith and Hope.

Hope is the smallest, most delicate person I've ever seen. She has a short-cropped pixie haircut fitting her elfish appearance. Her nose is tiny as well, though just the right size for her slight bone structure. She's wearing yoga leggings tucked into a pair of faux leather Doc Martens, and she carries a hemp bag slung over one shoulder. Even without makeup or jewelry, Hope exudes natural beauty. As the overly cute, complementary names suggest, Hope and Faith make an absolutely adorable couple, though their height difference is jarring.

"Before you ask," Vicki tells Faith, "the Library Room is mine. I've claimed it. Can't move in until the morning because these two lovelies are preparing it for the storm that's got everyone in a tizzy." She gestures to me and Rodrigo, who just entered the reception area. "Speaking of, how was your drive?"

"Long. The traffic out of New York was a bear, as always," says Faith, who has a sultry voice.

"We should have done it in two days," Hope adds. "But Faith, as usual, was worried about bedbugs, so no motels." As she removes her coat, Hope reveals a figure as delicate as a bird's.

Being a team player, I take her coat and hang it on the rack in the foyer.

"It's an epidemic," says Faith to Hope. "I promise if I see even a suggestion of a bedbug here, I'll be sleeping in my car." She cocks a grin, so we know she's kidding—at least, I think she is. "And what's the deal with doing this during a hurricane anyway?"

"We're not postponing a funeral," Vicki says. "And this storm is all hoopla and nonsense. It's going out to sea, or it'll be a little rain and that's all. Stop listening to the damn news."

Faith and Hope offer Vicki placating smiles. They've undoubtedly heard her rant about the mainstream media enough times.

I notice now that neither Faith nor Hope has any bags. Perhaps they're accustomed to New York bellhops and luggage carts.

"Where are your suitcases?" Vicki wants to know. "And your son?"

"Both are still in the car. I'll go get them," says Hope, who seems reluctant to retrieve her luggage—and perhaps her child.

Faith gives off an air of exasperation as she flips her thick, luscious hair back dramatically.

There's no better school for learning about human behavior than being a maid. You see it all in this job because nobody notices you're there. That hair flip is a clear sign of stress—and I bet the kid is the reason.

"After that long drive with Oliver, my nerves are utterly shot. I need a stiff drink," Faith says.

Bingo. Oliver must be her son, who's lagging behind in the car and has been driving his mother to drink. Maybe he's a sleeping baby. *Just what we need.*

"Did you call my psychiatrist, like I suggested?" Vicki prods.

Hmmm . . . babies don't usually need psychiatric help. It must be an older child.

"Say, Vicki, could you maybe, just for once, apply a little discretion? Please?" Faith looks directly at me.

I avert my gaze, thinking: *Don't count on it.* Clearly, Vicki will find a way to lord it over everyone, including her own sister.

Moments later, my question about Oliver's age is answered when he follows Hope into the hotel. Instead of a youngster, I see a teenager. It's hard to say, but he's probably around fourteen. Oliver is tall like Faith, with thin arms and gangly legs that support him with the grace of a newborn colt. He stoops forward, shoulders rounded as if drawing into himself like a hermit crab hiding in its shell. He struggles to make eye contact and doesn't offer so much as a smile to his aunt Vicki and uncle Todd, who greet him enthusiastically.

Oliver has dark brown, slightly greasy hair that lies perfectly flat against his bowling-ball-shaped head. His nose is small and his eyes are beady, although enlarged, thanks to the magnification of the thick lenses of his black plastic glasses. It's as if he's wearing a sign that reads: PLEASE BULLY ME.

I'm used to kids—many families stay at the hotel—but none have exhibited the same creep factor as Oliver.

"Ollie, go hug your aunt Vicki," Hope says.

Reluctantly, Oliver shuffles forward. His embrace is limp, without feeling. Vicki's isn't much warmer. Todd ruffles the kid's hair before not-so-discreetly wiping off his hands on his jeans.

"How are you doing there, champ?" Todd asks. "Enjoy the trip?"

"I've been in the car a while, lots of miles, too few smiles," says Oliver in a robotic voice.

"Oliver likes to rhyme," Faith explains for my benefit, as if feeling a need to excuse her son. "He didn't talk until he was five, and then he spoke in rhyming verse most of the time. I think it was all the books we read to him—his doctors still aren't sure. Hope thinks it's because he's . . . um, special. Who knows? Maybe he'll be the next Eminem."

Judging by his dress—dark jeans and a sweater vest that I can't believe he's willing to wear—I'd say Eminem doesn't have much competition from young Oliver.

"What's wrong with rhyming when you have good timing?" says Oliver, whose flat stare at nothing and nobody makes it impossible to tell whom he's addressing.

"The giant from *The Princess Bride* rhymes all the time, and that's Oliver's favorite movie," Hope says.

"I think he's just imitating, but it doesn't matter. We accept him for who he is, *always*," Faith adds, smiling with pride at her son.

Oliver remains placid, utterly expressionless, despite his mother's praise.

Standing next to his nephew, Todd lifts Oliver's arm as though inspecting an injured wing.

"Are you working out, buddy?" he asks. "You need to put some meat on these bones."

"You heard what my mom stated. I don't need my muscles inflated."

Todd takes a step back, as if Oliver's candor has shoved him. Faith and Hope remain impassive, probably more accustomed to his unusual ways.

"Oh, right, I forgot. For you, Minecraft is a sport." Todd seems proud of his retort, while Oliver, who I don't think has blinked once yet, doesn't respond. "Let me tell you, Oliver, video games won't make you strong. You need to work out. I'm benching 225 these days. Impressive for any man, not just someone my age."

"I'll take it under advisement," Oliver says, with such deadpan delivery I want to burst out laughing.

"Todd, since you're so strong and able, why don't you carry my sister's luggage to her room?" Vicki says.

Of course Rodrigo won't let that happen. He grabs all three bags before Todd can get one.

"Which room are we taking?" Hope asks.

"We've prepared the first-floor Gardenia Suite for you," says Rodrigo. "It's the only one with two bedrooms and a common sitting area. We thought it would be perfect for your family."

"Sounds great," says Hope, matching Faith's pleased expression as Rodrigo departs with their bags. Oliver falls into step behind, attempting a stealthy escape.

"And what's this about the Library Room being claimed?" Hope wants to know. "Is that a coveted room for some reason?"

"It was our favorite growing up," Faith says. "Our mother would have story time there. We used to pretend we were guests in the hotel, and we'd fight over who got to sleep there when it was available." She rolls her eyes. "Of course that wasn't the *only* thing we fought over."

I catch the telling look Faith sends Vicki's way. Vicki stiffens. It's obvious there's a bigger story here, one for which neither sister has let bygones be bygones.

"Oh, yeah, we had our squabbles over the years, that's for sure. But you're the competitive one, not me," says Vicki, lightening the mood with a playful inflection. "You hate losing more than anyone I know—even Todd."

Vicki has taken a liking to me, for she directs this observation my way as though we're confidantes. "Faith was our family tomboy," she says. "Best athlete northern Maine had seen in decades. All-State in hurdles and high jump. She was a good student, too. She was supposed to study hotel management and take over the business from Daddy, but suddenly . . ."—Vicki snaps her fingers to drive home the point—"Faith's not interested in the hotel trade anymore. Modeling is her new calling, and with barely a goodbye, she left at age eighteen and never came back—never until today. So welcome home! It's good to be together again under this roof, where we share so many wonderful memories."

A chill rips through me as Vicki and Faith lock eyes. I'm waiting for more explanation when, out of nowhere, I hear a loud clatter. I nearly jump out of my skin, my heart in my throat, afraid that it's Bree, that she's dropped something upstairs, and now everyone will go to investigate. But a moment later, Olga comes stomping out through the swinging doors to the kitchen.

"Sorry for the noise," she announces briskly, addressing the room. She's powerfully built, like a weight lifter. At this particular moment, what she's lifting is a large cardboard box filled with kitchen supplies. "I dropped some pots. I'll come back for them in a minute." Her tone is clipped. She's always been a hard woman, though smiles aren't easy to come by when you're cooking for twenty-plus people three times a day.

"Um, Olga, where are you going with all that stuff?" Vicki inquires.

"I'm quitting," says Olga as if it should be obvious. "I asked to be excused for the weekend because of the weather and was told no. I have to look after my house during the storm, and you act like your family is the only one that matters. So I quit. These are my personal cooking supplies, and I have the receipts to prove it."

"What do you mean, you were told you have to stay?" Vicki says to Olga. "Who told you? Nobody brought this to my attention. What are you talking about?"

"I told her," Todd says, stepping forward. "She called a few days ago and made her demands known. I took the call and said we had family coming and that she needed to cook for us."

"And you didn't think to consult me?" Vicki looks aghast. "Good God, Todd, you are more dense than petrified wood."

"No, I'm a businessman who knows that employees are expected to work for their wages and during the agreed-upon schedule."

"Well, I don't work for you anymore," Olga says.

"Olga, please reconsider," pleads Vicki. "You've been with us forever. My whole family will be here to settle Daddy's estate. We need a good cook. Can't you ask a neighbor to check in on your house?"

"I'm sorry," says Olga. "I truly am. But I've wanted to leave for some time now. I guess what I needed was a good hard push. Thanks for that, Mr. Todd. I've left you dinner for tonight. And good luck in this storm. I've been watching the weather. You're all going to need it.

The fridge is stocked—nobody will starve. But when the power goes out, be careful with the door. You don't want your provisions to spoil."

And with that, Olga stomps from the Great Room and out of the hotel, carrying her box and her grievances with her.

The room is silent for a time, until Hope breaks the spell.

"Don't fret," she says. "I've been taking cooking classes for a while now. I plan to open a restaurant specializing in sustainable, organic, vegetarian cooking. I've been a yoga instructor long enough. The time has come to expand my health and wellness business. I'll take care of all the meals."

"And just how many cooking classes have you taken?" inquires Todd, sounding skeptical.

"What are you nervous about?" Hope asks with a half-smile. "That I'm going to poison your food?"

She says this as a joke.

But nobody laughs.

Chapter 12

Olga's last meal was chicken noodle soup. She certainly didn't pull out all the stops for her culinary swan song. It didn't smell like Olga's best effort; it didn't look like it, either. A scattering of carrots floated on a briny sea of broth like a fleet of tiny orange ships. A few chunks of chicken lurked below the murky surface, rising to bump against a sprinkling of peas that I suspect came frozen. There was a basket of artisan bread, but Olga didn't even bother with the fancy butter balls, opting for a tub of margarine and a knife.

We served the meal buffet style, with no organization, and nobody sat together. Oliver ate in his room. Todd and Vicki ate in the dining room but seated themselves at opposite ends of the long wooden table polished to a mirror shine. It's not your typical hotel dining area; it's more like an old home where guests gather communally and eat together like friends and family. I guess Vicki and Todd didn't get the memo.

Todd spent much of the dinner hour drinking bourbon. Meanwhile, Vicki and Faith went together like mismatched socks, so they pretty much avoided each other entirely. Faith joined Hope in the kitchen, starting the meal prep for tomorrow night's dinner. That would be the formal meal with the attorney present to read the will. Boy, I'd love to be a fly on the wall for that event, but I'm sure I'll be like Oliver, eating alone in my room.

The disorganized dinner allowed me to sneak some soup to Bree, whom I find pacing in her room. Right away, I notice her lone black wheely bag is packed. The bed looks neatened up. The bathroom is spotless. It's clear that she tried to do part of my job for me. I certainly appreciate her thoughtfulness. She's wearing jeans and sneakers, ready to go at a moment's notice. After all her efforts, I'm here to explain that it's not happening.

"We have to keep you here at least one more night," I say as Bree plunks herself down on the bed. I hear the rain beginning to fall. The persistent pelting makes me think it wasn't wise of Vicki to discredit the news so wholeheartedly.

"Todd doesn't want to change rooms," I tell her. "He's drunk and annoyed. He's putting his foot down about staying in the Italian Room. They're still arguing about it, but Vicki relented for the time being. Since this room is off-limits per Vicki's orders, and more people are coming and needing rooms, this is the safest place to keep you. For now."

Bree glances warily at the wall separating her room from Vicki's. "I could hear him snoring," she says in a whispered voice.

"It's more important that *you* don't snore," I tell her, setting the bowl of soup and a plate of bread on the table.

"I sleep like the dead," Bree tells me, reaching for the food. She doesn't hesitate. Obviously, she's famished. It's been hours since I brought her that snack, but I'm taking a risk every time I come to her room. "But I suppose it's better to sleep like the dead than to be one of them," she adds. "Luckily, I haven't heard any more from Jake." She looks relieved, and so am I.

She slurps down a spoonful of soup.

"It's not Olga's finest, but the price is right," I say. "I guess Faith Bishop's wife is taking over the cooking duties from here on out. We might all end up starving. I think we're looking at vegetarian cooking from now on. Hope you're cool with that."

"Like you said, the price is right," Bree answers. "Thank you so much for helping me, Charley. I'll *never* forget this. Never."

Even though there's something in it for me, it does feel good to help someone in need. And there's a lot more emotion in Bree's grateful eyes than I've seen from the supposedly grieving Bishop sisters, that's for sure.

I leave Bree, promising I'll try to sneak her one more snack before bed, then head downstairs as quickly as possible before anyone can miss me.

As I descend the stairs, I catch sight of a tall young man standing in the middle of the Great Room. I almost trip over my feet, grabbing the banister just in time. Rodrigo enters from our dining area, and he, too, stops in his tracks. He looks at me, and I at him, and it's clear we're thinking the same thing.

Holy shit, he's beautiful.

Picture a teen movie where the guy pops out of a swimming pool, sparkling beads cascading down his glistening chest, his lush hair slicked back. That's the scene in front of us.

Quinn (for this must be him) is a hard-to-look-at kind of handsome. He's drenched from the rain, standing before us with tousled wet curly hair and alert hazel eyes that light up the room. He's carrying two suitcases, one pink, so I decide he's thoughtful and sweet enough to bring in his aunt's luggage. He sees me staring—okay, gawking—and sends me a bright smile. If a flash of teeth could knock you over, I'd be on the floor.

Standing behind him is a middle-aged woman with similarly soaked hair. I know this is a Bishop sister, but it's difficult to believe she's from the same gene pool. Vicki is composed. Faith is stunning. But this woman? It appears she's been dealt a much harder hand. Though remnants of a former beauty linger in her soft blue eyes, her gray, gritty skin hints at a life of hardship. A tight ponytail keeps the rain from turning her long, light brown hair into a tangled mess.

I've heard Iris struggled with drugs and alcohol, and I don't doubt it for a second. I've seen firsthand the toll that life can take.

She removes her rain-slicked jacket, revealing a thin frame underneath. While there's something fragile about her appearance, she's no pushover. Her frail forearms are decorated with tattoos, one of them clearly a Jesus fish.

Iris's eyes pierce the room with a quiet intensity reminiscent of a bird of prey. Fittingly, her impressive nose is somewhat beak-like.

"Where is everyone?" Iris asks, looking around expectantly.

As if on cue, Vicki emerges from the dining room, Faith and Hope following close behind. Iris's edgy exterior doesn't appear to soften at the sight of her sisters. It's as if she's been conditioned to be on the offensive, even in the familiar presence of her family. When I catch the icy stare she shoots Vicki, I suspect that family relations might be why she's on high alert.

"Iris, welcome," Vicki says, approaching. "So great to see you. And hello, Quinn, sweetheart. I'm glad you both arrived safely. How was the drive?"

"Okay, until the rain hit about an hour ago. Thank God for new tires." Quinn's soothing voice melts over me like warm butter. He shakes his head in disbelief. "Who thought having a reading of a will at the onset of a hurricane was a good idea?"

"Not you, too," Vicki laments. "It's just a storm. They happen all the time, and they've hyped it up, that's all. Besides, if it does hit, what better place to be than together in a hotel that's been standing for over a hundred years? By the way, did you lock up at home like I asked?" Vicki sends Quinn the worried-mother look. "I forgot to remind you to set the alarm."

Iris cringes ever so slightly when Vicki says *home*. This piques my curiosity. *Why would she care?*

"All you forgot is that you reminded me several times. So, yes, the alarm is on," says Quinn.

"Oh, good," Vicki says. "I'm glad I'm thorough and you're responsible." She eyes Iris strangely.

I don't know what to make of this odd exchange, other than discovering a new piece of the Bishop family puzzle that doesn't quite fit.

"Let me take your coats," I say, stepping forward, doing my best not to look directly at Quinn—and failing miserably. He catches me with eyes all over him, and I die a little inside. Luckily, the cold water beading off the coats thrust into my arms cools the heat of my embarrassment.

"Hi there, sweetheart," Faith says, embracing Iris in a way I now realize Vicki had not. "And, Quinn—look at you. You get more handsome by the day."

"Thanks, Aunt Faith." Quinn endearingly downplays the compliment.

Hope follows Faith's lead, giving hugs all around. "Are you hungry? I can reheat soup on the stove. We'll have a fancy meal tomorrow. I'm doing the prep tonight, but we're short on some ingredients, so I'll have to go to town in the morning," she says, wiping her hands on a crisp white apron.

"Are you cooking?" asks Iris. "I thought we had a chef."

"We did," Faith answers glumly. "Olga quit, so Hope's taking over."

"Quit, thanks to Todd," mutters Vicki.

"Did someone say my name?" Todd enters the room, holding his glass of bourbon that looks barely touched. I suspect he's refilled it already.

"Yes, dear," Vicki says. "I was just pointing out the mess you made with our former cook."

This earns a disapproving finger wag from Faith. "Are you entirely incapable of saying a nice word about your husband?" she asks.

"I would if he earned it. And what's happened to your New York edge? Has your New Age lifestyle softened your best asset?"

"Let's try to be kind, everyone." Hope steps forward as a referee. "We are all one family here—one great big interconnected family. We're really one with the universe, if you think about it. How we speak to each other matters."

"Spare me your airy-fairy kumbaya crap, Hope," Vicki snaps. "Even Todd would admit that he can be an ass."

"That's right, and proud of it," Todd says, puffing up his chest. "Nice people get walked over. Assholes get respect. I know how things should be done and hold others accountable. You don't get as far as I have in life by being a pushover."

"No, you get it by marrying a smart businesswoman who keeps making up for your financial mistakes," Vicki retorts with a grin that makes it clear *she* hasn't lost her edge.

Todd waves Vicki away. "Oh, please," he says. "Without me, you would never have taken any real risks. We'd be stuck in second gear. Faith is right: You should be thanking me, not criticizing me."

"*I* thanked you, didn't I, Todd?" Iris interjects with a grim smile. "Without you, I might never have found God."

Vicki scoffs. "Please don't feed his ego anymore, Iris. He already thinks he *is* God."

"Some people who act like God get struck down for being a fraud," chimes in a nasally youthful voice from the doorway.

Todd jumps, almost spilling his drink. All others turn to see young Oliver lurking behind them.

"Jesus Christ, you scared the crap out of me!" barks Todd. "What have I told you about sneaking up on people?"

I wonder how long Oliver's been standing there listening.

"Why don't you tell your kid not to creep up behind people?" Todd gripes to Faith and Hope. "And while you're at it, maybe get him to stop with the rhyming. It's weird."

Hope stands as tall as her tiny frame will allow. "Oliver expresses himself as he sees fit. And we accept him for who he is, without judgment. Maybe you could learn a thing or two about that yourself."

Oliver, who'd been primarily expressionless, sends Todd a chilling smile.

"Whatever. Just try not to scare people, all right?" Todd grumbles at his nephew.

Quinn approaches and pats Oliver on the back. The gesture of affection seems wholly lost on the boy, who doesn't react.

"I think Oliver's got a point about the God complex," Quinn says. "Words of wisdom from such a young man. You keep it up, buddy."

Finally I catch the first hint of light in Oliver's otherwise dull brown eyes.

"Right," says Vicki, clapping her hands with a loud thwack to dispel the mood and get everyone's attention. "Rodrigo, would you mind showing my sister to her room? You'll be in the Mohegan Room, Iris, which I know you love. I'm moving to the Library Room at some point, so sorry, it's taken."

Iris catches the shade Vicki tosses and sends it right back with a look of indifference. "The Library Room . . . of course you'd claim it first," she says to Vicki as Rodrigo collects her pink luggage. "Have you even read a book since we were kids? And reading conspiracy theories on Infowars doesn't count."

"Pooh-pooh it all you want," Vicki says, ignoring the dig. "Some people out there think it's good to question the status quo, unlike the rest of you *sheep*. At least someone in the family was smart enough to listen to Daddy."

"Daddy had questionable judgment in many ways," Iris says, her expression haunted. I get the distinct impression she's referring to more than his conspiracy theories. *How much does Iris know about her father's darker side?*

"Quinn, Charley here will show you to your room," Vicki says, interrupting my thoughts. "You'll be staying in West Indies. It's fitting—I know your father would like to take you there someday." She sends him an indulgent smile.

Quinn's eye roll is hard to miss. "Father-son bonding trip. *Great*."

Hmm . . . I get the distinct impression Quinn doesn't like his dad. *Iris and Vicki. Quinn and Todd. Todd and Iris.* Looks like I have a lot of Bishop puzzle pieces to try to fit together.

Chapter 13

Quinn collects his bag and heads for the stairs before I can carry it for him, as I would for other guests. I go to the office to get the key, then walk behind him as he ascends our grand staircase.

In no time, I'm alone with Quinn, strolling down an empty hallway with the key to the West Indies Room jangling in the pocket of my scrub dress. And that's when I realize—*crap, shit, fuck. I'm still wearing this awful scrub dress.* It's not that I want to impress Quinn, it's just that I don't want his lasting image of me to be that of a maid—even if that's what I am.

I suddenly feel small beside him, as though he's more worthy, simply because of our different backgrounds and his Abercrombie good looks.

"Was it a long drive?" I ask, immediately labeling myself the worst conversationalist in the history of human speech.

"Kind of," he says, leaving it at that, confirming my worst fears.

I'm nothing to him. A heavy sadness invades my chest. I don't know this boy, yet I'm surprisingly upset that he isn't immediately enamored with me.

Damn scrub dress.

"So, you're Charley, right?"

"That's right," I say, risking eye contact.

When he notices me looking, he breaks out the killer grin that I suspect a lot of girls fall for.

"My mom says you live in the hotel—is that right?"

"Yeah," I say. "Home sweet home." I shrug, but it doesn't dislodge my shame.

"How do you manage?" he wants to know. "It seems so desolate, so lonely. I didn't see a house for miles on the drive here."

"It's not that bad. It's beautiful, actually—and I have my nana, who lives close by, and Rodrigo," I tell him.

"The gay guy?"

I laugh. "How do you know he's gay?"

"I get hit on from both sides," he says.

I raise my eyebrows, wondering if he swings from both sides, too. I don't get that vibe, and I should find his cockiness appalling, but sadly I find it sexy.

"What about you?" I ask. "Where do you live?"

"Hanover," he says. "Last year of college at Dartmouth."

Dartmouth. Yikes. Smart, too.

"What are you studying?" I ask.

I expect him to say business, finance, something that will make more money in a week than I'll make in a year.

"Philosophy," he tells me. "With a minor in art history."

Well now, color me surprised.

"What made you choose that?" I ask. "Doesn't sound like the biggest moneymaking career path. What are your plans after you graduate?"

"I don't really know yet," Quinn says with a shrug. "I think I picked my major to spite my father. Todd is so crazy obsessed with making money that it kind of turned off my Wall Street ambitions. I told him I wanted to learn about art and culture, and he told me to do that at a state school. My mom refereed the subsequent blowout—luckily in my favor."

"I read a lot," I say as we arrive at the West Indies Room. "But I'm ashamed to admit, I don't know much about philosophy—or art, for that matter."

"All you need to know is that two things in life are infinite," Quinn says. "The universe and human stupidity—and I'm not sure about the universe!"

I laugh. "Are you quoting Plato or something?"

The competitive girl in me wants him to know I'm smart, too, even if I didn't go to college, let alone a school like Dartmouth. I can still name five or six famous philosophers, although I can't say much about their views.

"Not Plato, Einstein," he tells me, and when he smiles again, my knees go a little weak. "What do you like to read?"

I tense up. Maybe he *is* curious about me. Now I need to say something sophisticated. "Um, I like historical fiction and mysteries." Okay, not very sophisticated. But I keep going. "I like all kinds of books, fiction and nonfiction. I love getting lost in a story. I may be stuck in the boonies of Maine, but in a way, I get to travel when I read. It's always been comforting to me. The last book I read was actually an art book about the life of van Gogh."

It feels like I'm rambling. God, I'm such a bundle of nerves, so I change the subject to something related but not about myself.

"That reminds me," I say, "do you know anything about a mystery painting in the hotel? Vicki and Todd were talking about it. I guess it's worth big money, but there are so many paintings here, and most of them came from flea markets and yard sales. It would be cool if there was a real treasure."

A spark ignites in Quinn's eyes. "Hell, yeah, that would be cool! I haven't heard anything about it, but let's start looking. What do you know?"

I laugh because I've boxed myself into a corner. "I don't know anything," I admit. "Ask Todd. He's the one who brought it up."

Quinn's groan is telling. "My father? Oh, I wouldn't put much faith in anything he says. He's so full of shit you could mistake him for a port-a-potty. I actually used him as a subject in one of my philosophy papers. The title was 'Small Men Talk Big.'"

I laugh at his joke, or maybe it's not a joke.

"That's your dad," I say, surprised at his candor. "Kind of harsh, don't you think?"

Quinn shrugs it off. "It is what it is. He's my father, but he's not much of a dad. He's never paid a lot of attention to me. Let's just say, if it hadn't been for my neighbor, I wouldn't know how to throw a baseball."

I get the picture. I know how it feels to have a parent who's phys-ically present but mentally checked out.

"But he wants to take you places," I say. "So that's good."

"Places he wants to go, sure," Quinn says. "He wants a Sherpa not a son. There's not much togetherness when we're together—trust me on that."

I'm quiet for a moment. I don't know the situation well enough to comment, and I must be careful what I say to the Bishop family. But that doesn't stop me from passing judgment. Quinn might have a fraught relationship with his dad, but he's still the golden child. He's the type who can breeze through life with easy self-confidence. He knows he is distractingly good-looking and has had everything handed to him on a silver platter. Women probably fall all over him. I know exactly what to do with boys like that—*run*, don't walk. He'd probably use me like a dishrag before tossing me into the waste bin along with all the other discarded conquests in his life.

My rational mind keeps telling me this as I open the door to his room.

His smile widens as he checks out his home for the next few days. The West Indies Room is warm like the tropics, with butter-yellow walls and a gold and red area rug decorated in a palm tree pattern. A combination of rattan and teak furniture complete the look of the islands. Quinn's gaze goes to the hand-carved ceiling fan from Bali before traveling across the king-size bed with the inviting linen sheets and soft bedspread, also patterned with palm trees. He looks at me with those dreamy eyes. I could fall into them and get lost for days.

And I know right then and there I don't stand a chance in hell of listening to my rational mind.

Chapter 14

Friday

I start the day with my regular morning check-in with Rodrigo. He's looking dapper as always, in a white shirt so starched and wrinkle-free it's like it just came from the dry cleaner. There's not a single strand of dark hair out of place. He's impeccably attired in a black vest and a snazzy red tie. Light glints off the gold of his cuff links. You could travel hundreds of miles and not find a more distinguished and professional front desk manager.

"What's your plan for our frogger?" he asks, flashing me a dazzling smile while clicking away on the computer. "Cancellations are going into next week, so right now no reservations until next weekend. The storm really has everyone freaked out."

I'm not surprised. Even deep inside the hotel, I can hear the surf crashing against the rocks at the base of Gull Hill. I went out earlier to move the lawn furniture under the deck where we store it during winter; the winds had already knocked several Adirondack chairs over. The rain fell heavily, and forecasters say the storm will only worsen, with hurricane winds likely to hit Jonesport within the next twenty-four hours.

"Bree is staying in the Library Room for now," I tell Rodrigo. "Vicki and Todd haven't sorted out their move yet, and I don't know where she wants to put the attorney when she arrives."

"Do you know when she's expected?" Rodrigo asks. "There's no formal res on her, so I don't have any information to go on."

"No idea, so I'm keeping our frogger on her lily pad until further notice."

Without Olga around, I add some of her tasks to my daily list. First things first: I brew coffee in a large urn and set up a beverage station in the dining room. Rodrigo starts the fire and does a little storm prep, changing batteries in our flashlights in case of a power failure. Even though winters here can be rough, George never spent the money on a generator. He preferred to provide guests with the nostalgic ambiance of candlelight—battery-powered for safety—and stocked the freezing cold rooms with extra blankets in case the heat went out. Yeah, he really was that cheap.

"Have you regained your equilibrium yet?" Rodrigo teases me when we meet back up in the office. "I almost had to pick your jaw up off the floor."

I'm certain he's talking about Quinn. I fix him with my best mind-your-own-business stare, with hands clasped on my hips for emphasis. "You're more annoying than a nosy neighbor," I say, hoping to derail him with our made-up game, but he doesn't take the bait.

"Oh, come on, I've never seen you react like that to a guest before, and for good reason. Damn, he's hot." Rodrigo fans himself with his hand to cool down.

"I know when to keep my distance. That boy has all the DO NOT TOUCH signs I can imagine," I tell him.

"What? Good-looking, charming, and privileged?"

"Yeah, that's not going to play in my favor. Vicki called me a plain old Jane, so I'm not about to put myself out there to Prince Charming."

"*Plain Jane?*" Rodrigo sounds aghast. "That woman is like the adult version of Mean Girls. And clearly she needs glasses. You're Jayne Mansfield, if anything."

I google the reference and find pictures of an old starlet who resembles Marilyn Monroe. "I think *you* need glasses," I tell him.

Rodrigo places his arm around me. His touch feels comforting, as does the familiar scent of his spicy cologne. "One of these days, you're going to see yourself through my eyes," he says, "and realize how beautiful you are, inside and out."

I didn't have *crying* on my to-do list, but I can cross that off now. Tears are short-lived when I hear someone coming downstairs. I slip out of the office to investigate and find Hope headed for the front door, car keys in hand.

"I'm off to the supermarket before the weather gets worse," she announces. "I have my shopping list. Any last requests? But please, nothing that once mooed, clucked, or swam."

She sends me a beaming smile that I suspect Todd would label as virtue signaling. I can only think of breakfast food, so I suggest she pick up bagels or Danishes at Sunrise Stop.

Hope goes on her way, and I leave to get my cart.

A maid's work is never done.

While everyone goes downstairs for the continental breakfast of baked goods and coffee, I get to work cleaning the guest rooms. Tidying Quinn's room doesn't exactly make me feel like Jayne Mansfield, but at least he didn't see me scrub his toilet. That can't be a turn-on.

A couple of hours later, I come downstairs to vacuum the Great Room to find a suitcase in the middle of the foyer. I hear muted chatter from the dining room, but my attention goes back to the bag. What's it doing there? Rodrigo is always on top of these things. If the attorney had arrived, he would have taken the luggage to her room. What gives?

I find Rodrigo behind the front desk, but he's not his usual cheerful self. I don't even get a half-smile from him. He won't look me in the eyes. He's pounding on the computer keyboard so hard I'm certain he'll break it. A scowl creases deep lines into his forehead. He's clenching his jaw.

"What's going on?" I ask. "Is the attorney here? Is that her suitcase in the foyer?"

"It is," he says with fiery contempt. "And it can stay there for all I care. No way I'm carrying that *puta*'s bag for her."

I know a few Spanish words from our banter over the years, but that's the first time I've ever heard Rodrigo call a guest a bitch.

"*Puta?* What do you mean? What happened?"

I take a single step in retreat. Rodrigo's energy is combustible.

"Do you know who that attorney is?" he asks. Before I can say anything, he gives me the answer. "It's Brenda Black," he says in a scathing tone. He averts his eyes, as if embarrassed that I see him this angry.

"And?" I ask, prodding.

"And she's the attorney who almost got us deported." He balls up a piece of paper like he imagines crushing this woman in his grasp.

My eyes open wide. "What? How?"

"I don't have time to explain," he says. "Let's just say, not only is there racially biased policing, but the criminal justice system is totally corrupt. And *that* attorney, Brenda Black, is a *big* part of it." He makes a face like he just took a whiff of spoiled milk. "She's *no buena*, Charley."

Before I can ask for more details, I hear Vicki call my name. I return to the Great Room to find her standing next to a striking woman with sharp-edged features that look chiseled from stone. Her shoulder-length platinum-blond hair would hold its style in any windstorm thanks to hair spray. The leather shoulder bag she's holding and the suitcase Rodrigo won't touch are all she has for luggage. Hopefully, she doesn't get stuck here because of the weather, leaving me to do her laundry.

I notice her smart attire: a pencil skirt, boots, and a button-down off-white silk blouse under a fitted jacket. Vicki's no slouch, either. She's smartly dressed in blue slacks and a blazer over a rose-colored blouse. I suspect Vicki knew the attorney would arrive looking professional, and outfitted herself accordingly so she wouldn't be outclassed.

"Charley, this is Brenda Black. She's the attorney reading the will. I want you to put her in the Tiger Lily Room on the third floor. Nobody is up there, so it will feel like her own wing. She has an important job to do and doesn't need to be inundated with my family the entire time she's here."

Tiger Lily . . . that would be Vicki's childhood bedroom. There are certainly nicer rooms available, but if I've learned one thing, it's that Vicki makes the call, and you don't question it.

Rodrigo emerges from the office. His eyes are cold fury, cast in the direction of Black, but neither she nor Vicki takes notice. "I'll be finishing up a few things and heading home for the weekend," he says. "If you need anything, you know how to reach me."

I'm watching Brenda to gauge her reaction, but her expression remains neutral. Only Rodrigo is aware of their shared history.

With those parting words, he walks out the door, leaving Black's luggage untouched in the foyer.

Feeling responsible for Rodrigo, I get the key to the Tiger Lily Room and retrieve Black's belongings. Brenda has gone off exploring our collectibles, so she's out of earshot when Vicki motions for me to put the bag down.

"She's charging us five hundred an hour to read a piece of paper," Vicki tells me in a low conspiratorial voice. "At that rate, she can carry her own luggage upstairs."

I'm relieved. Hauling that thing up to the third floor would have been my workout for the day.

"And, Charley," Vicki says with a plastered-on smile, "I'd like you to serve the meal at dinner tonight. We all need to be focused on the task at hand. I know it's not in your job description, but we don't have anybody else. I'll put a little extra in your paycheck for the trouble."

She departs for the kitchen, leaving me with a feeling of dread. With this cast of characters, I have a strong suspicion that the main course on tonight's menu will be a heaping portion of chaos.

Chapter 15

Dinnertime almost feels normal at the hotel. So normal that I'm back in my scrub dress, in front of Quinn of all people—again. Vicki wanted to make it clear I was on duty this evening, so let the humiliation continue.

The pleasing aromas wafting out of the kitchen make me forget that Olga isn't cooking this meal. If the smells are any indication, Hope's future restaurant could be a real success. It's such a typical evening with people milling about, chatting pleasantly, that I momentarily forget I'm hiding a stranger upstairs.

Faith enlists my help in setting the table. She knows where we keep the sterling silver candleholders, the matchbooks, and the fine china as well. With Rodrigo gone in a huff, it was up to me to light a fire in the fireplace of our expansive dining room, which adjoins our Great Room. The crackle and distinct scent of burning cedar reminds me of the holiday season, as do the gold beeswax candles that Faith insists on displaying. She's breathtaking, Faith is, clad in a sequin-embellished flutter-sleeve dress, her glossy brown hair arranged in a casual bun atop her head, a few tendrils perfectly framing her striking face and immaculate complexion. She is flawless, and that incites sporadic glances of envy from Vicki.

"I can't believe everything is still where it was when I was a kid," marvels Faith as she retrieves a gold-embroidered tablecloth from an antique walnut hope chest. Together we unfold the covering and drape it over the long dining room table. Since I had never met the sisters before

George's death, it's easy to forget that this was once their home and these items are as familiar to them as Nana's belongings are to me.

I've been shuttling drinks and clearing dishes like a cocktail waitress, trying to listen without being noticed. I overhear Faith and Vicki discussing the trials and tribulations of the modeling business. I try to slink away, but Vicki catches my eye.

"Anyone could be a model these days, with Photoshop and filters," she says, looking at me, the Plain Jane from Maine. "It's all fake. Even Charley could have had a career, I suppose."

I want to shout: *Will you ever leave my looks alone and stop judging me?* But I know how to keep my job.

"Oh, you're prettier than those party girls on Instagram," Faith assures me as I arrange the silverware. "And trust me, honey, you're far better off staying away from that line of work. New York almost devoured me, and I can't imagine how *dreary* it is to be an influencer these days—all the pressure to document every moment of your life while trying to make it as picture-perfect as possible. No thank you." Faith turns her nose up at the influencer lifestyle in distaste. "I've barely worn any makeup since my last photo shoot, and I have no intention of going back to that world. Not ever."

"That's what you said about this place—no intention of coming back—and look, here you are," says Vicki without much cheer. "Home again, home again, jiggety-jig." Her speech adopts a singsong rhythm.

"We all know why I'm here," Faith answers curtly.

"Sure." Vicki sweeps her arms around the room in a grand gesture. "To stake your claim on what you never even wanted—what you ran away from, in fact—our treasured family hotel."

"I see it more as getting what I deserve," Faith replies.

"She means her inheritance," squawks Todd, clearly for my benefit. He's lounging king-like on a red leather armchair in a corner of the room, where he's been quietly draining his drink. I notice how he keeps the bottle close to him, like he's staked his claim on it for the evening, perhaps the entire weekend.

Vicki chuckles under her breath. "I'm not so sure getting what you deserve would actually *be* in your best interest." Her voice is thick with sarcasm.

Faith's sapphire eyes turn frosty as she stares down her sister. The clink of china and silverware as I continue to set the table seems to echo louder in the heavy silence. The intensity of the exchange makes me suddenly glad I don't have any sisters.

Todd tops off his bourbon, giving himself a more generous pour than last time. He strolls over to Faith, resting a hand on her upper arm with an ease and familiarity I find surprising. Vicki seems equally taken aback, quickly looking away before heading to the wine bar, where she snatches one of our more expensive bottles of Shiraz.

"Beautiful table," says Todd, leaning over Faith, his nose pressed up to her hair. He smiles charmingly, almost intimately, and I can't help but feel a twinge of discomfort.

"Thank you," Faith says, beaming.

Light from the fire and the antique lamps shimmers like miniature diamonds off the engraved crystal glasses at each place setting. I must say, Todd seems as self-impressed as George, but the compliment he pays Faith endears him to her.

From the kitchen, I hear Hope's lilting voice: "Dinner will be ready in thirty minutes."

"Good. That's plenty of time for me to get drunk enough to endure Iris." With that, Todd takes a swig.

Soon enough, everyone is around the dining room table, eagerly awaiting the meal that I'm to serve. Hope insists on helping me, saying it's practice for her future restaurant. Together we dart in and out of the swinging doors that lead to the kitchen, moving so quickly it's like someone hit the fast-forward button on a video.

In no time, the plates are filled with steaming piles of seasoned, sautéed vegetables. I feel sorry for Bree, who can't eat until I can manage to sneak her some food. As a side dish, each guest gets garlic mashed potatoes along with spears of buttered asparagus. Since this is my dinner as well, I guess I'm in for a night of bad breath and smelly pee—not exactly an aphrodisiac. However, the prospect of Quinn becoming more than someone to ogle from afar is dim at best.

The seating arrangement is Vicki's idea. She's placed Quinn, who looks handsome in a tight-fitting black jersey that accentuates his muscular frame, next to her and across from Oliver. He doesn't strike me as a mama's boy, but Vicki's been hovering ever since he arrived, checking in with him every few minutes, brushing lint off his shirt, fixing his hair, refilling his water like she's showing off her mothering skills.

The sound of the wind over the ocean has picked up, but nobody has been outside to see the change in the weather. Gusts come and go. Larry is an approaching giant, rattling windows with each exhale.

I have to lean down and get close to Quinn to serve him his food. I don't understand the mysterious alchemy that makes a man smell good. Whatever Quinn's scent is (ocean surf mixed with coffee? pine forest and licorice?), it sure works for him—and me. I probably smell like Windex, which isn't exactly alluring.

From my vantage point, it appears that everyone is taking this dinner for granted. Todd is getting drunk. Quinn and Oliver are distractedly looking at their phones, while Vicki keeps reminding them to put their devices away. Iris, dressed casually in cargo joggers and a short-sleeved gray T-shirt that showcases her many tattoos, absent-mindedly swirls the straw in her Diet Coke, her vacant eyes fixed on her plate. Brenda Black remains dressed in her officious business suit, projecting an air of formality, signaling she's here solely for business. Hope's finished helping me serve the meal and is now seated at the table, engaged in a quiet conversation with Faith. There's none of the joyful chatter one would expect from a family reunion, nor any of the somber murmurs marking the sad occasion of a father's death.

It strikes me that the Bishops don't realize how fortunate they are to have one another. It's been ages since I've had a family meal. In fact, my last dinner out was with Rodrigo, eating fried clams on a picnic bench outside a tractor-trailer diner, while country music blared from a cheap portable speaker. It was epic.

Quinn reaches across the table for the salt. As he's settling back into his seat, I catch him looking at me. I hold back a smile as I refill his water glass. But inside I'm tingling. I don't know what I want to have happen between us, if anything, but it feels good to be noticed.

Todd, who is seated at the head of the table, stares disapprovingly at his plate of food, then looks at Hope, confused.

"Is there more?" he asks.

"More what?" Hope replies. She looks to Faith for additional clarification.

"Um, food," says Todd blandly.

"It's on your plate," Hope tells him.

"This? This is compost," says Todd, tilting his plate, using a knife like a pointer. "I'm looking for the meat."

"I don't cook meat," Hope explains. "It goes against my beliefs. I strive to be in compliance with ahimsa."

"Uh-him what?" asks Todd.

"Uh-him-suh," Hope repeats slowly. "It's Sanskrit for 'noninjury.' My new restaurant will follow the ethical principle of not causing harm to other living beings."

"Very on message for these times," Faith adds with an approving nod before shoveling a forkful of potatoes into her mouth.

Iris, who is seated beside her, brightens. She's the only one at the table without a glass of wine, besides Oliver.

"I think vegetarian restaurants are great," she says. "We need more of them, and I'm excited to taste your cooking. It smells delicious."

Todd speaks up. "Ironically, organic fertilizer is composed of guano, dried and powdered blood, ground bone, and macerated day-old chickens—so eat up, everyone. Yum, yum."

"There are other options for fertilizer, Todd," Hope says with forced cheer. "Certainly, my restaurant won't use any product dependent on macerated day-old chickens."

Black speaks for the first time. "Did you know that chickens have complicated social structures and can recognize more than a hundred other chicken faces? They recognize human faces, too."

"Is that so?" Todd sounds sarcastic.

"Meat isn't good for our health, anyway," Hope says. "Heart disease, cancer—a lot of illnesses are caused by poor diets."

"We don't have healthcare in this country," Iris says. "We have sickness care."

Todd groans. "That's like one of those insipid self-helpy aphorisms you love to spout that sounds wise until you think about it and realize it's pretty stupid. The point of healthcare *is* sickness care."

"She means illness is preventable with a better diet," Vicki says.

"Well, why not just say it that way?" Todd asks. "Just be clear and maybe try thinking for yourself for a change. I'm not sure you have an original idea in your brain."

I've moved off to a corner of the room, on high alert to clear plates, fill wineglasses, whatever is needed, and essentially eavesdropping in the meantime.

To Iris's credit, she doesn't cower, but rather fixes Todd with a pointed stare. "Reading a lot of self-help books doesn't make me un-original," she counters. "It helps me to stay sober."

"I thought that was *Jesus's* doing?" Todd's tone suggests he hasn't been to church in a long while.

Iris says, "I take Jesus's teachings to heart, for sure, but there is a tremendous amount of wisdom to be gained from many spiritual leaders—Dalai Lama, Paulo Coelho, Thich Nhat Hanh—thinkers that people like *you* could certainly benefit from."

"People like me? Do you mean carnivores?" Todd quips.

"No, I mean narrow-minded people," Iris shoots back.

Todd rises from his seat without a retort. Off he goes to the kitchen, returning moments later, gnawing on a cold chicken leg.

"I wonder how many faces this tasty fellow saw?" he asks with a smug smile as he retakes his seat.

"Mom, are you just going to let him talk to Aunt Iris that way?" Quinn intervenes.

From across the table, I catch Iris flinch. Since she's clearly not intimidated by Todd, I question what suddenly made her uncomfortable.

"Thank you, Quinn, but I can handle myself," Iris says.

"Let's change subjects, shall we?" says Vicki.

"Tell me, Iris, does your parole officer even know you're here?"

Todd continues undeterred, licking chicken juice off his lips. "You still have to report your whereabouts, don't you?"

Parole officer? It takes all my willpower not to look at Quinn. *What is up with this family?*

"Not at the table, Todd, not here," Vicki says.

"Thanks for your caring and discretion," Iris addresses her sister bitterly. "And you, Todd—I'm sick of your high-and-mighty attitude. Please."

Iris's anger is bubbling to the surface. The tension is palpable, until she seems to catch herself. She closes her eyes. Her body appears to relax. Her scowl transforms bit by bit until a placid expression takes over.

"You know what?" Iris says, addressing the table. "My sponsor would remind me that I can't change the past. There's nothing to do except go on living in the present. Let go, let God, as we say in AA."

"We sure are giving Charley an interesting glimpse into our complicated family," says Faith with a wry smile, unfortunately drawing attention to me. "Relax, Charley," she continues as I try to melt into the corner of the room. "We Bishops are well known for putting the *fun* in dys*fun*ctional."

Vicki abruptly stands up, getting everyone's attention.

"Rather than endure more family chitchat, why don't we just jump right into the reading of the will, shall we?" She turns to Brenda Black, who appears apprehensive.

"What? Now? Before we finish the meal?" she asks.

"Yes," says Vicki, patting the table with an open palm to move things along. "No time like the present." She settles back into her chair.

I take this as my cue to give them privacy and slip back into the kitchen without anyone noticing. But now my curiosity is redlined. I open the swinging door that separates the dining room from the kitchen just a crack, enough to see and hear what's going on in the other room.

"Brenda, you do have the will to review with us, correct?" Vicki asks.

"I do," says the attorney as she pulls a folder from her briefcase. "And I'm glad we're all sitting down, because I think you're going to be quite surprised—and I suspect not all of you will be happy."

Chapter 16

The phrase *all the air got sucked out of the room* had always been just that—a phrase—until now. Worried glances pass around the table like a relay baton. Quinn straightens in his chair, Iris clasps her hands in a prayer position, Todd fixes Vicki with a menacing glare, and Faith holds Hope's hand.

I'm relieved to be safely hidden in the kitchen, peering out through a crack in the door. I find myself unable to look away, drawn to the unfolding drama in the same way people are compelled to gawk at car accidents.

"You certainly have our attention, Brenda," says Vicki. "I can't imagine what surprise Daddy has left for us. How do we proceed?"

"I'll read the document, then send copies for your review," Black replies in a crisp tone. She shuffles her papers, intentionally avoiding everyone's probing stares.

"Let's get this over with," barks Todd, his attention fixed on the antique crystal chandelier. George would boast to any guest who so much as walked near it that it had cost fifteen thousand dollars. The chandelier's lights flicker briefly. "The winds are picking up," Todd says. "Not sure how long we'll have electricity."

"Yes, of course," says Black, clearing her throat before beginning. "I, George Bishop, resident of the City of Jonesport, county of Washington, in the state of Maine, being of sound mind, not acting under duress or undue influence . . ."

Faith interrupts with a frustrated cry. "Jesus Christ, are you going to read all that horseshit? Can't we cut to the chase?"

Black remains impressively composed, and I can't help but wonder what kind of person can endure such verbal abuse without reacting. It must be someone with ice in their veins who could harass kind people like Rodrigo and his mother.

Brenda clears her throat. "I'll start with Quinn," she says, turning her attention to him.

Quinn, who doesn't look confident for once, braces himself.

"Your grandfather left you two hundred thousand dollars, which will be paid out in twenty-five percent increments over the next four years through a trust."

"Right on," Quinn exclaims before he adopts a more somber expression under Vicki's disapproving stare. He places a hand over his heart, a sad expression crossing his face. "Granddaddy was always so kind and generous," he declares. "I miss him. I'm truly grateful for his generosity, but obviously I'd rather have him back." He sniffs for added effect.

Oh, give me a break, I silently scoff. I'd be more inclined to believe Russian propaganda. *Kind and generous? Spare me.*

I can't blame Quinn for putting on a show. That would be life-changing money for me. But I do blame George for being a stingy bastard. I always knew he could afford to pay me more. Who knows, maybe he would have if I had given him what he *really* wanted.

"Quinn, we can help you set up some investment accounts," Vicki says. "With a solid rate of return, you'll have a good down payment on a nice house."

"Yeah, great idea," Todd says, his eyes rolling. "Give the kid a big anchor before he's twenty-five. Forget the house nonsense, Quinn. Let's go do ayahuasca in the Peruvian jungle. You haven't *lived* until you become a cosmic leopard dancing across the galaxies!"

Vicki groans loudly. "We all know how much you love to travel, Todd," she says with a hint of annoyance. "But let's not steal Quinn's money for your personal pleasure or encourage him to take psychedelics. Now, what about the rest of us?"

"Fine, let's get on with it," Todd murmurs.

The attorney reads from her paper. "Per the instructions of the will, the entire estate, which includes the Precipice Hotel, the assets within, and your father's cash and investments—a total value of six million dollars—is to be divided into thirds."

Six million! There it is again—all that money George could have used to be more generous with his employees. If Vicki decides to keep me on, I'm definitely going to ask for a raise.

"Thank you, Father," says Iris, looking up at the ceiling as if peering into heaven itself.

Black glances at her paper. "There are some stipulations you should all be aware of," she continues. "Vicki receives her third outright. However, the attorney for the estate, Brenda Black—that's me— shall hold Iris's share in conservatorship under the direction of Iris's brother-in-law, Todd Davis, her appointed conservator. This will con- tinue until Todd deems Iris cured from her chemical dependency, which has severely impacted her life. And, incidentally, mine."

Black clears her throat, trying to dislodge her discomfort. "Sorry, those were your father's words. He insisted on that exact language."

Iris doesn't seem to react to this news. Neither does Todd, for that matter. I get the impression that he *expected* this announcement. I'm not so sure Iris understands what just happened. But I do. Having navigated all the legal intricacies with my nana, I understand fully what a conservatorship entails.

Todd will be the one making all the decisions on Iris's behalf, in- cluding when she's fit enough to manage her own affairs. But watch- ing the greedy twitch dancing at the corner of Todd's mouth, I highly doubt Iris will *ever* be well enough to own her share outright.

It takes a moment, but eventually Iris seems to grasp the situation. Her eyes flare like a furnace igniting. "Wait? What? That can't be. There's something wrong," she stammers.

"I'm afraid there's no mistake," replies the attorney, who suddenly seems proud to be the bearer of bad news. She obviously knew the con- tents beforehand and yet still agreed to present it in person. Sadistic? Per- haps. Masochistic? That remains to be seen, as Iris has murder in her eyes.

"Well, I don't accept it," she fumes. "I'm not having Todd oversee my life. He's made a mess of it as it is. I have a good job in customer service and I've been clean for almost two years. This is ridiculous!"

"Unfortunately, you don't have a choice," Todd sneers. "Or are you still iffy on things like *laws*, Iris? Why don't you follow your own advice and—what was it you said? 'Let go, let God'?"

"Actually, it's more like *fuck you*, Todd," Iris roars, throwing her napkin onto the table.

"Don't worry, Iris," Faith reassures her sister, patting her hand. "I'll make sure the conservatorship is done away with."

Having been involved with the legal system myself, I strongly suspect she's talking out of her ass.

"I'm sorry to say there's more," the attorney says.

"We're all ears," mutters Vicki.

Faith smiles at Hope, looking like a woman about to get her due.

"The final third ownership share of the Precipice Hotel, including one-third the value of all the items within, goes to . . . Todd."

Vicki gasps, Faith's jaw drops, and Iris looks ill.

"Please explain," Vicki says, leaning forward in her chair as if she's about to pounce.

"Are you kidding me?" Faith spits out venomously. "This is a joke, right? I'll sue."

She glances about the room, as if looking for hidden cameras.

"It's definitely not a joke," says Black.

Faith looks like someone punched her in the gut. "I can't believe this," she says, shaking her head. "I can't believe Father would do this to me. I demand an explanation."

"Demand all you want, but these are your father's wishes," says Todd.

"You stole from us," Hope accuses him. "What did you say to George?"

"Me?" Todd points a finger at his chest, batting innocent eyes. "You must be confused, Hope. I didn't write the will. I have no idea why George gave me Faith's share . . . but he must have had a good reason."

Faith shouts back, "Bullshit! Don't tell me you had no idea this was coming."

"But it's true. I had no idea."

I believe Quinn's sappy speech about his granddaddy more than I do Todd's lame denial.

Even though he feigns ignorance, Todd tosses out one idea. "Maybe your father holds a grudge, Faith. Ever think of that? Running away from Maine, this hotel, your responsibilities . . . I imagine you weren't calling or writing home all that often. To be candid, George shared with me his reservations about giving you your share. To his credit, he didn't want to be unfair by giving it to your sisters, and besides, he worried they'd just give it right back to you. I had no idea he was going to pick me as the recipient, but in retrospect, it makes sense that he did. He trusted me to see that his wishes would be honored."

"That does make sense, to an extent," says Black, fanning the flames. "Per the will, if something happened to Todd, his shares would transfer to the executor of George's estate—to me, not to Vicki, so as to prevent any transfer to Faith."

"That's quite an interesting theory you've concocted," Faith says, her voice layered with sarcasm.

"Theory or no theory, those are clearly your father's wishes," Todd says.

Faith's face contorts with rage. She seems on the verge of either crying or charging at Todd with the butter knife she's clutching. It's hard to predict which.

Iris speaks up, directing her anger at Todd as well. "When I started working for you and Vicki, you said you cared so much about me. But ever since I got arrested, I've wondered . . . could it have been you, Todd? Did you intentionally leave that pill bottle for me to find? And I said no, that's impossible. Why would you? But now? I think maybe you did. Maybe you wanted me to relapse so you could set me up to take the fall for your embezzlement scheme. A bottle of prescription painkillers just left lying around in the staff bathroom I always used— how convenient."

Drugs? Embezzlement? What is she talking about?

"We do care, Iris. Or at least I do," Vicki asserts. "Todd, did you do or say anything, apply undue influence on our father? Did you betray my sisters in any way? If you did, I swear . . ." She trails off, eyeing her husband with absolute loathing.

"Of course not. I didn't do anything other than have conversations with your dad," he says. "Sure, I've helped with some of his business affairs over the years, but that's it. Maybe he just trusted me. What do I know?"

Vicki nearly chokes on her wine. "You? Mr. Get Rich Quick is suddenly a trusted advisor? Oh, please."

"Look, I didn't ask George for a conservatorship role, and I certainly didn't ask for Faith's share of the hotel. I gave you all my best explanation. Your father trusted me and didn't trust Iris—for good reason, I might add," he says with a sideways glance. "And he's bitter at Faith for abandoning him. So there, that all makes perfect sense to me. And given that you and I are married, technically, that makes my share worth two-thirds, and with the conservatorship—well, I suppose this place is more or less mine. Cheers to all!"

Todd raises his glass of bourbon and drinks.

"Our father would never have agreed to this," Faith says. "He did it because you did something or said something . . . there's cases of elder abuse, coercion—that sort of thing. I've read about it, and I'm sure that's what happened here." Faith's voice rises to almost a scream.

"You can always try to take me to court—if you can afford it." Todd smirks.

"I'm going to be sick," says Faith, but she doesn't get up from the table.

I hope she's speaking metaphorically.

"This is an absolute disgrace," Hope huffs. "We *will* take you to court, Todd."

"Brenda?" Todd says.

"The will is ironclad," answers Black. "It will stand up against any judge I know, I can assure you of that."

"Forget suing," snaps Faith. A dark stain of vegetable juice (or compost, in Todd-speak) seeps into the clean tablecloth. "There are other ways to get back at you."

Faith lifts her empty plate as she rises from her seat. Before I can blink, she's launched the ceramic object like a Frisbee at Todd's head. Ducking at an opportune moment, he avoids a direct strike. Instead of his skull, the plate smashes against the wall behind Todd, shattering on impact.

A stunned silence ensues.

Faith storms out of the dining room, with Hope giving chase. Iris leans back in her chair, glaring at Todd. Vicki is doing the same. Quinn's head is bowed, and if he could hide under the table, I think he would. Black maintains a stony expression. I'm peering at all this through the crack in the door, mainly focused on the stain where the plate had struck. Automatically, my mind spins through the list of cleaning products I'll need to tackle the mess.

But the bigger mess remains gathered around the table: the Bishops and Todd.

Chapter 17

*T*he front door is slightly ajar—the first sign of trouble. I push it open all the way, then take a few tentative steps inside. As I do, I brush snow off my hair, but I don't bother removing my boots. Something tells me not to get too comfortable. I pause to listen. Never has silence sounded so loud. It's like I can hear the apartment breathing, every pipe's creak and ping, the steady hum of the baseboard heat, the buzz of our ancient refrigerator. I can even pick up the beating of my own heart. But there are no other sounds. No footsteps. No voices. It's quiet as a crypt in here.

I make my way into the kitchen. The scent of stale coffee and cigarettes hovers in the air like a fine mist. Not very appealing for most, but for me, it's the smell of home. Something is different, though, and it's not just the open door. It's a feeling I have, a warning tingle that creeps up my toes and spreads throughout my body.

My eyes first land on the Kit-Cat Klock mounted on our yellowing wallpaper. The cat's plastic eyes move back and forth in a hypnotic rhythm. I always thought the clock was cute, but today it feels ominous, like it wants to tell me something.

A winter jacket dampened by melted snow is draped over the back of a kitchen chair. It's her jacket, my mother's. My gaze returns to the cat clock, and now I know what it was trying to say. It's 3:30 P.M., too early for anyone else to be home.

The open door. The wet coat. The silent house. A foreboding feeling sinks deeper into my bones, chilling me as if the January cold had trailed me inside. This is the kind of quiet I've been expecting . . . dreading.

I make my way down the hall, headed for the last room on the right.

Her room. I push the door open slowly. It's silent on its hinges. I step inside. The edges of the drawn shades glow otherworldly in the dim light.

In here, the smell of cigarettes is even stronger. The ashtray on the bed-side table is piled high with discarded butts. Half-open dresser drawers have clothes spilling out of them, some littering the floor. But it's the figure on the bed that draws my eye. She lies still under the afghan that Nana crocheted for her. One of her arms sticks out from underneath the blanket, a needle still in the spot where it had pierced the vein.

I approach the bed slowly, my eyes locked on my mother's angelic face. I've never seen her so at peace. There is a bluish cast to her skin. Her eyes are closed. Her mouth crests into an almost half-smile, her final moments at least having brought her some kind of pleasure. I don't want to touch her, yet I have to confirm what I already know.

My hand trembles as I place it against her cold, dry skin. Sadness fills my lungs so fully I could drown in it. I move my ear closer to her mouth and feel no breath.

As I turn my head to look at her once more, we are face-to-face. I see my-self in her features. Death has softened her hard edges, turned her younger. I'm about to kiss her cold cheek as a final goodbye when her eyes suddenly fly open. The whites are as yellow as our wallpaper. I leap back in fright. Her mouth contorts in a misshapen oval as a low moan escapes her lips. I scream in terror and she matches my fear note for note; only her scream grows louder and louder still, until it's a howling shriek that pierces my ears.

Mother sits up in bed, still screaming as if someone has taken that needle in her arm and plunged it into her neck. The blue of her face deepens, as does the yellow of her eyes. Her scream continues, while mine is silent. My mouth hangs open, but no sound comes out, no matter how hard I try to force it.

I jolt awake, drenched in a cold sweat.

For a moment, I'm convinced I'm back in the apartment where I lived with my mother until her death. As my eyes adjust to the dark, I realize I'm in my bedroom at the Precipice Hotel, surrounded by famil-iar furnishings, including all my books neatly arranged on the shelves.

But the scream from my nightmare seems to have followed me

into the waking world. I still hear it loud and clear, as though my mother's ghost is haunting me. I listen intently, and soon it becomes clear that the scream is quite real and extremely loud. By the sounds of it, someone in the hotel is in desperate trouble.

My heart rams into my throat as I leap out of bed. I don't bother with a change of clothes—sweatpants with a hole in the knee and a ridiculously oversize boxy T-shirt will have to do.

I race up our grand staircase, my balance unsteady, as I'm still waking up. By now the screaming has ended, but there's all kinds of commotion—noises, panicked shouts, utter chaos unfolding out of my view.

When I round the corner entering the main hallway, I see a cluster of people gathered outside the door to the Library Room and my unease compounds tenfold. The door is wide open. Has someone discovered Bree? But Faith and Hope are crouched on the floor with their backs to me, blocking my view of whatever holds their attention.

Quinn comes down the hall. He doesn't notice me as he's focused on the source of the distress—and then I see it, after Hope moves slightly to her left: a figure lying on the ground.

The figure is Todd. Vicki is on the other side of him. Her pink silk pajamas ripple as she feverishly pumps her husband's chest. She's pressing fast and hard, counting as she goes.

"One, two, three, four, five, six, seven, eight . . ."

"Call 911!" Faith shouts at Quinn.

I stand transfixed, unable to move a muscle, let alone offer any assistance. What happened to Todd? And where is Bree? Was she the one who screamed? Or was it Vicki? Why is the door to the Library Room open?

As rescue efforts continue, Vicki halts her compressions, and Hope takes over without prompting. Her fitted long-sleeved top reveals just how tiny this elf-like creature is—there's almost nothing to her. And yet she exudes an undeniable strength as she performs CPR, as if channeling some otherworldly energy.

Hope pauses and puts an ear to Todd's chest, but I doubt she'll hear a heartbeat. Her expression confirms my suspicion. Todd is dead.

Oliver walks by me like a zombie, saying nothing as he brushes past my shoulder. Hope takes notice and quickly gets to her feet, rushing to her son to shield him from potential trauma. As Faith takes over CPR duties, Vicki also rises to standing. But her focus is no longer on Todd—it's now directed to something—or more likely *someone*—inside the Library Room.

"He's gone . . . I think he's gone," says Faith to Quinn, who is on the phone with 911. Even so, she continues pumping on Todd's chest. But I'm watching Vicki, who is entering the Library Room.

She pauses at the doorway, turning to Faith.

"Keep doing CPR," she insists, not sounding hopeful. Then she's gone, disappearing into the room and out of my view.

"Who the hell are you?" she shouts. "And what did you do to my husband?"

"Nothing—I didn't do anything to him," Bree stammers.

I can only imagine the confrontation taking place within: Vicki encroaching as Bree retreats, until she's backed up against a bookcase.

"He was outside my door, banging to get in." Bree's voice is nearly a screech. "He was completely disoriented. I think he thought my room was his."

"Your room? There are no guests in the hotel other than us. Who are you again?" Vicki demands. "And what are you doing here?"

This is my cue. With my face twisted into an expression of shock and horror, I push my way through the gathering—Hope, Oliver, Iris, Faith, and Quinn, who is making a frantic plea to the 911 operator. The sight of Todd's inert form, mirroring my mother's ghostly pallor, momentarily paralyzes me, but I gather my composure and speak, my voice trembling.

"She's with me," I say, gesturing toward Bree, who is indeed cowering against a bookcase. "I can explain."

Chapter 18

Strobe lights outside the Precipice Hotel turn the dark sky into a blaze of color. Pretty much every emergency responder in the Jonesport area is on the scene. I recognize several firefighters who came to Nana's aid when she nearly burned her house down. I even see the paramedic who wheeled my mother away.

Everyone is downstairs, milling about the Great Room, wearing whatever they had on when we found Todd in the hallway. Bree is talking to a police officer, perhaps giving a statement. I wonder if she's telling him about Jake, inquiring about restraining orders, because it's doubtful she'll be permitted to stay here.

I'm doing my best to keep out of the way and avoid Vicki's death stare. She didn't say much about Bree, nor did she seem all that moved by her story of an abusive boyfriend or my need to cover Nana's rent increase at Guiding Way.

"You lied to me, Charley, and you stole from my family," she said in plain view of everyone. *Stealing* referred to the money Bree should have paid, not the guests I've fleeced, or else Vicki's anger would have been more visceral. Either way, it was enough to wound. Her words carved trenches in my brain where guilt settled like lead weights.

The shame was bad enough, but then things got worse.

"When this storm blows over, you're out of here, Bree," Vicki told her. "I don't care where you go or what happens to you. As for you, Charley, you're officially fired. If you want your full week's pay, you're going to have to work through the weekend, serving meals and keeping up with your cleaning duties. After that, you'll have to find a new place to live."

With that parting salvo, Vicki dashed into her room, emerging moments later with her phone in hand. She didn't look at me, not once. I was dead to her. She had checked me off her list. Now she had other matters to address.

I think of telling Vicki that she and her family owe me for all the years I endured George Bishop's abuse, but now isn't the time, not while Todd is being rolled out on a gurney with a white sheet draped over his body.

"Be careful with that table!" Vicki shouts to the paramedics navigating Todd through an obstacle course of antiques and breakables. Before the warning fully registers, a loud crash fills the room, and the remains of what was once an antique Hummel figurine lie scattered across the floor.

I want my full week's pay, so although I'm no longer the maid, I don't hesitate to sweep up the mess. George, who loved snagging valuable treasures at estate sales, bragged about buying the poor little ceramic girl and her dog for five dollars, knowing it was worth hundreds.

In the corner, Faith slumps on a plush armchair, her face buried in her hands as she sobs inconsolably. Her slender shoulders shake with each heaving gasp. Hope stands beside her, gently caressing her wife's long dark hair, which miraculously holds its style as if she never went to bed. Faith's reaction to Todd's sudden demise contrasts sharply with her angry display at dinner. It seems the only consistent thing about this family is their inconsistency.

"Faith, will you please get control over yourself?" Vicki snaps. "If I'm holding it together, you can do the same. And nobody is buying your act, anyway."

Faith's waterworks abruptly cease, as if a kitchen faucet were shut off. A second later, she's on her feet, an angry stare aimed at Vicki that somehow feels more authentic than her crying.

"What's that supposed to mean?" she says, closing the gap between them. If Faith didn't tower over Vicki by five inches, the two would be standing nose-to-nose.

"It means I don't believe your crocodile tears, or did you forget about your plate-throwing skills?" says Vicki. "You probably wanted Todd dead."

Faith backs up a step. "Are you suggesting that—well, what *are* you suggesting?"

Hope approaches from behind, followed by Oliver, who is wearing Star Wars pajamas despite being a little too old for them. As usual, he shows no emotion—it's almost possible to mistake him for a mannequin. I wish he'd blink more. And maybe wash his hair, which is plastered flat against his remarkably round head. But he does speak.

"It means because you were so mad, Aunt Vicki thinks you killed Quinn's dad." He looks directly at his mom, Faith, while delivering this latest rhyme in his trademark creepy monotone voice.

Conversation grinds to a halt as I shiver at the implications.

"I can't believe—I just—" Poor Faith has no words, but she looks more guilty than outraged.

"Ollie, you don't mean that," Hope says, pulling him to her side. "Vicki, you're not suggesting that Faith had anything to do with this, are you?"

"He didn't have a heart condition, so why the hell did he drop dead?" asks Vicki, her tone accusatory.

"That's what the medical examiner will determine," says Hope. "Faith may have a temper, but that doesn't mean she's capable of violence."

"Violence?" I recognize the baritone voice that rumbles through the Great Room.

Officer Dan Brennan works in the sheriff's department in Machias, a town thirty minutes north of Jonesport, around the block in Maine terms. I take comfort in his presence. Tall and lean, Dan isn't like most cops who harassed us kids at our beach bonfires and house parties, back when I went to them. He's a lot kinder, with that father-figure thing going for him, thanks in part to his gentle brown eyes and warm smile framed by a well-groomed beard. Plenty of Mainers grow beards for added protection during the harsh northern winters, but Dan's looks nicer than most.

Unlike his colleagues at the sheriff's department, who love flashing badges and drumming up excitement in the sleepy little towns of Washington County, Officer Brennan makes it clear he got into this line of work to *help* people. He was there the day my mother died, though I never did thank him for the shoulder to cry on.

"We're talking about what killed my husband," Vicki says, her voice rising and shaking with fury. In terms of the stages of grief, she's definitely in the anger phase.

"Appears to have been a heart attack," says Officer Brennan, offering the right touch of sympathy.

"Okay, but he was young, without any heart trouble," Vicki says.

"According to his driver's license, he was almost fifty, about the same age my uncle Earl was when he passed away. That's what I said about him," Brennan tells the room. "No symptoms. But he had SMI, silent myocardial infarction. Accounts for almost half of all heart attacks. One day he's out raking leaves and—*bam!*—gone, just like that." Brennan snaps his fingers, then looks remorseful for a gesture that could be perceived as uncaring.

"I know that doesn't make it any easier for you," he continues. "And with your father dying the same way, as I understand it, I know this is a lot to take in."

"My father was old and sedentary," Vicki replies, her voice laced with bitterness. "Everyone, including my father, expected he'd go out that way—*just like that.*" She imitates Brennan's finger snap.

"What exactly are you getting at?" Brennan's tone darkens.

"What am I getting at? My young, perfectly healthy husband just dropped dead, surrounded by people who can't stand the sight of him!" Tears spring to Vicki's eyes. Her body begins to convulse as red splotches break out across her cheeks. She buries her head in her hands. Her shoulders quake with each sputtering sob.

The tears subside as fast as they come on. Vicki stands up straight and tall, adjusting her pink pajama top to align perfectly with the bottoms. *There. All better.* She composes herself like someone hit a reset button.

She smiles tensely at her family gathered around—Faith, Hope, but not Iris. I don't see her in the Great Room. I think about the prison tats adorning her arms, references to parole officers, and her odd comment at dinner about Todd derailing her life. Where has she gone during this postmortem chaos?

I could ask Quinn, who just joined us. We make brief eye contact, and I see his grief. As soon as he looks away, my stomach shrinks to the size of a pea. Any chance of us being more than passing acquaintances has gone up in smoke. There's no room for romance after this family tragedy.

Besides, I know he overheard Vicki laying into me (okay, firing me). That certainly didn't make for a good impression. I suppose it would never work between us, anyway. At least I've spared Rodrigo from dealing with the aftermath of my broken heart.

Speaking of Rodrigo, I send him a text. We chatted earlier after he checked in on my nana, reporting that everything was okay. I take a chance that he's still awake. He is. I explain what's happened as best I can.

Surprisingly, or perhaps not so surprisingly, Rodrigo takes more interest in attorney Brenda Black than in the unexpected demise of Vicki's husband.

Is *la pendeja* still there?

> Yeah. She's hanging out with the rest of us. Looks pissed off, too. Don't know what about.

I'm pissed myself. Piss drunk, that is. At Cappy's. Gregg opened the place just for me.

Gregg is the bar owner. Cappy's is the bar. Gregg is a sometime fling of Rodrigo's. As long as Rodrigo's not drinking Hennessy, all should be okay.

On my third Hennessy.

Shit.

Maybe I'll come back there to tell
Black what I really think of her.

I grimace but spare him the emoji equivalent.

I thought you went home to
check on your mom?

She's fine. I needed something
to calm my nerves after seeing
Black. #triggering What's up
with Bree? Any fallout?

I can't bring myself to tell him I've lost my job because I'm not
ready to cry.

Not yet. They're too busy
dealing with Todd. I think every
cop in Jonesport is here.

So both of them?

I send three laugh emojis.

Is Dan Brennan there?

Rodrigo adds two heart emojis.

Yeah. Him.

Tell him I said hello!

He sends both the wink and the eggplant emojis.

I almost burst out laughing.

Okay . . . gotta get back to this shit show.

Tell attorney Brenda I'll see her soon enough.

What's that supposed to mean?

A shiver runs through me. It's out of character for him to be menacing. I don't get the expected three dots of an incoming response. There's no goodbye. This conversation is over. He's gone offline, and I'm left wondering what he meant by seeing attorney Black "soon enough."

Oh, well, this night has been plenty weird. Might as well pile it on.

While I'm busy pretending to do a whole lot of nothing, Quinn comes to me with a weighted gaze.

I didn't think it could get worse than my chambermaid outfit, but here I am in my pajamas. I have crazy bed head and can only imagine how many directions my hair is going in. I shouldn't be thinking about my appearance when somebody just died, but hormones aren't logical.

Unfortunately, Quinn looks cute as cute can be in his plaid pajama pants and slightly ruffled hair. He looks like he just shot a scene for some cheesy Hallmark Christmas movie—one I can't look away from.

"How are you holding up?" he asks. His voice is warm and caring. "I'm sorry about your job."

"I'm okay. I'll figure something out," I assure him, but I don't project much confidence. "But Todd was your dad. How are *you*?"

I'm all kinds of awkward, not sure what to say or do. I could offer him a supportive hug, but I barely know him. So I just stand there, looking and feeling ridiculous, not to mention sad for Quinn, and let's be honest, for myself as well.

"I guess I'm sort of in shock, maybe a little numb." Clouds pass over Quinn's eyes as he shakes his head slightly. His shoulders sag forward like he's caving in on himself. "Look, he wasn't the nicest guy or the best father—actually, he wasn't much of a father at all. I think he blamed me for holding him back from other things he wanted to do in life; I don't know. I always felt like he resented me for some reason, and I could never figure out why." He looks at me with a wounded expression, his mouth twisted in anguish. "I just don't know how to feel. It's too much to take in. On top of it all, my mom seems to think someone did this to him—like, maybe he was . . . *murdered*." He struggles to get out the word before continuing. "She's probably just being paranoid, but. . ." His voice trails off.

"Yeah, I just heard your mom tell Officer Brennan that she's not convinced it was a heart attack," I say.

Quinn gazes past me. "My mom reads into things too much. If there's a conspiracy on Facebook, she's sharing it. But she should be careful about raising any suspicions. If the police dig into their relationship, even a little, she'd be the first one they'd look at. Anyway, I'm sorry you've been dragged into my mess of a family, Charley. I'll talk to my mom later when things settle down and see if I can get her to change her mind about firing you."

Quinn wanders over to Vicki, who's waving to him, leaving me dazed.

Is he actually implying that his mom could be a murderer? Damn, I wish Rodrigo were here.

I should have asked Quinn if he knows where Iris is. I'm curious if Todd had something to do with his aunt going to prison as she implied at dinner. Do all *three* sisters have a motive to commit murder, or have I read too many mystery novels in the Library Room? Regardless, this family seems to harbor more secrets than the CIA.

In my peripheral vision, I see a figure moving into the room. It's Brenda Black. She's wearing her overcoat and boots, carrying her bags.

Officer Brennan notices her as she heads for the door. "Where are you going in such a hurry, Brenda?" he asks, halting the attorney in her tracks.

"I'm not sticking around here, Dan," she says.

It's not surprising that these two are on a first-name basis. Lawyers and cops would cross paths in such a small community. What does surprise me is that Brenda Black would try to leave in this weather, in the middle of the night. The wind is howling, and the rain's coming down in sheets.

"It's not safe to drive, Brenda," Officer Brennan advises. "There are a lot of fallen trees already. I suggest you hunker down for a couple days and ride out this storm."

"I have four-wheel drive. I'll be fine. But thanks for your concern."

"Well, that's not my only concern," says Brennan.

Black glares at him defiantly.

"It seems there's some question about the cause of Todd's death . . . doesn't look suspicious to me, but maybe it wasn't a heart attack. We just won't know until the medical examiner issues a report."

"That's all well and good," Brenda says, "but what does that have to do with me?"

Brennan smiles and says, "If something turns up that's suspicious, the first person I'd want to speak to is the one who ran out the door in the middle of a hurricane."

Chapter 19

Saturday

If I stand in the center of my room with my arms outstretched, my fingertips almost reach the opposite walls. It's incredible how I've transformed such a small space into a home. It's all about the simple touches. I painted my walls a soothing seafoam green, reminiscent of the color of the ocean on a bright summer day. On the rare occasions when I wasn't scrubbing toilets, I would steal a moment to sit near the edge of Gull Hill. There, I'd relax on an Adirondack chair reserved for guests as if I were one, watching the waves crash against the jagged shoreline below. At night, the walls of my tiny room made me feel as though the sea was cradling me in a loving embrace, gently rocking me to sleep.

A few framed photos of my family are displayed on a shelf that Rodrigo helped me install. I don't have a big collection, but my favorite is the picture of Nana, my mom, and me at Old Orchard Beach. The strip of asphalt at the ocean's edge holds a variety of amusement park attractions. Most of the rides are low-rent, the kind that get carted around from carnival to carnival. But to me, it was like Disney World—or the closest I'd ever come to seeing the Magic Kingdom on our limited budget.

I take the picture off the shelf, wrap it in newspaper, and place it inside a cardboard box I found in the kitchen. And that's that. Moving out has begun. *But where am I going to go?*

Tears prick the corners of my eyes. This place has been horrible for many reasons, with George Bishop topping the list and some guests not far behind. Still, it's been my home for the past two years, and now, home is no more.

I sit on my bed, the same one where George tried several times to coerce me into giving him a massage. I thought I might actually get to enjoy my living space now that he's gone, but such is life.

Leaving is for the best, I tell myself. Vicki Bishop did me a favor by firing me. I don't need this job, these memories, any of it. I'm fine on my own. But I know I'm lying. I need the work, if not for me, then for Nana.

I let out a weighty sigh as I remove the plastic bin that functions as a dresser from under my bed. I have a canvas bag under there as well, but I can't bring myself to start packing it yet. I guess I've got some time on account of the storm.

Looking out my window reminds me of going through a car wash. It's hard to believe these are only the outer bands of Larry. I can't imagine the damage it will do when it hits full force later today.

I call Nana to check on her but get no answer. Nothing unusual there. On her down days, when dementia-induced confusion takes over, she won't pick up the phone. I call Janice for an update.

"We're all fine here, Charley," Janice assures me. "Your nana is safe and sound, but I'm worried about you. How's the hotel holding up? And the Bishop sisters? Are they giving you any trouble?"

I have to tell her about Todd. She's surprised, but not overly so.

"Bad things always follow that family," she says. "You be careful. Don't get caught up in anything."

Too late for that.

I want to tell Janice that it's her fault for raising Nana's rent and making me desperate for extra cash. But I don't go there. Nana taught me not to blame others for my poor choices. That was my mother's approach, and I wasn't like Mary Beth, Nana would say—at least until she started mistaking me for her.

After the call with Janice, my attention drifts over to my bookcase. It might be small, but all the books on it are meaningful. I've arranged them chronologically by the year I read them, from earliest to latest. The book that catches my eye is on the top shelf, far left. It's the first and only story my mother ever read to me. Holding it in my hands, a wave of sorrow washes over me.

Each turn of the page transports me to a time when I felt safe and cared for. The peace, warmth, and joy of those memories envelop me like a cocoon spun by my mother's love.

I take it all in: the familiar room with its red balloon, a comb and a brush, a bowl full of mush, and that quiet old woman whispering hush.

Tears fall onto the page as I reflect back. My sobs mask the sound of Bree entering. I'm startled when she says my name. I close the book quickly as though ashamed of my sadness.

"Hey, I'm sorry to interrupt," she says. "Are you okay? I can come back."

"Yeah, I'm fine," I tell her, sniffing as I wipe my eyes with the back of my hand. "Just stupid nostalgia, is all." I hold up the book by Margaret Wise Brown.

Bree's expression brightens. Clearly, like most people, she knows this story well.

"Oh, I get it," she says, settling beside me on the bed. The old mattress creaks under her weight. I thought I wanted to be alone until Bree showed up. It's sad that a stranger is the closest thing I have to a girlfriend. Rodrigo checks a lot of boxes, but he's still a guy.

I sniff again, then force out a laugh. "It's the only book my mother ever read to me," I explain.

Empathy floods Bree's eyes. "I'm really sorry. And I feel awful that you got fired. It's totally my fault."

"It's okay. I didn't have to agree to it. I'll figure something out," I reply, but despair gnaws at me.

"I'll make it up to you. I promise," Bree assures me, determination in her voice. "I'll pay you extra, help you find a new job, anything."

How about finding me a new place to live while you're at it? And the money to keep Nana at Guiding Way? But I don't say this out loud. Bree looks too devastated and guilt-ridden for me to add to her misery.

"It's all right," I say. "Maybe I can move in with Janice for a while, or maybe Rodrigo and his mom will let me crash with them."

"Actually, I might have another solution for your problem. What if you don't get fired at all?"

I look at her, surprised. "What do you mean? We both heard Vicki. We're out of here."

Bree glances around nervously, as if someone might be listening. She gets up from the bed, gently closing the door.

In a quiet voice, she says, "There's something I have to tell you. It's about Todd."

"What about him?"

"Last night, when I heard him outside my room—I'm not a doctor, but that was no 'heart attack.' He was gurgling and making these thick, strangled sounds as he was dying, and there was foam at his mouth that dissolved before the others saw it. I know they're all saying it was a sudden heart attack, but this *wasn't* sudden. It was drawn out, long . . . and I hate to use the word, but it sounded *wet*, like he was choking on liquid filling his throat and lungs. It was more than just trouble breathing."

"Whoa," I say. "Why didn't you tell the police?"

"I think I was in shock. I had to process it all, but now, with some rest and a clearer mind, I have some serious suspicions."

"You think Vicki might be right about someone killing him?"

"He might have been poisoned," says Bree. "I mean, what else could do that to a person?"

"But you're talking murder."

Bree nods decisively. "Exactly that."

"Then that would mean the killer is here, right now, in the hotel."

"Is that so hard to believe?" Bree asks. "I overheard some of the will reading from upstairs. Okay, I confess, I snuck out of my room for a better listen. Not the best move, I know, but I was curious. You were down there, too; you heard them. This crew makes the Addams Family seem like the Brady Bunch. It could be *any* of them, even Vicki."

"Not Vicki," I say with authority. "She's the one *accusing* other people."

Bree's sidelong glance implies I'm being naïve. "Maybe she's creating a smoke screen to hide what *she* did. Last night I heard those two fighting in their room like cats and dogs. Couldn't tell you exactly what it was about, but it was intense."

"You think she . . ." I trail off, but Bree's expression answers my unfinished question. "Damn. That's pretty twisted," I say, grimacing.

"Sure is. Which is why I think we need to figure out *who* killed Todd. If we can prove that Vicki murdered her husband, maybe you won't have to live with Rodrigo."

A knock at the door makes me jump. "Who's there?" I ask.

"It's me, Rodrigo," comes the reply.

I let go a breath, relieved that it's not Vicki, before inviting him to enter.

Even though he's wearing an L.L.Bean raincoat, he looks like he's taken a dunk in the ocean. He takes off the coat, shaking the excess water into the hallway outside my room, then flashes the same toothy grin that instantly endears him to almost every guest at the hotel.

"What's going on?" he asks, noticing our grave expressions. "Uh-oh. Is there fallout from our stowaway?" He points to Bree.

Now I have no choice but to break the news.

"Yeah, I got fired. Vicki said I have to move out after the storm. Bree has to go, too."

"What?" Rodrigo's shock shifts into a faint I-told-you-so expression. "I warned you. I *knew* this would happen."

"Yeah, whatever. I don't need a lecture right now," I say. What I want is to go back in time and tell Bree I can't help her. But that's the problem with hindsight: it's painfully clear.

Rodrigo softens his reproachful look into one of compassion. "Oh shit, honey," he says, opening his arms for an embrace. I let him hug me, even though he's damp from the rain.

After we break apart, I go into debrief mode, filling Rodrigo in on the crazy family dynamics and accusations. I keep Bree's suspicions about Todd's death to myself. Rodrigo is worried about me enough as is. He doesn't need to think I'll be riding out the storm with a killer in our midst.

"You can stay with me and Mama as long as you need," Rodrigo promises. "I think she loves you as much as she does me. And as for you, Ms. Bree . . ."—Rodrigo's dimpled, reassuring smile flattens into a frown—"you can double what you promised so Charley gets some payback for the trouble you caused."

"I already told her I'd do that," Bree says.

"All right, double that, and do something else to help. You've made an absolute mess of her life," Rodrigo says, his frustration evident.

"No," I say, defending Bree, "*I* made a mess of it. She didn't force me. I agreed to help."

Rodrigo mulls this over for a moment. "I suppose so," he says grudgingly. "I guess we should save the retribution for people who really deserve it—people like Brenda Black."

"What exactly did she do to your family, anyway?" I ask. "You didn't get to tell me the whole story."

Rodrigo eyes Bree warily, unsure if he should trust her with his secrets, but relents with a shrug. "She's a criminal, no two ways about it," he says.

"How so?" I ask. Bree is off the bed, so we face each other in a football huddle.

"To explain that, I need to start at the beginning, when my mom was living in Honduras."

"By the beginning, you mean before you were born?" I ask, smiling.

"Trust me, it's important," he says, holding up a hand. He launches right into it. "My father met my mother at a hotel in Tegucigalpa. She was working at the bar, and he was staying for a while on a construction job. They hit it off and fell in love. After they got engaged, my mom could secure a nonimmigrant visa and move with him to the United States. But my father died before the wedding—a work accident at a new job. Fatal fall, that's all I know. My mother doesn't like to talk about it.

"Luckily, I had already been conceived, so I was born in Texas. That makes me a citizen, but *mi madre* . . . not so fortunate. When her visa expired, she had to leave the country by law, which meant either leaving me behind or taking me back to Honduras, where there was more gang violence than work.

"My mother and I fled to the East Coast—Portland, Maine, specifically, where she had a cousin. Can't say one of the whitest states in America was the ideal safe haven for a gay half-Hispanic kid, but I made the best of it.

"Mom jumped from one hotel job to another, taking me along for the ride, always trying to stay one step ahead of INS while I was dealing with the trauma of new schools and new bullies. I used to take my frustrations out by throwing rocks at bottles I set up in the backyard. Mom watched all of it. She was heartbroken for me. Little did she know I was inadvertently training myself to become a star pitcher on my high school baseball team."

"This is a great story and all," I say, "but I'm not seeing how Black fits into it."

"I'm getting there—patience, please," he says. "There are over eleven million undocumented immigrants in this country today living the daily grind—taking care of kids, shopping, paying taxes . . . that's right, many undocumented immigrants pay taxes without a Social Security number. And if you're like my mom, driving a car, especially in Maine where it's impossible to get anywhere without one, a traffic stop becomes a substantial deportation risk."

"But how can your mom get a driver's license if she's undocumented?" I ask.

"Maine didn't have a legal status requirement at the time," he says. "That's good, but it came with a big downfall. You get pulled over for a ticket, speeding, whatever, and before you know it, you're in front of an INS board getting your deportation papers handed to you. It happens a lot more than people realize. And Maine has its own traffic-stop-to-deportation pipeline. There are a lot of seasonal workers here and many black and brown people to target, but the pipeline my mom got caught up in was corrupt as can be—and Black was a part of it."

"How so?" I ask.

"A crooked cop, Black, and a corrupt judge worked together in an extortion scheme. It was simple. The cop pulled over potential marks and issued a citation. The violations were often made up, like in my mom's case. She wasn't speeding, but he said she was. Then they'd go before this corrupt judge, and Black, a public defender at the time, takes the case.

"The traffic stop isn't the big problem for people like my mother—it's a conviction in court that triggers the immigration penalties. So backdoor deals get made. That's the extortion part. My mom, and others like her, end up paying a portion of their weekly wages to these three criminals. No surprise the victims don't report the crime, because they don't want to risk being kicked out of the country.

"The racket shut down a while ago—I think the judge was feeling some heat and got forced into early retirement. And Black, she left the public defender's office soon after to go into private practice. Coincidence? I don't think so."

"What a prime piece of shit!" Bree seethes. I'm feeling equally enraged. "Why wasn't this a bigger story?" she wants to know. "Everyone's heard about those two Pennsylvania judges who sent kids to for-profit jails in exchange for kickbacks. Where was the news coverage?"

"Like I said, no witnesses. And I suspect the higher-ups in state government buried it. Bad for tourism and the image of the area. My poor mama, now she's got a bad heart, and I know it's the stress that did it to her. If her heart gives out, it'll be Black who's to blame."

Rodrigo, usually cheerful and professional, is almost overcome with rage. The intensity in his eyes unsettles me.

"I know a thing or two about that kind of murder," says Bree, who exudes her own palpable darkness. "Some bullets take a long time to hit their target." I've no idea what she's referring to, but she doesn't elaborate. Maybe it has something to do with her mother's death from cancer, but what or how? I couldn't say.

Rodrigo seems like he's going to press Bree for details, but before he gets the chance, we hear attorney Black's voice in the Great Room.

"I can't see her," he says, alarmed. "I might do something I'll regret. I just came here to check on things. I'm going to make one last trip to the store before the weather gets worse. Do you two need anything?"

"No, maybe just look in on Nana one more time before you go home. She's not answering her phone. The storm could be making her confusion worse. Think you can call me from her place so I can talk to her?"

Rodrigo gives a nod. I glance out the window at the tall pines bending like pipe cleaners in the fierce wind while the rain pours down.

"Are you sure it's safe to drive?" I ask.

"Well, it's not going to get any safer. And don't freak out, Charley. We'll figure out your situation together." He gives me a quick hug. There's no hug for Bree. Then he's gone, off into the hurricane, his emotions heavy as he heads out the door.

Meanwhile, I've lost my mojo for moving, but I've still got cleaning to do. When I tell Bree that I have to get to work, she surprises me.

"Why don't I help you," she offers. "We'll get it done faster together. I feel gutted about derailing your life, Charley. It's the least I can do."

Cleaning is a lonely business, especially when I'm not even wanted on the job. Who am I to decline a helping hand? As we head upstairs to fetch my Bessie, a dreadful feeling overcomes me—a premonition that something truly terrible is going to happen, something even worse than Todd's death.

I can't explain why, but when I see the door to Iris's room open and a crowd gathered inside, I know I'm about to get my answer.

Chapter 20

ris, Faith, and Vicki stand at the foot of the bed, looking with horror at the serpentine dresser made of tigerwood across from them. From the hallway, I can't see what's got them spooked, but I'm sure it's not their collective reflections in the attached mirror.

As I get closer, I see Oliver standing near the dresser. Hope is kneeling before him, as if he's about to anoint her with the gold lipstick tube he's holding tightly in his hand. She's petite to begin with, but down on her knees it's as though she's worshiping a giant.

Quinn is lurking in the hallway. His face is pale and emotionless. Everyone is accounted for, except for Black, whom we just heard downstairs. For her sake, I hope she doesn't run into Rodrigo.

"What's going on?" I ask Quinn.

"See for yourself," he tells me.

He takes hold of my arm, which sends a little tingle up my spine, before guiding me into the Mohegan Room. Because it's crowded, I have to slip in behind the three sisters, who are so fixated on the dresser that they don't acknowledge my presence. Bree slides in beside me, her hand touching my arm, and I can feel her nervousness sink into me.

I have to crane my neck to see over Faith, whose towering height is even more evident with her two sisters lined up next to her. It quickly becomes apparent why everyone is so distraught. Scrawled in bright red childlike handwriting on the mirror above the dresser is a poem so chilling and bizarre, I can't suppress a gasp. The letters seem to pulse with a dark energy.

As I silently read the words to myself, my mouth goes a little dry.

One of us will lose her life.
Another one will pay the price.
The last will mourn alone,
For the past she must atone.

I read the macabre poem several times, attempting to decipher its meaning. It's unsettling and menacing, that much is clear. My attention shifts to Oliver—our resident poet. Now that lipstick tube in his hand makes a lot more sense. I can also hear Hope's attempts to reason with him.

"Ollie, honey, you need to tell Mommy why you did this. Talk to Mommy, sweetheart. Why did you write this poem?"

"But I didn't write it," Oliver says weakly. His body is rigid, like rigor mortis has set in.

"Oliver, stop being creepy," Vicki orders. "We know it was you."

Rather than face his accuser, Oliver locks his dark, piercing eyes on mine through the mirror's reflection. It's as if he's held spellbound, peering into the depths of my soul. Then I catch it, as fleeting as the flicker of an eyelash. He sends me a glare so venomous, so ripe with loathing, that *pure hatred* is the phrase that springs to mind.

Hope's desperate voice draws my attention away from the boy's unsettling stare. "Ollie! Tell us why you wrote this," she insists.

But Oliver remains silent, standing still as a statue, his disquieting gaze still reflected back at me through the mirror.

"You're making him nervous, Hope," Faith says. "Take him out of here—now. Make him a cup of tea or something. We need some space to sort this out."

Hope doesn't object. Although she stretches, she can't quite reach Oliver's shoulder to put her arm around him. Nevertheless, it's enough for her to guide him out of the room without any protest.

As soon as he departs, Vicki turns to Faith, a fiery look in her eyes. "Your kid has certainly upped his creep factor," she says.

"Now just a second," Faith snaps back, wagging a finger at her sister. "We can't be sure that Ollie wrote this."

Iris harrumphs. "First off, it's a *poem*. Second, I walked into my room and found him standing in front of the mirror, holding a tube of lipstick. You solve the case, Sherlock."

"At first, I thought it was written in blood," Vicki says. "And it's obvious who wrote it, Faith. The question is why." She throws her hands up in the air.

"Frankly, I'm more interested in what the poem means," Faith replies. "It's clearly about *us*, right?" She points to Vicki, then to Iris, before tossing her hair back as if everything would be about her, naturally.

Vicki says, "What it *means*? Don't be daft. And yes, it's obviously about us. One of us will die, another will be accused of said death, and the last will spend the rest of her life grieving. Although at this point, it's unclear that any of us would actually mourn the departed. Either way, it's not difficult to comprehend."

Iris rolls up the sleeves of her black and gray flannel shirt, flashing her many tattoos like a peacock fanning its feathers. She takes a step to the side, eyeing the poem from a new vantage point as if that might clarify the mystery.

"That's part of it, Vick. But Faith is right. We need to figure out *exactly* what the poem is implying. Are we being threatened? It sure seems that way. And it's written from one of our perspectives. One of *us* will lose her life—not one of *you*, not *one of them*, but one of us three sisters. Now, why would Ollie do that? And besides, how would he even know about—"

Vicki cuts her off. "Stop right there, Iris." She grabs a handful of tissues from a box on the dresser, using them to smear the sinister parody of a child's scrawl into an illegible red stain that, as Vicki observed, does look a lot like blood. "There's nothing to know, and I won't let this silly poem rattle me. Obviously Oliver did this, and he needs to explain himself."

"Maybe Ollie is having some sort of mental breakdown," Iris suggests. "There's no rhyme or reason to this."

"Well, there is rhyme," Bree interjects. "But really, do you think Oliver would use words like *mourn* or *atone*? That's fairly sophisticated."

"Oliver is a very intelligent boy," Faith answers. "He reads a lot, so the vocabulary is *not* beyond him."

Funny, now that it involves praise, Faith seems to *want* Oliver to be responsible.

Silence, thick as fog, descends until Quinn speaks up for the first time.

"What's the big sin the poem referred to? That's what I want to know. Is there something the three of you would like to confess?"

"None of us are without sin," Iris replies eerily. Her probing eyes capture the room, casting a wide net that ensnares us all. "God did not send his Son into the world to condemn it, but in order that the world might be saved from sin through him. That's John, 3:17, paraphrased, but close enough."

"Please spare me the Bible verse," Vicki snaps. "What are you getting at, anyway? Just use normal words. Don't be cryptic like Oliver."

"And don't besmirch my son," Hope calls out as she returns to the room.

"*Besmirch?*" says Vicki, her voice rising. "Now that's a ten-dollar word." She leans back on her heels, directing a look at Bree. "Any questions about where Oliver got his advanced vocabulary should be settled now," she says.

A loud crack echoes outside the hotel, as if a large tree branch just surrendered to the wind. Nightfall is still hours away, but the stormy skies are so dark, time seems stuck at midnight.

"I don't believe Oliver wrote the poem," Hope says, addressing the room with authority. "At least not exactly. I think he's had an *episode*."

"An episode? What do you mean? What kind of *episode* are you talking about?" asks Bree.

"A psychic one," Hope says casually, as if that's a normal occurrence.

"A psychic episode?" repeats Vicki, making it clear that no answer could be more ridiculous.

"He's a special boy," Hope says. "He's got *the gift*. I've seen it. So has Faith."

All eyes turn to Faith.

"I mean, I have seen some things I can't explain," she acknowledges.

"Like what?" Vicki wants to know.

"He knew when Hope's mom died before we even got a chance to tell him," Faith says. "He just blurted it out when we said we wanted to talk to him: 'Grammy's gone, isn't she?'"

Hope uses the sleeve of her embroidered blouse to dab at her misty eyes. "That was so crazy," she says. "They were very close, Oliver and my mom, so I'm not surprised she reached out to him. And he knew that she had cancer. We never told him, but he knew."

"It was lung cancer," Faith elaborates, "and out of nowhere Ollie says: 'Grammy needs care, where she gets her air.' *Gets her air*—obviously that's her lungs. So he was tuned in. I mean, we both had chills."

Hope and Faith share a look of wonder.

"Hope thinks Ollie's rhyming tendency is because he's trying to process messages that come from the spirit realm," Faith says.

Quinn squints with doubt. "Aunt Hope, are you suggesting that Ollie got a message from the beyond, and that's why he wrote the rhyme on the mirror?"

"I'm not ruling it out," says Hope. "He's got the gift."

Iris sends Vicki a sidelong glance. "And you always treated *me* like the crazy one." She redirects to Faith. "If what you're saying is true, that would make this poem a—"

"Prophecy," Hope finishes for her.

"A prophecy that predicts one of us is going to die?" Vicki asks, her voice laced with cynicism. She glares over at Faith and Hope. "All this supernatural nonsense is just a distraction from the real issue at hand, which is what happened to my husband." Vicki's face contorts into a knot of grief, but I don't see any tears. "And Faith, I don't think you're being honest," she adds. "Same with you, Iris. You both have a motive for murder."

"Oh, go fuck yourself, Vicki," Iris claps back. "I don't need your accusations. Todd had a heart attack. Get over it. And he stole the hotel out from under Faith and me, so please forgive my lack of tears. And I certainly don't need to be the object of your innuendos."

"Please, let's all keep our tempers in check," Hope implores. "I believe Oliver is trying to tell us something important here."

"Well, how the hell are we supposed to know if this is a warning from another realm, or—more likely—your son playing a really sick game?" Iris wants to know.

"There's only one way I can think of," says Hope. "And it's a good thing I brought my tarot cards."

Tarot cards?

I study myself in the smudged mirror, my gaze unblinking, feeling a pressure building inside. If Bree's to be believed, Vicki has reason to be suspicious of her sisters, but is it just a smoke screen, a cover for her own crime? I desperately need to know more. Todd's death doesn't appear to be natural. The poem is totally creepy. Even creepier, Hope intends to invoke the spirit realm for answers.

But I have one big question on my mind: Just who ARE these Bishop sisters?

Part 2

THE BISHOP SISTERS

Chapter 21

Forty years ago

Iris's childhood seems idyllic in every way. Buttery sun-streaked afternoons melt into star-drenched skies, under which she gazes with wonderment into infinity. Far from the chaos of city life or the dull sameness of suburbia, Iris has the freedom to roam and explore as she sees fit. Her playgrounds are the woods and meadows, the shoreline with its cold water and sharp barnacles latched to rocks of all sizes, and the hotel itself.

Her family is happy. They live together on the third floor of the Precipice, she and her two sisters sharing a single room down the hall from their parents. She is the middle child, so she gets the top bunk—not the single bed, which goes to Vicki. No matter. Her sisters are her best friends, and life is good.

Summers here seem to last forever. The hotel bustles with activity, people coming and going, luggage in and out, meals prepared and dishes washed. Iris thrives on the energy of the place. When she's not people watching, she spends her days exploring and her evenings scouring the fields for fireflies, feeling an unusual kinship with these elusive critters. Like the insects that she chases and captures inside glass jars, Iris feels seen one moment and invisible the next. Her parents are too busy to pay much attention to her. And she's not the oldest, which comes with special privileges, nor is she the youngest, the baby who is doted upon.

It seems nobody notices Iris's glow no matter how hard she tries to shine. It's far more obvious with Faith. Everyone says she looks like an angel. Vicki is the smart one, always taking charge. But Iris has a quiet nature, sweet and gentle like the wildflowers growing in the garden that blossom into vibrant colors, but only when the conditions are just right.

The long winters bring piles of snow that collect up to the window-sills of the lower-level rooms. Storms that come and go encase the tree branches in thick ice, turning the landscape into a magical fairyland that glistens and sparkles like an endless field of diamonds. Dangling icicles cling precariously to hotel gutters in a display of ornate crystal daggers. This is the season of hot chocolate and snow days (rare for northern Maine, which prides itself on being hardy and resourceful at getting kids to school). Iris sleds down the steep driveway that cars can't climb when the road to the hotel turns icy and slick.

She loves making snow angels, pretending they're her friends. Biting winter winds push the snowflakes around, filling in the delicate wings, but Iris doesn't mind. She simply makes them anew. Although Iris is older than Faith by eighteen months, her angels are far shorter than the ones Faith creates beside her. The size difference makes Iris feel inferior: she's older, so she should be taller. It's her first real indication that life doesn't always align with her expectations.

After the long winter, springtime arrives, sending melting snow streaming into the creeks and rivers that flow to the turbulent sea. Iris spends her free time collecting shells on the shoreline while Father spends *his* time with the new young maid.

Iris sees them together often, and at first thinks of them as nothing more than playmates, friends who make each other laugh. But Vicki has a word for these encounters: *affair*. She has to explain what that word means, and when she does, it's as if Iris has taken a bite of the apple from the Tree of Knowledge.

Once she obtains next-level awareness that life isn't as it seems, that her family isn't what she believed it to be, things start to shift. Iris no longer feels as secure in her home as she once did, or as carefree stomping about in her many playgrounds. The fireflies don't glow as brightly as before.

One evening, Iris finds Vicki and Faith crouched outside the West

Indies Room, with their ears pressed up against the door. At their prodding, she gives a listen as well, hearing unfamiliar and frightening noises from within. The grunts and groans make her skin crawl.

When Mother arrives, she's angry—not at Father, but at her daughters for eavesdropping. She ushers all three to the kitchen, where she makes them grilled cheese sandwiches. Vicki wants to know why Mother isn't more upset.

"It's none of our business what your father does. He works very hard to provide for us. We should be grateful."

Iris knows she's lying. Pain is etched deeply in Mother's soft gray eyes, and she clutches her arms to her sides, as though trying to hold herself together. Mother pours whiskey into a glass tumbler and washes pills down her throat. Iris is too young to articulate what she suspects. The pills aren't for headaches, as Mother says, but for heartaches.

Father and the maid continue to play hide-and-seek behind closed doors (that's what Iris calls these encounters, for it's far easier to think of them as games). But she knows better. Father is being naughty right under Mother's nose, and she lets it happen! Iris doesn't like that one bit, but what can she do? She's only eight years old. Her idyllic life transforms; like a snow globe being slowly turned upside down, her world inverts and falls into countless pieces around her.

As the years go by, Father hires more pretty young maids. There's more eavesdropping and plenty more grilled cheese sandwiches.

Chapter 22

He doesn't care about them," Faith insists one rainy afternoon while the sisters are sifting through books in the Library Room. Iris, who just turned fourteen, wants to believe her, but Vicki is convinced this new one is different.

Her name is Christine, and Father is in love, or so Vicki believes. She's special to him, and it's easy to understand why. Not only is Christine young and beautiful, with flawless skin and a perfect body even a scrub dress can't hide, she's also smart and kind and a really hard worker.

Father is always buying her things: pretty scarves, fancy jewelry, expensive perfume—gifts he should get for Mother, but doesn't. Mother's drinking and pill habit gets worse. Maine is isolating enough when you have a happy marriage, and it's been a long time since they could say Mother was happy.

It's understandable that Iris blames her mother's misery on the new maid. Faith and Vicki do the same. Christine becomes an easy target. It's all childish, harmless pranks—name-calling, a marker thrown into her laundry, stealing gifts that Father bought for her, that sort of thing. But it doesn't matter what they do. Christine won't quit, and Father won't fire her.

Confusion becomes Iris's incurable infection. Sensitive, quiet Iris doesn't have the words to express herself, nor does she have much insight into her emotions, so it manifests in her behavior at school. Her grades begin to drop when she stops handing in her homework. Parent-teacher conferences don't seem to help. Some days, Iris leaves the hotel as if she's headed to school, but as soon as she's out of sight, she takes off and hides out in the woods. Sometimes she wanders into school late; other times she doesn't show up at all.

Mother goes through changes as well. She never used to yell at the staff. Now that's all she does. Nobody can do a good enough job anymore. She's always threatening to fire everyone—from Olga, the cook, and her handsome son, Samuel, who works with her in the kitchen, to the landscapers and other maids. But Iris never hears Mother yell at Christine—no, not once, not ever. In fact, those two never talk, and their silence says it all.

Christine is untouchable.

Two years later, and Christine is still there.

It's a dreary, depressing day—one of those gray days by the ocean where the sun never seems to rise, the chill never leaves the air—when Vicki hears her mother crying in the kitchen. She goes to check. No surprise, her mother acts like everything's fine, even though she's wiping her eyes to hide her tears. She smiles at her daughter.

"Hello, honey. Are you hungry? Want me to make you something to eat?"

Vicki knows what's on the menu, and she's in no mood for a grilled cheese sandwich. It's just after noon and already her mother's breath smells like the hard stuff. Vicki knows in her gut that her father has done something to upset her mother . . . again. The question is: What now?

It doesn't take long for Vicki to learn the answer. She peeks out the window, seeing a shiny new car in the parking lot of the hotel. Her father is showing it off to that awful maid, Christine.

Vicki is incensed. *Did he actually buy her a car? And is he really flaunting it in front of my mother? What a shit. What an absolute shit.*

She spies on Christine through that window, watching her inspect the vehicle. Christine brushes a hand gently along the smooth metal of the front fender like she can't believe it's real. But then, much to Vicki's surprise, Christine shakes her head as if attempting to refuse her father's profoundly inappropriate generosity. She reads the maid's body language—it's too much, she's trying to tell him, holding up her hands in a "no go" gesture. She wants to decline, but her father is being very insistent. He points to the tires, the interior, like he's trying to sell her on his own damn gift.

All this while her poor mother is at the kitchen table, drowning in tears and booze.

Vicki doesn't care that Christine seems uncomfortable, shrinking away from her father's touch. It's probably just an act, she decides. She's pretending to be the reluctant recipient, but she's just playing hard to get. The more she resists him, the harder he'll try, and the more she'll get. It's that simple. Vicki knows that Christine is not some sweet and innocent victim. No, she's more akin to a master musician, playing her father as though she were a world-class violinist and he the instrument made to sing her tune.

Something simply has to be done.

Vicki calls a conference that takes place in the Library Room. There she debriefs with her two sisters. She tells them about the car and how it's tearing their mother apart.

"It's going to kill her," she insists.

Vicki knows she's being overly dramatic, but she is seventeen, in her final year of high school, so drama comes with the territory. Faith sits on the edge of the bed, twirling her hair. Oh, how that girl drives her crazy! Faith thinks being beautiful actually fixes things. Ha! Eventually she'll figure out it's also a curse, but Vicki didn't summon her sisters to confront Faith about her vanity. Christine is the problem they need to address.

She makes an impassioned plea to her siblings. All the previous little pranks simply haven't been enough to drive her away. The time has come to take drastic action!

Banging her fist on a table for emphasis, Vicki must be convincing, for her sisters nod in vigorous agreement. But what are they to do?

Faith suggests trying to scare her away, somehow force Christine to quit.

Iris suggests framing her for stealing.

Vicki likes their thinking but doubts those ideas will work.

They start tossing suggestions around, brainstorming ways to rid themselves of the meddlesome young maid. Whatever they settle on, all agree it has to make a statement. Some of their ideas are too outlandish, some aren't terrible enough.

It's Faith, twirling her hair, ditzy, spacey as always, who actually (well, inadvertently) hits upon the best idea of all.

"Dad should be buying *us* a car, not her," she says morosely.

The car! Of course! Why didn't Vicki think of it herself?

Chapter 23

That slut of a chambermaid doesn't deserve such a nice ride, and their mother doesn't need to look at the shiny, expensive reminder of her husband's infidelity every single day—that's what Vicki has decided.

Her imagination goes into overdrive. The whole scenario plays out in her mind like a climactic scene in an action movie. The car must go, and they need to destroy it in such a way that they won't get caught. But Christine also needs to know it was a message directed at her to leave and not come back. Since there are always guests around the property, it's not safe to vandalize the vehicle in the parking lot.

And that's when Vicki settles on a plan she thinks is foolproof.

The sisters begin to study Christine like a primatologist would a chimpanzee. For several weeks, they compile notes in notebooks, sharing the results with one another at the end of each day. They learn when and where she eats, where she goes on breaks, and how well she does her job. They observe that she's friendly with the staff, but seems especially fond of Samuel, Olga's attractive son. The girls have even spotted Christine and Samuel holding hands, sneaking a kiss here and there, always on guard, as if George might be lurking around the corner.

Father's grown frustrated with Christine, that's what Vicki thinks. He keeps wanting to whisk her off into an empty room for an afternoon delight, but she's pushing back now. It's like she's got some big plan in mind that's giving her new strength and confidence. Seeing this shift doesn't change anything in Vicki's mind. She's convinced that it's all part of an act to get as much out of her father as possible.

After several weeks of studying, watching, and note-taking, the sisters settle on a course of action. They even pick the day to put their plan into action—a Tuesday, during a week when their father will be out of town on business.

That week, Mother uses Father's rare absence to torment Christine. She makes her work extra hard those days—giving her personal laundry to do, tasks that aren't in her job description, and even forcing her to clean bathroom grout with a toothbrush. It's grueling retribution, but nobody is feeling sorry for her.

Christine deserves that, and more.

Thanks to the sisters' painstaking reconnaissance work, they know exactly when Christine leaves the hotel each afternoon. It won't take much, Vicki figures. Some broken glass, perhaps a few cardboard boxes strewn about—something noticeable to make Christine swerve just as she reaches a particularly sharp bend in the road. Then, as she takes the blind corner at the wrong angle, she'll smash into a big log that they'll have strategically put into place, an obstacle she won't be able to avoid.

Vicki will ensure that Christine understands it was deliberate, without saying or doing anything incriminating. Perhaps she'll fix her with a scathing stare and say, "All actions have consequences, you know. You should be more careful next time."

There. Foolproof.

It's no big shock when, as the day nears, Faith and Iris start to get cold feet. They're worried that Christine could actually get injured, but Vicki assures them that won't be the case. Christine is an extremely slow driver, something Vicki's catalogued during the planning phase of the mission.

"You've seen her drive," Vicki reminds her sisters. "She goes at a snail's pace. She's very cautious, especially with the new car."

At the speed she drives, Vicki is certain the accident will damage the pristine vehicle, but nothing major will happen. It will be just enough to exact their revenge and send a stern warning.

Her sisters are well aware that when Vicki gets her mind made up, she can be quite insistent. She pushes and prods, layering on the guilt, until her sisters relent to the peer pressure. She smiles with self-satisfaction, knowing she can be just as persuasive as her father.

The sisters test the walkie-talkies they'll use to communicate and issue instructions. They've had them since they were little girls, for fun games and pretend play. But this isn't pretend. No, it's as far from that as possible.

Vicki is designated to be the lookout. It's her job to give the green light when she sees Christine driving along the road. They can't risk damaging the wrong car. When Vicki gives the command, Iris will scatter the boxes and glass to force the swerve. Faith will roll out the massive log. It takes the combined effort of all three girls to get the log onto the side of the road, but they've confirmed Faith can put it into position without any help.

On the appointed day, at the usual time Christine leaves work, Vicki spots the white car on approach. To her surprise, it's going much faster than she expected. She has no idea why Christine, on this day of all days, is in such a hurry. It's not like her. A nervous pang stabs Vicki hard. Even so, she radios to her sisters.

"It's go time!" she announces. "Nothing to worry about," she assures them over the air.

But a little feeling of doubt creeps in, warning her that she's never been more wrong.

As the car zooms past, Vicki's second thoughts return, this time even stronger. She considers telling her sisters to abort. Her finger is on the push button of the walkie-talkie. But it's too late. She's already given the order. The car has driven past her. It's only a matter of seconds.

Vicki doesn't see the crash, but she hears the impact: a loud squeal of tires, followed by a crunch of metal that seems to shake the sky. The sound of shattering glass chills Vicki's heart. But it's the skidding that's the worst of it. The screech, a discordant resonance of metal against pavement, seems endless. Vicki envisions sparks flying in all directions. She hears a loud *thwack* and wonders if the car has smashed into a tree, one of the many sturdy pines lining the side of the road.

Faith screams into the walkie-talkie: "Oh my god! Oh my god! What have we done?"

Vicki's horrified and sickened, but she's also smart. She radios back: "Get the boxes out of there. Hide them in the woods. Roll the log to the side of the road. And RUN!"

Chapter 24

Iris has a new companion—guilt—and it's with her every minute, every second, of every day. A year after the crash and she still can't shake it, or lock it away in a room, or drown it in the cold gray sea. It clings to her like a second skin, attaching itself leechlike to the fabric of her very being.

Nothing linked Iris and her sisters to the crash site. There were no eyewitnesses, no news reports other than a few paragraphs in the local paper that covered the basics. A car went off the road. It happened near the Precipice Hotel. There was a fatality.

Since nobody suspected foul play, nobody dug any deeper. But remorse had hollowed a pit in Iris's mind and soul, from which she couldn't climb out. It consumed her, changed her, owned her.

Thank God for drugs.

If Iris hadn't discovered them, she might have let the guilt slowly eat away at her until she vanished into nothingness. It starts with marijuana, a few drags at a house party. It doesn't take long before she graduates to pills. She likes how she can regulate her emotions with a swig, a puff, or a swallow.

At first she doesn't think much of it. She's sixteen now, in the midst of the teenage rebellion years. The rush she gets from each high is like being dropped into a warm river. She lets the chemical currents sweep away all her bad feelings—the hurt, confusion, pain, and sorrow that have been tormenting her night and day.

Subconsciously or intentionally—it's hard to say which—Iris begins using drugs not just to escape her life, but to destroy it. Her plan works to near perfection. She is booted off the math team, and soon after, she's kicked out of school entirely when a fellow student finds her passed out on a toilet in the girls' bathroom. The doctor informs her that she could have died from an overdose.

Whatever, she thinks. *Problem solved.*

Maybe it wasn't such a good idea to call her father a lying, cheating, child-molesting piece of shit during a big blowout argument over her expulsion, but who cares—it's all true, and the drugs help her say it.

Her parents—well, her father—tell Iris to leave home and not come back. So at eighteen, Iris moves to Boston—East Boston, to be precise, taking up residence in a one-room shithole apartment within spitting distance of Logan Airport. In no time, she can identify the type of plane flying overhead by the engine's sound alone.

She keeps her secret, the same as she does her guilt and addictions. What she has for furniture comes from the Goodwill reject pile. Filth is everywhere. She can't scrub the grime off the windows. The air is stale with cigarette smoke and spilled beer. Dirty dishes are left for weeks in the sink as the food remnants turn rank, but Iris grows as accustomed to the stench as she is to her loser boyfriend, whose name doesn't matter.

Money comes from, where else? Drugs. Dealing them, low-level stuff that barely brings in enough cash to keep the heat on in winter. Iris hustles for every dollar, which means doing things she never dreamed she could do. She doesn't speak to her sisters anymore or talk to anyone from her old life. They're all too quick with judgment and too stingy with money. They're of no use to her.

Every relationship in Iris's life is transactional, including the one with her nameless and useless boyfriend. The years roll on. She turns twenty-four, still living in the same crappy apartment city inspectors should have condemned years ago, but with a different useless, anonymous boyfriend. She spends her days working hard to avoid withdrawal symptoms, which means scoring more drugs.

She's had enough strikeout days to recognize the warning signs that her body desperately craves a fix: sweating, rapid heart rate, twitching, etc. But it's not the biological symptoms she fears most.

No, when her mind is drug-free, the lucid memories come flooding back to her—the sound of metal scraping across the pavement, her own panicked scream, the haunting crunch of a car slamming into an unyielding tree.

Iris is well aware that she's numbing herself to life, drowning her shame with a flood of dopamine, but she's no longer in control. The drugs create a toxic dependency. She needs them to feel good, and yet she is simultaneously killing herself by taking them. She hates herself for her weakness and often wonders if it would be easier to confess, go directly to jail, do not pass Go. But she doesn't feel strong enough to take that bold step, nor does she want to be the one to break the vow she made with her sisters never to breathe a word of that day. She might not be on speaking terms with her siblings, but there is honor among thieves, which she supposes applies to killers as well.

Iris keeps chasing her highs and catching them. It's what she's good at now. But imagine her surprise when she wakes up one morning after glorious oblivion to find herself surprisingly nauseated. Her heartbeat is erratic and she's sweating all over. This can't be a withdrawal, because she still has narcotics swimming in her veins.

The following day it happens again—vomiting, cramping, fatigue, and Iris is achy all over. She worries it's cancer. That would be a fitting outcome, a deserved one. Her good-for-nothing boyfriend won't take her to see the doctor, so she goes to urgent care on her own.

The doctor is actually a physician's assistant. Iris doesn't fully understand the distinction, but it doesn't matter. She dislikes all doctors, nurses, and now PAs equally unless they prescribe her painkillers. Unfortunately, everyone in Boston refuses to do so. She's burned all her bridges.

The PA is a few years older than Iris, but a look in the mirror offers a harsh reality check. Iris could pass for this woman's much older sister. Her cheekbones appear to have given way to sinkholes; she has the pallor of the dead and bags under her eyes big enough to weigh her down.

Iris can't stop fidgeting on the exam table, like she's an anxious toddler with an earache. The paper beneath her crinkles as she shifts. She's jonesing for a fix, but it's the anticipation of the devastating news that truly makes her restless. Whatever the diagnosis may be, it's certain to be much worse than an ear infection. The other shoe is about to drop. Cancer. That's what's causing her symptoms, and what Iris believes she deserves.

She flashes back to her innocent days when she would use the paving stones of the hotel walkway to play hopscotch or catch fireflies in the yard with her bare hands. Her glow, hidden as it was back then, is now about to be completely extinguished.

Her legs bounce continuously as the PA takes her vitals, looking into her eyes with some contraption that blinds her with its bright light. She winces, feeling entirely exposed, as if the light reveals her innermost thoughts and secrets.

"Do you use illegal drugs, Iris?" the PA asks patiently. "It's okay to tell me. I need you to be honest."

Iris feels no compulsion to lie. "Do you have any?" she asks.

The PA breaks into a wry smile before sending Iris to the lab to have her blood drawn and a urine sample collected. Iris waits impatiently for the results. It's a good thing she has some ground-up oxy to snort, because it's some hours before the PA returns with an update.

"How long do I have?" Iris asks, preempting the obvious.

"I'd say about seven months," the PA says.

The pang in her heart is hard and sharp, but Iris doesn't cry. "What kind of cancer is it?"

The PA tilts her head, and now there's a caring smile.

"Iris," she says, "you don't have cancer. You're pregnant."

Chapter 25

Two years after her sister Iris leaves Maine, Faith makes her own departure under the cloak of darkness. Her heart pounds like a ticking bomb, ready to explode. She'd been nervous for weeks, fearing her venture into the unknown. She knew it would be scary, but the reality is far more intense than she had expected. However, she has to go. There is no Plan B. The sounds of the ocean that had once lulled her to sleep now suffocate her. She craves the clamor of cars and bustling noise, hoping to drown out the looping thoughts in her head.

With just enough money for a one-way ticket, Faith boards a Greyhound bus destined for New York City. Her classmates always said she could be a model. She's done a few local fashion shoots, cheesy small-town stuff, but the photographers believed she had what it took to make it in the City That Never Sleeps. Now it's time to put that theory to the test.

As the bus pulls away, Faith reflects on all she's leaving behind. She's brought only a single suitcase of clothing. Her track and field medals remain on her bedroom shelves, along with a note for her parents. Her father will probably never forgive her. He's counting on her to take over the hotel because Vicki has already bowed out, and Iris is a hot mess. He'll have to endure the disappointment, as will Mother, because she's *never* returning to the Precipice.

The bus ride is long and tedious. To her disappointment, the passing miles don't ease the regret she hoped to leave behind. Perhaps time will heal her heart, but Faith doubts she can ever forgive herself for what she's done.

Eventually she arrives at her destination. New York is a cesspool. At least that's Faith's first impression as she emerges from the confines of the Greyhound bus and into the harsh urine-scented air of the cavernous Port Authority Bus Terminal. She is that girl—the one with wide, innocent eyes and a fierce determination etched on her youthful face, utterly convinced that she, like the lyric goes in the famous song, can make it here.

To the locals, she might as well have a piece of wheat sticking out of her mouth and blinders over her eyes.

Tucked under her arm, Faith carries a copy of *Backstage*, the one she'd ordered by mail some time ago. Inside is an address that the agency gave her, an apartment house specifically for aspiring models. Faith tells herself she won't be aspiring for long.

When she arrives at her new home, somewhere in the bowels of Alphabet City, a gnawing apprehension sets in. Has she made a terrible mistake? After the long bus ride, the five-floor walk-up feels like a trek to the summit of Everest.

Inside the apartment, a harsh new reality sets in. Having grown up in a sprawling hotel, Faith is accustomed to having room to roam, but here six girls share six hundred square feet. Their long limbs dangle over the sides of threadbare mattresses on the bunk beds where they sleep. The fridge is virtually empty, the models subsisting on cigarettes and protein bars that they nibble on in a sparsely furnished common room. Dust coats the walls like wallpaper. She knows hotels, knows quality accommodations, and this place puts the flea in fleabag. Adding insult to injury, she has to pay the agency over a thousand dollars a month for these squalid quarters. Since she doesn't have the money, they've advanced her several months' rent with the expectation that she'll repay it quickly, which means she's starting her career already in debt.

Unsurprisingly, it takes time to turn her killer smile into dollars. That debt—with interest, she discovers—starts accumulating quickly. *Work harder. Push yourself more.* That's always the answer when she brings up her concerns to the agency that hired her. When Faith finally lands her first paid gig—a catalogue shoot for a department store she's never heard of—she's financially so underwater, she's convinced she'll never be able to get out of her contract. They essentially own her.

She soon realizes that starvation and partying are big parts of the job. It's not long before Faith starts to run herself into the ground chasing gigs on too little food and too much caffeine. Eventually she sees the effects of her lifestyle in the dark circles under her eyes and the waxy tone of her skin.

The mirror serves as a wake-up call for her to cut back on the late nights and illegal substances to focus on what she's come here to do—model. But her good intentions take a back seat to the realities of the trade.

The industry is not a kind one. Faith has found that every cliché linked to modeling has elements of truth: underage girls *are* mistreated, drugs are consumed like candy, and sexual harassment is rampant. To speak about what she's witnessed and experienced firsthand, to write a flaming op-ed, or to complain to her agency would guarantee that the scarce jobs she has been getting would dry up like a puddle in the midday heat.

Faith works hard to maintain her thin frame but learns soon enough that the good advice she gets about diet and exercise is empty words, as toothless as a newborn. For an industry that is all about beauty, fashion is an ugly business. One poor girl she knows soaked cotton balls in juice and swallowed them as an appetite suppressant to cut down her daily caloric intake. It nearly killed her.

Faith isn't that desperate, but she does have a phase where she takes laxatives like they're Raisinets, enough to barricade herself in the bathroom for hours on end. Unfortunately, it works, so she does it again . . . and again, until her body says *no more.* Twenty cigarettes and a cup of coffee suffice just as well. Through willpower alone, Faith manages to maintain the desired body image, but it still isn't good enough to earn her the income necessary to get out of debt. She needs more help.

Her luck changes when she meets a dashing man at a local bar. He's just her type—tall with an athletic build, a thick head of lush dark hair, and piercing blue eyes that catch her attention from across the room. She obviously catches his eye as well, because it's not long before he makes his way over to her.

His opening line—"Do you come here often?"—is staggeringly unoriginal, but his good looks and charisma more than make up for it.

Faith smiles. "I bet you say that to all the girls," she says, matching his line with one equally trite. They share a laugh, and she feels a sizzle of energy pass between them.

Several drinks later, that sizzle is a fire. She feels like she's told him everything about her life (well, almost everything). He's a good listener and asks insightful questions. But she doesn't buy it when he tells her he has connections that could take her modeling career to the next level. Now *there's* a line she's heard a thousand times.

"You don't exactly look thrilled," he says, surprised.

Faith senses he's accustomed to making a big impression and might genuinely be wounded. She likes him enough to ease his pain.

"You don't have to invent things to impress me," she tells him. "Don't try so hard. I like you anyway."

"But it's true," he insists. "I have connections all over town." He pulls a business card from his wallet and hands it to her. "Look . . . I went to school with this guy. He's one of the top movers and shakers in the industry. I can get you a meeting."

"And what's in it for you?" Faith asks warily. He could have gotten that card from anywhere, and she's pretty sure she knows exactly what he'll want in return. But his answer surprises her.

"Sex and money," he says candidly. "Isn't that what everyone wants?"

Faith can't help but chuckle.

Two more martinis show up in front of them. Faith takes a drink. Twirling the olive in her glass, she says, "The sex part is easy, I get that— not that I'm saying *you'll* get it . . . but the money? How do you plan to make money out of this arrangement?"

She rests her chin on her hand, a playful glint dancing in her eyes, curious and captivated by this man's daring, unsure what might come out of his mouth next. The uncertainty is alluring.

"Truth be told, I'm an opportunist." The man's broad grin suggests that he hears opportunity knocking. "I've got a special skill for identifying a business potential and a knack for opening doors."

"That's good to know," Faith says, her defenses lowering slightly. "But again, what's in it for you? I get a check for the work, and my agency takes a cut of all my earnings. And I can't get out of my contract with the agency until I pay off my debt to them, so how exactly do you fit into this equation?"

"Here's my offer," says the man, leaning closer. She gets her first good smell of him—something clean and invigorating, the tangy scent of lemons and limes like he's just emerged from a shower. "I put you in touch with my friend, and if you get a job with a larger payday than any gig you've had before, you fire your agent and come work for me. If the gig doesn't cover your debt, I'll front you the money with no interest charged so you can break your contract."

Faith pulls back from the sheer audacity of his offer, but then finds herself leaning in again. She peers deeply into his eyes, searching for hints of deception or any suggestion that he's a two-bit con man offering nothing but false promises. But all she observes is his belief in himself, which feels oddly infectious. He *sees* something special in her; she's sure of it. Her mind zips to the future—the sweet satisfaction she'll get from proving all the doubters wrong. She looks for an angle, some way he can burn her, but his offer feels genuine and pretty risk-free. He's not asking for anything unless she gets the promised results. It's on him to get her that big payday. All she has to do is smile for the camera.

"The check has to clear," she tells him.

He grins at her over the rim of his martini glass. "Of course," he says.

"What about the other part?" she asks.

"The sex?" he asks.

"Yeah, that."

He glances at his wristwatch. "I'm in no rush," he tells her. "The lead-up is part of the fun."

She laughs warmly and touches his arm. "I can't just hand over my career to someone I don't know."

He extends his hand, looking to seal the deal. "My name is Todd," he tells her. "And I'm going to be the best thing that's ever happened to you."

Chapter 26

Vicki has been on the road for hours, but she doesn't know if it's the traffic or the stress of her recent breakup that's made her so fatigued. She's nearing the George Washington Bridge, which will get her into New York City with plenty of time to freshen up in the hotel before the big holiday party, which also happens to be Faith's cover reveal for *Vogue* magazine.

When Faith left Maine—escaped, more accurately—Vicki didn't know how things would turn out. She knew her sister had the looks, but she was also naïve, inexperienced, and about to go swimming with sharks. As Faith would tell it, it took a lot of luck, the right connections, and hard work to land on the cover of *Vogue*. It also took five years. Now Faith's modeling career is poised for lift-off into the stratosphere, while Vicki feels her life is going nowhere fast.

On the seat beside her lies the note from her boyfriend—or *former* boyfriend. It's a drawn-out apology, full of excuses for his bad behavior and rife with empty promises that he would change for the better. Some of her past lovers were discreet about cheating, but this one didn't even make an effort to hide it. She'd walked in on him fucking her roommate in their bed. His excuse? He thought her Pilates class went until noon—as if that somehow made it okay.

Oh, well. Another lousy boyfriend gone. There'd been a string of them, unfortunately. She keeps attracting men like her father—cheaters and liars. How on earth did she end up following in her mother's footsteps with her choices in men? At least she has the strength to leave them, even if she keeps dating the same type. Her mother died bitter, lonely, and depressed. Vicki realizes she's not much better off, considering she would describe herself the same way.

Her father taught her to be skeptical of the government, politicians, and the media, but somehow she's had no problem trusting the wrong people in her personal life. She's sure it's some kind of self-inflicted punishment, purgatory on earth, retribution for her past sins. It's a cycle she can't break, no matter how much she tries. Ironically, Vicki can control every other facet of her life—and does so with near-religious vigor—except for her impulse to hook up with bad men. A bunch of "dicks with dicks," a friend of hers took to calling them.

The only saving grace in these terrible relationships was that she'd never gotten pregnant. She'd like to have a child someday, but not if it meant being tied to one of these jerks. There was one guy she thought would be long term, and they stopped using birth control, but nothing ever came of it except an STD scare. When he was out of the picture, she went to the doctor, wondering why she hadn't conceived. The answer turned out to be abnormal hormone levels, which she was told made her a poor IVF candidate as well. It was hard news to swallow at twenty-six, when she supposedly had her whole life ahead of her.

The *Vogue* holiday party featuring Faith's first cover shoot is everything her sister said it would be and more. The Rainbow Room at the top of Rockefeller Center gets marketed as one of America's twenty most beautiful wedding venues, but tonight it's all about fashion. Vicki doesn't know the names of the agents trolling the floor, but she recognizes the faces of some models who have celebrity athlete and movie star boyfriends for dates.

The views of Manhattan from this height are nothing short of spectacular. The city pulses beneath them. Red taillights snake through the streets, while the twinkling city lights sparkle like a mini galaxy swirling below.

Gorgeous arrangements of flowers frame posters of Faith's cover photo, displayed prominently on gold stands strategically situated near the bars. If Vicki didn't know the occasion, she might have thought she'd stumbled into a black-tie memorial service for her sister.

She knows about the magic of lighting and makeup, but seeing Faith transformed into an ethereal being is astounding. It's like a Greek goddess had descended from Mount Olympus and taken over her sister's body. Faith's racy black lace top pairs perfectly with the issue's theme: "Soft, Simple, and Sexy Holiday Looks." The come-hither glint in her eyes conveys a woman in total command—a temptress, a seductress, a caster of charms—which is nothing like the woman Vicki saw on her last visit to New York. That Faith was a bundle of insecurity and nerves, her frame thin as a wire. But that was before she fired her agent and hired some new guy she'd met in a bar, of all places. Apparently, a lot has changed in a year.

"He's going to make it happen for me. I believe him," Faith had said when Vicki questioned her sister's judgment about this unknown man acting as her agent.

When Vicki asked for his name, Faith wouldn't tell her. She didn't want her sister digging up any dirt that would soil her dreams. Vicki didn't push the issue. The last time she'd exerted undue influence over Faith, it didn't end well.

Vicki drinks champagne, but her glass always seems to be full. Caterers in bow ties and crisp white shirts patrol the floor with the diligence and efficiency of a well-orchestrated team. Her head buzzes with the same effervescence as her bubbly drink as she swims through a crowd of beautiful strangers. These aren't her people. This world of rich, glamorous privilege is unfamiliar, but she takes it all in, gliding through the room with the wide-eyed wonder of a visitor to an exotic land, her heart in sync with the jazz music's bass pulsing through the air. The partygoers all seem to know each other and air-kiss greetings like it's some foreign custom.

Everyone here is classy and sophisticated, Vicki observes—well, everyone except one woman who's leaning against the bar, using it for support. She's strikingly gorgeous, though she appears to be in disarray. Smudges of mascara ring her eyes, and her high heels practically buckle underneath her. She's asking for another drink, but wisely the bartender refuses her repeated requests. *No* doesn't appear to be in this woman's vocabulary.

Her voice rises, her words slurring together as she begins to make a scene.

"I'm supposed to be the cover girl, you know," she almost sobs. "I bet I'd get whatever drink I want if I was. But you're late for ONE CASTING," she shouts while holding up her finger for emphasis. She wants the whole room to hear her gripe. "And you're out. Your career dries up, and some *nobody* gets all your glory."

She swings an arm in a wild arc in the direction of one of Faith's glamour shots. Before she can go on, a burly man shows up and gently takes hold of the drunk model's arm, leading her away from the bar, where she undoubtedly doesn't belong. Vicki watches as she vanishes into a sea of black and gold balloons. As she's escorted out, the model turns and spits on Faith's poster. A gooey glob of saliva dribbles down Faith's cheek, resembling a falling tear. Vicki is horrified, yet relieved Faith isn't around to witness the crude display of poor sportsmanship.

While Faith is a significant presence in the room, her picture displayed throughout, Vicki has hardly seen her all night. She's been fluttering about the room with the haphazard trajectory of a butterfly, going from person to person, receiving their congratulations, along with those customary air kisses and half hugs.

Ironically, the phoniness of it all feels the most real to Vicki. Nobody here genuinely cares about her sister; she's sure of it. The moment she's not cover-worthy, they'll discard her like yesterday's issue, or like a model who missed one casting call.

Seeing the money, though—the sparkling, glittering jewelry gracing all these lithe bodies—gives Vicki the idea that she could profit off the vanity. She's tired of her PR job and has been looking for a career change. Vicki was too headstrong to work for her father. He specifically wanted Faith, more of a people pleaser, amenable to doing things his way, to carry the Bishop torch forward at the Precipice. Faith had agreed, until she disappeared, leaving only a note to say goodbye.

Like her father, Vicki wants to work for herself—become an

entrepreneur, if only she had a niche to explore. Now it seems fate has come to her. Vicki resolves to seriously consider opening a high-end jewelry store when she returns to Boston, maybe one that sells other expensive gifts. A new challenge could be just what she needs to scrub her brain of the image of her boyfriend writhing in ecstasy beneath her former roommate.

The party itself is a helpful distraction from that painful memory, and when Vicki catches the eye of a handsome man, she reminds herself that she's a free woman. The gentleman with Cary Grant's good looks is lingering alone near a bank of windows that offer a breathtaking view of the Empire State Building, lit up in holiday green and red. He's drinking a Budweiser from the bottle as if it's a middle finger to the glitterati trying to out-pose each other with fancy cocktails and even fancier outfits. Finally, someone she can relate to, and it doesn't hurt that he's so damn good-looking.

Vicki moves in. She's not shy. She's also glad to have on a scoop-back satin maxi dress that showcases her ample cleavage. She looks like a million bucks, though the dress cost her only eighty-five at a discount store.

"Are you here modeling for Budweiser?" she asks, pointing to his bottle. "Because I didn't see that on the menu."

The man flashes a half-smile that weakens her knees. "The bartender is my cousin," he says. "I can get you one if you want."

She holds up her champagne. "Thanks, but I'll pass. So are you a model?" she asks. "No offense, but you don't strike me as one."

The man playacts being hurt, touching his heart as if she'd stabbed him with her words. "Most people think I'm beautiful."

She thinks they wouldn't be wrong, but she's not about to inflate his ego with the truth. The man might lack taste in beverages, but she can tell he isn't short on confidence.

"It's not your looks," she assures him. "You're off by yourself while everyone else here is making connections and working the room."

"I used to be in the business," he explains. "But lucky me, I got out with my soul mostly intact. I still get invites to the good parties, though, and I can't pass up a night of free food and beautiful women."

He looks at her when he says this, and she's certain he's not referring to the models roaming the floor. How does this fine-looking creature not have a date?

"Not everything here is beautiful. There was a pretty ugly scene at the bar just a moment ago." Vicki tells him about the drunk woman who spit on Faith's poster.

The man shrugs it off. "That's Kate Monroe," he says. "She was in the running for the holiday cover, and now she's bitter because she lost out to another model. It was her own fault. She didn't show up on time for the final casting shoot. Instead of taking responsibility for her actions, she's blaming the winner. It's so sad, but I'm glad they escorted her out. She shouldn't have come here in the first place."

He flashes a radiant smile that enchants her, making Vicki forget about Kate Monroe's unfortunate display. The next forty-five minutes are the most invigorating of Vicki's life. The party slips into the background; the four-piece jazz band barely registers a note in her ears, which are buzzing from the instant connection she feels with this attractive individual.

They talk effortlessly. It's not what he says, but how he says it that intrigues her. She's sworn off men since her latest fiasco, and yet here she is, hoping that he doesn't live on the other side of the country and that he wants her number. She's completely at ease with him, their conversation so natural that he gives her a feeling of coming home. *What's that all about?*

They flirt all night. He never leaves her side, even when he goes to the bar for another Bud. Her stomach is doing a tap dance the whole time, and she feels drunk on love, even though she knows it's probably just champagne.

Something tells her that this is a turning point in her life. She's sure of it. No more loser men. No more falling into the same horrible pattern as her mother. She's going to break the spell that has cursed her days. There's nothing she can do about the past. But the future is wide open, and it keeps smiling at her between sips of his beer.

"So, any interest in meeting the star of the night?" she asks.

The man lights up, but not in an overly eager way, which is a good sign that she's his focus and not her sister.

"She hasn't exactly been approachable," he says. "Do you know her?"

Vicki's eyes glint mischievously. "Just a little," she says.

Minutes later, she's leading him through a crowd of gowns and suits gathered in a corner of the elegant room. Faith brightens when she sees Vicki approach.

"Hey, sis," she says, flashing her cover-worthy smile, "I've barely seen you all night. Are you having a good time?"

Vicki pulls her newly acquired date forward by the crook of his arm. "Better than you can imagine," she says. "Faith, this is my new friend, Todd Davis."

Faith's rosy glow dims. For someone on top of the world, she suddenly looks defeated. Vicki is not surprised. She knows her sister is accustomed to getting the attention of the cutest guys, and she's probably jealous because Todd is by far the best-looking man in the room.

Chapter 27

There's a cold squirt of jelly, and a moment later, Iris is looking at an image of her unborn child. The ultrasound shows the baby is healthy. The fetus is not even out of utero, and thanks to the miracle of modern medicine, Iris already knows where it measures on various scales. She gets the fundal height, measured as the distance from the top of her pubic bone to the top of her uterus. Her doctor now has a better estimate of the gestational age. But the only calculation Iris needs is the one that tells her she's too far along to turn back now.

The sight of the baby in her womb—floating in a black abyss, moving inside her like some parasitic alien—frightens her initially, but soon there's a shift. A warm, radiating energy encases Iris like a velvety cocoon. She can't help but smile—timidly at first, then broadly as her eyes fill with tears of absolute, unadulterated joy. She's never felt so close and connected to anything in her life. In fact, she's never felt like she genuinely mattered to anyone, until now. All the wrong she's done, the harm she's caused, somehow feels balanced out, perhaps even eclipsed, by the magnificent being flailing its tiny little arms and legs inside her.

Iris has been working with a social worker named Simone since she found out she was pregnant, and she's there, offering Iris emotional support during the appointment. It was Simone who supported Iris as she wrestled with the choice to keep the pregnancy. The idea of motherhood isn't what kept Iris up at night drenched in a cold sweat. It was the dreadful notion—no, make it the soul-paralyzing fear—of what it would take to come off the drugs and stay clean so she could give birth to a healthy, happy baby.

Throughout it all, Simone has been a hero, never wavering in her support or commitment to Iris. She helped guide Iris in making the best decision for herself. When Iris was certain, Simone found a doctor who put her on a step-down plan to wean her off the opioids. It took more willpower than Iris knew she possessed, but miraculously it worked. Simone drove Iris to all her medical appointments. Those visits were always fraught. Worry that her past behavior would harm the baby haunts Iris day and night. But for all her obsessing, every checkup has shown a normal developmental trajectory. Why God seemed to be on Iris's side, she couldn't say, but she is deeply grateful.

It would be nice to share this news with her family, but Iris still isn't on speaking terms with her father, and she hasn't heard from her sisters in years. She has little support, including from her loser boyfriend, who got her pregnant and then abandoned her for another woman two days after she broke the news. But Simone has been a rock since the beginning. Without her care and encouragement, Iris knows she wouldn't be looking at these magnificent images of a life force within her, something pure and good. It's as if she's growing her own second chance.

Iris watches the screen as the doctor explains the ultrasound like she's the narrator of a nature film. "Black is fluid. Usually, white are bones," she says. "The tissue in between will be whitish gray."

Iris can see the baby's face and chin, and the impossibly small white spots are the sides of the ribs. She's been feeling the baby move inside her for a few weeks, but somehow, seeing it happen before her eyes while simultaneously experiencing it in her belly brings the reality of the moment into clear, sharp focus. The ultrasound machine is a magic portal that facilitates a deeper connection between Iris and her unborn child, cementing a bond that feels as immutable as the universe itself.

"And these are the knees, and here are the feet, and oh." The doctor stops herself mid-sentence before looking at Iris thoughtfully. "Do you want to know the gender?" she asks.

Iris doesn't hesitate, not for a second. It's just one less unknown in her life to contend with. She gives a nod.

"That right there," says the doctor pointing to a spot on the image, a pleased smile on her face, "is what makes this a baby boy."

The romance of being a new mother doesn't last long. The baby is born healthy, thanks to her abstinence. And thanks to Simone, Iris has a safe place to live. With the help of St. Mary's Catholic Charities, Iris is now a resident of a boarding home for unwed new mothers. Instead of renting, Iris must subject herself to random drug testing and attend regular Narcotics Anonymous meetings. It's a price she's willing to pay for a roof over her head and no cockroaches in the sink.

But as soon as her baby enters the world, he has needs beyond what charitable assistance can provide. St. Mary's keeps them warm in the cold Boston winter. Food stamps keep her from going hungry. Breastfeeding keeps her baby from starving. But money remains tight. Diapers aren't cheap, and neither is childcare.

Iris hardly sleeps. The baby cries constantly—a colicky newborn, a nurse from St. Mary's explains. It's nothing to be worried about, but Iris suspects she's losing her mind.

She finds work as a housecleaner to make ends meet, impressing her colleagues with her can-do attitude. She doesn't tell them that she trained for this job in Maine for years. It's a grueling gig, but the cleaners don't complain, so Iris doesn't, either. She's trying to save for an apartment so she can finally move out of the boardinghouse that has a sad story in every room.

Before Iris knows it, her son turns one, while her back feels forty-one. He comes to work with her most days because she can't afford day care *and* her bills, so one had to go. The choice wasn't hard to make. Lucky for her, her coworkers love doting on her son, taking turns caring for him while Iris does her best not to fall asleep on the job.

She doesn't like how her body feels or how her face looks—ashen gray, the color of the dust her vacuum sucks up. Every day it's harder to get out of bed. Depression creeps in on her, starting at the toes and working to the crown of her head like she's submerged in a tub that's slowly filling with water. It's hard enough to be a new mom, but craving drugs while sleep-deprived is downright cruel. The hunger will never go away. She understands that each day is a choice not to use, to deny what her body desires—a quick fix for the pain.

Adding insult to injury, she can't always tell the difference between her urges and her symptoms of depression. They're very similar, causing mood swings, crying spells, crushing anxiety, hopelessness—and that's on a good day. She still attends her regular NA meetings, but they're not as effective as they had been. What initially felt like a sprint to give birth to a healthy baby has turned into a marathon for which she has neither the training nor the will.

On a particularly challenging day, after only two hours of sleep, Iris shows up to work running on fumes. Caffeine is no help, and her baby's incessant crying feels like someone is taking a chisel to her skull. As she's cleaning a bathroom, down on her hands and knees, scrubbing the tub while gritting through the pain, she decides to do something she's never done, not once, not in over a year of cleaning houses.

Iris looks at herself in the medicine cabinet mirror, her vacant eyes peering back, empty of life. She opens the cabinet, and like a skilled bloodhound hot on a scent, she finds exactly what she was hoping for. She holds a bottle of Vicodin in her shaky grasp. Down go a few pills. The rest of that day passes in the blissful, drug-induced euphoria she's missed so much. It's the best she's felt in ages. Now she looks forward to work. She always volunteers to clean the bathrooms without anyone guessing why. In time, she learns which homes yield the biggest score.

For a while, she's careful about how many pills she steals. But her recklessness grows in proportion to her dependency. It's not long before it all comes undone. Iris loses her job when a client complains. The nuns discover she's using again, and they're mandated by law to report her to DCF, the Department of Children and Families. She's kicked out of the boarding home and ends up back in some new shithole apartment with some new shithead guy who has a bad temper that gets worse the more he drinks, and he drinks plenty. She has no money for rent, but there are other things he wants from her, though she's more careful this time. Another kid would be a disaster.

DCF threatens to put her son in foster care, but it takes time, and the system is overwhelmed and inefficient. Meanwhile, Iris worries her new boyfriend will hurt her son. He hurts her instead. She'd just returned from the Dollar Store with groceries but forgot his cigarettes. It wasn't the first time he'd hit her, but it definitely was the worst. She's afraid to leave her son alone with him to go to the hospital, so she brings him to the emergency room with her. X-rays show she has a broken arm and several cracked ribs. The police are notified. Eventually the boyfriend is arrested, but now Iris has no place to live, and DCF is breathing down her neck.

She doesn't know if the number still works, but she has no one else to turn to. The phone rings once, twice, three times. She's about to hang up when she hears someone answer, a familiar voice, like a ghost from her past whispering *hello*. Iris feels her breath catch in her lungs. She's not sure she can respond.

"Hello?" the voice asks again, this time clearly annoyed. "Is anyone there?" Pause. "You know, I can hear you breathing. Is this a prank call?" Pause again.

Iris tries to speak, she really does, but no sound comes out.

"Well, goodbye then," says the voice on the other end. But before the call disconnects, Iris somehow, by the grace of God, manages to blurt out, "Vicki, please don't hang up. It's me. It's Iris. I'm in big, big trouble, and I need your help."

Chapter 28

Faith shows up at Brilliance Jewelry and Gifts in Boston, the store that Vicki and Todd opened soon after they got married. She hasn't seen him since the wedding and, even then, she'd been careful to avoid him lest Vicki catch on that they have a secret history.

She puts extra effort into her appearance that day, knowing Todd will take notice. She doesn't do this to impress him—she certainly doesn't want him back. She has to leave all that in the past for her own well-being. Even so, before she opens the door to the jewelry store, she touches up her lipstick, fixes her hair, and adjusts her casual, fitted dress, which she knows shows off her curves in all the right ways.

On some level, Faith realizes she's spent most of her life hiding her insecurity and self-loathing behind a gorgeous, perfected, and largely false exterior. At this point, not only is her hair dyed, but her eyelashes are fake, her lips are enhanced with injections, and she's considering Botox even though she's only twenty-seven. It's one thing to wear a mask, but something else to embody one entirely. And to take it off means seeing something hideous underneath, a vision Faith can't bear to look at, not since that day in Maine. Nobody can know her true self, including the man she once loved.

She has mixed feelings about seeing Todd again. He might not have been a good guy, but to his credit, he delivered everything he had promised her, and more. He got her the job that surpassed anything she'd ever earned before, and staying true to her word, Faith fired her agent and hired him. That first shoot opened doors, and her career began to climb steadily, but Todd wanted more, and he had convinced Faith that she deserved a chance at the big time.

Scoring the cover of *Vogue* magazine was a moonshot at best. But it happened, just as he said it would—though luck and connections weren't all it took to make her the magazine's final choice for the cover model. No, Todd had orchestrated a little bit more, and that was the beginning of the end of both their business and personal relationship. This also meant saying goodbye to some of the most intense passion she'd ever experienced.

She had no choice but to leave him, especially after what they had done. Guilt was what turned her relationship with Todd sour. It was why Faith couldn't bring herself to come clean to Vicki about her history with Todd, or even that she knew him at all. Letting her sister in on who Todd really was meant owning who *she* was as well. Todd wasn't even supposed to be there that night. She had told him in no uncertain terms that he wasn't welcome, but he never listened to anyone but himself.

When Vicki brought Todd over for an introduction, Faith speculated that he was trying to make her jealous so she'd take him back, but that was *never* going to happen. She wasn't too concerned when the pair left together that night. She assumed any romance between Todd and her sister would fizzle out quickly. He lived in New York, and she was in Boston. That couldn't last even if there was chemistry between them. And besides, Vicki and Todd were nothing alike. Their relationship had all the staying power of a fashion trend; Faith was sure of it. But instead of ending, it accelerated like a rocket ship—married within a year, running a store together soon after.

There was simply no time or space for Faith to come clean about her sordid history with the love of her sister's life. She didn't have the will, either. Shame and guilt not only robbed Faith of her voice, but stole her common sense as well. And if she was being honest, part of her believed Todd and Vicki deserved each other for what they'd both done—Todd for his sin and Vicki for hers.

But Faith knows she's no better.

Now her actions and Todd's have profound consequences that go far beyond anything she could have imagined. The latest news is so shocking and terrible that she felt compelled to deliver it in person.

It's her first time setting foot in Vicki's new store. The pictures she'd seen didn't do it justice. Where their father had been an eclectic collector, Vicki has far more refined taste and a discerning eye. Every piece in the elegant glass cases is a work of art. The overhead chandeliers cast a broad light that turns the jewels into a vibrant presentation, like a miniature fireworks show. *Brilliance* is a fitting name for the new business, but Todd's smile when he sees Faith eclipses all the gems on display.

He emerges from behind the counter, his tailored suit revealing that hard work hasn't taken a toll on his muscular physique. As always, his eyes draw her in, a magnetic force she cannot escape.

"Well now, this is a wonderful surprise," he says. "What brings you here?"

He pulls her into a hug that Faith barely reciprocates. When they break apart, Faith doesn't draw it out. Her hand goes into her purse, and a moment later, it comes out holding a newspaper clipping—a story about a woman who plunged to her death from the top floor of her Tribeca apartment building.

"She killed herself," Faith tells Todd while he's busy reading the article about Kate Monroe's suicide.

Reflecting on it now, Faith isn't sure if her attraction to this man was genuine or if she was simply captivated by the future he painted for her. Either way, she had stars in her eyes when she fell into his arms and bed. Their fling lasted longer than she expected, but Faith didn't initially see it as anything serious. It was more practical. Todd connected her to the life she'd come to New York to find, and in return, she gave him what all men wanted from her—her body and a beautiful trophy to carry on his arm.

For a while, things were light and happy. The opportunities became more plentiful as Faith's star ascended, but the stakes got higher as well. She believed a few more high-profile shoots could put her on the map and in the driver's seat of her career. This was why, when *Vogue* offered Faith the chance to compete for the cover, she knew her moment had arrived. It all came down to her and a rival model with more experience and cachet in the industry than Faith could dream of having. Success, she thought, could never have been so close and yet so far away.

She discussed her concerns with Todd. When he wasn't busy gallivanting on one of his wild adventures, he lived with her in a small New York City apartment. She'd become dependent on his big talk and big dreams. Without him, she felt adrift in a sea of hustlers, con men, and girls who came younger and prettier. When Todd asked how far she would go to get what she wanted, Faith forgot there was a price for everything. She couldn't help but imagine her face plastered on billboards in Times Square, walking the runway in Milan, or appearing in fashion magazines from Tokyo to London.

"All the way," she told him. "I'll do anything."

Anything. How foolish.

When Todd revealed his plan, Faith recoiled. This was going too far—*way* too far. She already had enough regrets for one lifetime. She felt like she was back in Maine, like she had never really escaped. And just like before, Faith went against her better judgment and didn't say no.

Nobody will get hurt, she assured herself. Besides, it's a cutthroat industry. Everyone does what they have to do to get ahead.

On the night before the final casting, there was a party. There's always a party in this line of work. All the big names in the industry were present, and of course, her rival, Kate Monroe, was also in attendance. Kate looked as stunning as ever in a sequined cocktail dress that hugged her body like a Formula One race car owning the track. She already looked like she was on the cover of *Vogue.*

"Just relax and let me do all the hard work," Todd whispered in Faith's ear.

The hard work, it turned out, meant trying to charm the cocktail dress right off Kate's amazing body. As the night was winding down, Faith became increasingly confident he was going to succeed—and a little too well. Kate was draped over Todd like a curtain.

"This is your big plan? Fucking Kate?" Faith growled at Todd in a moment alone.

"Have some faith, Faith," Todd said, cracking himself up.

He left the party with Kate on his arm. Faith knew this was part of the plan, yet she still felt confused, angry, and in a way, betrayed.

The next day, the day of the big cover shoot competition, Faith was the only one of the two models to show up.

Kate arrived three hours later as the crew was breaking down the lighting rigs. She looked like she had just crawled out of a grave, poor thing. Her skin was shockingly pale. Her hair was a tangled mess. Only a model could have designer bags under her eyes.

"I don't know what happened," Kate told the casting director, tears streaming down her face. "I didn't think I had *that* much to drink last night . . . but I slept right through my alarm. I'm so sorry. Can I still audition?"

A shake of the head gave her the crushing answer.

Kate might have been confused, but Faith knew *precisely* what had happened. Todd had orchestrated the whole mishap by slipping something into her drink.

Later, Todd swore he hadn't taken advantage of Kate in her compromised condition. All he did was ensure she got home safely, was unharmed, and simply missed the photo shoot. But when he went for the hero's kiss, Faith pulled away. She was still attracted to him, but at that moment, she couldn't stand the sight of him—or herself.

She got the job. Her career took off as expected, but at the cost of her relationship with Todd, and much of what remained of her self-respect. She'd assumed he was out of her life forever until Vicki found him at her party. And now Faith was here with the tragic news of Kate's death.

"We did this to her," she tells him. "This is *our* fault." She feels on the verge of tears.

Todd shakes his head grimly. "We didn't open the window and throw her out. She did that to herself," he says. "She made her choice."

"But we *helped* her," Faith says. "We gave her a push."

When Todd touches Faith's arm, she's flooded with a familiar rush of conflicting emotions.

"Your heart's too big for this world, Faith."

But she knows that's a lie and a line, and yet she feels herself falling for it again, the same as before. Her heart is too *small,* if anything. Too weak. If she closes her eyes, Faith believes she can hear Kate's final scream as she plummets to her doom, just as she can hear the screech of metal across pavement and the loud crash of the white GTI slamming against a tree.

Chapter 29

The courtroom isn't like the ones Vicki has seen on TV. It's window-less, with a dropped ceiling and bad lighting. A utilitarian judge's desk is on a dais, flanked by an American flag and another flag displaying the Great Seal of the Commonwealth of Massachusetts. There's no jury box because, in this courtroom, the judge is the single overseer of the law. Instead of a gavel, a pen will seal the decision to transfer the parental rights over Quinn Bishop from Iris to Vicki.

Vicki and Iris sit at opposite tables, as though one is the plaintiff and the other the defendant in a criminal trial. Although there's no crime being adjudicated today, it feels like there's a victim, someone who has suffered an irreparable loss—and it's not Vicki.

Iris bounces Quinn on her lap, his tiny head turning in all directions, taking in the sights through his wide beautiful eyes. Despite all the hardships he's been a part of during his two-plus years on the planet, Quinn is a remarkably buoyant and healthy child. Thank goodness he won't remember a thing about this day.

Iris holds her son so tightly it's clear she's desperate not to let go. But it was Iris who, with the help of DCF, agreed to relinquish her parental rights to Vicki and Todd. Now, both are mere moments away from going from Quinn's foster parents to his adoptive mother and father.

In a different courtroom, at a different time, Iris addressed criminal theft charges and completed a rigorous drug court program that spared her any prison time. While Quinn lived with Vicki, Iris's downward spiral into full-blown relapse was quick and destructive.

She continued lying, cheating, and stealing to get her high, never quite finding bottom until police discovered her with a needle stuck in her arm in a parked car that was reported stolen. Proving necessity is the mother of invention, Iris had embroiled herself in a car theft ring. Her job was to deliver the vehicle to be scrapped for parts, but she couldn't make the five-mile drive to the chop shop before getting her fix.

By that point, DCF, with Iris's blessing, had already placed Quinn in Vicki and Todd's care. The hope was that it would be a temporary arrangement until Iris could get her life back on track, but as time went on, it became increasingly clear to everyone that there wasn't a track for Iris to return to, at least not in the foreseeable future.

Vicki suggested a more permanent solution while Iris was out on parole.

"We can provide him with the stability he needs. Let's be honest, Iris. You might be clean right now, but that doesn't mean you're in any shape to raise a child."

Vicki could have gone in the opposite direction and propped Iris up with words of encouragement. She could have supported Iris and Quinn financially and allowed them to stay with her for a time. They had two stores now, intending to open a third. Business was good. Very good. She had the means, but not the will.

Vicki never told her sister that in the short time she fostered Quinn, she couldn't imagine a life without him and the special role she played in his life. Out of nowhere, in the most unlikely of ways, she now had the child she always wanted and a husband with whom to raise him. It had been years since she used any birth control, and the doctors who had informed Vicki that her irregular hormone levels would prevent pregnancy seemed to be correct.

Enter a miracle.

Since the day Quinn came to live with her, Vicki has felt a love she'd never known before. Every morning, when she sees Quinn's cherubic face gazing up at her from his crib with an expression of innocence and awe, it's harder for Vicki to think of him as anything other than her son.

It didn't take much convincing for Iris to believe Quinn would be better off with Vicki and Todd. That conversation took place when Iris was at her lowest point—stripped of all her dignity, feeling worthless, useless, and out of control. Vicki found it hard to even look at Iris; she appeared so skeletal her collarbones were sticking out. In Iris's diminished state, Vicki's words alone were enough to knock her down and keep her there. Iris couldn't oppose her sister, especially not when she believed she would never get healthy and pull her life together— and Vicki thought the same. Not everyone attending NA meetings becomes a success story. Vicki told herself she was protecting Quinn, but in moments of quiet self-reflection, she understood that she was also protecting herself.

The judge, a sixty-year-old balding man with tired eyes and a caring face, speaks solemnly from the dais. "Adoptions are usually a highlight for me," he says. "I see a lot of sad cases here and not enough happy endings. This one is a mix. Iris, I want to commend you. I know what you're doing today is extremely difficult and emotionally fraught. I'm certain this is not a decision you came to lightly."

Iris clutches Quinn even more tightly. "Thank you, Your Honor," she says, her expression pained. "And I want to thank the court for being compassionate in this difficult time. I know this is best for Quinn, and it's comforting that he'll be with my family and part of my life forever."

Everyone in the courtroom appreciates those sentiments—all but Todd, who whispers loudly in Vicki's ear, "So we lose the money from the state for being foster parents and get all the burden of Quinn's ongoing expenses. Great deal, Vic! You really crushed this one."

Vicki cringes, worried the judge will overhear him, but she doesn't linger on this thought. She catches her sister's expression. Regret floods Iris's eyes, but it's too late now. Everything has been set in motion.

To Vicki, the judge says, "And I know this is a bittersweet day with complicated emotions for you as well. But I trust you'll do right by your sister."

Vicki cherishes the role of savior. "Of course, Your Honor. Children weren't in our plan, but I guess God had other ideas for us," she says.

Todd coughs out a quiet laugh. "*God?* I think you mean *Vicodin.*"

The judge clearly isn't enamored with Todd, but he, too, prefers that Quinn remain with family.

"And I promise Iris will be a part of Quinn's life forever," Vicki adds.

Todd grouses loud enough for all to hear: "Great, I'll start saving for bail money."

After the notary seal is pressed into the papers and all the signatures are obtained, it is done—Quinn is officially Vicki and Todd's son.

As though it's the final step in a somber ceremony, Iris walks over to Vicki, tears of sadness and gratitude in her eyes. Without words, she kisses Quinn on the forehead, then lovingly places him in Vicki's arms. A heavy moment of silence passes between the sisters before Iris finally speaks.

"Take good care of my boy," she says, her voice breaking.

Vicki clings to Quinn. His smell, warmth, and touch make her sister's plea sound distant and irrelevant. But like a reflex, she responds, "He'll be safe with us. I'll be a good mom, a great one," she promises. "We'll give him the best of everything and we'll take care of you, too. Todd and I have talked it over. You get clean, stay clean, and you'll have a job with us in our business. You'll have money, a safe place to live, and a chance to rebuild your life. All of that can be yours. But, Iris, you have to understand something. I'm Quinn's mother now. For his own good, he can never know his past. It's too confusing and traumatizing for a child to process. He must know me only as his mother, and you will always be Aunt Iris."

Part 3

THE EYE OF THE STORM

Chapter 30

Everyone is gathered around the dining table again, finishing up lunch before the tarot reading. I'm back to my waitressing gig, shuttling drinks and food in and out of the kitchen, feeling dismal about myself and my prospects. But money is money. Besides, I have no leverage to fight Vicki, and I don't know yet if Quinn will have any sway with his mom.

Still, a girl can dream . . .

Mixed in with the fine china and gleaming silverware are near-empty bowls of hummus, tabbouleh, salads garnished with olives and orange slices, and white bean croquettes made with artichokes (which I find surprisingly delicious). Most everyone drank the health water, consisting of lemon slices, cucumber, and sprigs of rosemary. Hope and Faith were the only ones who wanted the beet juice.

The mealtime conversation I overhear while serving the food is strained at best, with the attorney doing a lot of the talking, most of it centered around her departure.

"The weather forecast says we're going to have a little lull before the brunt of the storm hits," she informs the room. "I was thinking I'd use that opportunity to head out. You don't need another person to feed."

I notice how daintily Black dabs at the corners of her mouth with a cloth napkin, leaving behind a small red smudge where it catches her lipstick. I also observe that the shade of her lips matches the color of the poem written on the mirror. I can't help but wonder: *Where was*

Black during all that drama? Although she's not a Bishop sister, that doesn't put her above suspicion.

Unlike the others, Black shows up to lunch dressed as though she's still on the clock. She's wearing a tailored pin-striped skirt coupled with a matching jacket, white blouse, and high heels—not a practical choice for a casual meal or an early departure during a storm.

Vicki smiles tersely at Black. "Didn't we discuss this already? You should stay until Officer Brennan has had a chance to thoroughly review Todd's death. If something turns up, everyone needs to be available to answer questions."

Black sits up straighter in her chair, lowering her hands to her lap, her lips pulled tight as if holding back a frown.

"I can't imagine anything will come of that," she says. "We all know what happened."

"We don't know what the poem means," Iris says in a clipped tone.

Hope rests her hand on Oliver's shoulder. "We'll know soon enough. If Oliver was compelled by spirits to write it, it's crucial we understand why. The cards will tell us what we need to know."

Despite being thrust into the spotlight, Oliver remains composed, appearing as prim as a Catholic schoolboy. Firelight illuminates the grease marks smeared on the lenses of his thick black plastic glasses. His chambray shirt, buttoned all the way to the top, is more like an attempt at asphyxiation than a fashion statement. There is simply nothing comfortable about this young man, and yet it seems as though everyone (or at least Hope and Faith) is placing their collective trust in the boy.

"The cards? What do you mean?" asks Black, her eyes probing the room.

Iris rises from the table. "Hope thinks Oliver is a vessel for supernatural forces and that he wrote the poem on my mirror in some kind of freak trance."

Vicki stands as well. "She's going to have him read tarot cards to prove it, and I for one want nothing to do with this charade."

She sends Hope a disapproving stare before departing, leaving me to clean her place setting without so much as a thank-you.

"I think I'll join her," says Iris with a hint of disgust. At least she has the courtesy to bus her own dishes. She vanishes into the kitchen through the swinging door.

"If you're going to stay for the reading, please have a seat," Hope says to me after Bree and Quinn help clear the table.

It's an invitation I can't pass up. I settle myself across from Oliver, next to Bree, who is seated beside Black. I'm surprised she decided to stay as well. Quinn's on the opposite side of the table, sitting near Oliver, who is sandwiched between his two mothers.

"Ollie and I read together all the time," Hope says. "He's very astute. If the spirits are communicating through him, we'll know it."

I watch with growing interest as Hope lays out a blue velvet cloth in front of Oliver. The color matches her billowy paisley palazzo pants. Without a word, Oliver accepts the wooden box Hope hands him with great care, as if there's a delicate egg inside. Oliver opens the box, revealing a deck of cards adorned with an intricate filigree pattern and bright gold edging. The cards are cradled in an ivory satin lining.

"We must have a clear question in mind before Oliver shuffles the deck. This is crucial," Hope says, pausing in an overly dramatic fashion. "Please, everyone. Concentrate on the following: What does the poem mean, and what should we do with this information?"

Hope prompts us to close our eyes, and I comply. In the dark, ensuing silence, I can almost hear the question projected into the universe. Seeing all eyes open simultaneously, as though our energy has been aligned, is mildly astounding. Only then does Hope encourage Oliver to take the cards from the box. His delicate fingers caress their gold edges. I'm surprised to see him rock back and forth in his chair, at first subtly, then more noticeably, as if the movement is a necessary precursor to a psychic link. He shuffles the deck with the skill of a seasoned magician.

"Please keep the question in mind," instructs Hope. "Oliver is doing a simple three-card spread representing the past, present, and future."

To my astonishment, the atmosphere in the room has shifted. The air crackles with an electric charge, causing the hair on my arms to rise and a prickling sensation to travel down my neck.

Oliver splits the deck with a practiced hand and carefully places the top three cards facedown in a row onto the velvet cloth. He reveals the leftmost card first, turning it over gently. It depicts a detailed drawing of a full moon cast against a dark night sky. The moon's glow barely illuminates a winding path that leads to two towers. In the foreground stands a small pool, beside which a dog (or a wolf, for the drawing makes it hard to distinguish which) howls at the glowing orb above.

Hope's voice is grave. "The Moon. A Major Arcana."

"What does it mean? Is it a bad omen or something?" Black sounds oddly concerned, her eyes worried, as though she's taking this very seriously.

"The Moon card can signify deception or a projection of fear," Hope explains. "Since it represents the past in this spread, it suggests we need to shine a light on a painful memory. But only part of our awareness will be illuminated. There's a dark side to the moon as well, which could indicate that others are lying to us—or potentially, that we're lying to ourselves."

The room stays quiet as everyone reflects on the Moon card and its symbolism.

The next card Oliver turns over shows a tall stone tower built high upon a rocky hillside. The structure reminds me of the Precipice Hotel and its perch close to a cliff's edge. A bolt of lightning strikes the tower at midpoint, turning the stone into rubble and dislodging a crown that capped the top of the building. Two figures fall from a great height in a desperate attempt to escape danger, while flames shoot out of the tower's two dark windows.

Hope announces, "This is the Tower, another Major Arcana."

"Looks grim," Bree says.

"This represents our current circumstances. It warns us to expect the unexpected," Hope replies. "A massive change is happening . . . a profound upheaval. And there's no escaping it. There's no more hiding from the truth," she whispers, as if her words flow from an unseen source. "The lightning bolt cuts through the lies and illusions. Now all will come crashing down before us in ways we could never imagine."

"Lovely," Quinn remarks.

"A life built on secrets and misdeeds does not have a sturdy foundation," Faith says. "It must come tumbling down. We have no choice but to surrender to the chaos. Only then will the truth be known."

Faith continues, "Oliver, turn over the final card—the most important one in the reading. This will reveal the outcome of our current circumstances."

Oliver sits in a trance, his head bowed, his eyes shut tight, his right hand hovering over the last card as though afraid to touch it. Eventually, he lifts an edge and turns it over slowly.

Faith gasps. I slide closer to Bree. Black bristles next to me, while Quinn's eyes widen. Hope remains motionless.

On the card is a picture of a skeleton dressed in black armor, riding a white stallion, and carrying a black flag decorated with a white, five-petaled rose. The horse's hooves appear to be stomping on the word DEATH written below the Roman numeral XIII.

"Now, now, don't get too upset," Hope says in an authoritative voice. "This is one of the most misunderstood cards in the tarot. It doesn't mean anybody else is going to die, so relax. The Death card can be one of the most positive cards in the entire deck. It often means that one door must close before another one opens."

"Not in this case." Oliver's tone is flat and his eyes, magnified behind those thick glasses, are devoid of all emotion. "Death is coming, coming again, and soon. That's what the card means. Death is near."

Hope leans toward him, her face etched with concern. "Ollie . . . what are you suggesting? Are you still here with us, Oliver? Is it even you?"

"Is this a message for my sisters and me?" Faith asks nervously, locking her hands in prayer.

Oliver's eyes remain fixed to a spot on the wall opposite him. I turn my head to follow his line of vision, but I see nothing out of the ordinary. His dark stare implies that he's seeing something we cannot.

"Uncle Todd had a secret, and he took it to the grave," Oliver says, his voice adopting a singsong lilt. "Now we're all in danger, so we must be brave, for a killer walks these halls, and some will not be saved."

He slumps in his chair as if deflated. When he looks up again, little color remains on his cheeks.

The room is silent. The thick air makes it difficult to breathe. The message Oliver delivered is provocatively clear: Death is coming to the Precipice again, and there's nothing we can do to stop it.

Chapter 31

Okay, how creepy was that?" Bree asks as I prepare a mug of herbal tea in the kitchen. We both need something to settle our nerves. Naturally we're curious about the secret Todd took to the grave, but Oliver's done spouting cryptic messages, and everyone else claimed ignorance.

I will admit, I didn't leave the session a full-blown skeptic. After the reading, Oliver appeared drained, as though the experience had depleted him of his life force. Hope escorted him out of the room, his limbs like those of a limp rag doll. He needed a nap to recuperate, or so his mother had said. Brenda Black returned to her room, perhaps more determined than ever to pack and leave before any more suspicion could be cast her way.

While I might be a convert of sorts, Quinn shared his contrary opinion with me immediately after. "What an utter, gigantic pile of pure horseshit," he whispered in my ear, chuckling to himself. "Oliver was just putting on a show for his mother. Obviously, Hope is guiding all of this. She's loopier than a roller coaster."

Now that Bree and I are alone, we can debrief privately. She leans up against the oven, sipping her tea. Her designer shirt reveals just enough cleavage to induce a twinge of envy. She seems so put together, and I wonder if Quinn's noticed how hot she is, especially compared to me—*the plain old Jane*. Granted, she's older, but what difference does that make when you have eyes and hormones?

"Do you think it was real?" I want to know.

Bree thinks it over. "I was doubtful at first, but I gotta admit, that was bizarre," she says.

"Part of me wants to agree with Quinn, but if that was fake, it was quite the performance."

"So, you think there's a chance Oliver tapped into something supernatural?" Bree asks.

"I dunno, maybe," I say with a shrug. "I usually think of psychic stuff as fairy tales for adults—we believe in it to make ourselves feel better."

Bree frowns. "Feel better about what?"

"Life. Just being here, struggling to survive, all of it," I say. "I mean, everyone has problems, right? The idea of a spirit world gives people hope, makes us feel better about all the shit we have to put up with here on earth."

"Is that a bad thing? Shouldn't everybody have a little hope?"

I like that Bree cares about my opinion and shares her thoughts like we're equals. Even though she has much more life experience than I do, she's not talking down to me.

She continues, "I've got an obsessive ex-boyfriend, no job, too much debt, and a guilty conscience for all the trouble I've caused you. And it's entirely possible I'm trapped in a hotel in Maine with a homicidal maniac in our midst—so yeah, I'll take as much hope as I can get, even if it comes from a deck of cards."

A faraway look settles in Bree's eyes, and I sense we share the same feelings. We both want Oliver's gift to be authentic. We long for more than our loneliness and pain. We want to connect to our mothers, let them know we love and miss them desperately, and get a message back, clear as a phone call, that they heard and love us, too. Overhead, lights flicker as if someone is playing with the switch. Or maybe, just maybe, it's my mom, nudged by the tarot, reaching out to say hello to me the only way she can.

Despite the thick walls separating us from the outside world, I can still hear the wind shaking the trees. I'm concerned about Rodrigo. I've texted him several times, but he's not responding. It's possible he lost electricity and can't charge his phone. But still, I'd love an update.

According to Janice, he never stopped by to check on my nana, and that's all she knows.

I'm worried. Bree is, too, but maybe for other reasons. She shoots me a suspicious look over the rim of her mug. "I think the secret is that Todd knows he was murdered, and he somehow communicated it to Oliver."

A foreboding tickle creeps up my arms.

"And I think there may be more to come, Charley."

"More what?" I ask.

"Death. Murder."

Her words make me gasp. The sound is sharp and cruel, like a judge handing down the final sentence.

"Who, though?" My mind races through possibilities.

"Who what? Who killed Todd? Or who's next?" Bree raises an eyebrow. "If we believe the poem on the mirror, then it has to be a sister, but which one will be the victim, and which is the killer?"

Since I don't have the answer, I stay silent.

Bree continues, "Oliver's prophecy made it clear that none of us is safe, and I agree. No murderer would think twice about killing again to protect their secret." There's zero doubt in Bree's voice. "That means we're in real danger. I heard Todd's slow, strangled death. It wasn't natural."

"So we go to the police."

"With what?" Bree raises her mug. "What evidence do we have? Oliver's supernatural talent? A mirror smudged with lipstick?"

"I mean—yeah. The mirror. That seemed like a pretty direct threat," I say, realizing the urgency of our situation.

"Against whom? By whom? And then what?" Bree asks. "Say the police come here, assuming they can even get here in this weather, and investigate. What if they find nothing? The killer will feel threatened, giving them a reason to strike again. I have nowhere to go, and neither do you. It's too risky to call attention to ourselves like that."

"Then what do we do?" I ask, gulping.

"I say we keep our eyes on the Bishop sisters. And thanks to Rodrigo, we know Black is no good, so we watch her as well. As for

Hope, she's too good to be true. One of them took out Todd. Has to be."

"What about Quinn and Oliver?" I ask. There's trepidation in my voice. "Quinn told me he had a super strained relationship with his dad."

"Jury is out on Oliver . . . I think he's harmless enough, but that kid is off, and young killers aren't unheard of these days. And Quinn, well—I think he's all right. I've got a good radar for crazy, and he isn't raising any alarms."

I sigh with relief, but feel a need to remind Bree that her intuition didn't raise alarms with Jake, either.

She seems to take it in stride. "It's true. I think Jake would kill me if he got the chance. I'm sure of it. And why? Because it's always the husband, or the boyfriend, the one closest to the victim. In Todd's case . . . the wife."

"Vicki? You think Vicki did it?" My voice drops to a whisper. Reaching behind me, I grab a dish towel from the stainless-steel prep table to dry my sweaty hands.

Bree says, "Those two were going at each other like cats and dogs last night. Woke me from a deep sleep. Plus, Vicki doesn't seem very broken up about her husband's death."

"You didn't meet him," I say. "That guy was high up on the hard-to-feel-for scale."

"More reason for her to do him in," Bree says, stepping forward. She places a hand on my shoulder. "Look, Charley, if we can get some evidence, we can call the cops. Without the murderer in our midst, it'll be safe to ride out the storm together. When it's all over, I'll go my way, you'll go yours, and I'll send you the money I promised—and more, like Rodrigo said."

"What are you suggesting?" The dish towel in my hand has become a stress ball.

"You've got access to the guest rooms and a reason to go in them. You still have to clean, right?"

"Yeah," I say. "I guess I'm still the maid."

I frown as I say it, feeling self-conscious. Bree is a hip and cool bartender, and I'm basically the dishrag I keep wringing out in my hands.

Sensing my discomfort, Bree says, "You're not your job, Charley. But you *are* in the best position to take action. When you clean Vicki's room, search it thoroughly. See what you find. If we dig up any real evidence, we call the police. Simple as that." She says it like an order.

Aside from Janice, who was mainly a life preserver thrown my way, I've managed on my own for years. Suddenly Bree is in the picture, and I like the idea of having a partner.

But I don't relish messing with these Bishops. For all I know, Iris may have shanked someone in prison. And to Bree's point, I doubt Hope and Faith are as sweet as they seem. Then there's Vicki—the real wild card, and potentially a homicidal maniac.

The idea of searching her room freezes my heart.

Bree sets her tea down with finality, leaning back against the stove as if she's trying to give me space to think it over.

I don't need long. Searching rooms for hidden stuff is kind of my expertise, even if I don't want Bree to know *that* whole story. Who knows, maybe if I don't find the smoking gun Bree's hoping for, I'll score a little extra cash to help out my nana.

"You keep Vicki distracted," I say, with false bravado. "If there's any evidence in her room, any at all, I'll find it."

Chapter 32

I may have sounded tough with Bree, but I'm scared shitless as I walk down the corridor to Vicki's room. I have Bessie with me, which makes my nervousness all the more absurd. Cleaning is my job, and one Vicki has *asked* me to do. I've done this work day in and day out for years. But this time, it feels dangerous.

We never moved Vicki because of the chaos after Todd's death, so she's still in the Italian Room. I'm fishing around in my scrub dress for the key when a man clears his throat behind me.

I stop short, knowing who it is.

Turning slowly, I try to wipe the guilty look off my face before confronting Quinn. There he is, casually leaning against the wall, eyeing me with playful curiosity.

"I straightened up my room to save you the trouble," he tells me.

Instinctively, I step behind my cart, using it like a shield to hide my embarrassment and fear. While Quinn doesn't know my ulterior motive, I can't stop imagining I've raised his suspicions. Making matters worse, I'm back in this stupid maid outfit.

"Thanks. I'm happy to clean it, though," I say. "Maybe your mom will see that I'm a good worker and let me keep my job."

Taking a deep breath, I force myself to look at Quinn. We hold each other's gaze for a moment, and I notice that the playful look has vanished. In its place, I see . . . *interest?*

"Yeah, about your job . . ." he says, as if it's been weighing on him as much as it has on me. He takes a step closer, causing my heart to speed up. "So much has happened, I haven't had a chance to talk to you about it."

I shrug. "What's there to say? I hid Bree here against the rules. I did it to myself."

"Seems to me like you were trying to help someone in need and you're being punished for it. That's not right in my book."

At that moment, I want to know all about *his book*. The Quinn story is one I'd like to read over and over again. The last boy I kissed was a year ago—a high school senior here on vacation, looking for a good time and not finding it with his family. We went to the beach on my day off and had fun together. We fooled around a little, nothing major, before he went back to high school. However, cleaning his room afterward was an ego-bruising experience that I swore I'd never revisit.

And yet here I am, getting lost in Quinn's blue eyes and dazzling smile. Despite all my reservations, I want to believe that he *could* be interested in me.

"Look . . . I feel awful about what happened and that I haven't done anything about it." Quinn sounds sincere. "My mom sometimes acts impulsively," he says, "and I don't think she fully understands how much this job means to you."

"It's my home . . . it's how I survive," I tell him. "And my grandmother relies on my income here."

That's all it takes for the tears to start. Part of me wants to run away, but my feet won't move. Before I know it, he's reaching for my hand. I'm so nervous I almost flinch, but I don't stop him. The warmth of his touch envelops me as our fingers interlace. I can sense a connection between us, an energy I can almost feel. All I want to do is pull him closer, know how his body fits against mine.

But I have a mission to complete, so I pull my hand away. Quinn looks crestfallen. I don't want him to think I'm not interested. This is going to take some careful handling.

"Sorry, I'm just a little overwhelmed," I say. "I don't want to put my problems on you. You and your family have so much to deal with already."

Quinn gives me a sweet half-smile that's a little sad, but also suggests that he's undeterred. He takes a step back, giving me the space I asked for, but our connection isn't completely broken.

"I know you're not asking for my help, but I want to give it to you anyway. I'll talk to my mom. It's the least I can do. I'll tell you how it goes," he says as he turns to leave.

Part of me thinks he might try for a kiss, and part of me is disappointed that he doesn't. I watch him walk away, wanting him to look back at me before he disappears around the corner. And he doesn't let me down. He throws me a charming grin over his shoulder before vanishing.

After Quinn departs and my racing heart finally slows, I realize that he doesn't seem very broken up over Todd's death. Nobody, in fact, is exhibiting the sort of grief one would expect from the passing of a close family member. As I slip the key into the lock, I wonder if I'm about to find out why.

Before I enter, I check down the hall to make sure the coast is clear. Bree promised to keep Vicki distracted and warn me if she was on her way, but I don't have much time. In addition to searching, I have to make the bed and clean the whole room, which only adds to my anxiety.

We usually keep the door ajar while working, but this cleanup requires more discretion. After softly shutting the door behind me, I survey the room, unsure where to begin.

Two suitcases rest on the bureau, half unpacked. I start there, picking the one with boxer briefs folded on top, thinking it must be Todd's. Trying to avoid making a mess, I sift through clothing a weekend golfer might wear, finding nothing out of the ordinary.

I unzip a section of Todd's suitcase and discover his wallet inside. Vicki must have put it there after the police looked through it. Inside the billfold I find two hundred dollars in twenties. Old habits really do die hard. I stash eighty bucks in the pocket of my scrub dress, feeling confident nobody will miss it. As I'm returning the rest of the cash to his wallet, I notice something small and square tucked behind his license and credit cards. I pull the mystery object out, surprised to find a condom. Strange. Do married men typically use them? I don't have time to contemplate.

Next, I search Vicki's luggage, finding nothing unusual. I keep checking my phone while I look through her stuff, watching for a text from Bree. I can justify tidying up the room, but I won't be able to explain snooping through her belongings. The clothes within are all classy-casual brands like Lululemon and Anthropologie, neatly folded and organized, fitting Vicki's uptight personality, so I leave everything as I found it.

I make the bed, do a little dusting, and go back on the hunt. A laptop is on the desk, but when I open it, it asks for a password, so I close the lid and move on. There's nothing special here. It's the usual mess any guest would leave. I take a peek inside the bathroom. There are so many beauty products on the counter, it looks like someone robbed a Sephora. In typical Vicki fashion, all the bottles are perfectly arranged as though she's preparing for an Instagram video promoting her skin-care regimen.

Turning back to the living area, I notice a half-empty bottle of bourbon resting on the bureau, reminding me of Todd's drink of choice. I wouldn't be able to tell if Vicki had poisoned the bottle, so it's of no use to me. My hands start shaking. I'm running out of options and time.

I should check the bureau drawers. That's a logical place to hide something.

The first drawer I open contains Vicki's underwear. I dig through a pile of silky fabrics, stuff I could never dream of affording. I'm semi-horrified that while in the process of committing a crime, or at least a misdemeanor, I'm thinking about wearing something sexy like this for Quinn. Then I realize, this is his mother's lingerie—*ew!* That crushes the sexy vibe.

Just as I'm about to abandon my search, my hands brush against something concealed in the far corner of the drawer. I remove a plastic bag from within and hold it to the light. It's full of dark berries, round like midnight pearls, and a scattering of green leaves and stems. The berries appear to be fresh, the same as the leaves. I can't say I've ever seen a plant like this growing here.

I stand motionless in the center of the room, transfixed by the contents of the plastic bag. *What in the world is this?*

I grab my phone, snapping a quick pic before opening my texting app to compose my message to Bree. But before I type a word, a message from her pops up on my screen. It takes a moment for the meaning of her message to register. When it finally does, my blood goes cold.

QUICK! SHE'S ON HER
WAY! YOU HAVE TO GO—
NOW!

Bree added three alarm emojis for extra emphasis—all caps. Supreme urgency.

Shit.

I quickly close the bureau drawer and turn to leave, the plastic baggie still in my hand. But as I go to grab my cart and make my way out, the door swings open, and in steps Vicki. Her lips are pulled as tight as her ponytail. My hand flies to my chest in surprise. I have to brush this off as perfectly ordinary—just a maid cleaning a room. But I catch the strange look on Vicki's face. And that's when I realize, the hand that went to my chest is the same one holding the mysterious plant.

"Why was the door closed?" she asks sharply. "Our policy is to keep the door open when cleaning. You should know that."

I pause long enough that I seem guilty of something. Eventually my mouth catches up to my brain. "Oh, um, I just forgot, sorry," I stammer.

Vicki closes the gap between us, her keen eyes probing mine. She moves the fancy purse she always carries from her right shoulder to her left as she snatches the plastic bag from my hand.

"What's this?" she asks.

We're standing close enough that I can smell her perfume. If money had a scent, this would be it. The gold belt cinching the waist of her white capri pants sparkles like the dazzling necklace she's wearing. Up close, I get a better look at Vicki's overly highlighted hair and perfectly applied makeup. But her fractured expression is in sharp contrast to her otherwise put-together appearance.

"Where'd you get this?" she asks, holding up the baggie of berries.

I go completely blank. The room turns dark; I don't have a good answer. And since I just found the baggie in Vicki's drawer, she should know where I got it, so it's no use lying to her. I don't know what comes over me or where I get the courage, but Nana's advice rings loudly in my ears. *Sometimes the best defense is a good offense.*

I stand up straighter, hoping my height advantage will be intimidating. I send Vicki something of a pointed stare and say, "I should be asking you that question. I got this from your underwear drawer. You've been saying all along that Todd's death seems suspicious, and this seems suspicious to me. Lots of people heard you two fighting last night. I think you have some explaining to do."

Vicki's expression quickly shifts from stunned to ... *impressed?* She tilts her head slightly to one side, surveying me as though she's never set eyes on me before.

Admittedly, I'm a little proud of myself. I've been pushed around so much in life that taking a stand feels empowering.

A smile creeps across Vicki's face, holding me transfixed. With our gazes locked, I neglect to look at her hand, which evidently slipped inside her purse while I wasn't looking. Her smile remains frozen as I catch some slight movement below. I shift my focus downward, and as I do, I find myself staring directly into the barrel of a gun.

Chapter 33

"Family meeting, everyone! Family meeting—right now!" Vicki's lilting voice floats down the grand staircase with the forced cheer of a preschool teacher. "Everyone to the alcove. Hurry! Hurry! Out of your rooms! Let's go! Tout de suite!"

When I appear on the upper landing with Vicki hovering directly behind me, I see Bree waiting downstairs, resting a hand on the ball cap of the curved mahogany banister that runs from the ground level to the second floor. She's craning her neck to see what's going on above. My wide, petrified eyes must convey that something has gone awry.

Iris and Brenda Black join Quinn in descending the stairs behind us. Everyone seems uncertain and bewildered—everyone, that is, except Vicki. She wears a cheery, plastered-on smile as fake as the silk flowers decorating the reception desk.

When I reach the bottom step, I mouth the word *gun* to Bree. Then with a closed fist and fully extended index finger, I pantomime a weapon to ensure my message is clear. Bree looks like she's about to speak out, but I quiet her with a subtle headshake. Vicki is obviously a loose cannon, and I've no idea how she'll react if she's pushed too hard.

"You too, Bree," Vicki says as we pass her. "You're part of this now. Let's go."

Hope and Faith, who are staying in the Gardenia Room on the first floor, step into the Great Room, wide-eyed with confusion. Oliver, who is staying in the same two-bedroom suite with his moms, shows up soon after. He's still sleepy and disheveled, a cowlick sticking antenna-like from the back of his head.

"Everyone, take a seat in the alcove," Vicki instructs in a sugary sweet tone.

Quinn and Iris set about arranging the chairs in a semicircle. They switch on a couple of antique lamps. The warm glow casts deep shadows across the confused faces of those crowded into the sitting area. I plop down on a plush chair beside Vicki with Bree to my left.

Now that I'm closer to the boarded-up windows, I can hear the storm more clearly. From the sound of it, Larry is strengthening as the updated forecasts predicted. The plywood sheets keep out the driving rain, but the wind finds plenty of cracks to seep through in the drafty old hotel. I can still hear the continued popping and cracking of trees, like a team of lumberjacks hard at work. The barricaded windows make the room darker, smaller. The whole alcove seems to be shrinking as if the walls are closing in on us.

I use the panicky commotion of the group to camouflage my whispered warning in Bree's ear. "The gun is in her purse," I breathe.

Stealing a glance at Vicki's Fendi bag, Bree must see that the latch is undone, making it easier to access the weapon inside.

When the nervous chatter sputters to a stop, Vicki wastes no time.

"So," she begins, "I have a simple question, and I'm looking for a straightforward answer. I would like to know who is trying to frame me."

A palpable sense of uncertainty sweeps through the room. Without elaborating, Vicki reaches into her purse. I tense, expecting she'll draw her weapon. But thankfully, she removes the plastic bag of leaves and berries she had taken from me back in her room.

"What's that?" asks Iris, leaning forward to get a better look. "And what are you talking about? Framing you for what?"

Vicki casts a suspicious glance around the circle. "Well, murder, obviously," she says, her voice sharp. "Todd's murder, to be precise. And I'd like to know what this is. Charley claims to have found it in my underwear drawer." Vicki glares at me with spiteful eyes. "What a maid is doing rifling through my undergarments is beside the point.

For the time being, I believe Charley when she tells me she didn't put it there. But the rest of you, except for my son, are *not* above suspicion. Now, I want to know which of you is trying to take me down?" Her voice rumbles, dark and menacing.

"Let me see that." Hope motions for the bag, which Vicki hands over without objection. With keen eyes, she studies the contents intently, assessing the dried leaves and berries like Sherlock Holmes.

"*This . . .*"—Hope holds it up for all to see—"is *Atropa belladonna*, more commonly known as deadly nightshade." She turns toward Vicki. "What the hell are you doing with belladonna?" Hope's voice is sharp and surprised. "Do you know how dangerous this stuff is?"

Vicki glares back at Hope before snatching the bag from her hand. "Obviously I thought it was dangerous, or I wouldn't have made a big deal about it. Belladonna, melladonna, telladonna, what do I know about plants? I sell gems and jewelry. But I do know someone *planted* this in my room."

"And why would any of us do that?" Faith asks, flipping her hair again, which I now recognize as a nervous habit.

"I'm guessing Todd's tox screen is going to come back positive for this substance, and someone wants to blame me for his death," Vicki says.

Quinn looks skeptical. Although he harbors suspicions about her, he also knows his mother loves a good conspiracy. He's locked in on his phone, most likely reading about the deadly nightshade. "Who'd even use belladonna, anyway?" he asks. "That's such a book-club way to die."

Faith manages to furrow her wrinkle-free brow. "Quinn, we're talking about your father. Show some respect, please."

Quinn sends his aunt a telling glance. "If you spent more time with us, then you'd know we didn't get along. I'm sorry he's dead, but I'm not going to play the grief-stricken son."

I don't see a lot of Todd in Quinn's face, but there's certainly a family resemblance on the Bishop side. They all have a look that's a little hard-edged, cut sharp like the diamonds in Vicki's fancy stores.

"He resented me for some reason," Quinn goes on. "And if we're being completely honest ... maybe that's why *you* didn't like him, either, Mom."

Vicki looks rattled, but only briefly. She sighs as she slips the baggie into the pocket of her pants. "Your father wasn't perfect, but he did love you. And I loved him—I would *never* have hurt my husband."

Iris raises her eyebrows. "Is that your defense, Vic?" she asks, sounding doubtful. "That you loved him too much to kill him?" She let loose a short laugh. "I'm not so sure a jury would buy that. Scratch that. They *won't.*"

"Let me be blunt," Vicki continues. "Hope, you know herbs and plants and that sort of thing better than anyone here. That's pretty interesting, don't cha think?" She pauses for effect. "And you and Faith most likely want your share of the hotel back, am I right? In my opinion, that gives you both a motive to kill Todd and frame me for it. It seems in line with the creepy poem on the mirror—a poem your son just happened to write.

"And speaking of Oliver, I assume he has easy access to your herbal home remedies, Hope. Ever think of that? Psychopaths are coming younger and younger these days, especially with all those hormones in milk, and 5G and cell towers and whatnot. We can't discount that possibility—no offense, Ollie, just calling it like I see it."

"The boy who does the rhymes also does the crimes," Oliver says, offering no indication that he took offense.

Hope guffaws. "I've never heard such bullcrap in all my life."

Vicki rolls her eyes. "The word is *bullshit,* Hope, or are you too good to swear? And what about you, Iris? You have a vendetta against me for your prison stint that somehow you think is *my* fault. Or perhaps you were murderously angry with Todd over the conservatorship?"

Brenda Black speaks for the first time. "Never trust a former convict."

Vicki's attention shifts to the attorney. "And *you,*" she says, aiming her finger at Black like it's the gun concealed inside her purse. "What happens legally if I'm, say, incarcerated?"

Black clears her throat uncomfortably. "Well, in fact, um ... Yes, in the event that you, the only beneficiary with an outright ownership share of the property, were unable for any reason to oversee caretaking duties, there's language in the will that would, um . . . Let's just say, as the executor of your father's estate, I would assume caretaking duties of the hotel, until such time as the conservatorship dissolved, and then Iris could take over if she wished."

"And now that Todd's gone, who determines when the conservatorship dissolves?" Iris wants to know.

"Per the will, that responsibility lies with me," Black says grimly.

"So, if I'm in prison, you'd essentially own this hotel. Well now, I would call that motive," Vicki says.

"Why on earth would I want this place?" Black asks the room. "It's nothing but a headache. I don't know a thing about running this sort of business. I think the shock of Todd's death and being cooped up together has made your imagination run wild."

"Maybe it's not the business you want, but what's *in* the hotel that you're after," Quinn suggests. I can almost hear neck bones cracking as all our heads swivel in his direction. "Charley mentioned something about a valuable painting that's here," he continues. "Maybe that's it."

Gathering her composure, Black responds sharply, "I don't know anything about a valuable painting, and I certainly don't want anything to do with this hotel, aside from leaving it, which I plan to do as soon as possible."

Black has traded in her skirt and pumps for jeans and more sensible shoes, a far more practical outfit for making a quick exit.

"Quinn, your father was full of tall tales. He exaggerated everything. If any of this artwork is worth more than a flea-market price tag, I'd know about it," Vicki says. "But we're getting off track."

She clutches her Fendi bag to her side, stalking the circle with her eyes, going from person to person as though she can pinpoint the liar in the group simply by looking hard enough.

After a lengthy silence, she seems to tire of the wait. "Okay, I can see we're not very interested in being forthcoming." She offers a tense smile. "No worries," she says sweetly. "We'll just try a different approach."

To everyone's surprise, Vicki gets up from her chair and quickly departs the alcove, passing through the Great Room on her way to our office. We all watch in confusion, even after she vanishes from view.

"What is she doing?" I ask nervously, but no one has a good answer. In fact, no one has any answer at all.

A moment later, I jump in my seat when a loud pop goes off, like a firecracker exploding indoors. No mistaking it: It's the sound of a gunshot.

Quinn rises to his feet in alarm. "Oh my god," he sputters. "Did she just shoot herself?" He moves to rush after Vicki, but Iris grabs hold of his shirt before he gets two steps away, pulling him back forcefully.

"Stay here. It's not safe," Iris tells him. "She's clearly unhinged."

"But she might be hurt." Quinn twists to break free.

Iris holds firm. "Just wait. I don't need you acting impulsively, too."

Faith and Hope huddle around Oliver, trying to shield him from the tragedy that has apparently unfolded out of sight. Next to them, Brenda Black sits thunderstruck.

Bree and I exchange looks of utter disbelief as the distinct odor of gunpowder fills the air. I imagine Vicki slumped lifelessly on the floor, blood seeping from a bullet hole to the head—a hasty choice made when she felt hopelessly cornered and helplessly trapped.

Quinn, undeterred, finally pulls free from Iris, bolting out of the alcove with sprinter's strides as he heads for the office.

"Quinn, wait, no!" Iris calls out. But it's too late. He's gone around the corner, out of view, and a second later, another shot rings out.

"Oh my god!" cries Faith, her hand flying to her mouth. "She shot Quinn!"

Iris crumples in her chair as though she's the one who'd been shot. Thankfully, their fear, and mine, is short-lived. A few seconds later, Quinn reappears in the Great Room, returning to the alcove with Vicki marching behind him. Relief sweeps over the room like a great wave. To everyone's astonishment, Vicki has a gun in one hand and something unidentifiable in the other.

When she reaches the alcove, Vicki tosses the mysterious object into the circle's center. It lands on the floor with the clunking sound of broken plastic.

"It's time you all took me seriously," she says, using the gun to indicate her purse. "Put your cell phones in my bag—*now*. That was the router I just shot. There's no internet access anymore, so computers are useless. Once I have your phones, you'll have no contact with anyone outside this hotel. Consider yourselves under house arrest until I figure out which one of you is trying to frame me for murder."

Chapter 34

Iris says what everyone must be thinking: "A gun, Vicki? What the *hell* are you doing? Have you lost your mind?"

"Don't have a conniption," Vicki says. "I'm not going to shoot you—yet—but I need you to put your cell phone in my bag. Now."

I don't know where to direct my focus—the gun or the decimated router on the floor. Our vital communication link is nothing but broken pieces of plastic and shattered electronics. Vicki's right. Without our phones or internet, we're essentially cut off from the outside world, unless we're willing to brave the hurricane. Given how the hotel keeps shaking under these unrelenting winds, I'd say that would be ill-advised.

Quinn and I make brief eye contact, but it's long enough to receive his telepathic apology. He's obviously deeply distressed. It's written all over his face. I want to impress him with my fearlessness and composure, but seeing Vicki's gun triggers me all over again. With a few shallow breaths, I manage to slow my racing heart by a couple of beats. Guns are as common as grasshoppers in Maine, but I've never had one pointed at me.

"I'm serious. I want all your cell phones, and I want them now," Vicki says again, using the gun to indicate the Fendi bag open on the floor in front of her.

"Vicki," Brenda Black says in a soft and soothing voice, "I think you're confusing house arrest for . . . um, hostage taking."

"No shit," huffs Iris.

"What are you talking about?" Vicki claps back. "I'm merely demanding justice and defending my civil rights."

"You've got a gun pointed at *us*," Faith reminds her. "Whose civil rights are being violated?"

"I don't *want* hostages, and I don't *want* to use this weapon," Vicki assures everyone, mostly Quinn. "But I'm being forced into a corner. You know me. I'm not a psychopath."

Hope laughs derisively. "Yeah, the jury is still out on that one."

I'm taking note of Vicki's appearance. Her crisp tennis whites are in sharp contrast to her messy hair, which is half out of its ponytail and sticking haphazardly in all directions. Her makeup is smeared from wiping beads of sweat off her forehead. After seeing her so poised and controlled, it's unsettling to watch her unravel. The loss of her husband and the fear of incrimination have clearly taken a heavy emotional toll. I'm witnessing a person breaking apart right before my eyes.

Iris is a calm sea compared to Vicki's hurricane. Her expression is neutral, and her body language is indifferent. She likely learned how to control her emotions while in prison, and it's paying off right now. But she's sharp, and her hawkish eyes assess every slight movement that Vicki makes. Her muscles are tense, sinewy like wire pulled taut. I get the feeling that, at any moment, she might pounce on her sister and go for the gun.

But of everyone here, Oliver is the least reactive. He seems completely disengaged from this craziness in a lights-on-but-nobody's-home kind of way. Perhaps the spirit world showed him how this all plays out, and we'll be just fine. Or the opposite could be true, and he's resigned himself to a much darker fate.

"I, for one, have had enough of this nonsense," Faith says. "I'm calling Officer Brennan. He'll straighten this out."

I'm too scared to check my phone to see if we still have cell service. The cell tower goes out in less severe weather, but that's seldom a problem because our Wi-Fi for internet calling is delivered through fiber-optic cable that's far more reliable—or it was, before Vicki shot the router.

Faith ignores the mandate (and common sense) as she unlocks her phone. Seeing the expression on Vicki's face, I'd put that cell phone away in a flash, but Faith resumes her call. Before she can hit send, Hope snatches the phone from her wife's hand and, with equal quickness, tosses it with bull's-eye accuracy into the awaiting cavernous purse.

"This is *not* a gamble I'm willing to take," Hope says. "I'm not risking my family over this." She puts her phone in the bag along with Faith's.

"Smart move," Vicki says. "My phone and Todd's are already in the bag. Now the rest of you. Follow Hope's lead."

Vicki uses the gun again to show where she wants the phones deposited.

Black gives in and drops hers into the bag, muttering, "I don't get paid enough for this shit." She glares at Vicki before adding, "And just so you know, when this is all over, not only am I going to *sue* your ass, but you're going to prison just like your jailbird sister." Black thumbs at Iris.

"Who are you calling a jailbird, bitch?" Iris seems to grow ten feet tall. "I'm guessing you coerced my father into writing that shoddy will. You better watch yourself, lady, because I think you'll be joining Vicki behind bars when all this is done."

I have a flash of Black and Vicki, prison cellmates, locked in a catfight, but now isn't the time to indulge in daydreams.

Everyone eventually complies, including me, each of us placing our cell phones into Vicki's designer bag. The last holdout, Iris, finally caves, relinquishing her phone with a grunt of displeasure.

With the bag full, Vicki surprisingly hands it over to Oliver. "Ollie, honey, Aunt Vicki needs you to rush this to her room. It's unlocked, and the safe is open. Put it in there, close the safe door, and lock it with the bag and all the phones inside, then come right back here."

Oliver takes the bag agreeably and lopes off toward Vicki's room.

"Why are you bringing Oliver into this?" Faith gripes. "He's just a kid. Leave him alone."

Vicki waves off her sister's concern. "Out of everyone here, he's the most likely to follow the rules—a little too obsessively, in my opinion, but whatever," she says. "Now, let's get down to it. One of you killed my husband, and you're trying to pin it on me. I don't think it's you, Charley, or your freeloading friend." Vicki looks at Bree, then back over to me.

I shrink under her scrutiny, hating myself for appearing weak in front of Quinn.

"I hope you're including yourself in the list of suspects," says Faith. "You and Todd were always arguing, and last night's fight was probably one of the worst."

It's a bold statement, considering Vicki has the gun on her lap.

"That was nothing. Couples fight all the time," Vicki says. "I know that I'm innocent. And I doubt Oliver's involved, but really, with him, who knows? And it's definitely *not* Quinn. That leaves my two *loving* sisters, who believe Todd double-crossed them, and you, Ms. Black."

"Me?" says Black, her hand going to her cheek.

"Oh, don't act so innocent," Vicki says. "It's obviously going to be difficult for me to wrangle the estate out from under you if I'm behind bars." Vicki's voice dips slightly. "And I agree with Iris that you coerced our father into writing that terrible will, knowing you'd have the controlling shares if Todd should be out of the picture."

"Exactly," thunders Iris.

"Which means," Vicki continues, "we're all staying in this cozy little alcove until I get the truth."

Silence falls. Then, in what I suspect is her prototypical courtroom voice, Black declares, "Confusion is the criminal's best defense. The smart ones distract and evade. Charley caught you red-handed with the poison. What else can you do but deflect blame onto others? Even your young nephew isn't safe from your wild accusations."

As if on cue, Oliver reappears empty-handed. "The phones are now where you asked, so I guess I have completed my task."

Kudos to him; his rhyming skills are still on point.

"You did wonderful, Ollie," says Hope, who can't seem to pass up an opportunity to praise her son.

Oliver retakes his seat. "What did I miss?" he asks, like someone who'd gone to the bathroom during a movie and wants a recap.

"You haven't missed a thing," Quinn says, unable to hide his disgust. "My mother is just as crazy as when you left."

"Oh, good," replies Oliver, which is the closest thing to actual enthusiasm he's shown so far.

While Oliver is getting a weird thrill out of this entire spectacle, Iris is not. She stands defiantly, crossing her tatted arms in front of her.

"You don't scare us," she says, staring down Vicki, who counters her sister's rebellion by aiming the gun directly at Iris's face as she rises to her feet.

"Really? Don't push me, sis," Vicki threatens. "Your prison stare doesn't intimidate me. I have the gun, remember?"

"Yeah, and you're going to give it to me right now and get control over yourself," Iris says.

Instead of obliging, Vicki inches closer to her target.

"It's okay, Aunt Iris," Quinn says with forced calm. "Don't push her."

"Stay out of this, Quinn," Iris answers tersely. "I know my sister. She's all talk and no action. Hand over the gun, Vicki. Enough of this nonsense."

But Vicki holds her ground. Tension rises. The air holds an electric charge. I'm thinking of the greatest standoffs in film history, movies I watched with my nana before her memory declined. Darth Vader versus Obi-Wan Kenobi. Harry Potter versus Voldemort. The Ghostbusters against the Stay-Puft Marshmallow Man.

Then I remind myself that this face-off is real; it's a real gun, with real bullets and real lives at stake.

Vicki's right eye twitches ever so slightly. The left corner of Iris's mouth lifts a degree, forming a twisted smile. Everyone else is frozen in place.

"You know what's scarier than a gun?" Iris asks the room before answering her own question. "The truth. You keep asking for it, Vicki.

You want to threaten *us*? Well, let me threaten *you*. Give me the gun or I'll tell everyone in this room, right here, right now, our big secret—and I'm not talking about the maid."

Me? I think. *What do I have to do with any of this?* But Iris isn't looking at me. She's still locking eyes with her sister. Then I remembered my conversation with Vicki on our walk-and-talk, when she told me I reminded her of a woman who worked here named Christine. Could that be the maid Iris is referring to?

Vicki's face turns ashen. She recoils as if Iris's threat is a different sort of weapon. "You wouldn't dare," she says, her voice cracking with emotion. The shadows in the room seem to move on their own, as if animated by the escalating conflict. The lights join in the dance, flickering on and off intermittently as the mighty wind gusts ebb and flow.

"Don't test me," Iris says.

In response, Vicki stands a little straighter as she tightens her grip on the weapon. Iris doesn't waver. She holds out her hand expectantly.

"The gun or the truth," Iris says.

Vicki looks pained as she takes careful aim. I see murder in this woman's crazed eyes.

Iris shrugs off the danger. "Have it your way," she says resignedly, ready to reveal a truth I can't imagine. Turning to Quinn, Iris announces: "I'm not your aunt . . . I'm actually your mother."

And that's when the lights go out.

Chapter 35

I've been in dark places before, but this is on another level. The blackness engulfs me, dulling my senses. Even with my palm pressed against my nose, I can't see my fingers. But I can hear just fine. Everyone must be fumbling around, stumbling into each other, because it sounds like a bar brawl, with heavy footsteps and a mix of frightened voices that adds to the chaos.

"Where's the gun?" That's Faith asking.

"Let go of me!" Maybe Vicki? I'm not sure.

Someone grunts nearby. Somebody pushes against me. Something crashes loudly; perhaps a lamp has fallen over.

I stay put, bracing for the shot, a flash in the dark, fearing a bullet might strike me should I make a move. The voices of mass confusion blend into one jumbled uproar. That's when I realize I haven't heard anything from Quinn. Is he okay? Did he pass out? Is he in shock? What Iris said, if true, changes everything. His whole world has been turned upside down. I want to hold his hand and offer comfort, but I can't find him in this blackout.

"Get us some flashlights, Charley! Go get us flashlights!" I think it's Iris shouting at me, but I can't be sure.

"If only we had our phones." I have no trouble identifying Hope as the complainant.

Much as I'd love some light, it's too dark, not to mention unsafe, to go look. The flashlights and candles are in a storage closet off the kitchen, but again, I'm rooted to the spot, too scared to move. The last thing I need is to bump into Vicki and get a bullet in the stomach for my troubles.

The chaos recedes into an unsettled quiet, the void now dulling my sense of time. We're in a collective freeze. It's impossible to say how many minutes pass with us trapped in this profound darkness.

Just as quickly as the electricity went out, it flickers back on, casting a glaring light that leaves me squinting. Gradually my vision adjusts to the sudden brightness. I take in the scene around me, everyone standing perfectly still, deer in the headlights, their faces etched with relief, as though we've narrowly escaped disaster unscathed.

One of George's favorite stained-glass lamps has been knocked over and smashed to pieces on the floor. The lights continue to flicker, threatening to plunge us back into darkness at any moment.

There's a lot of chatter as the group regains its composure. Everyone's moving about the alcove freely now, checking in with one another as if they hadn't been arguing moments before. Hope and Faith are busy fawning all over Oliver, as usual. They look spooked, like they'd just emerged from a haunted house. For a moment, everyone has forgotten that Vicki still has a gun.

Everyone, that is, except for Vicki.

"Hey—hey, we're not finished here," she trumpets, waving the weapon around, motioning all to retake their seats. She's acting like a bomb hadn't been dropped just before the blackout.

Quinn turns to his mother, gutted. "How could you?" he asks.

Vicki lowers her weapon, crestfallen. Love brims in her eyes, sorrow lurking just beneath the surface. She reaches out her hand for Quinn. He shrinks from her, as if she's a live wire not to be touched.

"And Todd?" he asks, his voice shaking. "Is he even my father?"

Vicki looks to Iris. Her visible emotions speak the words she cannot. *Look what you've done. Are you happy now?*

I've never known one sentence to do so much damage. It stole a mother from her son and stripped a mom of her identity. It's hard to witness.

I look at Bree, who meets my eyes with disbelief.

She mouths, *Holy shit.*

Dismay eclipses Vicki's face. "He's your father because he raised you, and so did I. I'm still your mother," she says to Quinn. Next she whirls around to Iris, keeping the weapon at her side lest her ire manifest itself as an unrecoverable trigger pull. "You selfish bitch," Vicki says, her emotions boiling over. "You've just gone and upended Quinn's life for no reason at all. Everything was fine, and now you've screwed it up forever."

Iris barks out a laugh. "Everything was fine? You're holding us all hostage, you loon. I gave you plenty of chances to be reasonable. And it was never *fine* for me. You had me backed into a corner, and I had no choice but to bow to your wishes. I gave up everything for Quinn. I needed help, but instead of offering support so I could get back on my feet and still be a mother, you stole him from me. My mistake here, if any, was trusting that you would do right by me and allowing this charade to continue for far too long. Now you'll have to live with the consequences."

Iris's face goes slack. For a moment, the anger leaves her and she appears on the verge of tears. But Quinn does not look like he's about to offer emotional support. His eyes are ablaze—full of outrage and confusion.

"As far as I'm concerned, you both lied to me," he says, switching his focus between what are apparently his two moms.

"We did it for your own good," Vicki says. She's still trying to get near Quinn, but he keeps backing away. "Iris was on drugs. She couldn't take care of herself, let alone a child. So we agreed that I'd take you in, become your mother, and offer you a stable family. It would have been too much for a child to understand that his aunt was his biological mother. We all agreed it was better this way."

"Agreed?" Iris's voice shoots out like a cannon. "Bullshit! You outright threatened me, saying I could be in Quinn's life, but only if I kept my mouth shut. You've been controlling me, my son, everything for years!" Iris is shouting, her face red, muscles flexing.

Hope's quiet voice somehow manages to cut through the tumult. "Let's calm down, everyone. Anger isn't going to do any good."

Quinn whips his head around to confront Hope. "And did you

know, too?" he asks. "Aunt Faith, how about you? It seems like everyone but me was in on this. So nobody here can judge my reaction."

Hope smiles sweetly at Quinn, with no sign of hurt or agitation. "I understand how you feel, but remember that your family loves you. It's complicated, and mistakes have been made, but let's not lose sight of the love. Love is the energy that binds us together. It connects us in heart, body, and spirit. Your mothers—yes, they are both your mothers—have wanted nothing but the best for you. Let's use this opportunity for healing and growth."

"Oh, give me a fucking break," Vicki groans.

However, Hope holds firm, undeterred and seemingly surrounded by a soothing aura that dampens the currents of rage and sadness coursing through the room.

Overwhelmed, Quinn slumps back into his chair with his head in his hands. Vicki sits back down, and the rest of us follow suit.

As everyone retakes their respective places, I notice something is amiss—or, more accurately, someone is missing. The others seem to notice as well. We all find ourselves staring at the same empty chair where attorney Black should be seated.

Chapter 36

Vicki spins in all directions, refusing to believe what she is (or isn't) seeing. Black is nowhere to be found.

"Well, well, if that isn't suspicious, I don't know what is," she says. "Where did she go?" Vicki searches the faces of those remaining in the alcove as if someone will have an answer, but I know better. Black is gone; that much is obvious. And Quinn is angrier than before.

"My whole sense of self . . . everything I've known is a lie, and all you can do is think about yourself," Quinn says to Vicki, his voice rising in disgust.

Vicki offers him a half-reassuring smile at best, clearly distracted. "Quinn, your life hasn't really changed. I'm still your mother. Just like always. But I'm facing a potential murder charge, and now Brenda Black has vanished. I'm sorry, but I need to focus right now."

"Of course you do," Iris says tersely, tossing Quinn a sympathetic glance, but he can't bear to look her in the eyes.

Vicki calls out into the gloom, "Brenda, you better get your ass back here and retake your seat! We're not through!" Her voice echoes in the mostly empty hotel.

Brenda doesn't answer. Smart. I wouldn't have come if she called me, that's for sure.

Vicki seems torn between her desire to search for Black and her need to maintain control of the room. Her eyes dart in all directions, the gun shifting as she scans the alcove. She's even more agitated than before.

"Jesus Christ, Vicki, you're being a maniac," Faith practically yells. Her eyes harden. "She can't have gone far in this weather. She's probably hiding in her room, trying to escape *you*. And I don't blame her one bit!"

Vicki grimaces. "The fact that she took off in the blackout makes me think she's the one who planted the belladonna." She gives us a brief show-and-tell before putting the baggie with the plant back into her pocket.

"Well, what do you want us to do, Vicki? Call in the National Guard?" Hope asks.

"Is this over yet?" Oliver wants to know. "Can I go back to my room now? I have to pee." His cheeks puff in and out like fireplace bellows, suggesting he can't hold out much longer. But if the boy is traumatized in any way, it doesn't register on his face.

"No, you cannot go anywhere," Vicki says, annoyed. At least she had the wherewithal to lower the gun when speaking to her nephew. "We're going to find Black, and you're all staying right where you are until we do."

"I'm not staying anywhere near you," Quinn says. "Feel free to shoot me in the back. You already stabbed me there."

Vicki looks crushed. "Quinn, honey, please."

"I have to pee," Oliver insists.

Vicki grumbles to herself, "Everyone is so damn *needy*." Her frustration gives way to a hint of compassion. "I suppose I can't deny a kid a bathroom break," she says. "Bree, I want you to take Oliver to the bathroom."

Bree's eyes squint with confusion. "Me? Why me?"

"Yeah, why her?" asks Hope with a touch of annoyance. "I think I can take my own son to the bathroom, thank you very much. Not that a fourteen-year-old even needs an escort."

She springs to her feet, but Vicki puts a quick end to any idea of Hope leaving the alcove with a vigorous headshake. "Sorry, Ollie needs someone to go with him because Black is loose in the hotel and potentially dangerous. But sadly, I trust a stranger more than my sisters—and that includes you." Vicki turns to address Bree. "Use the bathroom off the Great Room. I don't want you two going far.

If you're not back here in five minutes, Charley has no chance for redemption," she says.

"What does that mean?" I ask, blinking in confusion.

"It means that you *might* be allowed to keep your job, Charley—*if* you and Bree don't cause any trouble and you agree to help me out."

My brow furrows as I consider working for this lunatic. At this point, I might be better off without this job, but I keep that thought to myself.

Quinn rises to his feet. "I need some space. Tell you what, *Mom*," he says with sarcasm. "I'll go look for Black."

"Quinn, I don't want you wandering off by yourself when you're this upset," Vicki says, ignoring his jab.

"I could use some time alone, actually. But whatever. I'll take Charley with me," Quinn responds as though the decision has been made, and it's not up for discussion.

Vicki bites her lip. While she's mulling this over, I grow increasingly anxious at the prospect of time alone with Quinn, unsure what to say or how to offer support when I hardly know him.

"Fine," she relents. "We need to find the attorney . . . Charley, keep an eye on my son and remember what I said about your job. *Don't* double-cross me."

Jagged energy radiates off her, hot and sharp, as I rise to my feet. There's not much time before this simmering pot boils over.

Bree stands as well. "Come on, Ollie," she says.

Hope grudgingly plops down in her chair, submitting to her captivity once more. Rolling with the punches, Oliver accepts a bathroom escort without complaint. He takes his time navigating around the broken glass from the fallen lamp. Bree pauses, waiting for him. I fall into step with Quinn, walking behind Bree and Oliver, and the four of us head into the Great Room together.

As we walk, Bree drags me aside and whispers in my ear. "I need you to pull the fire alarm. Cause a distraction."

Fire alarm? What?

I can't decide if Bree is brilliant or insane. "Shit, are you planning what I think you're planning?" I ask as quietly as I can.

Bree's steely eyes are sharp and certain. "The sudden noise will throw Vicki off guard, then I'll take her by surprise and get the gun. Simple as that."

Simple as that? It sounds like a catastrophe in the making. My worried face catches Quinn's attention.

"What's going on?" Quinn asks as Ollie heads for the bathroom.

Bree subtly shakes her head, and I know she's trying to convey the importance of secrecy. I get it. Despite the bombshell news about his secret adoption, Vicki is still his mother, and family bonds are strong. Fraught as the circumstances are, it's doubtful he'd want to conspire against his mom with a stranger. And Bree might have to use force against Vicki if it comes to that.

"Oh, Bree was just reminding us to be careful," I say, stumbling over my words. I've always been a shitty liar; just ask my nana.

I'm hoping Quinn will interpret my voice's flutter as nerves instead of dishonesty. For the moment, he seems to accept my explanation. But when he isn't looking, I mouth to Bree, *Are you crazy?*

Bree's calm demeanor offers silent assurance that all will be well. If she believes it, I can, too. Someone has to take control of this situation, and better her than me.

We hear a toilet flush, and soon after Oliver emerges from the bathroom. He tosses the paper towel he used to dry his hands into the trash bin.

"Are you okay to go back?" asks Bree, sounding easygoing.

"Yeah, fine," Oliver replies blandly.

"It's okay if you're scared, but everything is going to be fine," she tells him.

"Fine for me, if you think that's true," says Oliver in a deadpan voice. "But I highly doubt it'll be fine for you." His delivery is pure ice.

The words put Bree back on her heels. Her body stiffens as she lifts her chin to meet his stony stare.

Quinn steps forward. "Stop creeping everyone out with your weird rhymes, Ollie," he says. "We've got enough on our plates without you pretending you can predict the future."

"Whatever you say," Oliver answers before starting his march back to the alcove.

Bree moves to go with him, but I reach for her arm again, holding her back.

"Be *extra* careful," I suggest, hoping my imploring look makes my meaning unmistakably clear. "Oliver knows things. I can't explain how, but he seems to *know.*"

Bree gives me a warm smile that doesn't ease my apprehension.

"I promise I won't do anything foolish," she says.

I nod, but I know a promise that can't be kept when I hear one.

Chapter 37

As soon as Bree leaves, my first thought is: *Holy shit, I'm alone with Quinn.* I still don't know what to say or do that will help. I try to put myself in his shoes, but it's too crazy to imagine that your whole life is based on a lie. He's been so sweet to me throughout this ordeal and I just want to be there for him.

His emotions are running hot. I can't see the flames, but I feel the heat, like he'd burn me if I touched him. Even so, I'm compelled to put my hand on his arm, and when I do, he looks at me with a wounded expression that absolutely tears my heart. His eyes are two wells, deep with despair.

He pulls away from me, but I don't take it personally. Something tells me he's withdrawing into himself, that it's too much to share his burden, his new reality, with anybody, even himself. He wants to run from this; that's the vibe he's giving off, anyway. But he has nowhere to go, so I bravely touch his arm again, gently. This time, he lets me.

He steps closer, and suddenly I'm enveloping him in a hug. His arms wrap around me. For a moment, I'm afraid that he'll cry. That might make me cry, too, seeing this beautiful young man shed raw tears, and we'd be a blubbering mess, enmeshed in an embrace, feeling all the feels. I'm scared to be so vulnerable in front of him. But that's what we should do, get it over with, let it all out in a great rush of sadness, hurt, and pain. I'd cry for myself, Quinn, my nana, my mom, and Rodrigo, for all he's endured.

But instead of some profound letting go, Quinn gently pulls away, standing tall and subtly wiping his eyes. His expression has shifted, hardened.

"We should get the hell out of here," he says. "I can't be in the same building, let alone the same room, as those two."

He thumbs toward the alcove and his two moms. I suppress the urge to offer an opinion. But I do have firsthand experience with parental disappointment. I want to tell him that Vicki and Iris did what they thought was best for him and still love him despite their deception. Nobody is perfect. We all fall short of our high standards sometimes, and forgiveness is a gift we give ourselves as well as others. But he doesn't look like he's in the mood for a lecture. Besides, I suppose getting away from a crazy woman with a gun is the smart choice, so I nod my agreement.

"My car keys are in my room. I'll just run and grab them," I say.

I won't mention what else is weighing on my mind, how worried I am about Bree's plan. If we leave the hotel, I won't pull the fire alarm, and Bree won't do anything risky that might get her or someone else injured—or worse. I don't feel great abandoning her, but I know I can't talk her out of it, so leaving and getting help is best.

Quinn glances over to the exit. "Okay," he says. "I'll go outside to scope out the weather, see if this is even possible. And I'll check for Black's car while I'm out there. Meet me in the foyer near the front door as soon as you have your keys."

I hurry to my room. When I return, Quinn is standing in the entryway, drenched as if he just showered with his clothes on. His face is as pale as a full moon, and he shakes his head like a dog, spraying water everywhere.

"There's no fucking way we're leaving," he tells me, his voice hoarse. "It's crazy out there. I've never seen anything like it. Tree branches are scattered all over the place. I could barely walk against the wind to get to the parking lot. Black's car is still there, and there's a huge tree that's fallen over. It's blocking the driveway. We're stuck here, Charley."

My first thought: *shit*. Second thought: *I like how he said my name.*

"Okay, then," I say, "we stay." The howling wind outside shakes the walls, rattling my nerves with each gust. "We just do our job and try to find Black. She must be here somewhere."

Quinn is quiet as he squeezes more water out of his curls, his eyes reflecting the dim glow of the many lamps. I realize we should start a fire in case the power goes out again, but Quinn interrupts my thoughts before I can suggest it.

"I've got another idea," he says, and I forget all about the firelight.

"And that is?" I lean toward him, instinctively wanting to reach out and touch his hand like we did before, but I let the powerful force of good judgment hold me back.

"Money," he says, with a vengeful eye.

"Money?" My brow knits. "Why does money matter at a time like this?"

"Not just money," he says, his voice low and conspiratorial. He steals a glance over his shoulder before pulling me toward the reception area.

"A lot of money," Quinn clarifies once he's sure we're alone and out of earshot.

I don't like the sinister tone in his voice.

"That painting," he says. "Do you think we can find it?"

Tension leaves my body. At least he doesn't have some violent revenge fantasy in mind.

"Do you think it even exists?" I ask. "Todd, um . . . Well, he doesn't seem like the most reliable source."

Quinn doesn't appear dissuaded. "Look, this news about my adoption . . . it's all kinds of confusing," he says. "But it does help me understand one thing, and that's Todd. Now I get why he was so distant, not very fatherly, and why he seemed to resent me. It wasn't my imagination. He probably *never* wanted to adopt me, and my mom—well, *Vicki*—she can be forceful, to say the least."

"Tell me about it," I mumble.

"But if there's one thing about Todd you could always trust, it was his nose for money. He could sniff out a cash opportunity like a bloodhound. I know I said he was full of crap, but what if I'm wrong and there really is a valuable painting here? I guess after all the crazy shit that's gone down, I'm willing to believe anything is possible."

And I'm ready to believe him. Damn, he's convincing.

"Trust me, Quinn, if I knew which wall had a priceless painting hanging on it, I'd certainly let you know."

Quinn's knowing look suggests he's one step ahead of me. "That's my point exactly!" he exclaims. "It's probably not even hanging up."

"You think it's in storage somewhere?"

"Well, yeah," he says. "Isn't there an attic here or something?"

"Not *or something*," I say. "There's an attic."

"Then that's where we should look."

Quinn's enthusiasm is contagious, but I still need more information. "What are you going to do if we find it?" I ask.

Quinn's disposition blackens. "Vicki and Iris both deceived me," he says bitterly. "Even Aunt Faith and Hope were in on it. And Todd never wanted me. So I'm going to take my revenge. I'll get the inheritance from my grandfather and take the painting—the painting they don't even believe exists—for myself, and maybe I'll never see these people again."

That sounds like a terrible plan to me. "Quinn, they're still your family. They still love you," I say. "I mean, at least you *have* a family. I don't know my father, my mother is dead, and my grandmother who raised me is hardly there. Don't take the people who care about you for granted. Even if you're hurt and angry, don't push them away. You'll regret it. Trust me."

I don't know where my little speech comes from, probably a place of deep sadness and longing, but my words seem to connect with him. Quinn's expression softens and he appears to be considering my advice.

"Okay," he says, nodding. "You make several good points there, got to admit. Maybe *you* should be the philosophy major."

I laugh a little as he sinks into a thought.

"Tell you what, I won't make any big decisions about my family just yet," he assures me.

"Glad to hear," I say.

"But that won't stop me from taking the painting and the money," he adds. "Payback's a bitch, right?" The gleam in Quinn's eyes is moderately unnerving. "Let's search for it while we look for Black," he suggests. "This is my chance."

He probably sees the disappointment percolating in my expression. There's something else he isn't realizing. Quinn acts like he cares, but now he seems like just another privileged guy expecting others to cater to his whims. He doesn't realize the impact this could have on my life. If we get caught going rogue, he'll still have a place to live, but what about me? I have a chance to get my home back. And no matter what, Vicki isn't going to shoot *him*. But I'm as disposable as the trash.

"Hey," he says, touching my arm, "you've got a shit deal, too. If we find the painting, I'll help you out as well. I promise. You won't have to worry about working in some crappy hotel for unappreciative owners and living in an oversize closet, that's for sure."

Well, if that doesn't sum up my existence in an embarrassingly concise manner, I don't know what does. Despite his cringeworthy assessment of my life, I'm floating again. Maybe I got him all wrong, and he actually gets it. Even so, I remain cautious. It's hard to completely trust your feelings when they change so rapidly.

"Okay, Boy Genius, I'm game," I tell him. "But how are we going to identify it? Neither of us has a clue what we're looking for."

"Simple," he says as if he's already given this much thought. "We search everywhere we can. Take any valuable-looking paintings that are not already hanging on a wall and sneak them to your car after the storm passes. I should have some clue what we're looking for. I am an art history minor, after all."

I love that he seems so sure of himself, while I'm thinking: *It's only a minor.*

"Then what?" I ask.

"Then we can take whatever we find to that art museum in Rockland sometime next week. They'll know what we have, or they can recommend someone who can figure it out."

His plan and awareness of the Farnsworth Museum impresses me, but I see one small wrinkle to iron out.

"What if we're wrong and the valuable painting is already hanging on the wall? Someone will notice a big empty space and start asking questions."

Quinn has an answer for that as well. "If we suspect it's one on the wall, we'll find a way to swap it out for a print. I've got a great camera." *Of course he has a great camera.* "We can make a high-end copy using a digital printer, nobody will notice it's missing. Trust me, Charley, this will be as easy as taking candy from a baby."

I manage to suppress a groan. "Have you ever heard a baby wail nonstop?" I ask him. "There's *nothing* easy about that. Remember, every action has an equal and opposite reaction. There's always a consequence. Like you said, payback can be a bitch."

Chapter 38

Quinn's plan doesn't sound half bad, but it doesn't sound half good, either. Minus the potential pitfalls, I like the idea of hitting a jackpot, so I agree with his wild scheme. More than that, I appreciate the feeling of camaraderie, like we're in this together.

But before proceeding, I remind Quinn that we should still look for Black.

"Let's do a quick search of the first floor, then head upstairs and check her room. After that, we'll move on to the attic and start looking for the painting. Sound good?"

Quinn endorses my plan with a nod, and we're off.

The first-floor search is a bust, so we head upstairs. Quinn makes a pitstop at his room to change out of his wet clothes. Then we head to Black's room, which is locked. I knock out of habit. I'm not surprised there's no response. I use my key to let us in. The Tiger Lily Room on the third floor is nondescript, with a king-size bed, a modestly comfortable sitting area, and a full bathroom. While many upper-level rooms have balconies, not all offer seating for two or scenic water views like the Tiger Lily Room.

I try to imagine this as Vicki's childhood bedroom. There's certainly space for a bunk bed and a twin. But were the girls happy here? Was this a room filled with laughter and love? Judging by what I've seen of the sisters' interactions, I'd say that's highly doubtful.

Down the hall is George's old bedroom. What went on in there? Yikes, that's all I can say. I let the creep vibes pass through me like a chill.

The curtains are drawn, so I pull them apart to have a look outside. Night is falling, but in this weather, it's impossible to tell dusk from dawn. It's dark and gloomy, though I can see debris strewn across the lawn. It certainly looks as bad as Quinn had described.

On the plus side, Black appears to be an ideal guest, in that she likes to keep her room spotless. The bed is made the way I would do it. There's no trash on the floor, no crumbs scattered about, and even the towels are neatly folded, left hanging on the rack as though they hadn't been used. On the minus side, she most certainly is not here. It doesn't take long to search 273 square feet to figure that out. I can't help but check the white tip envelope on the desk (a hard habit to break), and I'm not surprised to find it empty. *Oh, well.*

Inside the closet, we discover Black's shoulder bag, along with a pair of navy blue suitcases. The smaller of the two, a foldable canvas travel bag, has a green tag on it. I have no idea what that tag is for until Quinn explains it's used to easily identify luggage on an airport carousel. I don't have the courage to tell him that I've never flown on a plane. All the coat hangers are empty, so perhaps Black is packed and ready to go. But where has she gone without her luggage?

"If her car is here, her luggage is here, then she *must* be here," I reason. But something is nagging in the back of my brain. There's something off about this room.

"Let's go check the attic," Quinn says.

"Fine," I say, but I can't shake the feeling that something in *this* room is amiss. Since I can't put my finger on it, I let it go.

Then another troubling thought tumbles into my mind, this one about Rodrigo.

"I texted him a bunch of times before Vicki took our phones, and didn't hear back," I say. "That's not like him at all."

Quinn shrugs off my concern. "Maybe he's busy with the hurricane, or he lost power and his cell phone died. Who knows?"

"Maybe," I say, frowning slightly. "It's just . . . I'm worried, is all."

"About him?"

"Yeah, him *and* Black."

I peer off into the distance, debating how much of his story to reveal. Before I can stop myself, I'm unburdening a heavy secret. Because we've limited time, I keep it to the highlights: Black's illegal deportation scam with the courts, the devastating impact on Rodrigo's mother, and the burning vengeance I saw in his eyes.

Quinn's no dummy; he knows where this is going. "You think Rodrigo might have something to do with Black's disappearance?" he asks.

I nod slowly, a constricting weight settling in my chest. "What if he's been hiding out in the hotel this entire time?" My stomach flutters. "Waiting for the right opportunity to make his move. And when the lights went out—boom!" I clap my hands loudly, startling Quinn. "He took it."

He eyes me as if stress has short-circuited my brain. "Isn't he a friend of yours?" he asks, squinting in confusion. "Do you really think he's capable of something like that?"

"After the past twenty-four hours, nothing would surprise me." I wipe my sweaty palms on the hem of my dress. "The last time I saw him, he wasn't himself. He was dark, angry, threatening even . . . I'm not saying he *did* anything. I don't know that. I'm just saying I'm worried, and it seems a little coincidental that Black is gone, and I haven't heard from Rodrigo."

Quinn doesn't know what to do with that information, and I don't, either.

"Let's just go to the attic," he says. "And hopefully we won't find Black dead and your pal holding the knife."

I shudder at the image that pops into my head.

To access the topmost floor, I have to use an ancient brass skeleton key that's been on my key ring for two years and used only twice. As I push the door open to a narrow wooden stairwell, a strong odor of cedar and mothballs hits us with force. We tread the rickety staircase carefully, ascending to the attic in single file.

There isn't much headroom up here, but Quinn can stand upright without stooping. The walls aren't as well insulated as the rest of the hotel, so we can hear Larry's roar loud and clear.

I'm searching for more light switches, feeling the knotty pine of the wall panels, worried they might not withstand the force of the winds. The wide-plank floorboards creak under our collective weight as we cross the room together. While the dark atmosphere is undeniably creepy, there's also something kind of romantic about it. We're far away from prying eyes, alone in the dim light, hunting for a priceless work of art and a potential fugitive.

Romantic notions soon give way to reality when I realize the herculean task in front of us. If we're going to find this mystery painting, we'll have to search maybe a hundred boxes. They're piled haphazardly on top of each other. Many are coated with mildew. Others are draped in cobwebs. The dust is making my allergies act up, which is totally not sexy, but what's a girl to do? Cool girls sneeze, too, which I do—loudly. And bless Quinn, who blesses me.

"Attorney Black, are you here?" I call out.

No answer.

Quinn's eyes dart about as he peeks in corners and around piles of boxes. "Definitely not here," he says. "But how are we going to search this place for a painting? It's packed with crap."

Quinn realizes what I've already determined. Besides the boxes, sheets are draped over antique furniture and God knows what else. There are lots of lamps and old box fans that couldn't compete with the cooling power of AC.

"We don't have a ton of time," I say, "so let's assume this painting is pretty big if it's valuable, and focus only on the larger boxes. We should check under all these sheets, too."

"I don't think we should assume bigger is better," Quinn says, then pauses. "I mean, sometimes it is." He smiles.

I cringe. "Are you making a sex reference right now? Really?" His embarrassment is enough for me to give him a slight smile, to let him know I'm teasing. "Okay, you're right. It could be small and pricey," I say. "I'm just trying to narrow it down, but whatever, let's just start looking."

Quinn nods.

We begin on opposite sides of the room, shuffling boxes around as quietly as we can and peeking under drop cloths. It doesn't take long to feel frustrated. We could be here for days.

George's paraphernalia are an amusing distraction, though. I occasionally get lost examining the odd figurines and artifacts scattered throughout the space. Every piece is a curiosity, but a solitary box tucked in the corner draws my attention. It's separate from the others, like it's been abandoned, and maybe that's what attracts me to it. I kneel down in front of the box, brushing dust that flies right into my eyes. *Ugh.*

Carefully, I lift the cover, hoping against all odds that the painting will magically appear. Instead, I let out a disappointed sigh. Inside are just a bunch of old scrapbooks, family photo albums, a collection of personal memories that aren't related to my search. But the Bishop family is so bizarre and their history so murky, I can't resist taking a look. It's difficult to picture crazy Vicki, glamorous Faith, and hardened Iris as young children, but here they are.

As I riffle through the yellowed pictures encased behind tacky plastic film, snapshots of George's younger years pass through my hands. He was handsome in his youth. Plenty of photos appear to show a blissful childhood growing up in the glory days of this hotel: three sisters playing on the rocky beach, looking super cute and innocent. I see them posing on the grass and the porch and selling lemonade to the guests. What turned them from these sweet creatures into a gun-toting maniac, an ex-con, and a somewhat aloof model who seems to hide behind her good looks? It makes me feel sad for them—even Vicki, who's taken me hostage. Are these the early stages of Stockholm syndrome? When you read a lot, you learn a lot, which is how I know about the feelings of trust, even affection, that some victims of kidnapping or hostage taking can feel toward a captor.

Another dusty album has photos of the Bishop sisters in their teens. There's Vicki, dressed to the nines in a slinky outfit, probably on her way to a school dance, her hair somehow defying gravity in every shot. Faith has a few magazine cutouts from her early days as an aspiring model—local stuff mostly, small department store ads, and one for a sporting goods shop where she convincingly poses as a bass fisherman.

A picture of Iris shows her holding a certificate of achievement for a math competition. English was my best subject; numbers make my head spin. Would Quinn think less of me if he knew I got my GED, but never a diploma? I hope not, but my choice carries a stigma that no certificate can erase.

I'm taking too much time, but as I return the album to the box, a loose piece of paper falls out, fluttering to the floor. Even in low light, I can tell it's an old newspaper clipping. I pick it up carefully, feeling the brittle paper crinkle between my fingers.

The headline reads: FATAL CAR CRASH NEAR FAMOUS PRECIPICE HOTEL. The photo of a white car looks vaguely familiar to me, its front end completely demolished against a tree.

As I read the article, my hands begin to quiver.

More details have been released about a deadly crash Tuesday night on Route 187 that claimed one person's life.

Washington County sheriff's deputies say the crash involved a Volkswagen GTI that veered off the road near the entrance to the Precipice Hotel.

Investigators say the driver went off the right side of the roadway and lost control, causing the car to go into a 180-degree turn facing north before leaving the road, where it collided with a tree.

The crash was reported around 6:30 P.M.

Deputies are not releasing the identity of the victim pending notification of the family. The cause of the crash is still under investigation. No other injuries were reported.

I've spent long enough studying the picture to catch Quinn's attention. He comes over and kneels beside me, perching his hand on my shoulder. I hardly register his touch.

"What's going on?" he asks.

"This car," I tell him. "I've seen it. I know it."

"How? That article looks ancient." His probing eyes search mine as if I may be delusional. And there's a date at the bottom. I might not be great at math, but it doesn't take long to figure out this article is thirty years old.

"I'm telling you, I've *seen* this car before," I insist.

And that's when it hits me. As soon as the realization takes hold, I'm ready to go—on the hunt now for something other than lawyers and artwork. Quinn trails me down the stairs to the second-floor hallway. We come to a stop facing a wall of staff photos that have been hanging here for years.

There's the photo of Sam in the kitchen with a stack of freshly washed dishes to his right and his mom, our former cook, Olga, beaming at his side. But it's the photograph next to it that I want Quinn to see. I hold a newspaper clipping up to the image for a point of comparison, and Quinn gets it right away.

"That could be the same car," he says, as if he's just made some great discovery.

I resist the urge to say *no shit*.

Quinn takes a closer look at the photograph. "Who's the girl?" he asks, his gaze lingering, examining her near-flawless features as though entranced. "She's pretty. Reminds me of you, actually."

I feel myself blush, but I don't need to look. I've seen this photograph enough times to practically have it memorized. "I don't see it," I say.

Quinn studies the picture for a second time before gazing deeply into my eyes. "I don't think you see yourself the way I do," he tells me. "You do look like her, Charley. But you're more than just pretty. You're a beautiful soul."

Now my whole body is red from embarrassment, and I'm totally overwhelmed. Nobody has said anything that sweet and kind to me in a long time, maybe ever, unless my nana counts.

"I've always related to her . . . a young, kind of sad maid from a different time." I check the date on the newspaper clipping again. "Now I think I know when—thirty-some years ago."

"Well, she's about your age here, and she *definitely* looks like you."

A sudden feeling of vertigo overwhelms me. This isn't the first time someone in this family has remarked that I look like a former maid. My throat goes completely dry.

"Your mom—well, Vicki—she kind of said the same thing to me. This must be who she was referring to when she told me I looked like a girl who used to work here."

A tingle rushes from my feet to the top of my head. Why didn't I think of it before? I stop breathing, and it's not from Quinn's compliment. I feel an even deeper connection to this girl than I did all the times I passed her photograph while vacuuming the hallway. She is me. I am her. We are the same. Chambermaids. Young women. Victims.

I'm starting to put a lot of puzzle pieces together, and I don't like the picture it's forming.

"Quinn," I say, my breath sputtering, "I think this is the same person from the newspaper, which means she *died* in this car crash." I hold up the clipping for reference. "You agreed it looks like her car."

Quinn compares the two images. "I said it could be, but I'm not sure. Even so, what does that have to do with anything? I mean, not to sound cold, but it doesn't help us find Black—or the painting."

"It's not about that," I tell him, trying not to be impatient. "I think this is Christine," I whisper.

His face screws up with confusion. "Who's Christine?" he asks.

I see no reason not to tell him. "Vicki told me I looked a lot like a maid who worked here named Christine. And I think she and your grandfather may have had an affair—I don't know the details, but there was something between them, I'm sure of it." I intentionally omit that his grandfather was a predator who wanted to sleep with me as well, and that it's possible Christine wasn't a willing partner. Quinn's had enough family disillusionment for one day. "And just before the lights went out, Iris alluded to *two* secrets—one about you and the other about *a maid*. And let's not forget about the poem on the mirror—something about atoning for the past, for something *they did*."

"So?"

"So?" I say, surprised he's not getting it. "There's some big secret about a maid who had a fling with your grandfather. Maybe there was anger, rage, who knows what, and then it looks like she died an untimely death, and they saved the article about it. So . . . what if this car crash *wasn't* an accident?"

Chapter 39

I feel numb as we head down the hallway, back on the lookout for Brenda Black and the valuable painting. We have plenty more rooms to search, but Quinn's a lot more focused on this mission than I am. My thoughts are still whirling about Christine. There was a time I wanted to know *more* about these Bishop sisters, and now part of me wishes I knew less.

Quinn doesn't seem to be buying the idea that his aunts (or his mothers—Lord, how confusing for him!) could harbor a dark and nefarious past. But I have no trouble believing it, especially now that I've experienced Vicki's erratic ways. Who knows what she's capable of underneath that phony, friendly veneer. Mrs. Calm, Cool, and Collected is really Cunning, Calculating, and Crazy.

We check all the unoccupied rooms—no sign of Black. So far, our search is a bust, as is the painting hunt. There's a lot of artwork hanging on the walls, but most of it is junk. You don't need a degree in art history to know that.

I can feel Quinn's disappointment as we head to the staircase. But before we go down, the fire alarm on the second-floor landing catches my eye, and I remember I have another mission. Since I can't very well pull it and justify my actions to Quinn, I need a way to make setting it off look like an accident.

Nothing comes to mind, and we're getting closer to the stairs. I could miss my chance. We're five feet away from the alarm when an idea comes to me. There's one thing that I could do that would make pulling it seem inadvertent, but if I think about it one second longer, I'm going to lose my nerve.

Taking Quinn completely by surprise, I push him up against the wall, almost dislodging an old framed photo that's behind him. I hesitate for half a second at most. I can't believe I'm doing this, but when I see the look in Quinn's eyes—a flash of disbelief along with a spark of desire—I know it's worth it.

Moving quickly before I can talk myself out of it, I press my lips against his. At first I do it as a necessary distraction, but then I feel the warmth of his body, the soft brush of his breath, and I melt into him. The kiss deepens as Quinn wraps his arms around me. My lips slowly part, allowing his tongue to gently caress mine. We begin to explore each other, his hands running up and down my back, pausing at my waist, grasping hold of my clothes as though he wants to tear them off. I'm momentarily swept away by the rush of unexpected feelings. Eventually, the turbulence of our wild kiss subsides, we catch ourselves, and during that pause, Quinn pulls away.

"Whoa now, that was quite a surprise," he says breathlessly, a huge smile on his face. "Maybe not the best time and place, but *wow*." His face lights up with an expression that begs for more. He pulls me against his body, and I go willingly.

Much as I'd like to, I can't let this go on forever. I have a job to do. Luckily, Quinn's back is up against the wall when I pretend to stumble, so it looks like I need to steady myself by grasping hold of anything within reach, which just happens to be the plastic lever of the fire alarm. I pull down. A piercing wail erupts above our heads and all around us. Lights over our exit signs start flashing. Quinn cups his ears.

"Oh shit—how do I shut this off? I totally screwed up!" I scream, thinking my performance is good enough to sell it as an accident. I actually know how to shut it off. There's a breaker I can flip, Rodrigo showed me, but Bree needs time to enact her plan. Unfortunately, I don't believe the alarm is connected to our mostly volunteer fire department, so I'm not counting on anybody else coming to our rescue. We found this out when a little kid pulled it a few weeks ago and no fire trucks showed up. George didn't have enough time to fix the issue before he died.

The continued wail of the alarm makes it hard to think, let alone hear, but we both turn our heads when a loud commotion—shouting, screaming, crashing—manages to cut through the noise. I know what's going on, but Quinn does not. While my ears are bleeding, I half expect to hear a gunshot.

Quinn shifts into autopilot, breaking away from me and moving toward the disturbance downstairs. I don't want him charging into danger, so I grab his hand and pull him back toward me.

"CHARLEY," he screams to be heard over the continued screeching. "Let's pick this up later, okay?"

But I don't let go. It's not great that he thinks I'm some sort of deranged nympho who wants to keep kissing while the alarm is going off and there's a disturbance downstairs, but I feel obligated to keep him alive.

"Don't go. It could be dangerous!" I shout.

"I have to," he says. "It's my family down there."

And that's when I know Quinn will eventually put the betrayal behind him. Family is everything, and as strange as these circumstances are and as weird as this family is, I'm genuinely happy for him. But I'm not thrilled about what he's running into.

He tries to slip away, but I apply some force to hold him back. "Let's at least go slowly," I scream. "Don't forget, Vicki has a GUN."

Oh, my ears. I hate this plan, but I do hope it works. I've had enough of being a prisoner.

Quinn agrees reluctantly, letting me set the pace down the stairs, which I make frustratingly slow. As we reach the bottom step, the struggle seems to have subsided.

The alarm, however, has not. I want to shut the blasted thing off, but I can't leave Quinn alone when I don't know if everything is all right. But then we see Bree, her back to us, standing at the entrance to the alcove. Her clothes are disheveled, her shirt is torn, but she has it—she's holding the gun.

The tension leaves my body like I've sprung a leak, and now I think it's safe to leave Quinn. I race to the office, and a moment later, there's silence. Thank God!

When I return to the alcove, it's quite the sight. Vicki is sitting in an oversize plush chair, slumped forward. Her tiny frame in such a large piece of furniture makes her look sadly defeated, childlike even. There's a nasty scrape on her chin, but other than that, she seems unharmed. The other sisters, and Hope, look relieved. Oliver looks the same as before, as if nothing has happened.

"Bree is our hero," Iris thunders, grinning triumphantly, her hands together in prayer, the Jesus fish tattoo on her arm catching my eye.

Being the dutiful son, Quinn flashes a conflicted look at Bree before taking gentle hold of his mother's hand. "Mom, are you okay?" he asks.

Mom. That's another good sign he'll forgive his family.

"I'm fine. I'd be better if I had my gun, but Bree went all commando on me. I think I pulled a hamstring."

Vicki stands, rubbing the back of her leg like she's a lame horse.

"I'm sure your Pilates studio can live without you for a while," Faith says.

"All right, everyone, let's settle down," Bree says. "I'm in charge now."

Bree motions for Vicki to retake her seat, the gun being an effective tool for ensuring compliance. When that's done, Bree fishes the plastic bag containing the belladonna out of Vicki's pocket. "I'll give this to the police when they get here," she says.

Iris speaks up. "How about you give it to me now, and I'll go make my darling sister a nice warm cup of *tea.*"

Quinn bristles beside me. "Come on, Aunt Iris," he says. "Have a little empathy, will you? Obviously, my mom is under a lot of strain."

"Thank you, son," says Vicki, brushing her hair to one side and sitting up straighter, as if trying to recover a shred of her dignity.

"Yeah, I'm not sure you should be calling me that . . . I don't even know if I should still be calling you Mom," Quinn says, wounding Vicki further.

A smear of blood on Vicki's torn white shirt, through which I can see flashes of her bra, adds insult to injury.

"But I suppose I'll always just be Aunt Iris."

"Please, everyone, now isn't the time for this," Bree pleads. "We just need to regroup and refocus."

Out of nowhere, Oliver says, "Well, this sure has been interesting, but now it's come to a head, so if you'll all excuse me, I'd like to go to bed." He lets out a big yawn to emphasize his need.

Vicki nods in vigorous agreement. "That's exactly what I want to do as well. I need to shower and get out of these gross clothes, and then I could use a good night's sleep," she says, moving to her feet.

Bree pushes her down with some force.

"That's not going to happen," she says, brandishing the weapon. "We can't let you have free range in the hotel, not when you clearly have a few screws loose."

Vicki snorts. "I'm perfectly sane, thank you very much."

"Mom, I think all of your conspiracy theories have warped your sense of reality," Quinn says with heartfelt compassion. "You see nefarious plots everywhere, including here. Chances are, some guest left that bag of belladonna behind, and Charley didn't see it when she cleaned the room."

I hold my tongue. I'm good at my job and would have found that baggie if it had been in the room before Vicki and Todd moved in, that's for sure. But it's more important that we keep Vicki contained, because she's dangerous.

Vicki groans dramatically, clutching her head, seeking any sympathy that might get tossed her way. Nobody bites.

"I might have a concussion," she moans. "I need to change my clothes and go lie down."

"Actually, you're not supposed to lie down if you have a concussion," Hope says.

A few end tables are knocked over, as well as an armchair, adding to the general disarray of the alcove. Perhaps Vicki hit her head in the scuffle. But she's not getting any special treatment from us, that's for sure.

"We'll get clothes for you," Bree says, "and let's move into the Great Room. This place is a mess."

One I'll have to clean, I think.

"Charley, can you get a fire started for us?" Bree asks. "And we need something to tie Vicki up."

"Tie me up? Are you insane?"

"That's sort of your territory," says Iris, who stands off to the side with her hands on her hips.

"There's some garden twine in the supply closet in the kitchen," I say. "We could use that if you think it'll work."

Vicki's eyes shoot daggers at me. "Well, you can kiss your job goodbye, young lady," she says.

Quinn steps forward. "Mom, really, this isn't the time to be making employment decisions."

"Oh, whatever," I say, while silently appreciating Quinn coming to my defense. "This isn't the safest working environment anymore."

"Agreed," says Bree.

Quinn takes charge. "Here's what I think we should do. Ollie, you took the phones earlier. Go get them. We need them back. We've got a missing person, my mom is clearly . . . um . . . not herself . . . and none of us knows for sure what happened to Todd. Let's get the police, and they can help us sort all this out."

"Hear, hear!" Iris and Faith say in unison. Must be a sister thing.

Bree appears distracted but doesn't oppose the plan. She inspects her torn shirt. "I want to get these clothes off as well," she says. "I'll get changed. Oliver can grab something for his aunt to wear when he goes for the phones. Let's all reconvene back here in twenty minutes."

Oliver starts to leave. He probably wants his job over and done with so he can go to his room.

Vicki reaches out, grabbing the arm of his shirt before he can depart. "Oliver, do *not* get those phones. I don't want the police here until I have answers about what happened to your uncle Todd."

Oliver takes a step back, but as he does, Hope comes forward. "He's our son, and he'll listen to us, not you."

To this, Oliver finally has some reaction—he looks utterly bewildered.

"Oliver, do not get those phones," Vicki repeats, baring her teeth at Hope as if she's grown fangs.

"Oliver, go get them now," says Hope.

This goes on several rounds, with Oliver looking to his mom, then to his aunt, and back again, unsure whose order to take.

In the end, it's Iris who settles the matter. "Ollie, go. Do as your mother says. And grab something for your aunt Vicki to wear while you're at it."

This time, Oliver doesn't hesitate. He's off like a rocket. Nobody, not even Vicki, counters the challenging look in Iris's eyes.

"What do we do with Vicki?" I ask.

Before I know it, Bree presses the gun into my hand. The cold steel is foreign in my grasp. I'm surprised by the heft of it, too. The weight makes everything feel all the more real—and terrifying.

"What do you want me to do with this?" My voice squeaks.

"I trust you, Charley. You're in charge while I'm gone. You do know how to use this thing, right?"

"I know that you pull the trigger," I say in a way that conveys my lack of experience.

Before I can offer anything more, Iris crosses the room, extending her hand for the weapon.

"You're not tough enough for this kind of job, sweetheart," she says. "I can take it from here."

Bree shakes her head vigorously. "Last thing we need is another Bishop sister with a loaded weapon. Charley's in charge while I'm gone. I know she can be tough as nails when she needs to be." She turns to me and continues, "Just hang on to it and keep things under control. I'll be back in twenty. Quinn, can you start a fire in the Great Room?"

"Sure," he says with the confidence of a former Boy Scout.

"Terrific," Bree continues. "Faith and Hope, get the twine from the supply closet and secure your sister. Iris, if you want to play pit bull, that's fine by me, but you'll do so with fists, not a firearm. Understood?"

Nobody objects, and Bree departs the alcove, leaving me behind holding a gun on my former boss and the mother of the boy I just kissed.

Vicki eyes me with pure disdain, making my skin crawl. "I can only imagine why my father raved about you so much," she says.

My face screws up with confusion. "What's that supposed to mean?" I ask.

"You know what it means," she says.

I don't feel like engaging, but I'm not about to let her bogus innuendo go unchallenged.

"For your information, I *never* let him touch me," I say. "And way to go blaming the victim." I'm angry, but it's sad to see this powerful woman rendered helpless. "Look, I get it. You're pissed off . . . but you brought this on yourself, Vicki. We *had* to do something. You were threatening us, and we don't know what you're capable of."

At this, Vicki smiles. "Oh, Charley," she says as if I'm the dumbest person on the planet, "you have no idea how far I'll go to protect my family."

Chapter 40

Thirty minutes later, Bree returns to the alcove, looking refreshed. She's showered and changed into comfy clothes. I managed fine without her but hated pretty much every second of it. The gun feels extra heavy in my sweaty hand, and I'm eager to relinquish the weapon. On the plus side, Quinn said nothing about my holding his mom at gunpoint. Part of him was probably celebrating it.

Vicki and I were the only ones who didn't take advantage of the lull to change outfits and freshen up. My conversation with my former boss/captor during that time was strained at best, and I'm relieved that Bree is back in charge.

She comes over and unhesitatingly takes the gun from me, no questions asked. Relief washes over me the moment the gun is back in her possession. Bree gives me a faint smile, sending a quiet thank-you my way before shifting her focus to Vicki. Struggling in vain to break free from the twine restraints that Faith and Hope have tightly wrapped around her, Vicki grunts with every twist, turn, and pull, only succeeding in driving the binds deeper into her flesh.

The sight of Vicki tied to a dining room chair, wrapped in knotty green twine like a straitjacket, brings a satisfied smile to Bree's lips. I'm sitting on a chair across from Vicki, watching as Hope and Faith check over their handiwork, testing the knots in different places to ensure their durability. With the prisoner tied up, the gun must feel needlessly aggressive because Bree tucks the weapon into the back pocket of her jeans—hopefully, with the safety on.

After giving one final and enraged thrust, Vicki explodes, "I swear to God, you untie me this instant, or you all will regret it!"

Sitting on the staircase landing in the Great Room, just outside the alcove, Iris runs a hand through her damp hair. "Why don't you pipe down and give us all a break until the police get here?"

Quinn, listening nearby, tosses another log onto the roaring fire before rejoining the group. "Speaking of the police, where is Oliver? How long does it take to get some clothes and our phones? He's been gone for ages now."

"No shit," says Vicki, using her eyes to draw attention to her ripped and bloodstained attire.

"I thought you were going to check on him when you went to get the twine?" Faith snaps at Hope.

"No, you said *you* were going to check when you went to get us some water."

She points to the pitcher filled with lemon slices, cucumber, and ginger. Faith has on a new, figure-flattering outfit consisting of a deep blue button-down shirt paired with hip-hugging black pants. And did she put on lipstick? Leave it to Faith to broadcast to the world that she's still attractive and stylish, even during a crisis.

Vicki spits out a laugh. "You are both idiots," she bellows. "If you recall, I'm the one who suggested Oliver have an escort to the bathroom for his own safety. Black is still somewhere in this hotel, and you just let him wander off alone. A fourteen-year-old left to the clutches of a potential murderer? You should be ashamed of yourselves!"

Hope flinches. "There's no reason to think Black would harm Oliver."

Faith's shoulders sag in silent disagreement. "No, I specifically told you that I was worried . . . and you said you would check on him."

Iris stands, looking up the stairs, craning her neck as if it might give her a view of the second floor. "Prison brain," she says flatly. "We'd get it all the time. Stress does that, you know? And in a group setting, that kind of collective amnesia can work like a virus, spreading from one person to another until someone snaps the spell and remembers the thing that everyone else forgot."

Faith pushes past Iris and hurriedly ascends the stairs. When she's halfway up, Oliver emerges from the kitchen as silent as a cat on the prowl. He steps into the center of the room, shoving potato chips into his mouth, with crumbs falling as he chews. He stuffs his free hand back into the crinkly bag for another scoop.

Faith catches sight of him and swiftly spins on her heels, graceful as a gymnast on a balance beam, before rushing down the stairs to Oliver.

Hope hastens to his side as well, getting there first. "Ollie, thank God," she cries, drawing him into a smothering embrace, which he resists, pulling away so he can continue munching on his snack unperturbed.

Hope cocks her head in confusion. "Where have you been?" she asks.

Oliver lifts the chip bag in response as if to suggest the answer should be obvious. "My stomach was grumbly and I wanted something crumbly," he explains before shoveling another handful of chips into his mouth.

That might be his cutest rhyme yet, I think.

Faith arrives at his side, clearly thankful. "But you've been gone for a while now. What took you so long?" she asks.

"I've been around," Oliver replies with a shrug. "Nobody noticed me, so I grabbed a snack."

Hope frowns. "Ollie, you know how I feel about processed food. It's basically poison," she says.

"And why didn't you tell us you were back?" Faith wants to know.

Oliver responds in typical fashion—with a blank stare.

Iris comes over to him. "What a truly strange bird you are," she says, ruffling Oliver's hair on her way to the fire.

"What about the phones, Oliver?" Bree wants to know.

"And my clothes?" Vicki adds, turning as far as she can in her chair to address Oliver directly.

"Clothes are still upstairs," Oliver says. "I took a hike to get something you'd like, but I didn't know what that would be, so sadly you get nothing from me."

Vicki rolls her eyes.

"The phones, Ollie," Quinn wants to know. "Why didn't you at least bring those?"

"They're still in the safe," he says, talking with a mouthful of chips. "I don't have the code."

"Oh shit," Faith sighs.

"Charley, can you get us the master code?" Bree asks.

"Only George knew it," I say. "He never trusted the staff enough to share it with us."

"And only *I* know where my father keeps it," Vicki says, triumphantly. "And I'm not about to tell you all."

I deflate. "Sorry, I probably should have mentioned that. I figured Oliver must have known the code, or he wouldn't have gone upstairs. I guess I was rattled and wasn't thinking it through."

"Prison brain," Iris says again.

Bree removes the gun from her back pocket and points it at Vicki. The room lapses into an uneasy silence. "Give us the code," she insists in a low voice.

Vicki's face shows firm resolve as she stares down Bree. It's as if she's challenging her to pull the trigger.

"Or what?" Vicki asks. "Are you going to shoot me in front of everyone? Cold-blooded murder with how many witnesses?"

"Six, Aunt Vicki," Oliver says, his words garbled as he chews.

"I'm pretty sure she wasn't looking for an actual number, Ollie," Quinn says with a shake of his head.

All eyes are on Bree, waiting with bated breath to see how far she'll take it. There's a stony standoff for several beats before Bree stuffs the gun back into the pocket of her jeans. A collective relief sweeps the room.

It's short-lived. We all tense again as Bree extracts a large folding knife from her other pocket. Where she got this knife, I have no idea. But it makes sense for a woman on the run to be armed, so I don't question it much. As she unfolds the sharp blade, it locks into place with a click. A devious gleam lights up Bree's eyes as she approaches Vicki, holding the weapon lancelike before her.

Vicki's arrogance drains in a flash, replaced with a look of terror as Bree moves the blade closer to her heart. Iris cries out, "No, don't!"

Vicki swallows a scream like she's gulping down her final breath. She closes her eyes tightly as Bree slides the knife underneath the twine. Then, with one strategically placed upward thrust, the sharp blade slices through the string holding Vicki to the chair as easily as if she cut a stick of butter.

She cuts again, releasing more tension from the twine. At last Vicki can move her arms, but she keeps them still while Bree slices open the last remnants of her restraints.

With a final cut, Bree finishes the job, but the knife slips at an inopportune moment, and the blade's tip carves a thin nick into the palm of Bree's left hand, less than an inch long. A trickle of blood begins to seep from the small wound. Though it isn't a severe injury, there's enough oozing for Bree to rotate her palm to avoid staining the carpet.

Iris storms over to Bree, ignoring the injury, and gets right in her face with fire in her eyes. She points an angry finger at Vicki. "Why'd you free her?" she challenges. "She's my sister. I don't want her dead, but I don't think she should be roaming around the hotel."

"This has gone too far," Bree answers calmly. "Someone is going to get hurt. I guess I needed a little pushback to come to my senses. And I trust we've made our point clear, isn't that right, Vicki? No more weapons, no more hostages or house arrests. We're all in this mess together."

"Speaking of mess," I say, pointing to Bree's injured left hand, "that looks like it hurts. You're going to get blood all over your clean clothes."

"Serves her right," Vicki gripes, spitting out her disgust as she rises to her feet. With a dance-worthy shake and shimmy, she dislodges the last bits of twine from her body.

I examine Bree's injured hand with a slight grimace at the sight of the blood. "I'll go get the first-aid kit in the office."

Meanwhile, Quinn approaches with a wad of tissues taken from a box put out for guests.

Bree presses the wad to her cut, applying pressure to stanch the bleeding. "Thank you," she says quietly to Quinn and me.

I depart for the office amidst the background noise of Bree and the others cajoling Vicki into giving up the code so we can get our phones. We have a mysterious death and a woman missing; we need the police. As I grab the first-aid kit, though, something unusual catches my eye. The antique typewriter by the reception desk is where it's always been, but for the first time in my recollection, there's a piece of paper in the roller.

Naturally, I take a closer look. Something tells me to be on guard, and my instincts prove correct. As I read the typewritten note, the room tilts as if the hotel has come off its foundation. I reread it to make sure I'm not mistaken. I'm not. The ominous message hits me with the force of a punch. Is the tarot about to come true?

I stagger into the Great Room in a daze, holding the first-aid kit in one hand and a single sheet of white paper in the other. I'm sure I'm as pale as a vampire. I feel unstable on my feet.

"What's wrong?" Bree asks with alarm.

I present the paper as an offering for anyone to take. Since Iris is the closest, she snatches it from my trembling hand.

"I found it in the old typewriter, in the reception area. The typewriter still works, but we don't use it—although someone did. They left us this."

Iris holds the paper up and reads aloud for all to hear: "You must confess your sins tonight, or another dies before the light. And if you're looking for attorney Black, I suggest you check out back."

Larry's blustery winds and pelting rain fill the gaping silence that follows.

Bree scans the room, seeking answers she doesn't find in the blank stares looking back at her.

I speak up. "There are only two ways to get to the typewriter in the office—through an unlocked door by the reception area and through a door in the kitchen."

One by one, everyone turns to look at young Oliver, who stands remarkably self-possessed and composed. Potato chip crumbs decorate
his clothes like confetti, evidence of his trip to the kitchen during his
extended absence from the group.

Chapter 41

Before you accuse Oliver, there are other possible explanations." Hope states her case from the center of the Great Room, the roaring fire crackling behind her. But my verdict is in: It seems obvious that Oliver snuck into the office through the kitchen, and I have no doubt Bree is on the same page.

"And what other explanation might there be?" Bree asks.

Faith's rage comes on like a gas stove catching flame. She steps in front of her son as if to shield him from further charges. "It could have been Black herself, for all we know." Faith tosses out the idea while ignoring things like logic and reason.

Meanwhile, Vicki couldn't care less about any of this. Her focus is on herself—as always. She examines her skin for any damage the twine wrapping might have caused.

"I'm going to go get changed," Vicki announces with queenly contempt as she breaks for the staircase. "I want out of these ripped, bloody clothes this instant."

Iris returns the paper to me before maneuvering to block Vicki's way out. "Not without someone to watch over you," she insists. "You can't be trusted."

Vicki's dumbfounded, eyeing her sister as though she's gone mad. "Don't be cruel, Iris—at least, no more than you've already been."

But Iris isn't budging.

Quinn steps forward. "I'll get you something to wear," he says, eager to keep the peace between his two moms.

Iris relents with a huff, stepping aside to grant him access to the stairs like she's a nightclub bouncer.

Up he goes, and my eyes follow him as he retreats. Before I know it, my mind jumps back to our moment in the upstairs hallway—the taste of his lips, the lemony smell of his skin. I shake my head to refocus on the situation at hand.

Hope steps forward, looking ready to make an announcement. "We would have heard him typing," she begins. "We've all been in this room. We're not far from the office. Someone would have heard the clacking of an old typewriter. We didn't hear anything, so it couldn't be him."

"Nice try," Iris says. "But obviously someone typed it, and nobody heard it, so that doesn't prove anything. Oliver is our poet—so there's no question he's the author, just like he wrote the poem on the mirror. With the storm, the winds, the yelling, and our *distractions* . . ."—she glances over at Vicki, who sulks on the bottom step with her head resting against the railing—"it's no great surprise we didn't hear the typewriter."

As if to prove that point, a particularly loud gust of wind rumbles through the hotel, causing the timbers to creak and groan like we're in the belly of an ancient ship.

I'm used to Bree taking the lead, but she's busy applying a bandage from the first-aid kit to her wound. I step forward.

"Hey, I just want to add something." My voice sounds uncertain, but I've got to speak my mind. "Most of us have been in and out of here at some point over the last hour or so. And there's a back staircase that runs from the third floor to the kitchen, so someone could have gone that way to access the office."

While everyone considers my contribution, Quinn returns to the Great Room with clothes for Vicki. She sends him an appreciative smile before heading to the bathroom to change.

Iris follows to stand guard.

"What did I miss?" Quinn asks, reading the gravity of our expressions.

"I was explaining how anybody in this room could have written the new poem, although most of us are pretty sure it was Oliver."

But a pulse of doubt stabs me. Maybe the author is someone who *isn't* in this room. I still don't have my phone, but I doubt a message from Rodrigo will be waiting for me when I get it. Could he be hiding in one of the hotel's many rooms or various dark corners? Was he waiting for an opportunity to take revenge against Black? I can't imagine him writing the poems, unless he did so to keep us distracted and throw us off his trail, like Black suggested criminals often do. I don't believe Rodrigo could be a criminal, but I can't dispel the notion entirely.

Quinn takes the poem from my hand. "Ollie, did you type this?" he asks.

"No," Oliver says blandly.

Quinn shrugs and heads over to the fire. For a moment, I think he's going to burn the paper, but instead, he gives a red-hot log a few quick jabs with the poker until a flame catches. "If Ollie says he didn't do it, I believe he didn't do it."

I have to admit, Quinn is convincing. I want to agree, but at that moment, Vicki and Iris return to the alcove from the bathroom. I suppress a laugh as I gawk at the ridiculous outfit Quinn chose for his mother. Still, I guess Vicki packed it, so this Jolly Rancher–colored lime-green velour tracksuit with white piping on the legs is technically her choice on some level. Something tells me that Quinn searched out the most embarrassing ensemble as petty retribution for his mother's deception. Score one for the kid.

Both sisters get a quick debrief, and Iris, no surprise, isn't buying Oliver's denial. "So what? We just take his word for it, then? Well, that was easy," she says sarcastically, wiping her hands mockingly as if the issue is all cleaned up. "The boy speaks in *rhymes*. Come on, people, don't be dense."

Bree finally weighs in. "I think we're all ignoring two critical things."

All eyes, mine included, fall on her.

Vicki taps her foot impatiently. "Well, well, well . . . our little stowaway seems to have *all* the answers. And pray tell, what might those *very* important things be?" Despite her tone, she doesn't come across as very threatening in her ridiculous lime-green tracksuit. She reminds me of Oscar the Grouch, and I'd love nothing more than to plop her inside a trash can.

To Bree's credit, she doesn't take the bait. Somehow she remains calm and composed in the face of all this adversity. She counters Vicki's sentiments with a determined glare.

"Whoever is behind this, you Bishop sisters are being called upon to confess your sins," Bree reminds the room. "Both poems made it quite clear there's dirty laundry to air. If we want a chance to get out of this mess—whatever it's all about—you three need to start talking, and pronto."

Faith straightens. "Confess our sins?" She makes it sound like another death would be the preferred option. "And what's the second thing?" she asks.

Bree sets her hands on the back of the chair where Oliver is seated and says with foreboding, "We should do as the poem says and look out back for attorney Black."

Chapter 42

At last I've managed to take off this stupid scrub dress, but the replacement outfit isn't much of an upgrade. Now, I look like I'm auditioning for *Wicked Tuna*, wearing a yellow rain suit I found in the same supply closet where the twine is kept. Underneath, I have on jeans and a COOL AS A MOOSE T-shirt, the only clean and comfortable thing I had to wear. I still have the newspaper article from the attic with me, folded up and stuffed in my back pocket. I want to show it to Bree and get her take, but now isn't the time. We've got a missing person to find.

There were actually two of these Crayola-colored rain suits in the supply closet, and I've given the second one to Quinn. He and I make up the entire Attorney Black Search Team. At least I won't be the only walking banana around here. Bree is staying behind to watch over the sisters. If we take the poems as gospel, none of the Bishops are safe, and none can be trusted.

I also grabbed two flashlights with fresh batteries—one for me, and one for Quinn, who is off somewhere putting on his rain gear. As I slip the flashlights into the front pocket of my rain suit, I notice the bandaged cut to Bree's palm and the purplish bruise on her forearm. I remember her telling me how her ex-boyfriend, Jake, had gripped her arm with such force that he left that mark behind.

"What about Jake?" I ask her.

Bree eyes me, perplexed. "My boyfriend? What about him?"

"What if he traced you to this hotel, and *he's* the one who typed the note?" I suggest.

Bree's not buying it for a second. "Why would he play games with the Bishops or want to hurt Black? He doesn't even know them. If there's anybody besides the sisters who would want to hurt Black, my money would be on Rodrigo."

I nod grimly. "I've been worried about him, too."

"I've also started wondering about Quinn."

Bree tosses this out like an afterthought, while my stomach drops.

"Quinn?" I grimace at her innuendo. "You said he was all right, that you had good radar for crazy and he wasn't it. Why would you suspect him now?"

Bree shrugs. "The adoption bombshell changes things."

"What things? He's the most stable of the bunch, and besides, what would his motive be?" I ask.

Bree's ready with an answer. "Revenge. You've got to look at things from every angle, Charley, and you can't rule him out. Maybe he somehow discovered Iris is his mom, and he's gone a little haywire, or more than a little."

Shit. Now I wish I hadn't started the conversation.

Bree sees the concern on my face. "Don't stress," she tells me. "It's probably not him. Just watch yourself, is all. Don't fall too hard. I wouldn't trust anyone in this family."

Guess that's a point we can both agree on.

We meet up with Quinn in the Great Room. He may be yellow as a pencil, but he's still adorable. Glad I didn't make a promise to Bree about falling too hard. And the more I think about it, the more absurd it seems that Quinn could have anything to do with the threatening poems.

But I don't have time to dwell; I want this search over and done with. Judging by the antsy way Quinn's bouncing from foot to foot, he feels the same.

It's dreadful to think I'm voluntarily going out into the whipping winds and hard-driving rain that sounds more like hail. I'd much rather stay in the Great Room, which is now peacefully quiet. The fire is down to a low flame, with lots of red embers that give off plenty of heat.

Vicki is still in her green tracksuit, sipping brandy from a crystal snifter, the bottle on a table beside her. She's enjoying the comfort of a cushy chair set at an angle in front of the fireplace.

Iris lingers nearby, acting like a prison guard, hovering close to Vicki.

Hope passes us on her way to the kitchen and announces in a surprisingly lighthearted voice, "Faith and Ollie are resting in our room. I'm going to start dinner." Her manner certainly doesn't fit the circumstances. Instead of wishing us luck or showing even slight concern, she floats into the kitchen without a care—no encouraging word for us, or Black, for that matter.

Quinn sneaks me a suspicious glance. "She's oddly jovial," he says in a low voice. "I think I know where Ollie gets his emotional detachment." He places his arm over my shoulder, bracing himself while reaching for the door handle. "Ready?" he asks.

I give him one quick nod—no turning back now.

The moment he opens the door, a blast of wet, cold air and a smattering of blown leaves hits us hard. I'm momentarily stunned at the storm's ferocity but manage to step outside. The wind feels alive. It spins, darts, dips, and lifts with the cunning quickness of a predator. When I turn my head one way for protection, the gale slams into me from the opposite side. There's no avoiding it or blocking out the rushing sound of the storm's power.

Hurricane winds whip up sticks and small stones, hurling them at us from all directions. I'm forced to shield my face with my hands or risk injury. We have to lean into the wind to advance. Rain streams off my hood like a waterfall. The flashlight in my hand casts a feeble glow on the soggy ground, but following Quinn is easy. His bright yellow raincoat is a beacon in the dark.

Even with the wind's steady rumble, I can still hear powerful ocean surf pounding against the rocky shoreline at the bottom of Gull Hill. No person in their right mind would be out here. If Black *is* out back, she's in serious trouble.

We pass cautiously over a tall pine tree that's become uprooted, just missing the hotel's beloved porch, where guests like to admire the breathtaking ocean views. But there's no sightseeing tonight. I aim my flashlight under the porch, where Black might have thought to take shelter, but all I can see is darkness and muddy earth.

I shout her name but get no reply. We have to keep looking.

We reach the spacious outdoor area behind the hotel, where, this time of year, we'd usually find the colorful Adirondack chairs. But even those large pieces of furniture would have become projectiles in this weather. Despite the protective gear I'm wearing, my cheeks feel red and raw. Quinn staggers as the wind pummels him. He wipes rain from his eyes, shouting instructions I can barely hear.

"Say that again?" I yell back, but he shakes his head while pointing to his ear. Damn. To speed up communication, he grabs my arm, dragging me forward with urgency toward the stairs built into the cliffside.

Hell, no. I am not going on those stairs in this weather. Turns out that's not even an option. Waves and wind have washed away a good portion of the staircase, making any descent to the shoreline treacherous.

Unfortunately, Quinn's undeterred. He yanks me to an area near the cliff's edge where a section of the wooden fencing has been knocked out. As he pulls me along, I struggle to maintain my footing on the wet grass. I understand now why he picked this spot. He wanted the quickest and easiest access to the edge of the drop-off.

Wisely, he keeps some distance to avoid a fatal fall, but he's not close enough to see down. Even leaning his body forward, he can't peer over the side, so he moves perilously close to the brink.

"Quinn, NO!" I shout, but either he can't hear me or he intentionally ignores my warning. A fierce blast of wind rips off the ocean, pushing Quinn off-balance. His arms flail as he fights to regain equilibrium on the waterlogged ground. His flashlight beam dances in the dark. I have a horrifying image of him tumbling to his doom, his scream unheard over Larry's wrath.

I pull him back, using all my might.

"It's NOT SAFE," I holler.

Quinn nods, which sends a torrent of rainwater cascading off his hood. "You're right," he yells back. "It'll be easier if I lie down on my stomach. Hold my ankles, so I can look down."

Before I can protest, Quinn is on his belly, sliding forward like a snake. I've no choice but to lie down and hold on as instructed. Luckily, a piece of the broken fence remains—a sturdy post buried deep into the ground—and I wrap my leg around it to provide more support. I'm trying not to drink puddles of rainwater while I hold on to Quinn. My flashlight lies on the ground next to me, and it isn't exactly where I want it, but I can't let go to redirect the beam.

I don't know if Quinn is being brave, stupid, or both. He keeps inching forward on his stomach. I try to tighten my grip, but my fingers are frozen, and the rain makes everything slippery. Summoning strength I didn't know I had, I manage to hold on while Quinn shimmies right up to the big plunge. He's close enough now to get his flashlight beam aimed directly down, illuminating what's over the edge.

For a second, I think we're going to be okay. Quinn's got his head and shoulders beyond the ledge of the cliff, surveying what's a hundred feet below while my grip holds steady. But then all of a sudden, his body jerks forward unexpectedly, straining my already tenuous grasp. The glow from his flashlight vanishes instantly, and I think I hear it clatter on the jagged rocks. I'm horrified when Quinn's body starts sliding forward, taking me with him.

I scream, my fingers digging into his flesh like talons, my feet searching for any purchase to try and arrest his slide. He's thrashing about, kicking his legs this way and that, instinctively fighting a losing battle against gravity. In the chaos, one of his heavy rain boots catches me hard on the cheek. A searing pain rakes across my face. I let out a loud yelp, but somehow manage to maintain my grip. I yank so hard that the tendons in my arms strain to the breaking point.

Quinn continues his slide. And then, as if my prayers are answered, he finds a foothold, digging his boot deeper into the soft earth. Our combined effort is enough to pull him safely from the ledge. He flops onto his back. Rainwater fills his mouth as he gasps for breath. I'm lying on my stomach close by, reeling from the shock of nearly losing him.

"She's down there!" Quinn's shrill voice carries over the booming waves and snarling winds.

My blood turns colder than the air. Flipping over onto my side, I adjust my flashlight on the ground until the light illuminates Quinn's pale face.

He gasps one more time, his chest heaving up and down. "Black," he spits out breathlessly. "I saw her, Charley. She's down there—on the rocks. She's dead. Black is dead!"

Chapter 43

We return to the hotel, drenched, my chapped cheeks badly scraped. Mud is caked on my forehead, rimmed around my eyes, and speckled throughout my matted hair. A smattering of grass clings to my skin and rain gear.

Quinn and I must look like soldiers returning from the battlefield. His eyes are especially haunted, sunken and sad. We don't bother disrobing in the foyer, instead allowing water to drip off our rain gear and onto the hardwood floor and carpet as we solemnly march into the Great Room, where the others are clustered by the fire, awaiting news.

Vicki and Iris rush Quinn, showering him with frantic attention as though competing for the Mother of the Year Award, which neither is likely to win.

"Honey, are you okay? What happened?" Iris asks, peering into Quinn's eyes like a neurologist performing an exam. Not to be out-done, Vicki touches his forehead as though he may have developed a fever after fifteen minutes in the wind and rain.

"I'm fine," he says, his eyes downcast. "Really, I'm fine." He moves away to get some space. "Attorney Black, on the other hand . . ." Quinn's voice cracks.

Vicki's hand flies to her mouth. "You found her? Is she all right?"

Iris puts an arm around her son's shoulders, but Quinn pulls away, shaking his head before moving over to me and taking hold of my hand.

He struggles to get the words out, choking on the emotion.

"I almost fell over the cliff trying to find her. Charley . . . she, she saved me."

Prison may have hardened Iris, but tenderness for her son shines brightly in her loving eyes. Vicki, too, is brimming with relief and gratitude—enough to embrace me. I'm too surprised to return the gesture.

"What the hell happened out there?" she asks.

"Quinn saw her," I explain. "She went over the cliff. She's down there, on the rocks . . . she's definitely dead."

Bree comes over as Vicki and Iris contemplate the unfathomable. "We've got to go down and get her," she insists.

Faith, who is listening nearby, agrees. "You can't know for sure she's gone."

"Nobody could survive that fall," Quinn tells her. "And there's no safe way down anymore. The storm blew out a good portion of the stairs."

Everyone sits pensively, absorbing this news, until Hope breaks the silence by offering to make some tea before dinner.

"Since there's nothing we can do, we'll just have to ride this out," she says before walking off to the kitchen, providing comfort in a way that makes sense to her—with a warm beverage. Faith goes with her.

No surprise, Oliver stays out of this. He's found a book to occupy himself. Iris, meanwhile, paces about the room like she's back in lockup, walking the yard. Vicki returns to her chair and the comfort of her brandy by the fire. She acts as though nothing calamitous has just occurred, to which Iris takes some exception.

"A woman is dead, and you're just relaxing by the fire? What's *wrong* with you?" she asks.

Vicki appraises her sister with slight bemusement, as though it were she who had taken the wrong approach to the crisis. "Iris, that woman is dead. You heard them. There's no way down there and nothing for us to do," Vicki says.

"We might not be able to get to her, but the police could. They have ropes, rescue equipment, ways to rappel down a cliff," Iris says. "So get your lazy, uncaring, scrawny little ass off that chair right this

instant, and go get us our phones! And if you don't, we'll tell the police
you hindered a potential rescue. She may still be alive down there, and
if they find her dead, you'll be partially responsible because you knew
she needed help, yet you prevented us from calling."

Vicki mutters a string of unpleasantries as she rises to her feet.
"Fine," she says brusquely. "I'll go get them, and you can call the police.
I suppose another body requires it. But nobody better mention a thing
about the belladonna, or mark my words: *you will regret it.*"

She marches off in a huff, stomping up the stairs, spilling brandy
onto the carpet runner with one particularly angry step. Iris trails
behind, likely to make sure her sister keeps her word.

Shortly afterward, Faith returns from the kitchen carrying a silver
platter with a teapot and several cups. "Let me know if anybody wants
cream or sugar," she says, pausing to look at the empty chair where
Vicki had been sitting. "Did I miss something?"

"Aunt Vicki is pissed, that's all you missed." Oliver doesn't bother
to look up from his book.

"Pissed about what?" asks Faith as she sets the tray on a table.

"Getting us our phones," Bree answers. "Vicki finally agreed. We
should be able to call the police soon."

"Well, it's about time," says Faith with authority. "But I doubt
they'll be able to get here very quickly. The storm is only getting worse.
At least dinner is almost ready, and there should be ample to share in
case help arrives." Faith flips her hair like she's proud of something
she's accomplished. "Poor Brenda Black," she adds, speaking with a
reverence I don't believe is authentic.

After Faith departs, Vicki and Iris come down the stairs, Vicki
clutching her Fendi bag full of phones. She hands them out one by
one, like holiday gifts: Quinn first, then Oliver, next me, Iris, and last
is Bree. It's like a magic trick, some kind of collective hypnosis. Without our phones, everyone was making eye contact, but the moment we
have them in our possession again, we're all hunched over our devices,
eyes glued to these small screens—me included.

It doesn't take long for the problem to emerge.

"I don't have a signal," Quinn announces.

"Me neither," Iris says morosely.

One by one, we all confirm that Larry must have taken out cell service.

"I'm not surprised," I say. "There's only one tower, and it's prone to outages in bad weather. But no worries—that's why we use Wi-Fi calling most of the time, so we can still get help."

It takes only a second for me to realize my mistake. Quinn apparently arrives at the same conclusion, for he marches over to the alcove and returns a moment later with the blown-apart router dangling from its useless cord.

"Yeah, I don't think the Wi-Fi will help us," he says without cheer.

"Motherfucker," Iris seethes at Vicki. "Look what you've done!"

"Me?" Vicki points to herself incredulously. "I didn't kill Black or Todd. I'm not the one who put belladonna in my dresser drawer. And I certainly didn't conjure up a hurricane to take out a cell tower."

"You can't take responsibility for anything, can you?" Iris hisses.

Faith and Hope emerge from the kitchen, taking in the unhappy faces surrounding them. "What now?" asks Faith.

"The phones don't work, no cell service. And since Rambo here took out the router, our phones are useless," Iris says, thumbing over to Vicki.

"Oh, Jesus, Vicki. Way to go," Faith says. "What do we do now? Just wait out the storm and hope that Black doesn't get washed out to sea?"

Vicki responds by pouring herself a refill from the bar cart. "Do you have a better idea?"

Faith rolls her eyes. "Hope is making linguine with eggplant and tomato sauce. I talked her into heating up some chicken kebabs that were in the freezer for anyone who's interested—they were already dead, so she didn't protest . . . too much. I suggest we all just have dinner and ride this out. The storm can't go on forever."

The suggestion of food sparks a realization that I'm actually famished, my stomach suddenly rumbling in anticipation. But as everyone moves from the Great Room to the dining room—Oliver included, book in hand—Bree pulls me aside. She drags me to a spot in the foyer near the reception desk where we can converse in private.

"What's wrong?" I whisper.

"First Todd, now Black . . . do you notice a pattern?" She looks around nervously, as if afraid to be overheard.

I hesitate, thinking it through. "Other than both of them being dead, no. What am I missing?"

"The poems make it seem like the Bishop sisters are in danger, and it's all about them, and yet they're all fine, and *other* people are dying," she whispers. My muscles tighten as her words sink in. "So far the victims *aren't* direct family members—which means *we* might be in much more danger than we thought."

"What do you suggest we do?" I ask, my voice barely audible.

"We have to follow the instructions in the last note," Bree says. "Specifically the part that says, 'confess your sins tonight, or another dies before the light'—and that other could be you or me." She points at us both with her bandaged hand. "If we're going to make sure that doesn't happen, then you and I have to put our collective heads together—fast—and find a way to get the secret sins out of these three bitches."

Chapter 44

The fire dims, and there are no dry logs left to rekindle it. We're waiting for the wet wood that Quinn dragged inside to dry out, hopefully before the dying flames are extinguished entirely.

Everyone's acting as though things are perfectly normal, which I find super unsettling considering there's a body at the base of Gull Hill. I can't wrap my brain around the fact that Brenda Black is dead. It's such a final thing. Breathing one second, gone the next. But I know from firsthand experience how death eventually comes for us all—unexpectedly for some, like my mother, Todd, and now attorney Black.

I'm trying not to let my thoughts get too dark as I help Bree set the table for dinner. I didn't dare look over the cliff's edge, so the picture I have of Black splayed out on the jagged rocks below—her neck twisted grotesquely, her skull caved in on one side—is only in my imagination. Quinn saw her, though, and he's been withdrawn ever since, keeping to himself in the Great Room and drinking whiskey. I think back to what Bree said about him. It's hard to imagine that sensitive Quinn wrote those poems just to spite his family, but I suppose anything is possible. Oliver continues to find his escape in a book, sitting in the same cushy chair in the dining room that Todd once occupied with his drink in hand. If we still had cell service, Ollie would be lost in a device instead.

Vicki seems comfortable in her lime-green tracksuit, drinking from her glass, fixated on her phone as though willing the internet connection to return. It takes ages in better weather to get service restored, so she'll be waiting a long time. Meanwhile, the only thing

Iris keeps her eye on is her sister. She's barely left Vicki's side, refusing to relinquish her role as a self-appointed watchdog.

Scattered across the table are open bottles of wine. Bree is hoping a few drinks may loosen lips and prompt confessions. Once again, my mind goes back to the tarot cards. If all goes well, our plan will, oddly enough, align with the reading—we'll cast light on the lies so the tower may fall and maybe we can prevent death from visiting us again.

Hope bubbles into the dining room, carrying a large serving bowl filled with steaming pasta. The aroma tickles my nose as I pick up hints of garlic, onion, and rosemary. Olga used to keep a rosemary plant in the kitchen—it was her favorite herb—so I'm familiar with the smell and find it comforting. Thinking of Olga also calls to mind Sam, her young son, his photograph still hanging in the upstairs hall-way next to a picture of my counterpart and kindred spirit, the lovely Christine. She looked so youthful and full of potential next to her white GTI, where death found her in an untimely manner as well.

Is Christine's death the secret sin we must get the sisters to con-fess? If so, which sister is pushing the others to come clean, and why here and now?

Faith follows Hope out of the kitchen, carrying a basket of warm bread. The salads are already plated, waiting for people to take their seats and start the meal. Hope invites everyone to gather. This time I'm not the waitress. I have an actual seat at the table, and it just hap-pens to be next to Quinn. We fall into a strange yet familiar pattern, as if we're one big happy family sharing a meal together.

Before anyone takes a bite of food, Hope announces, "Let's have a moment of reflection for Brenda Black. Please stand and join hands."

Nobody objects. Quinn's hand is warm as it wraps around mine. It's surprising how some of the awkwardness is going away already. In such a short time, I've grown closer to Quinn, and judging by the way his thumb gently caresses my skin, the feeling is mutual. Knowing my luck, we're probably just trauma bonding.

Hope lowers her head in solemnity, so I feel obligated to do the same.

"Let us all wish Brenda an easy journey as she crosses over into the next realm—her eternal home. She is now a boundless being of light, surrounded by the unconditional love of the source energy, the great consciousness that gives rise to everything there is and all that will ever be. May she rest easy until her beautiful soul is called once more to this earth."

"Amen," says Iris, coaxing out a chorus of the same.

"Reincarnation, my ass," Vicki says, her lips pursed. "That woman is fish food now, and that's all she'll ever be."

"Wow, heartfelt as always, sis," Faith says.

Hope, trying to preserve the spiritual vibe, ignores the exchange and urges everyone to eat.

It's hard to chitchat after Hope's heavy and awkward eulogy, so for a time, there's no sound aside from the clink of forks against fine china, sips of wine from all but Iris and Oliver, and an occasional chair scraping as someone adjusts their position. No one seems to mind that I'm underage as I pour myself a second glass of wine. Usually I don't drink, not after what my mother went through, but Quinn might have the right idea tonight.

Iris voices what's been on my mind, and likely what others have been wondering as well. "What was Black doing outside on a night like this?" she asks. Her gaze goes from person to person, but nobody answers.

The relentless wind and rain serve as constant reminders that it would have been foolish to venture outside willingly.

"She kept wanting to leave," Vicki says between bites. "I'm assuming she did just that—she snuck out during the blackout, got disoriented in the weather, and fell to her death. It's not complicated."

Faith furrows her brow, unconvinced. "And then one of us typed a note directing us to her location? Did someone witness her fall but not inform the group? That makes no sense to me—none at all. And there was nothing friendly about that note, either. It was a threat."

"Agreed," Iris says. "I don't think someone saw it. I think someone *did it*."

"Did it? Killed Black? But who?" Hope wonders. "No one here would want to harm her—and the poems are about you three sisters, not Black."

"*No one here would want to harm her?*" Bree asks, incredulous. "Iris and Faith lost the hotel to Black. And Vicki gets Todd's controlling shares now that Black is out of commission. The way I see it, all three of you Bishops benefit from Black's death, and Todd's as well."

Now, if that's not a mic-drop moment, I don't know what is.

Hope's face falls. "But nobody's been outside."

Quinn slowly raises his red-rimmed eyes to Hope. "All of us have been out of sight, at least briefly, since we last saw her. Every one of us," he says, his words slightly slurred.

"Not me!" Vicki objects. "I was tied to a stupid chair, remember?" She portrays herself as an innocent victim. "So it couldn't have been me."

"Or me," says Iris, "because I've been watching Vicki, even when she went to the bathroom."

"You took a shower and changed," Quinn reminds her. "And Faith did the same. As for you, Vicki—" I notice it's Vicki now, not Mom, and I'm pretty sure that's the booze talking. "How do we know that you didn't conspire with Faith or Iris to take out Black?"

"Quinn's right," Bree says. Leave it to her to be so bold. "What was it Black said about criminals? Distract and evade? All this bickering between you three over the hotel could be for show, the poems, too, all of it—to keep us distracted and off guard while you take out Todd and Black. Sisters helping sisters."

"That's a fine theory you've concocted," Vicki says. "But you're missing something important. This hotel is a gigantic pain in the ass. Why would any of us want *more* control over it?"

"I'll say the same thing to you that I said to Black: maybe it's not the hotel you want, but what's inside it," Quinn shares. He raises his eyebrows and brings his glass to his lips. "What if you made sure Todd couldn't get his cut so your sisters could get theirs?"

"Oh, so we're back to this absurd painting again?" Vicki takes her own long drink of wine before slamming her glass on the table. "There are a few things I'm sure of in this world: the existence of Bigfoot, UFOs, and who shot JFK—it was the CIA, just so you know—and you can now add one more thing to this list. I'm absolutely certain that there's nothing, and I do mean *nothing*, valuable hidden in this hotel. And are you really accusing me of murder? Your own mother?" Vicki's voice rises sharply. "After all I've done for you?"

"You lied to me for my entire life, so forgive me if I don't feel too bad about my accusation."

While Quinn makes an excellent point, I don't think we should push Vicki to the brink; we've all seen what she's capable of.

"Maybe what Quinn is trying to say is that the *rumor* of a priceless painting is going to raise some red flags with the police," I suggest. "If the two people who stood in the way of your having full ownership of it are suddenly out of the picture, I'd be suspicious, too."

Vicki's scathing stare is meant to pulverize. "Well, looky here, will you?" Her eyes bore into me. "The ex-chambermaid is now our resident Miss Marple." She laughs scornfully. "I'd fire you again if I could." Her smirk disappears inside her wineglass as she takes a gulp.

"But I don't think you're the only one with a motive," I continue, undaunted. "Rodrigo is unaccounted for, and he *really* had it in for Black."

"Rodrigo?" Vicki sounds surprised.

I look around the room, reminding myself of all the hidden corners of this rambling structure. It's possible he could stay out of sight for days, just as I'd planned to keep Bree.

"He and Black have a long and complicated history, lots of bad blood between them. And Rodrigo was here when you all arrived, so he met Oliver and heard him rhyming. But I admit it's hard to believe he'd write these poems, and if he did, I can't explain why he'd threaten your family."

"I think I can." Vicki's mouth is long and mean. "He and Daddy butted heads all the time. Sure, he was good at his job, and good employees are hard to find, so Daddy kept him on, but their relationship was strained. And if we're being honest, nobody in Jonesport likes us very much. We're rich, and they're jealous. So could be Rodrigo didn't just have it in for Black. Maybe he's targeting us as well." Vicki points to Iris, Faith, and finally herself.

Bree rises to her feet. "Look—we could theorize all night about what happened to Brenda, and to Todd, for that matter. But I think we're missing the point. There's a ticking bomb, a real threat, and we've *plenty* of reason to take it seriously—two dead bodies. And they're not Bishops, which makes Charley and me extremely anxious. No more bullshitting. It's time to tell the truth. The last rhyme was quite clear: Confess your sins *tonight* or another dies before the *light*. So? Who here has a sin to confess that's worth killing over? Because the life you save might be my own."

A jagged energy zooms through the room. Everything goes oppressively quiet. The tension is suffocating. The sisters stay silent. Bree's not finished pressing her case, and good for her.

"Oliver, don't be shy," Bree encourages. "It makes sense you wrote these rhymes, and there's got to be a reason. I suspect you're trying to tell us something important, and now is the time to let it out. Just come clean."

Quinn has had enough. "Ollie, spit it out," he presses. "We're done keeping secrets. Somebody else might die because you're talking in riddles. You don't want that on your conscience. Just tell the whole truth, dammit!"

Nobody speaks. Oliver is playing with his food, avoiding eye contact. Eventually he adjusts his glasses, signaling his readiness to address the room.

"I don't want to be responsible for anybody else getting hurt," he says in a quiet voice.

Oliver slowly rises to his feet. As he pushes back his chair, the scrape against the hardwood floor goes right into my teeth. He stands still like a picture. No expression. No smile. The boy with no outward emotion has us all under his spell.

I'm not surprised when he chooses to communicate in the manner that makes him most comfortable—a poem. He doesn't pause, doesn't stumble over the words. It's as if he's waited a long time for this moment to arrive, practiced it over and over so he could deliver a flawless rendition of what may be his poetic masterpiece.

He says:

"When I was only four,
A man came to the door.
Hope was out of town
When he came around.
Faith thought that I was sleeping,
But I was good at creeping.
So I stayed out of sight
While I listened to them fight.
From an unknown man I believed
Is how I was conceived.
But in their whispered yells
A different story they did tell.
I felt my face grow hotter,
To learn my uncle is my father."

Chapter 45

For a moment, no one even blinks. The only sound is Vicki's ragged breathing. It takes a few seconds for me to put it all together, and the moment I do, Bree blurts out the conclusion I just reached.

"Holy shit!" she exclaims. "Todd is your dad?"

Vicki's expression contorts with anguish as she hops up from her seat and immediately goes on the offensive. Dressed in her silly track-suit, she's like a lime-green missile streaking over the table, her sights set on Faith. Her hands and feet move with astonishing speed and agility. She knocks over bottles of wine like bowling pins, spilling plates of food and shattering crystal glasses during her mad scramble. With outstretched hands, it's clear she's going for Faith's neck, pushing aside anything and everything in her way.

Surprisingly, Hope hardly reacts, maintaining a stony stare similar to Oliver's.

Iris lets out a high-pitched whistle, as if this behavior is reminiscent of the chaotic days in the prison cafeteria. Then to my surprise, she moves lightning fast, seizing hold of Vicki's ankles and pulling her back across the table before she can grab Faith. As she travels in reverse, Vicki's body smears food and red wine, creating an abstract image on the white tablecloth like an artist's canvas.

Quinn helps Iris get Vicki off the table, holding her back in a bear hug.

"You lying, fucking, backstabbing bitch!" Vicki shrieks. She twists and turns, exerting all her might, trying to escape Quinn's hold.

"Mom! Mom! Calm down!" Quinn tightens his grip, his arm muscles bulging under the pressure.

Using her son as leverage, Vicki pushes against his chest, lifting herself off the ground, her legs bicycling in the air in a futile effort to deliver a good swift kick to Faith's ribs.

"I knew he was cheating on me, but I didn't know it was with my goddamn sister. Let me go, Quinn!"

If the sight of Vicki looking like a food-stained glow stick trying to wriggle out of Quinn's arms wasn't so tragic, it might be comical.

"How could you?" she pleads with Faith. "How?"

Faith's eyes are empty, and so are Hope's.

I watch the fight leave Vicki's body as she visibly relaxes. She goes limp in Quinn's arms, no longer struggling. He releases his hold but remains on alert, tense like a panther.

"That's karma for you right there," says Iris, addressing Vicki without a trace of sympathy. "This is what you get for screwing me over and covering up for Todd. I bet you knew his whole scheme from the start. Who better to take the fall for his embezzlement than a recovering drug addict? Was it your idea to leave the pill bottle for me to find? Don't bother answering. I won't believe you anyway. I guess this is some kind of payback."

For the first time, I see actual distress on Oliver's face. "I didn't want someone else to die, so I had to confess the secret sin. I had to," he says.

The lack of rhyming makes me think he's speaking more from the heart than the head. He turns to Faith with regret; she gives him a faint smile in return. "It's okay, honey. I should have been more honest with you. And you, too," she says to Hope.

Hope appears unimpressed as she retorts bitterly, "By that, you mean you shouldn't have lied about going to a special fertility clinic in Colorado and not wanting me to accompany you because you believed my presence would only add to your anxiety? Which made me feel terrible, by the way."

"There was so much pressure—you were so desperate for a child, and you knew I wasn't as certain," Faith explains. "You wouldn't even listen to my concerns. It was all *go, go, go, get pregnant.* And when it came to undergoing IVF yourself—no, you didn't trust the hormones or pharmaceutical companies. But somehow it was *fine* if I did it. With you, it's all natural or nothing," she continues. "No surprise it all fell on me. I can't even talk to you about Botox, which I use all the time, by the way, and it's perfectly safe. You want to believe what you want to believe, and that's all there is to it."

Ah, so Hope's homemade creams weren't the miracle cure after all.

"But you didn't even use hormones, Faith," Hope says. "You had the most natural treatment of all—a good, old-fashioned penis."

"Tell me you two didn't get it on in one of the rooms last night," Vicki interrupts.

Faith hesitates but then shakes her head. "It was a long time ago," she says, but Vicki definitely doesn't believe her.

"Liar," she exclaims. "Which room was it? Sunset? Gardenia? It better not have been the Library Room, or I swear . . ." She hurls her dinner plate onto the floor, smashing it into countless fragments.

Great, another mess for me to clean up. Still, I feel bad. Of course I do. But the broken plate serves a purpose as I watch the anger drain from Vicki's face.

Faith's remorseful expression deepens, her eyes misting over. She shifts her focus to Hope, not her furious sister. "How can I ever make this up to you?" she begs in a shaky voice. "I love you . . . I didn't want to deceive you. Todd and I knew each other from a long time ago. He's the one who got me the *Vogue* cover job."

"*Todd* got you that job?" Vicki blurts out. "So on the night I met him, you'd already screwed him? Good God, Faith." Vicki can't seem to believe it, and neither can I.

Faith looks sorrowfully over at Iris. "Just so you know, I think you're right about Todd intentionally leaving that pill bottle for you to find. It's exactly something Todd would do. He drugged my competition so that I'd get on the *Vogue* cover. He said it would make my career—and he was right. I just didn't understand at what cost."

A light goes on in Iris's eyes like she's been vindicated. "I knew it! That son of a bitch," she shouts. "He basically drugged me, too."

"I broke it off with him after I won the competition," Faith tells Hope.

"I wouldn't exactly call that *winning*," grumbles Vicki.

Faith ignores the barb. "The guilt was too much. I told him I never wanted to see him again, but he came to the big party anyway and that's where he met you." Faith turns her attention to her sister. "I didn't dare reveal how Todd and I knew each other because I couldn't face up to what I did. I went into denial mode, lying to myself, trying to forget him and what I agreed to let him do on my behalf." Faith pauses. "I've lied to myself a lot, I guess—about my career, about Oliver, even how I've kept up my youthful appearance."

"I can't believe you did *Botox*," Hope says with disgust. "After all the literature I gave you."

"Oh, Hope. I know it's disappointing, but everyone does it," Faith answers.

I think we're all surprised that Hope emphasizes the Botox over her wife's affair.

"Anyway, just to be clear, Todd and I reconnected many, many years ago . . . and, well, it got out of hand for a little bit. And then it was over. I've tried my best to leave the past in the past."

Hope rests a hand affectionately on Faith's arm, a sign of an unbreakable allegiance. "Since we're being honest, I have a confession to make as well." All eyes are on Hope now. "I've actually known for years that you weren't telling me the whole truth. I couldn't find any records of your treatment, so I suspected a man was involved, and I forgave you a long time ago."

I guess that explains why she's more upset about the Botox—sort of.

Their eyes meet, Faith's brimming with gratitude. But Hope's posture is rigid, and her strange distant expression unsettles me. She tightens her hold on Faith's shoulder, her knuckles turning pale and tense. Gradually her lips start to tremble ever so slightly. I observe her eyes twitching as if she's on the verge of tears.

"Oh, God, isn't Hope just always the better person?" Vicki says with contempt. "Whatever," she continues. "Why do I even care? He's dead. And I knew he was getting it on with someone—found all kinds of explicit messages on his phone—just didn't think you had that kind of language in you, Faith. Goes to show how much we *really* know each other."

"So that's what you two were arguing about last night?" Iris asks. "As a helpful suggestion, Vicki, maybe don't share that detail with the police if you want to stay out of prison. And how do you know it was Faith who wrote those messages? Todd probably had other women in his life. We're talking about an affair from years ago—*before* Oliver was born."

Vicki storms over to Faith, standing beside her chair, her upper lip curled into a snarl. "Tell me the truth right now," she demands. "Were you and Todd sleeping together? And I don't mean fourteen years ago, but recently—in other words, are you the girl who sent my husband enough eggplant emojis to open an Italian restaurant?"

Faith shakes her head vigorously. "No, no. Iris is right. That was ages ago. After Todd had given us the baby Hope and I so desperately wanted, I broke it off with him.

"We promised we'd keep it a secret. He didn't want you to know, Vicki. But he agreed to help out financially, which is mostly what we argued about—I'm sure Oliver overheard one of those fights. Models over thirty don't command top dollar, and Hope wasn't earning much teaching yoga. We *needed* the money, but that's all Todd was—a source of cash and a sperm donor. Nothing else happened between us after that." She sounds frantic, begging Vicki and Hope to believe her.

Out of nowhere, Hope bursts into a wild laugh, like a poor imitation of the Wicked Witch of the West—an honest-to-God cackle. Her breathing grows labored, verging on hyperventilation, while her eyes resemble those of a rabid animal—wide and full of crazy. She glares at Faith, revealing a dark side I didn't know she possessed. "Bull—fucking—shit, Faith."

Hope lifts her hand from Faith's shoulder and runs her fingers through her short hair, pulling at it as if she might tear out a clump.

"You've been seeing him . . . for years. And all this time, I've turned a blind eye, doing everything in my capacity to keep our family intact." Hope is almost spitting as the anger and betrayal pour out of her. "Come on now, tell the real truth, Faith, like the poems demand."

"I am telling you the truth. I haven't slept with him since I got pregnant with Ollie, and I certainly haven't been sexting him, if that's your worry."

Hope breaks. "Oh, what a load of crap!" she explodes. "The truth is, you'd *still* be fucking Todd if I hadn't killed him."

Chapter 46

Out of everyone in this whack-a-doodle family, Hope is the last person I'd suspect of being a murderer. It's unsettling, to say the least, how she maintains a calm facade, donning it like a veil as she sips from her glass of water, acting as though she's said nothing of consequence and admitted no crime.

She's seated at the table. I can hear her deep, steady inhales and exhales come and go through her nose. Maybe she's using a yoga breath technique, as if that could magically make everything okay. The table itself—the cloth stained red with spilled wine, plates overturned, glasses upended, food scattered about—looks like another violent crime took place.

Vicki slinks back to her seat, her tracksuit a soiled mess. The adrenaline must have left her, because she makes no effort to confront Hope. It seems we're all stunned into silence.

Poor dear Quinn. He's rubbing his eyes, perhaps hoping it'll wake him from this nightmare. He manages to get to his feet, sidling over to Oliver. He sets his hands on the boy's shoulders in a show of support, while looking desperately in need of support himself.

I'm sitting as quietly as can be. I don't do or say anything, fearing a wrong move could cause an unforeseen domino effect.

Iris shakes her head in disbelief. "Out of all of us, the 'peace and love' yogi who can't even bring herself to eat an animal is a *murderer*? I've seen a lot of shit in my days, but this one blows me away. You'll be eaten alive in prison, Hope. You'll be candy on a stick. I do *not* envy you."

Slowly, as if it causes her great agony, Faith forces herself to look Hope in the eyes. "That's not possible . . . Tell me, Hope, tell me that you didn't. Please tell me this isn't true. I—I *loved* him. And I love you!" Tears spill out in a great flood. Her hitched breathing turns to heaving sobs, making it impossible for Faith to say more.

"Don't you see? That's exactly why I had to get rid of him," Hope says. "He was going to tear us apart."

"What are you so broken up about, anyway?" Iris asks Faith. "He loved you so much that he took this hotel right out from under you."

A sudden movement to my left catches my eye. I turn my head to Bree. She's pointing the gun, which she never relinquished, directly at Hope.

"All right, someone has to take control here, and I vote for the person who's armed," Bree says, peering down the barrel as she takes aim.

"I did what I had to do to save my family," Hope says. "And honestly, I did all of you a big favor." She sits up straighter, confident and poised, no doubt delusional.

"Todd was nothing but a menace to each of you," she says. "To Iris, he was a thief who stole from his family business and sent her to prison. Vicki, not only did he steal from you, but he cheated and lied to you for years and used that terrible lawyer to coerce your father into giving him a controlling share of this hotel.

"And as for you, Faith, he strung you along, never supported Oliver like he promised, and stabbed you in the back with the will. He was resentful of Quinn over the adoption he never wanted, and made sure he knew it his entire life. He despised Ollie, his own son—our gifted, beautiful, special soul. But even Oliver, with his unique abilities, couldn't see Todd for who he really was: a lying, cheating, stealing charlatan."

"How did you do it?" Bree asks. "I heard him outside my room, dying. I'll never forget that wet, wheezing rattle. What did you do to him?"

"It's a plant called oleander," Hope says impassively, like someone listing an ingredient in a recipe. "It's such a beautiful, flowering shrub—soft petals, pink and purple as a new day, but also very deadly.

It's because of the cardiac glycosides." She shares this as if the question on everyone's mind is *Why is oleander so deadly?* rather than *What the hell is wrong with you, Hope?*

"The molecules are in every part of the plant—similar to digitalis, which is commonly used in heart medications. In small, controlled doses, the glycosides manipulate the ion pump of heart cells, which causes an increased force of heart muscle contractions. But in larger doses, like I gave Todd in his bourbon, it messes with the heart's rhythm—and you get other symptoms, too. Nausea, cramps, vomiting. Not pleasant, but he wasn't a pleasant person, was he?"

Faith speaks up. "Why are you confessing all this? Do you think the medical examiner will find out and you'll be caught anyway? I don't get it."

Hope laughs off the questions. "No, I guess I'm confessing because I couldn't listen to your lies anymore, and I snapped. That's it, I just . . . snapped." She snaps her fingers to punctuate the point.

"But when I get that strong of an instinct, I know it's my spirit guides working through me, so this was *meant* to be. It's better this way. Dark secrets breed dark energy. The truth is always liberating because it means less resistance. You know the reason we suffer in life is because of resistance . . . trying to force external conditions to match our inner desires. Surrender is the path to true freedom.

"And Todd is now free—he's not dead, you know. Not in a spiritual sense. He's with us right now, in fact. I can assure you that he's listening to this *very* conversation. And he knows, as do I, that a medical examiner checks for only about a hundred compounds, and oleander isn't one of them. They'd have no reason to order any additional tests unless one of you tips them off. But keep in mind how I truly did you all a favor."

Quinn says, "I thought you said dark secrets breed dark energy."

"Well, this one is for the greater good," Hope answers.

"This is the craziest crap I've ever heard." Iris takes a step back from the table. "We need the police. Are the phones working yet?"

I check mine and give her a thumbs-down. No go.

"There's no way we can drive for help," Quinn says. "There's a big tree blocking the road, and it's not safe anyway."

"She can't just wander around free. She's way more dangerous than any of us knew." Bree makes her observation with the gun still leveled on Hope.

"And yet *I'm the one* everyone wanted tied up. Where's the damn twine, anyway?" Vicki turns to me for the answer.

"I think we used it all up on you," I say.

Vicki glowers, recalling her brief confinement. She rounds the table to confront Hope directly, crouching right in her face. "That was my husband you murdered, Hope. Mine!" She stands, poking Hope's shoulder, giving it several stiff, sharp jabs. "He may have been a total shitheel, but he was *my* shitheel, and you had no right to do what you did—none! I will see to it that you rot in jail, you crazy bitch." She balls up a cloth napkin before hurling it into Hope's face.

Hope doesn't even flinch.

"Why now?" Faith sounds crushed. "Was it the hotel—the will?"

"No . . . no," Hope answers flatly. "I was going to do it this weekend regardless. The will, I admit, was an added push. Either way, it was now or never, Faith. You and he were plotting your joint escape for months. You think I didn't know?"

"I knew," Oliver says softly.

"Of course you did, Ollie, of course. You have the gift." Hope sends him a tender smile, glowing with pride. "Listen, I did everyone a favor, and you all know it. Everyone wanted him gone . . . Vicki, you won't admit it, but you wanted him dead, too. The only one who didn't want this was probably Faith, and he had her so manipulated she'd never find her way out. I had to help her . . . for the sake of the family, I had to help, and now that he's gone, I hope you'll all come to your senses and help me."

"Help you? Really?" Vicki sounds incredulous.

"The hotel can be ours again," Iris says, as though she's actually giving the crazy idea serious consideration.

"What about them?" Vicki points to Bree and me. "You have

witnesses who aren't family. They won't keep this secret even if you want them to, you dumbass."

"I guess you'll just have to decide how to handle that." Hope offers this suggestion indifferently, with none of the sympathy that she insisted *all* creatures deserve.

Bree is aghast. "If any of you have ideas about harming Charley or me to protect this secret, you better think twice." She displays the gun for all to see.

Quinn comes over to me, standing close. Despite all that's happened to him, he's acting as *my* protector. "Nobody is doing anything to anybody," he says. I watch Vicki, Iris, and Faith hold a silent conference with their eyes. They may not be on the same page as Quinn.

Hope rises from the table, ignoring the gun leveled at her chest. "Look, I'll make it easy for you. Is there a room where you can lock me up until you figure out what you want to do?" she asks.

"My room locks from the outside," I say. "It was a storage closet before I moved in. We can put her in there."

"Quinn and Charley will secure Hope," Bree tells the room. "I'll stay here and keep an eye on the rest of you." She reorients the gun toward Iris and Vicki.

Hope passively allows Quinn and me to escort her out of the dining room, though she pauses at the doorway and turns to face the gathering.

"For your information, I brought oleander to the hotel, not belladonna," Hope says. "I have no idea where that came from, Vicki, or how it ended up in your dresser drawer. And if anyone is wondering, I *didn't* kill attorney Black."

Chapter 47

It feels like being in the eye of the hurricane. Once Quinn and I get Hope settled, an uneasy calm descends on the hotel. But it's an illusion. The storm outside continues to rage. Still, there is some closure knowing we've solved the mystery of at least one sudden death.

My room is small, like a prison cell, and now it's become one. We leave Hope with water and a plan to check on her later for a bathroom break. I turn the key, lock her away, and that's it.

On our way to the Great Room, Quinn repeatedly apologizes for having such a screwed-up family. I remain silent rather than add to his shame with reminders that Hope subtly (or not so subtly) threatened my life. Although I trust Quinn, I worry the Bishop sisters will side with Hope and turn against Bree and me. The gun offers some security, but I'm still on edge.

What I'm not going to do is drink away my troubles. A couple of glasses of wine are plenty. I've already got a little headache, and I need my wits about me.

Quinn, however, is a different story. He goes to his room to freshen up and takes his whiskey bottle with him.

When he leaves, I notice the fire is nearly out, but the wood is far too wet to get it going. I hope the electricity stays on, despite the wind having a different agenda. The overhead lights flicker with increasing frequency, as if issuing a warning to be prepared. I set the flashlights on the fireplace mantel for the likely event that we lose power.

Faith and Oliver are nowhere to be found. As strange as that boy is, I feel for him the most. He didn't ask for this mess. He tried to do the right thing by bringing Faith's secret into the open. But I'm still not sure all the sins have been confessed. If we're to believe that Hope isn't Black's killer, as she claims, then not only do we have a lot of unanswered questions, but we may also have a murderer still in our midst.

When Quinn returns to the Great Room, he plops himself onto a plush couch, whiskey in hand, saying nothing, leaving me to guess how he's processing everything. Judging by his bloodshot eyes, I'd say rather poorly.

Since Quinn's not interested in conversation, I leave him with his whiskey to check in with Bree. I'm not ready to tackle the mess in the dining room. The last thing I want to do is clean up after these psychopaths. And I'm certainly not putting that scrub dress on again, that's for sure.

Bree, Vicki, and Iris have assembled in the alcove, sitting in front of our boarded-up windows. Bree is occupying Black's old seat, a blue upholstered wingback chair riveted with bright brass buttons. Is Black still down on those rocks, I wonder, or has the tide carried her out to sea? It's too grim to dwell on the thought for long.

Aside from the noise of the weather, the room is silent. Bree has the gun by her side, but my eyes are drawn to her left hand. She's bleeding through her bandage, leaving a small stain on the cuff of her long-sleeved pullover.

"It looks like that needs to be changed," I suggest.

Bree glances down, turning her hand to see the issue.

"Oh shit . . . I love this shirt," she laments.

I have to smile. It's a relief to think about something as mundane as a clothing stain.

"I'll grab the first-aid kit and go get cleaned up," Bree says. "Thanks for pointing it out. I had no idea the cut reopened—I don't think I'm feeling much right now. I must be a little numb."

"We're all a little numb," Vicki notes in a dry, muted voice.

I follow Bree out of the alcove, biting my cheek to avoid blurting out what I have to tell her. The first-aid kit is still in the Great Room. I retrieve it for her, carrying it into the ransacked dining room, thinking we can speak there without being overheard.

Unsure where to start, I remove the folded-up article from the attic out of my back pocket, handing it over to Bree. "What's this all about?" Bree asks, giving it a quick read. "This car accident is from a long time ago."

I explain to her about Christine—what Vicki said during our walk together.

"And you remember when Iris hinted at some secret involving a maid who worked here?"

"I've been wondering what that was about," Bree remarks.

I fill her in on how Quinn and I found the article in a photo album while we were looking for Black.

"We think this might not have been an accident. Do you know anything about cars?" I ask.

"A little," Bree says. "Jake is big into vintage rides—took me to some car shows, one of the better things we did together. Why do you ask?"

"There's a picture of Christine and her car hanging in the hallway near your room. Quinn and I think it's a white GTI, same as the one referenced in the article, but we don't know for sure. If it is, this might be the sin they're supposed to confess."

"That's kind of far-fetched," Bree says. "But after this night, I'm willing to believe anything. I'll go have a look."

"Good," I say, feeling a rush of gratitude. "I'll see if I can coax more info out of Vicki and Iris while you're gone. Vicki's had a lot to drink. Maybe she'll talk. I'm just not sure Faith's confession is the last of it. We could still be the next to die before the light."

Bree frowns, turning her head in the direction of the Bishops. She holds the gun out toward me. "Do you want this for protection?"

"No," I say. "Just don't be long."

When I get back to the alcove, Faith is there, but Oliver is not.

"He's staying in his room until further notice," Faith informs me.

I can hear Quinn snoring in the other room. His head is tilted back, mouth slightly open, splayed out on the couch as if he's not waking up until morning.

"I need a drink . . . anybody else?" Faith asks.

It's no surprise that Vicki doesn't want anything if it's coming from her, and Iris already has sparkling water. When Faith returns to the alcove, she's got a wineglass in one hand and a bottle in the other. "It's going to be a long night," she says.

Vicki stands to leave, but Faith grabs her arm before she can go. "Please—stay," she pleads. "We have to talk about this."

"I can leave," I offer, but Vicki raises her hand to stop me.

"No, I need you here as a potential witness. Think of it as a disincentive so I don't end up killing my sister."

"All I know is that my sobriety must be rock solid if this night hasn't knocked me off the wagon." Iris lifts her water glass and toasts the heavens. "Thank you, Jesus," she says.

Vicki sits back down, changing seats to put as much distance between herself and Faith as possible.

Bowing her head, Faith allows her beautiful long locks to curtain her face, concealing her shame and her glassy, watery eyes.

"I am so sorry," she whispers to her sister, her breathy voice cracking. "What I did was beyond hurtful."

Vicki's not disagreeing.

"You hate me—and fine, I deserve it. I'm not offering any excuses for my behavior . . . but please know I never meant to hurt you. After we reconnected, I just fell back into an old pattern . . . but it wasn't about him. It was about me.

"On the surface, I project what people expect from a model— confidence and poise. But it's just a facade. I've always needed attention to feel good about myself, even when it came from the wrong people. And Todd filled a void inside me that I couldn't fill for myself."

"I know what *void* he filled," Vicki mutters. But her fiery anger has dimmed. "Oh, whatever," she says. "I should have divorced him years ago when Iris went to prison."

"Divorce him?" snaps Iris. "You should have gotten me out, you jackass. And thanks for basically admitting you knew I'd been set up."

"This isn't about you right now, Iris. I'm the one suffering!"The old Vicki returns, getting fired up again, though it doesn't last long.

I can almost feel the weight of her guilty conscience, as if it were a new presence in the room.

"If you did know Iris was innocent, you should confess," I say. "We need all the skeletons out of the closet—tonight. I don't want to be the next dead body."

"Charley's right. You knew all the ins and outs of your business the way Dad knew how to run this place," Faith says. "You had to know Todd set Iris up."

Vicki wilts on the spot. "I—I—didn't know. Not exactly," she stammers.

"What's that supposed to mean?" Iris asks, looking from Faith to Vicki.

"It means I figured it out later, after you were already incarcerated." Vicki throws her hands up in surrender. "And yes, Faith, you're right. Todd embezzled money to cover the losses from one of his stupid schemes. He wanted Iris to relapse, making it easier to frame her for his crime. But, by the time I caught on, Iris's prison time was almost up. And by then she was clean and sober again, doing quite well. She had finally found some real direction in life."

"What I found was Jesus," interrupts Iris. "And I sure as hell need him right now." She again lifts her gaze to the ceiling.

Vicki exhales a heavy sigh. "If I had come forward, it would have ruined our lives," she says. "Repaying the insurance money alone would have bankrupted us, not to mention Todd would have been sent to prison. And God knows what all that might have done to Quinn. Keeping quiet was my best option, so that's what I did. I kept my mouth shut . . . So there, are you happy now? I've confessed my sin—just like you asked, Charley." She crumples in her seat, burying her face in her hands as she shrinks in on herself, too exhausted or drunk to care that she's still wearing a food-stained tracksuit.

"If you're looking for absolution, you're going to have to wait a long while to get it from me," Iris says. "Jesus might be all-forgiving, but I'm not."

"Maybe I deserved to be cheated on," says Vicki, turning to Faith. "At least someone was getting something out of that man. I sure wasn't."

"Yeah, because he was getting it elsewhere." Iris delivers her assessment with cold directness, taking some joy out of her sisters' misery.

Faith ignores the remark and addresses Vicki. "I think what we need to do is forgive ourselves," she says. "I've been working with a therapist for a few years now—she's helped me understand so much about where my insecurity comes from, this feeling I can't shake that there's something wrong with me.

"Iris hinted at the root cause tonight—the *other* secret. We have to face it, Vicki. It's never left me. The guilt has clouded my entire life. I've made so many bad decisions with partners—including Todd— because of it. I thought my relationship with Hope was going to be different, healthier. I mean, sure, I saw some warning signs with her—"

"Warning signs that she was a psychopathic killer, you mean?" Iris interjects.

"More like a little mood instability, reactivity, and some eccentricity," Faith says calmly. "But I had no idea how unhealthy she was. I don't even know what I'm trying to say here, really . . . I guess just that Todd is a perfect example of my terrible decision-making, and how I would choose the wrong person because I felt bad about *myself*. And if I'm being honest, I was angry with you, too, Vick, for what we did all those years ago. But, I'm still really sorry for hurting you."

Vicki draws in a long breath as her hard shell cracks just a sliver, enough to reveal a softness underneath. Her whole body seems to go slack. "I get it . . . I do. It's been difficult for us all."

And here is where I probably should have just kept my big mouth shut. That's what maids do, right? Stay quiet and clean up the mess, but like Faith, I can't seem to follow my better judgment.

"You're talking about Christine, aren't you?" I blurt out. "What did you do to her? Did you somehow cause the car accident that killed her?"

Bree took the newspaper clipping with her, so I don't have the evidence to show them. Regardless, the three sisters gawk at me like I just spoke gibberish, so I repeat myself.

"I found a newspaper article about her car accident in the attic when Quinn and I went looking for Black. Is that the secret about the maid, Iris? What happened? Did you three do something horrible to that poor woman?"

Before I can dig my hole any deeper, Bree returns to the alcove. She has a new outfit—a blue oversize sweatshirt and black leggings—and a fresh bandage on her hand. That same hand is holding a framed picture that she's taken off the wall.

"I went looking for the photograph of Christine just like you asked, Charley," Bree says, addressing everyone, not just me. "The picture frame was there all right, but someone turned the photo around and wrote another poem on the back. Our third. Three poems for three sisters."

She holds up the frame for everyone to see. This poem is written in childlike block printing. The ink of the black marker bleeds into the white paper in spots. It's reminiscent of the poem on the mirror, both suggestive of a young hand—a young poet. As I read the poem to myself, I'm overcome with a fright unlike anything I've ever known.

> Sisterly bonds have a limit.
> We've all been pushed within it.
> For what we did that fateful day,
> Another's life is the price to pay.

My blood turns to ice. It feels like I'm the one who has gone over the cliff, freefalling into nothingness. This isn't over—not by a long shot. And we've hours to go before the morning light.

ris holds her breath, inflating her cheeks. Faith stifles a gasp. Vicki has the empty eyes of someone under hypnosis.

"Where is Oliver?" Bree questions, acid in her voice. "And what did you three do that's put us all in danger?"

I step forward, shaking. My nerves are so frayed I'm not sure how much more I can stand. I'm one small fall away from cracking into a million pieces. But I'm not going to be intimidated anymore.

"One of you is out for revenge." I point first at Vicki, then at Iris, and finally at Faith. "You're Oliver's mom. You would know if he's behind this or if Hope's been coaching him. Maybe you're both in on it. Did you know Hope was going to kill Todd? Is this about Christine or is it about the will?"

A mighty gust of wind turns off the lights, plunging everyone into darkness. The firelight, long gone out, fails to provide even faint illumination. The flashlights with fresh batteries are still on the stone mantel of the fireplace, far out of reach.

My panic lasts only a second or two. As soon as the wind dies, the lights return as if Larry were a person playing with the switch.

The sisters look at each other, a quiet conference, a silent understanding passing among them.

"I *know* this is about Christine," I continue, undeterred. "Please . . . please, just tell us the truth, and maybe all this will be over. Iris, you're the one who brought up the secret involving the maid—"

Vicki breaks in before I can finish my thought, or perhaps to keep Iris from responding. "We sisters need to talk," she says. "Alone."

Vicki, Faith, and Iris look to each other in silent understanding. Without another word, all three depart the alcove, marching off in a line like the von Trapp children from that movie my nana loves, headed for the dining room where they'll be able to converse, free from prying eyes and ears.

I watch them go, crossing and uncrossing my arms nervously. Bree's scowl follows the sisters out.

"I don't like this one bit," she says in a low warning tone.

"Agreed," I say. "Maybe we should have the gun ready?" I hate the tremor in my voice as I glance toward the dining room.

Bree wiggles the weapon out of her back pocket. "God, could this night get any more screwed up? And nobody answered me when I asked about Oliver. Where is he?" she wants to know.

"He's supposedly sleeping," I say. "But I'm wondering about Rodrigo. Remember what Vicki said?"

"Yeah, the Bishops haven't built up much goodwill around here. I certainly believe that," Bree says.

Angling her body, she peers through the Great Room toward the dining room. All is quiet except for Quinn's snoring.

Bree wrinkles her nose as though she's an animal sensing danger. "Look, Charley, I don't feel good saying this." Bree checks behind her at sleeping Quinn. "But he knew about the photograph . . . and he was upstairs for a while, out of sight."

"You think Quinn—?"

But I don't get to finish the thought because the Bishop sisters return. They brush past Bree to reclaim their prior positions, standing in line with their backs to the boarded-up windows.

Bitterness overcomes me as I observe their determined, self-righteous stares. What game are these three playing?

"We've come to a decision," Vicki announces, her eyes drawn to the weapon in Bree's hand. "But we're not about to negotiate under duress."

Bree's fingers tighten around the gun grip. Behind us, Quinn remains blissfully unaware of the escalating tension. I refuse to believe he's involved, yet Bree's suspicion is impossible to ignore.

Vicki takes notice of the flickering lights that are giving off a strobe effect, battling to stay on as the wind intensifies. "Iris, dear, fetch the flashlights," she says. "I don't think the power will be on much longer."

Bree and I look at each other. I'm guessing she also keyed in on the affectionate *dear*, and the significant glance the two sisters shared. The dynamics clearly shifted during the Bishops' conference.

Iris departs the alcove as instructed.

Vicki doesn't wait for her return to issue her ultimatum. "We're willing to propose a compromise, but we won't discuss it under threat. Give me back my gun, and we'll talk this over like civilized people."

Even though Bree and I aren't sisters, I feel close to her now, and want to believe we have the ability to communicate as if we were. A single glance is all I give, and I hope Bree guesses my intended meaning.

"I don't think you understand who is in charge here," Bree says, hoisting the weapon.

Bingo.

"It's you who doesn't understand."

Out of nowhere, something wraps tightly around my rib cage. It's the perfect amount of pressure—light enough to allow me to keep breathing, but it wouldn't take much to compress my lungs or crack some ribs. I have barely enough air to spit out a fear-filled gasp. I know I'm in trouble, but for the first few terrifying seconds, I don't understand what's happening.

When my rush of panic subsides, I realize that Iris snuck up behind me, and it's her arm snaking around my chest. Her other hand holds a kitchen knife with a blade sharp as a wasp's stinger, pressed to my neck. She must have thought I was the easier target.

"Prison taught me a lot," Iris says. "The biggest lesson being, I never want to go back." My eyes shift to the blade, but I can see only the wings of Iris's butterfly tattoo rippling as her biceps twitch. But I can feel the knife tip dancing perilously close to a pulsing vein on my neck.

Bree stands frozen, like a motor that's seized up.

My eyes dart between the butterfly tattoo and Vicki's cold, dead stare. The anticipation of being stabbed in the neck, that first pinch of pain, sends terror coursing through my body. My throat convulses as I struggle to get air into my lungs, and Iris's firm grip around my chest isn't helping.

"This shouldn't be a tough call, Bree." Vicki holds out her hand expectantly.

I know Bree will comply. Even so, I don't dare relax, not for a second. With my mouth pressed tight and my gut in knots, I try to slow my breathing as Bree hands over the gun, the cold metal slapping against the flesh of Vicki's waiting hand.

Vicki's lips curl into a self-satisfied smirk. Iris releases her grip, the knife falling to her side. I stagger away from her, my eyes ablaze.

"What the hell is wrong with you all?" I shout, gasping for air.

"What's the offer?" Bree asks, her voice sharp. "You've got the gun. Tell us what you have in mind."

Faith steps forward, looking sympathetic. "We're sorry it's come to this," she says, her voice ringing with remorse. Then she straightens. "But you're bringing up dangerous questions."

"You want answers, and we want to keep the past in the past," Vicki says, brandishing the weapon as if we needed the reminder that she's back in charge.

"And we don't want Hope to spend her life in prison," Faith adds. "I have a lot to make amends for, and Oliver needs both his mothers."

"Again, what's your offer?" I can hear Bree's patience is wearing thin.

"We want to buy your silence," says Iris, who has come around to stand in line with her sisters. "Vicki has agreed to return the hotel shares to Faith and me, so we're offering you both five percent of our annual profits."

"That's a generous lifelong payday, Charley," Vicki says. "You'll be able to support yourself, your family, without working here . . . and you, Ms. Bree, you could start that new life of yours away from your threatening ex-boyfriend. I'd call it a win-win for everyone."

I can see a fantasy percolating in Bree's eyes. "Charley and I need to talk this over *privately*," she says.

"Talk over there." Vicki uses the gun to direct us to a spot in the Great Room not far from snoring Quinn. While I struggle to believe Bree's suspicions about Quinn, it's easy to see why someone would want to take revenge on these sisters. I sure do.

"We'll wait right here—and we're watching everything you do, so please, don't try to be clever. I'll tell you what I told Charley earlier: you have no idea how far I'll go to protect this family. We may not seem close—or even kind—to one another, but at the end of the day, blood is blood, and that bond is sacred. Go, talk it over, but be quick about it."

Bree gently guides me by the arm, turning her back to the Bishops as we exit the alcove.

I speak first. "Are you actually considering this crazy deal?" I whisper harshly. My eyes widen as I peer over Bree's shoulder into the alcove. "Hope is a *murderer*."

"No, I'm not considering it. But, Charley, if we reject their offer, we're putting ourselves in immediate danger. We don't know what they're going to do to us."

I feel desperate. "So, what should we do?"

The lights dim to half power, then regain full brightness. "I suggest we play along for our safety. But if I get the chance, I'm going to try and snatch the gun back from Vicki. So, Charley—when the lights go out, and I'm sure they will, don't hesitate, not for one second. Get as far away from the alcove and the Bishops as you can."

Chapter 49

I follow Bree back to the alcove and the awaiting Bishop sisters, realizing it would be much easier to take the cash and shut my trap. Part of me wants to do just that. Rodrigo's given me a peek at the hotel's ledger, and my cut would be worth around fifty thousand dollars a year. No way could I skim anywhere close to that amount. Bree's financial future isn't rosy, either. But I'm happy to know our integrity is worth more than a payoff.

I certainly don't love the idea of leaving Bree, if it comes to that. We're supposed to be partners in this and have each other's backs. But, I made a promise, and I'll try to make a break for it if the lights go out.

As soon as we're back in the alcove, Bree steps forward, confident and poised. "We've talked it over, and we accept," she says.

Vicki gives us a crisp nod, gloriously impressed with herself. "Glad you both have good sense," she replies. "We don't want these unfortunate events to cloud our collective futures. What's done is done. We can't change the past."

Faith's whole body relaxes as she sinks into one of the comfy chairs. "Should we let Hope out now?" she asks.

"Yeah, I suppose we can go get her," Iris says, eyeing me apologetically. "And, Charley, I'm sorry about all that. I know it wasn't very Christian of me."

"Ya think?" I'm in no mood to hold back. "To love thy neighbor certainly doesn't mean putting a knife to their throat. I think you may have mixed up Jesus and Judas."

There. I knew my CCD education would come in handy, eventually.

Iris's mouth dips into a frown. "Not my finest moment . . . but we had to do something. We couldn't be threatened any longer."

"But it's okay if *we* are?" Bree says—annoyed, and I don't blame her.

"Forgive as the Lord forgave you," says Iris.

This makes me even angrier. I want to shout at them all—scream at Faith for being so selfish, at Iris for being vengeful, and at Vicki for being greedy (not to mention pretty unhinged). But I try to maintain control.

Vicki inhales audibly, seeming to shift gears. "We're going to make some tea and relax. We'll let Hope out of her mini-prison and ride out this storm together."

"What about Oliver? Christine? The poems? Rodrigo? Black—all of that?" I throw my arms into the air in exasperation.

"And don't forget the belladonna," I add, unable to control myself. "We don't have the whole story there, either. You say you're buying our silence, but we should at least know what we're being silent about!"

Vicki inflates her small frame. "Just trust us, Charley, and let it go."

"Trust you?" Bree asks. "Charley doesn't have any reason to trust you, and neither do I."

Vicki's cold stare could cut stone. "Then fine, maybe we can't trust you, either. In that case, this deal won't work. It's a shame. You've already seen a bit of what we're capable of, but I can assure you, that's not everything."

The power flickers on and off, as if the hotel is taking a dying gasp. I draw in a breath and hold it, but thankfully the lights come on as the wind dies down. It's cold comfort. In a matter of time, they'll go out again, and eventually they'll stay out. Driving rain pelts the exterior like thousands of fingers tapping against the roof and walls. Larry is knocking to get let in.

Behind me, Quinn is snoring louder now. He's of no help if we lose power, and the wood is too wet for the fire, so there's no backup light coming from the Great Room. And Iris, who collected all the flashlights when she got the knife, doesn't seem to be in a sharing mood. Darkness and the Bishops seem as deadly a combo as a glass of bourbon mixed with oleander. Bree's instructions bounce in and out of my brain.

If the lights go out—don't hesitate, not even for one second . . .

I get it. When the power goes out, Bree will try to get the gun. The best thing I can do for my safety is follow the plan and run.

I scope out my surroundings, planning my escape route while the lights are still on. Soon enough, a fresh gust gradually crescendos into a loud roar. The hotel shakes, and just as I feared, everything goes dark. My breath catches in my throat as a band of fear pulls tight across my chest. Now's the time.

I turn around, taking a tentative step forward, trying to orient myself in this void. Memory is my guide. Moving through the dark, I try my best to remember the layout, attempting to avoid any obstacles in my path. My breath sputters no matter how I try to calm myself.

"Where are the flashlights?" It's Faith's voice I hear over Larry's howl. "We need to keep an eye on them!"

Just when I think I'm nearing the foyer, my foot connects hard with what I'm sure is a table leg. The contact makes a loud thud, but worse is the sound of breaking glass when something (a tall vase, perhaps?) tumbles to the floor. I go completely still, eyes pointlessly probing the inky gloom, ears fighting to pick up any noise other than the wind.

There's no question the Bishops can pinpoint me now. I'm not surprised when a flashlight beam cuts through the dark. The spotlight passes near me, but I stay frozen in place, afraid the blood thrumming in my ears will give my position away. But before I can think what to do next, I hear a loud pop behind me. In the same instant, I see a bright flash reflected in the mirror above the fireplace. It looks like a lightning strike indoors. There's another pop and flash . . . and another still . . .

Soon, the pungent smell of gunpowder fills the air. Behind me, I hear the crash of a body—one or two—falling to the floor. *Oh my god, Bree.* The blackout is short-lived and the room brightens in a sudden flood of warm white light. I should continue on my way—Lord knows outside is safer than inside—but I'm too worried about Bree to make

a hasty departure. I spin around, my eyes pained by the sudden illumination. When my focus returns, I can't believe the sight before me.

Bree is kneeling, crouched before Vicki, who looms over her,
pointing the gun at Bree's head. Faith and Iris are crumpled on the
floor off to the side, bleeding onto the carpet.

It doesn't take me long to figure out what happened.

It appears the Bishop sisters are not a united front after all. Vicki
must have double-crossed both Faith and Iris, and Bree, my stowaway,
is most certainly her next target.

Chapter 50

I hurry to the alcove, but stop short of entering. Bree gazes up at Vicki, whose eyes are bursting with madness. Her face is pale, near bloodless. She's gone somewhere else, lost in a haze of mania.

I put the odds of Bree being shot at around 50/50 at best. Not because Vicki wouldn't dare pull the trigger, but because her hand trembles so violently that hitting any target, even one at close range, would be a challenge.

Unsteady or not, Vicki is still a viper, a dangerous animal wielding a lethal weapon. She needs to be disarmed. But how? Bree's eyes dart around for some escape, but always return to the gun pointed directly at her.

Hopefully, being down on her knees sends a clear message to Vicki: *Please don't shoot!* I think about rushing in, diving at Vicki's legs, but probably would get a bullet in my back for the effort.

I can't believe both Faith and Iris are down, bleeding out on the floor. Hard to say if either is still alive, but neither is moving. It's insane what happened in one brief, dark moment.

She shot her sisters.

Something shifts in Vicki. Her gaze bores into Bree. Her jaw is set tight, her eyes narrow. Her finger twitches on the trigger, but she doesn't pull it.

Behind Bree, Faith moans in agony, expelling a wheezing cough that draws Vicki's attention. I have to look. I see blood dripping out of Faith's lipstick-stained mouth. There's also movement from Iris, who grabs her left arm, groaning as she curls into a fetal position.

"Oh my god," Vicki says. She turns to face her sisters, Bree temporarily forgotten.

This is my chance.

I ready myself to dive at Vicki's legs. Who knows? Maybe I'll get lucky and survive. Either way, I'll go down fighting. But before I can launch into a suicide scramble, a flash of movement comes at Vicki from my right side.

Quinn, who had gotten off the couch without me realizing it, barrels out of nowhere, propelling himself over the tea table, and tackling his mother in one swift movement.

As they both tumble to the ground, Vicki's head connects hard with the edge of the table. I hear the sickening *thwack*. She releases the gun on impact. It slides across the floor, landing just out of Bree's reach.

Bree dives for it, seizing hold of the weapon before righting herself with a grunt of effort, standing tall.

"Quinn! Oh my god, are you all right?" Bree says, scanning casualties in the alcove: three sisters on the floor, two bleeding and in evident pain. Quinn is also down on his stomach, half on top of his mom, Vicki, who holds a hand to her right temple, whimpering.

Quinn presses himself up awkwardly, staggering to his feet, swaying side to side.

"Yeah, no, I, uh . . ." He can barely get out the words. "I think I'm gonna be sick." He sprints past me into the Great Room, moving like an off-kilter jackrabbit, slamming his shin against one of the armchairs in his mad rush to the bathroom.

I scamper to Bree's side, sizing her up and down for injuries, before turning my attention to the Bishop sisters.

"We need to help them. What are we going to do?" My anguished voice tears through the room.

Dropping to my knees, I assess Faith and Iris first. The smell of blood mixed with gunpowder is a blend I won't soon forget. I've never seen a person shot before. An ominous dark stain spreads out from Faith's abdomen. As for Iris, the wound to her arm appears less grievous, but if the bullet struck an artery, her time could be pretty short.

"They're losing a lot of blood," I say in a panic. "We've got to do something." As I look around, something in my mind clicks into place. I rise quickly, rushing to the bank of windows, where I untether a tassel tieback from one of the curtains. I'm not much with knots, but I use the tieback to create a makeshift tourniquet around Iris's left arm. Almost immediately, the bleeding slows.

Faith's wound is internal, so I can't do the same for her.

"We need bandages and antiseptic at least—the bare minimum, and then we've got to get an ambulance here," I say to Bree.

Though I might not have formal medical training, I still have common sense.

During my brief exam, Vicki manages to get off the floor enough to prop herself up against a chair. She's hurt, lacking the strength to make it up to the seat. Groaning, she rocks back and forth on the floor as if that might end her misery. She could be severely concussed, but I don't see other signs of major trauma.

Quinn returns to the alcove, his skin pale, looking clammy and sweaty. He immediately goes to Iris, gripping her hand and touching her forehead before checking her pulse like he knows what he is doing. "It's going to be okay, Aunt Iris," he says, then catches himself. "I mean, Mom . . . we'll get help here soon." Looking at me, his expression deeply grateful, he adds, "The tourniquet was clever."

"I've been shot," Iris wheezes in disbelief.

"Don't talk," Quinn says. "Save your strength."

Vicki removes her hand from her head, her mouth falling open as if readying to speak, but Bree is quick with the gun, flashing it in front of her face.

"That advice also applies to you, *Ms.* Vicki," she says with contempt. "Not a word out of you. You've caused enough damage as it is."

A grief-stricken Quinn looks at his mother scornfully. "How could you?" he says. "They're your *sisters*. We're family."

Vicki stares into the barrel of the gun Bree holds inches from her face. She's a wise woman and doesn't say a word.

"I'll get the first-aid kit and some clean towels to try and slow the bleeding," I say. "Quinn, go get ice for Vicki's head. I'll be back in a minute."

Off I go, suspecting that a minute might be too long for Iris and Faith.

Chapter 51

I rush to the office, but when I get there, the first-aid kit is nowhere in sight. I'm looking all around, frantically ripping open drawers, knowing time is of the essence. Then I remember: Bree took it to her room when she changed her bandage. I make sure my key ring is in my pocket as I pass Quinn on my way to the staircase.

"I'll be right back with the ice," he says, looking seasick-green. "Are you okay?"

"Fine," I spit out. "I think the first-aid kit is upstairs. I'll be down in a second."

We don't linger. There's nothing between us other than our shared concern.

Up I go, racing to the Library Room as quickly as my feet can carry me. I unlock the door and step inside. Has it been only four days since I readied this room for Bree? It feels like a lifetime ago.

I don't allow my thoughts to drift. I'm on a mission. It doesn't take long to find the first-aid kit, which Bree left open on the bathroom counter. But as I'm about to leave, something else catches my eye.

Two suitcases on the floor next to the bed in a hotel room aren't wildly out of the ordinary. I should just vacate—nothing to see here. I need to get back downstairs with the first-aid kit and clean towels I grabbed from the bathroom. Yet I'm drawn back to those two suitcases. My subconscious is trying to tell me something. It's not odd that Bree is packed and ready to go; she was planning to change rooms. But something else is wrong. I can't seem to put my finger on it.

Then it hits me. The realization is so powerful it momentarily knocks me off balance. I know now why I was troubled when Quinn and I searched Black's room. *Two* suitcases and Black's leather work bag were in the closet. But when Black arrived at the hotel, I distinctly remember that she had only one suitcase with her—one, not two pieces of luggage. I remember it vividly because Rodrigo wouldn't carry the bag for her, and Vicki told me to let Black do it herself.

And now one of the pieces of luggage belonging to Black—the smaller of the pair, with the green tag that's helpful for identification on an airport carousel—is on the floor next to Bree's bag, the one she arrived with.

What is Black's luggage doing in Bree's room? Naturally, I can't let that question go unanswered. It's not like I haven't gone rifling through guests' personal belongings before, so I'm not even remotely troubled about it now, even if Bree is my friend.

Placing the suitcase on the bed, I undo the zipper to open the top. Inside, I find rumpled clothing, professional attire I'd seen Black wear. She'd done a hasty packing job, to say the least.

As I'm sifting through the clothing and undergarments, I hit something that feels out of place: rough fabric wrapped tightly around a hard smooth object. My hands brush over this mystery item, trying to make out what it could be, like I'm guessing a gift in Christmas wrapping.

I feel around for the edge, my fingers soon finding it. My heart races as I carefully remove the item from within. One of our hotel towels falls away, revealing what was concealed.

I'm looking at a rowboat, but I don't think it will stay afloat. The stern of the boat appears to be filling with water, pushing the bow upward, angling it toward a gray and gloomy sky. There's a patch of dark land in the background, but I see no people, animals, or life of any kind on it. This is one of the most lonely, bleak paintings I've ever seen, but it looks classic, a familiar rocky coastline that could be New England, even Maine. The overcast sky takes up two-thirds of the canvas. The choppy water is dark and ominous, with a few whitecaps touching the horizon. The rowboat's future may be questionable, as is my understanding of art, but I can almost feel the value.

I wish Quinn were here to give his opinion on what I suspect is the alleged priceless painting. He might only be minoring in art history, but I think he'd agree the quality is tangible. Even in this hotel, with its overabundance of artwork, I'd have stopped to look at this painting. But it never hung on any of the walls. Believe me, I've dusted them all. George must have hidden it away, and his attorney knew where to find it.

But how did Bree know it was in Black's suitcase, and why is that suitcase now in Bree's room?

This raises so many questions, but the most pressing question of all is: *Who the hell is Bree Bradford?*

Chapter 52

I sneak quietly back downstairs, stopping in the kitchen to procure a weapon, just in case. With a sharp knife in hand, I return to the Great Room, but I don't announce my presence. It's in my best interest to assess the situation from afar. I stand to one side, using the shadows to conceal me.

Quinn is tending to Iris and Faith, doing his best to keep them alive. The kitchen towel he's placed on Faith's wound is stained dark with blood. He double-checks the curtain-tie tourniquet that's likely keeping Iris conscious.

Vicki hasn't fully emerged from her stupor. She sits propped up against a chair, holding a bag of ice to her head. Despite all the commotion, Oliver is still nowhere to be found. One would have to be a supremely heavy sleeper to nap through this ordeal, so I suspect he must be hiding.

Was he really channeling the spirit realm? I can't believe how much the scene in front of me is actually "mirroring" the prophecy on the mirror. As things stand, Faith will probably die from the gunshot wound to her abdomen. Vicki will pay the price for her murder. And poor Iris, whose injury is not nearly as severe as Faith's, will be left alone to mourn all she has lost.

But it seems there's a missing part to the poem and prophecy, for which Bree must offer an explanation. I take a step forward but stop when Quinn speaks.

"Just relax and take it easy," he tells Faith, trying to get drops of water from a wet cloth into her mouth. "We're going to find a way to get you help."

Judging by the wind and rain, Larry is in no hurry to cooperate.

Quinn casts a panicked glance over to Bree. "We need to get to a neighbor or a phone quickly," he says. "There's a big tree blocking the driveway, so I'll have to walk."

"In this weather?" Bree sounds doubtful. "Not sure how far you'll get."

"Have you checked the cell service?" Quinn asks, alarm rising in his voice.

Bree pulls her phone from her back pocket. She's mostly been watching Vicki, who is slumped on the floor, too dazed and confused to pose even a modest threat. I watch as Bree checks for a signal. Quinn's hopeful expression falls when she shakes her head slowly.

"I'm going to have to risk it," he tells Bree. "I don't know how long Faith can hold on."

"What happened?" Faith's weak voice forces out the words. It's encouraging that she's coherent, but her chest rattles as she takes a shaky breath. Time is not on her side.

"Your sister double-crossed you both," Bree says, holding the gun and her attention on Vicki. "I guess she didn't want to share the fortune with her family after all." She makes a disapproving *tsk-tsk* sound. "Are these really all the sins you're supposed to confess: adoption, an affair, and some embezzlement? The poems suggest you three are hiding something bigger, a *shared* secret that must come to light." Bree crouches in front of Vicki, her eyes never leaving her face. "I think there's something else . . . something darker, something worth shooting your sisters over. It's now or never, Vicki." Bree uses the tip of the gun barrel to lift Vicki's chin ever so slightly, enough that their eyes are deadlocked. "Confess your sins."

And I take that as my cue to finally step out from the shadows. "Actually, Bree, I think it's time you told us *your* sins."

Bree whirls around, no doubt shocked to see me standing there, holding a knife against the canvas painting.

Chapter 53

Bree's slack-jawed expression lingers on the painting as Quinn springs to his feet.

He points to me. "Oh my god, is that—?"

"Yup, I think we've found our priceless work of art," I say, though my attention is fixed on Bree and the gun in her hand. Still leaning against a chair with an ice bag pressed to her head, Vicki winces as she tries to focus on what I'm holding.

I've positioned the knife to quickly puncture a hole in the rowboat and put an irreparable gash through the canvas. I'm confident Bree understands my intent. If I'm right, I'll be safe confronting her, at least for now.

"Where was it?" Quinn asks, stepping forward. He still doesn't realize that he's in grave danger. But I do. I just don't understand why.

"It was in attorney Brenda Black's suitcase," Bree answers for me, her tone bitter. She cranes her neck, assessing me, my knife, the whole situation.

Quinn looks to Bree, no doubt puzzled by it all. "How would you know that?" he asks, standing too close to Bree for his safety.

Boys. They're not the brightest.

I puff up, countering Bree's threatening stare with one of my own, despite the fact that I'm scared shitless. "She knows because Black's suitcase was in her room—next to her packed bag. You've got a lot of explaining to do, Bree."

Bree's face reddens. The mask of sisterly affection she's worn so convincingly washes away in one hateful glare. "What were you doing in my—" She stops mid-sentence. Her demeanor softens as some new revelation takes hold.

"Well, I'll be damned. Iris was right," Bree says, her voice filled with wonder. "Prison brain—I had fucking *prison brain*."

"What the hell are you talking about?" Quinn asks.

Feeling bolder, I take a few steps forward, being careful with the knife, which I continue to hold to the painting as though I've taken a live hostage.

"I forgot I had brought it to my room," Bree says. "So simple, yet so damn important."

"What did you bring to your room?" Quinn looks puzzled.

"The first-aid kit," I answer for Bree. "She forgot the kit was in her room when I told her I would get it."

"But what on earth made you look inside that suitcase?" Bree's dumbfounded, struggling to puzzle it out.

"When Quinn and I were searching for Black, we checked her room, and I saw *that* suitcase in her closet. It caught my attention, but at the time I couldn't figure out why. Then I saw the same bag with the green tag in your room, and that's when it hit me: Black had brought only one suitcase for a short stay. Now I think she packed that extra bag to take the painting out of here.

"It wasn't until I saw the suitcase in your room and recognized it that I realized something strange was going on. I had to look. And thank God I did. Apparently, you were ready to sneak out with it." I hoist the painting higher to draw attention to the treasured object. "What's the deal here, Bree? Did you kill Black to get this painting? Are you and Vicki working together? Is that why she shot Iris and Faith? Are you double-crossing everyone? Who are you, and what's this all about?"

I press the tip of the knife blade against the painted wood of the rowboat, careful (for now) not to poke a hole that would sink its value.

"She's not working with me, Charley," Vicki says as she removes the ice bag from her temple. "She's a monster." Vicki makes a staggering attempt to stand like a novice on ice skates.

Bree whirls around. "Sit your ass back down." The gun, an effective motivator, works like a charm, and down goes Vicki back on the floor.

"You're one to talk, Vicki. You shot your own sisters," I say.

A look of profound sadness washes over Vicki's face. She's utterly brokenhearted. Is she just feeling sorry for herself because her plan is now derailed? It's not lost on me that she's also concussed, confused, and dangerous.

"I . . . didn't shoot the gun," Vicki stammers. "It was so dark and disorienting, but I would know if I fired my weapon."

"You were holding the gun when the lights came on," I remind her. "I saw it in your hand."

Faith groans, drifting in and out of consciousness. Iris shifts her position to get more comfortable, releasing an agonized moan. Both have lost a lot of blood. We don't have time to sort this mess out—and we're all at Bree's mercy.

Vicki seems lost in her thoughts. I can almost hear the gears turning in her head before she blurts out, "The gun was fully loaded. Count the bullets. The magazine holds fifteen rounds. I fired twice at the router. If there are thirteen bullets left, then you'll know I didn't shoot anybody."

Quinn advances, his hand outstretched. "Let me count," he says to Bree, who twitches like a cornered animal.

Instead of complying, she switches targets from Vicki to Quinn.

I gasp. Vicki shrieks. Quinn recoils.

"Whoa, whoa, whoa!" he exclaims, instinctively throwing his hands in front of his face as if that would somehow stop a bullet. "What's going on here?"

"Obviously, she doesn't want you looking at the clip," I say. "Probably because Vicki's right. But I don't get it. If the bullets are still there, who shot Iris and Faith?"

Bree turns to me, lifting her baggy blue sweatshirt to reveal the handle of a black metal gun tucked into the waistband of her stretchy pants.

"I did," she says with frightening nonchalance. She keeps the pistol pointed at Quinn, holding him at bay.

Two guns. Stupid me. I should have known.

"I'll shred this painting if you don't give us both weapons this instant," I say. Again, Quinn sends me a thankful look. "And Faith and Iris need medical attention, right away. Bree, this has to stop."

She mulls over my threat, unperturbed, then lets loose a crazed laugh, so chilling and unexpected that the force of it sends me scurrying backward.

"Has to stop?" Bree asks, incredulous. "I've planned half my life for this moment, so the last thing I'm going to do is stop. Sure, things haven't gone exactly how I envisioned," she admits. "But I'm so close to getting what I deserve, I can almost taste it."

"What are you talking about?" I ask. "What exactly is going on here? You didn't come to this hotel to run away from Jake, did you?"

Bree laughs again, twirling a strand of hair, trying to determine what to do next. Even though she's distracted, Quinn doesn't dare approach, and I don't blame him. As her face relaxes, I sense Bree has settled on some course of action. "The Jake I told you about doesn't exist. I invented all that. But there is a real Jake. He's the private investigator I hired to dig up all the details on the Bishops . . . and you, Charley. I had to know everything I could about all of you before I put my plan in motion."

I blink rapidly, trying to process those words. "The text messages? That bruise on your arm?"

"The texts I wrote myself—had them auto-sent from a different phone. And the bruise wasn't hard to self-inflict—a little bourbon and a few thwacks against a doorframe was all it took."

"Why?" My voice is brittle. I've never felt so shattered. This was purposeful and evil—deceit that I never could have imagined. I trusted her.

"Charley, I never meant to hurt you. In fact I still won't unless you back me into a corner. And if I were you, I'd be *extremely* careful with that painting. Depending on how this all goes down, it might just change your life."

"How what goes down?" I ask, totally overwhelmed.

Bree turns her attention back to Vicki. "Confess," she says, preacher-like. "I'm still waiting. The poems have been clear, but you've all danced around the real sin from your past. Time to fess up, Vicki. Confess yours, and I'll confess mine; then I'll leave you all be. Hopefully, we'll finish this quickly enough for Iris and Faith to survive."

"Oh my god, Bree, this isn't story time!" I practically scream. "We need medical help immediately."

"Sorry, Charley. My gun, my rules," Bree says. "I came here for accountability and justice, and I'm not leaving without it. It's in your hands now, Vicki. The faster you own up, the faster your sisters get help."

Vicki touches her forehead, defeated, the bag of ice at her feet. "You win," she says morosely. "I don't know why you care, but I know what sin you want me to confess. And yes, Charley, you're right. It is about Christine."

Without further prodding, Vicki launches into a story about the sisters' anger, hurt, and heartache over their father's infidelity and cruel treatment of their mother. She describes how George flaunted his affair with Christine, and the harm it did. Her tale turns darker when Vicki details how she, Iris, and Faith plotted to destroy Christine's car, a white Volkswagen GTI their father had gifted the young maid. Only what was meant to be petty revenge went horribly wrong as they miscalculated the car's speed, causing far more damage than expected, culminating in one, tragic fatality.

"I knew it. I just knew it!" The heat rises in my cheeks. "You were responsible for Christine's death."

"Not exactly," Bree cuts in. "Do you want to explain it, Vicki, or should I?"

Vicki stays silent, her nostrils flaring.

"What does that mean—*not exactly?*" asks Quinn, his face screwed up in confusion.

Bree reflects for a moment before responding. "I suppose it's my story to tell," she says without urgency while two people are bleeding out on the floor. Quinn haplessly continues to apply first aid, changing blood-soaked bandages and adjusting the tourniquet around Iris's arm, but it's of little use.

Bree gives the injured pair nothing more than a cursory glance as she paces in front of Vicki, gun in hand, flaunting her control. She seems to take pleasure in their suffering.

"This is all still about Christine, Charley," Bree confirms. "Just not in the way that you think."

The confusion on my face must say it all.

"Allow me to explain," Bree says.

Part 4

THE SISTER'S SECRET

Chapter 54

Twenty-two years ago

"It's all right, Mommy . . . I'm here, Mommy." Bree stretches her tiny arm across the starched hospital sheets to take hold of her mother's frail hand. Her mother's skin, once so warm and comforting, feels as brittle as a winter leaf. She doesn't like how her veins stick out. Many are covered by adhesive tape that holds the plastic tubes in place, delivering medicine from the IV drips. But not one of these drugs, and there are many, is working. It's not like when Bree had fevers that her mother could reduce with Tylenol. The doctors can do nothing for her now but help manage the pain.

Even though they can't save her mother's life, Bree can do her part and be there for the bedside goodbye. She is committed to being the last thing her mother sees before she's gone. It must be her angelic face, the eyes of love, that fade from view until her mother sees no more. She's alone in the hospital because there's nobody else in her life. She has no grandparents, no aunts, uncles, or cousins who can support her. Her mother is her world, and her whole world is dying.

Dark circles of pain ring her mother's beautiful blue eyes. Her skin clings to her bones. And Bree, who used to think that only magicians could make people disappear, now sees it happening far from any stage. She turns her head to hide her tears, wiping them away as discreetly as possible. She has to be strong and brave so her mother will have less to worry about, but it's a hard job, and each day it gets a little harder.

She hates how this place smells. It confuses her that so many powerful cleaners can't mask the odor of sickness and disease. People here treat her like a child because she is one, but she knows more about her mother's illness than the doctors and nurses give her credit for.

Her cervical cancer is from the HPV virus, which her mother contracted from Bree's birth father. This is Bree's early understanding of the birds and the bees: sex can create life and destroy it. Her birth father wasn't devoted to her mother. He slept with many women, and that's how he passed the deadly virus to Bree's mother, who will take it to her grave. Bree tamps down the molten pool of anger that always bubbles up when she thinks of him, her birth father, he-who-shall-not-be-named.

Her emotions calm when she looks at her mother. "Mommy, can you hear me?" Bree asks.

Her mother doesn't have the strength to talk, but there's a slight uptick in her mouth, a little hint of a smile. That's the extent of her language now. A flow of love rushes from Bree's heart, filling her whole body with warmth. She squeezes her mother's hand a little tighter.

"I love you so much," Bree says, her voice breaking.

She can't pretend it doesn't hurt, just as she can't pretend she isn't scared about what will happen next. Who will take care of her? She's never had a father. She was supposed to have a stepfather, the man who planned to marry her mother and make Bree his daughter. But life isn't always fair. In fact, sometimes it's downright cruel.

Her mother's lips look bloodless and chapped. She needs an ice chip, but there's none in the cup. Bree knows how to find the ice machine for the same reason she knows the names of every nurse and doctor on this floor. This has been her home for the last two weeks. Her place in the world is by her mother's side. Bree makes a quick dash down the hall, not even stopping to thank the kind nurse who had brought in a portable speaker so her mother could enjoy some music.

She returns to her mother's bedside with a cup full of ice, but something is wrong. Her mother's expression hasn't changed, not even a little. She still has that faint hint of a smile. "Mommy, can you hear me? Are you awake?" *Please . . . please . . .* Bree begs, her stomach sinking. But she knows . . . she knows.

Bree takes her mother's limp hand in hers. It feels cold to the touch. The doctors have explained that her mother could stop breathing at any moment. But they didn't explain how much this would hurt. It feels like all her mother's pain has somehow jumped from her lifeless body and burrowed inside Bree. Her one and only job was to make sure the last thing her mother saw was her face, a face of pure love. But what did she see instead? A tiled ceiling and recessed fluorescent lights. Now, when she needs those tears, they won't come.

Bree is eight years old and she's just learned that some pain stays inside forever, with no way to let it out.

Chapter 55

Bree directs her grief and rage at the man responsible for her mother's death. Her hatred fertilizes a poisoned seed inside her until it sprouts roots that grow deep into her core. She carries this inner tempest with her from foster home to foster home, using it to defend herself against people who should never be trusted as caretakers. It's no wonder she earns all the bad labels: difficult, troubled, oppositional, and so on.

The social workers warn Bree that she's making adoption an unlikely prospect; she needs to change her behavior and attitude if she wants a forever home. But her pain is fused into her bones, running like a river through her blood, making her too angry to care.

Eventually the state finds someone willing to take her in, a stern middle-aged man along with his subservient wife. The couple spouts bullshit lines about wanting to give back to the community when all they're after is money from the state.

The man is warned about Bree, but he assures those in charge that he's up to the challenge. There are visits, of course—social workers aplenty come to check on the problem child in her new environment.

A model citizen, the man tells them during one such visit with a smile plastered on his smarmy face, gripping Bree's arm as a warning to be agreeable. *Such a joy. We're so blessed.*

They've told her to wear long-sleeved shirts to hide the bruises for these surprise popovers, though most of her wounds are on the inside, hidden scars of her torment at the hands of her foster father.

She barely does her schoolwork. Fear, hopelessness, and helplessness are her *real* education.

One night, Bree wakes up in a completely dark place—as in can't-see-a-hand-in-front-of-her-face kind of dark. Some places, like her mother's hospital room, she can identify by smell alone. This is one such place. The damp mildew stink of the basement is unmistakable. It shrouds her like a suffocating blanket drawn over her head.

She's not restrained, but it doesn't matter. There's no way out of here. There are no windows, and the only door is at the top of the stairs. She's gone through this routine enough times to know the door is locked without checking.

Bree hears footsteps overhead. He's up there, walking around in his heavy boots. A sharp pain radiates from her left side, a reminder of the swift kick he delivered to her ribs before dragging her down the stairs.

He threw her to the basement floor with force, then stomped on her back once more for good measure, before storming away. She heard the door close and the unmistakable click of a lock engaging.

All this because of a stupid Diet Coke.

Her crime? She'd taken the beverage out of the fridge without asking. That's a big no-no around here. She knew it, too. Rules were rules; that's what he always said. But being aware of the risk did not make her immune to temptation. At the time, the desire for immediate gratification overtook her better judgment. Nobody had fed her dinner that night. That was nothing new. With her stomach rumbling, she snuck downstairs after everyone had gone to bed to get something to eat. There was no food in the fridge, but then she saw it—a shiny silver can with red lettering, just begging for her to drink it.

The next day, she figured it was over and done with, that she'd gotten away with it. But he came into her room after lights out. Gripping her arm hard, he turned on a bedside lamp, blinding her briefly. She cried out in pain. How could she not? She was only ten. Her arm bones were saplings in his bruising grasp.

He leaned down, putting his mouth near her face. His breath smelled like gasoline. His eyes were red as a rat's. She hated him. If she had a word for something stronger than hate, she'd use it, but her vocabulary wasn't advanced, so *hate* would have to do.

"Did you drink my Diet Coke?" he seethed, practically growling.

She didn't answer him. She knew better.

He dragged her out of bed. Bree stole a glance down the hall. She always hoped her foster mother would save her, but she never did. The door to their bedroom was closed. She was probably in there right now, listening to Bree beg for mercy.

He brought her to the fridge.

"Open it," he commanded.

Bree did as she was told.

"Look inside," he said.

A shiver rippled through her.

"Do you see what's missing? You know the rules. You're supposed to ask. You don't touch my things without asking."

He threw her against a wall, and she fell to the floor. She knew what was coming, but that didn't lessen the pain. His swift kick to the ribs was just hard enough to bruise without sending her to the ER.

"Ungrateful little bitch," he rumbled. "We don't have to feed you at all. We could let you starve, and this is how you repay our kindness?"

Another kick, this one a bit harder. He hoisted her off the ground.

"Down you go," he said. "Another night in the basement for you. Maybe this time you'll learn your lesson."

And down she went into the black.

As the years wear on, she thinks of dying almost as much as she does of running away. She's long given up dreaming of a kind, loving family like all children deserve. She hasn't dared hope for one, not since the fairy tales her mother shared about her one true love, the man she *almost* married. He would have been her adoptive father, someone who would have cared for them both. But Bree's life wasn't destined for a happily ever after.

Each day brings a new test of survival; her life has come down to simply making it through another day and hoping, somehow, she'll gain her freedom. In the cracks of time when she's not suffering, her hatred grows and grows, like a different type of cancer spreading, blackening her heart.

It's no surprise that a desire for revenge takes hold, one so powerful it consumes her, a fire burning within. She swears he'll pay the price for her misery—not her foster father. No, he's just a symptom of her disease. The object of her scorn is the *cause* of all her suffering. That's who must pay: the man who killed her mother. And that's just the start.

She's fourteen now. Her mission is clear, the outcome all but decided. The how, when, and where remains to be determined.

At sixteen, she is old, wise, and strong enough to finally run away from foster care. She becomes a statistic. Half a million children go missing each year, but almost all are found. She is the exception. She looks older than her age. She uses this to her advantage to manipulate men into giving her what she needs.

Life isn't easy, that's for sure, but she's proud of her shrewdness: how much she's done and how far she's come. She's like the wind. Men try to hold her, but she always slips through their fingers onto the next, careful not to get too close. She only wants to hurt the people who hurt her.

She discovers her trade—bartending—before she's legally allowed to drink. By that point, the state has stopped looking for her. Alive or dead, she doesn't matter to them now. The years pass in a hazy delirium of late nights, youthful antics, and regrets. She may have lost herself along the way, but she has never forgotten her purpose.

He *will* pay. They will *all* pay.

She has just enough knowledge of her past to locate her target. However, this isn't a straightforward hit; she needs to gather as much information as possible to carefully plan her next steps. Deciding to hire a private investigator is the moment her scheme solidifies. She pieces everything together: His name is George Bishop, he owns a business called the Precipice Hotel, and her mother, Christine, worked there as a maid. She even finds an article about the accident.

She's methodical in her preparations, ensuring she has everything in order. When the time is right, she takes the next big step.

She emails him, presenting herself as a salesperson for a whiskey that she hopes he'll carry at his hotel. She includes a picture of herself holding the bottle with enough cleavage to ensure that she gets an in-person meeting—somewhere private, as she suggests in her message to him.

"George, it's nice to meet you," she says when he greets her at the door to his home in Jonesport. She flashes him a dazzling smile. He thinks he's getting more than a sales pitch, and in a way, he's right.

She takes her time with her prey but doesn't lie about her identity. She drops the salesperson charade quickly and presents herself factually as his offspring. She provides the evidence to prove it, too. Producing her birth certificate, which shows her mother's name and her year of birth, is not sufficiently convincing for George. As such, he agrees to take a paternity test, which they purchase at Walmart for a hundred fifty dollars. As expected, the results confirm a match. It's a little unsettling how easy it is to present herself as the smiling and sweet prodigal daughter when she knows what she's come here to do. But she's convinced herself she's not a psychopath. If anyone else had endured her loss and suffering, they'd understand her decision.

She and George quickly form a bond. To her amazement, he takes pride in fathering her—actual *pride*. Guess he loves the idea of more of his genes out in the world, no matter how that came to be.

She gets to know him over the course of several weeks. He thinks she's being personable, when in reality she's grooming him—gaining his trust. During their conversations, he makes it known how much he values loyalty. It's *everything* to him, he says. She's unsure why he's telling her this but gets the answer soon enough when he presents her with his last will and testament.

He always knew he had a daughter because her mother told him that much. She wasn't kind about it, either. No, she wanted to rub the revelation in his face.

You'll never see her. You'll never meet her. She'll be mine alone.

Her mother knew this would enrage him. He presents this fact like he's the victim, but Bree knows he's a controlling monster and nothing more.

It must have driven him mad to think of a daughter living in this world without knowing her all-powerful father. She almost laughs. Hubris. Pride. How quickly and effortlessly she wins his trust because, in her eyes, he sees only reflections of himself. *Look at me shining through in this other being! My beautiful daughter!*

Her story of hardship and suffering doesn't matter to him, so his death won't matter to her. The whole wretched family will pay a heavy price for her misery.

His chest inflates with self-importance when he shows her the will. He's unsure how long he'll live—he has heart troubles. His last heart attack was what inspired him to draft it. Not one will, but two—a secret will, this one just for her. She's in there, he insists, his unnamed daughter. All that's required to claim her inheritance is genetic proof that she is his biological child.

And what's in this secret second will that's exclusively for her?

An item purchased at an estate sale for twenty-five dollars, that's what. Twenty-five measly dollars—that's her cut of his life. There are some stipulations, he points out. She must not reveal her identity to her siblings. He doesn't want them to know about his dirty little secret—the child he conceived with one of his *very* young employees. But in his mind, fair is fair, and blood is blood, so Bree is entitled to a share of his estate.

This secret inheritance changes her plan, but only a little. It actually makes it sweeter . . . better.

As he sips his tea, he reiterates how deeply he values loyalty. He warns that the will can be changed at any time if she goes public. He mentions explicitly one daughter of his, a model, who years ago turned her back on him. She's paying a hefty price for that betrayal. He chuckles as if the joke is on her.

She smiles at him from across the table when he clutches his chest. She knows what's coming, even if he's just started to suspect the worst. She sips from her tea, which is different from his. His tea is loaded with belladonna . . . also known as deadly nightshade.

He seems dazed and feverish. His pupils grow large. She can almost smell his fear. It won't be long now. His heart rate is rising along with his blood pressure.

"You had all the power over her and you abused your position to get what you wanted. But you can't just go around screwing everything in a tight little skirt and not care about the consequences—or do you not know how HPV spreads?" she tells him as he gurgles. "But maybe I wouldn't have been born. Honestly, for you, that would have been for the best."

He makes one last sputtering gasp before face-planting on the table. She cleans up the mess. Removes the evidence. Then she's gone. There's no changing the will now.

She knows the value of the twenty-five-dollar purchase he left to her. Andrew Wyeth was one of the greatest artists of the twentieth century, working predominantly in the regionalist style. His painting of a rowboat, hers now, is worth about two million dollars at auction—or a quarter of George Bishop's entire net worth.

But she's not done. Not yet.

She has another score to settle.

George killed her mother, Christine, a maid at his hotel, with his careless disregard for her health. But his daughters killed the man who had vowed to wed her mother and raise the girl growing in her belly as his own.

This young man gave Christine a ring, while down on one knee at the edge of Gull Hill as the ocean churned below, and the sunset bathed them in a warm evening light. Christine wore the ring only in his presence. It had to be kept secret. Who knew what jealous, vengeful George might do if he found out about them? They both worked at the hotel, saving money as best they could while planning their escape. Christine found the strength to push back on George's sexual advances, but she wasn't a fool. She took the car. Of course she took it. That was how they were going to get away.

Samuel, the handsome son of Olga, the cook, did everything for his love, including picking up dinner one evening when she was forced to work late—retribution from George's bitter wife, who blamed

Christine for her husband's abhorrent behavior. Samuel took the new GTI down the long, winding road from the Precipice, eager to return to his beloved Christine. He revved the engine, angry at George, angry at George's wife, pressing harder on the gas.

They had big plans. A happy ending that would never be. Samuel never made it back with dinner that night. He never made it back at all. A horrible crash ended his life. A collision that was orchestrated, calculated, and left poor Christine alone, heartbroken, months away from giving birth to a daughter, and years away from developing cancer from the virus George had given her.

But now Bree is at the Precipice Hotel, ready to settle a long-simmering score with her three sisters.

Chapter 56

'm shocked beyond measure, but also deeply saddened. My friend is far more depraved than I could have imagined.

Bree pulls her gaze away from Vicki, redirecting it onto me.

"You're a Bishop," I whisper in disbelief. Pointing with the knife, I gesture to Faith and Iris. "These are your sisters. You shot your sisters."

Bree nods. "My mother told me it wasn't an accident—she knew it but could never prove it. After it happened, she ran for her life fearing she would be next, not knowing she'd already been given a death sentence. Whenever we talked of Samuel, her one true love, she told me three siblings who used to torment her at work were responsible for the tragedy. Years later, when I identified George Bishop as my father, it was easy to figure out exactly who those girls were. My darling sisters," Bree says with a twisted grin. "If they didn't kill Samuel, he would have been my father. No foster homes. No abuse. I would have had a *good* life . . . but these three took all that away, caused Olga unimaginable heartache, and what price did they pay? None. None at all."

"You fucking bitch," Vicki hisses. "You killed our father."

"Yeah, and he killed my mother," Bree counters. "And the three of you destroyed my future. So I'm calling it even."

I think back to the poems, all the references to sisters and sisterly bonds that convinced me either Faith, Iris, or Vicki had to be the author. Now I know it was Bree all along. *She is a Bishop. She's one of them.*

Faith moans from the back of the alcove.

Quinn passes me a look of alarm. "We can't let her die like this!"

Her breathing sounds labored. Even from across the room, I can hear strangled exhales, a gurgling in her chest.

"Look, this isn't how I planned it. It was supposed to be much cleaner." Bree shrugs. "I'd use belladonna to kill Vicki and frame Iris, who's an easy target given her prison record. And Faith would be the lonely sister left behind. But once Hope killed Todd, I decided to improvise, starting with the first poem. Credit to Ollie for the inspiration." Her satisfied smile shows just how impressed Bree is with herself.

"I was sure Todd was poisoned," she said. "I saw what that looks like with George, and it was similar. I figured Vicki did him in because I'd heard those two fighting, and *it's always the spouse*. I'd have killed him, too, if he were my husband. Either way, even with all my preparation and research on this screwed-up family, I didn't figure Peace Out Hope was a killer.

"After Todd died, I simply reworked my plan. Vicki would go down for his murder. Then I had to decide if I'd take out Iris or Faith and pin that on Vicki as well. That's why I encouraged you to search her room, Charley, because I knew you'd find the belladonna that I planted there. I didn't warn you in time that Vicki was coming because I *wanted* her to catch you. Then, it would be out in the open. She'd be rattled, and it would start to create suspicion that would pit my sisters against one another. But I didn't expect her to go rogue. Once again, I adjusted my plan to get my confessions, get my revenge, get my painting, and get the fuck out of here."

Bree points to the painting in my hand. "Nobody else has to die, Charley," she says.

I don't like the icy detachment in her voice.

"Look, there's a way to call 911 without Wi-Fi. Give me the painting, and I'll tell you how to do it. That painting belongs to me. It's in the will. You can look at it if you want. I have a copy in my suitcase. Attorney Black had a copy as well. That's how she knew about it, knew where George kept it, and why she was trying to get out of here so quickly. I realized that early on and, in the blackout, whisked her off to my room at gunpoint. When I had the chance, I—well, let's just say, I got her out of the way."

"Got her out of the way how?" I ask.

"Thanks to you flipping the breaker, I was confident that the alarm wouldn't go off when I used the fire exit to go outside for an evening stroll along the cliff's edge. And in case you're wondering, I asked you to pull the fire alarm for two reasons, not just to distract Vicki."

I want to be fierce and defiant, but my practical side is speaking loudly. Faith is in dire need of medical attention; Iris, too. What do I care about Bree and her money? Lives are at stake.

"I give you this, and you'll go?" I say.

Bree nods.

"Okay. But first, tell us how to call 911."

Bree ponders silently before shaking her head decisively.

"You hand over the painting, *then* I'll tell you how to do it. I've taken care of you, Charley. You don't know it, but I have. I promise. You'll know what I mean when the time is right. Hell, you're the only friend I really have."

"Do it," Vicki orders. "Just give it to her."

Quinn looks pained. He knows the value of what I'm holding, but he also knows life has no price tag.

I can't drag this out. Both Faith and Iris are losing too much blood. I approach Bree and carefully set the painting on the floor beside her.

"Now tell us," I say. "How do we call for help?"

Bree doesn't answer right away. "Get me a plastic bag and some tape. Hurry."

I don't delay. I'm in the kitchen, grabbing the supplies as quickly as possible. My mind flashes momentarily to Olga and her loss. So much grief and sorrow. I run back to the alcove, hoping with all my heart that I can prevent more suffering.

"Wrap it," Bree orders, unwilling to take her eyes off Vicki even for a moment. I do as I'm told, abandoning my instinct as a maid to make things neat and tidy.

In no time, Bree has the package securely tucked under her arm, now protected from the elements. Outside, it sounds like hell and fury, but Bree is determined to go. She pushes past me in a rush to the exit.

"How do we call for help?" Vicki pleads.

Bree pauses, sending her a wistful, almost apologetic smile. "You wait until you get cell service, then dial 911."

Vicki seethes, her nostrils flaring. She bolts to her feet and takes a single step in Bree's direction, but the gun holds her back. "You lied," she rails. "You murdering bitch!"

"No, I promised to give you a way to call 911 without Wi-Fi, and promise kept." She points to Faith, groaning on the floor in delirium. "And that's another promise kept. One of *us* *will* lose her life. Looks like Faith drew the short straw. Goodbye, sister." Bree whirls to leave but stops to look at me. "And I'm sorry about all this, Charley. I never meant to hurt you."

With those parting words, Bree snatches a rain slicker drying on a coat rack in the foyer, and she's out the door in a flash.

Before I can catch my breath, a blur of motion rushes past me. It takes a moment to realize that the blur is Quinn.

"What are you doing?" I cry out as he speeds by.

"That painting is ours," he shouts back. "I'm not letting her get away with it."

I lunge for him, but he's too damn quick. My fingers only brush the fabric of his shirt.

Vicki moves for the door, anguish in her face. "Quinn, no!" she cries.

But he doesn't stop. He keeps on going.

And me, stupid me . . . I go chasing after him.

Chapter 57

B ree is walloped from behind so hard she thinks a falling tree has struck her. She'd been making her way quickly along the curved walkway en route to the parking lot, intending to hike the winding road to her car tucked away at the bottom of the hill, when something knocks her off the path into the muddy grass.

Breath flies out of her in a rush. Bree lands hard on the wet ground, cold mud coating her face like an oil slick, seeping into her ears, nose, and mouth as she tries to suck air into her lungs. Vicki's gun tumbles from her grasp on impact, blending into the darkness, vanishing from her view. The painting slips from her other hand and, like Bree, lands in a muddy pool of water. Thankfully, Charley's handiwork will protect the valuable piece of art.

Buckets of rain dump over her. The trumpeting winds feel powerful enough to lift her off the ground, but something, or rather *someone*, holds her down.

Whoever had bowled her over is pressing the side of her face deeper into the mud, making breathing nearly impossible. She hears a voice—a man's voice, definitely not Oliver's, so it must be Quinn's.

Bree thrusts her hips, using all her strength in a futile effort to dislodge him, but no luck. He's too strong and weighs too much.

Pain stabs her thigh. It takes a moment to realize that her second gun, the one secured in the waistband of her pants, is digging painfully into her flesh. No matter how she twists and turns, Bree can't squirm out from under Quinn. Exquisite pressure builds against her ribs.

Despite her evident disadvantage, Bree knows she won't go down this way. She's invested far too much time, effort, and energy to allow anyone to undo a lifetime of work.

Quinn rises, straddling her hips, perhaps maneuvering to get his hands on her shoulders to hold her down more firmly. As he does, Bree tries rolling to slide out from under him, but his legs hold her like a vise.

Deep breaths . . . don't panic, Bree tells herself.

What she needs is her gun. As she wriggles to break free, Bree digs her foot into the soft earth, using the added leverage to lift the right side of her body ever so slightly off the ground, creating just enough space for her fingers to grip the weapon's handle. Then she lets her body go slack, still as the dead. Cold rainwater seeps into her mouth, but she dares not cough.

The instant she relaxes, Quinn loosens his hold. He's not a killer . . . perhaps he's worried she's drowning in the mud.

Bree doesn't hesitate. She uses this moment to throw an elbow, striking the soft part of Quinn's abdomen. He grunts in pain, crumpling in on himself. When his hands reflexively go to his belly to guard against another blow, Bree throws one more elbow jab, this one connecting hard with his shoulder.

Quinn tumbles sideways, falling to his left. Unfortunately for Bree, his landing spot puts him closer to the painting. She scrambles forward on her hands and knees, still clutching the gun, desperate to beat him to the prize. The fingers of her left hand claw into the damp earth, both feet sliding behind her as she fights for traction, pushing against the force of the wind.

Charging forward, Quinn makes it a race. He stretches out his arm like a baseball player going for the steal. His fingers brush the frame of the painting at the exact moment Bree dives for his feet. Her cold hand and his sodden jeans make it impossible to get a good hold. A quick twist of his ankle is all Quinn needs to break free.

Youthful agility helps Quinn as he staggers to standing with the painting clutched securely in his hands. Bree, looking like a savage beast—her hair tangled, face mud-streaked—lunges at him again, but he's too fast.

A bullet would be quicker, she thinks.

As he darts away, Bree clambers to her feet, breathing hard, the wind plastering the rain slicker to her chest. Floodlights offer only spotty illumination.

In the rain and dark, Quinn can't see that he's run right through the broken section of fencing abutting Gull Hill. Another few steps and he'd have gone straight over, but he skids to a stop just before he'd have made a fatal plunge.

Now he has no place to go.

Bree approaches slowly, moving in an arc. The gun in her outstretched arm divides the rain that splatters against the black steel barrel.

"You can't go anywhere," she yells, her words disappearing into the storm. The ground shakes, and Bree is aware of soggy, wet footsteps running in her direction.

"No! Put the gun down!" screams Charley.

Pivoting, Bree adjusts position until her gun is aimed at the one person she's sworn not to harm.

"Get back, Charley!" Bree yells, rain beading off her nose, filling her open mouth. "This isn't your fight."

Charley emerges from the gloom, a sodden waif with medusa hair and the look of a warrior. She advances as if Bree were unarmed. "It's not yours, either, Bree. Quinn did nothing to you . . . just let him go. Leave us and go."

"Not without my painting," Bree says.

"With this?" Quinn hoists the painting over his head. The wind nearly turns it into a kite, but he tightens his grip. "I'll toss it over the cliff if you don't leave!" he screams. "This belongs to my family or to no one. I mean it. I'm not fucking around. You go—or this goes."

Bree faces off with Quinn, not liking how close she is to the edge, but she isn't about to let her prize vanish into the sea. Charley stands off to the side, forming a triangle that takes Bree's attention away from Quinn, if only briefly.

"Put the painting on the ground and back off," Bree demands.

Quinn doesn't budge.

Does he think she's bluffing? Does he think this is a game? *This guy has a lot to lose and no way to win.* That should make him cooperate, but he's as stubborn as he is foolish.

"I'm not joking, Quinn," Bree says.

Even in the pouring rain and dim light, Bree can see Charley approaching in her peripheral vision. She spins around, using the gun to halt the advance.

"No!" she shrieks before turning back to Quinn. "I'm counting down from five."

Bree knows he hears her. She widens her stance to better brace against the winds. Her body shakes from cold and adrenaline, but her commitment remains steadfast. Quinn will die. He is a Bishop—guilt by association.

Good enough.

"When I get to one, I'll shoot. Put the painting on the ground . . . five."

"Back off!" Quinn yells.

"Four," Bree says. Her heart rate redlines.

Charley must see the determination in her eyes. "Do it, Quinn. Put it down. It's not worth it." The winds turn her scream into a whisper.

"Three."

"You'll get nothing," Quinn yells back. His face is a knot of rage.

"Two!" Bree lifts the gun an inch higher, her aim dead-on.

"No!" screams Charley. She breaks into a run, coming after Bree with quick strides, but there isn't enough time to cover the distance.

"One." Bree pulls the trigger.

Even a hurricane can't swallow the sound of a gunshot.

Chapter 58

Something streaks out of the darkness an instant before I see the gunshot flash. It's like a meteor flying through the night sky. The outdoor floodlights illuminate this mystery object ever so slightly. As Bree fires her weapon, her head snaps back strangely. Her body bows like the branches of the battered trees.

When the gun goes off, there's a sound like thunder. Everything slows down. It's as if I can see each raindrop as it falls. Bree and Quinn's bodies are shadows against a canvas of black. I take it all in— the streaking object cutting sideways through the rain and wind, the gun, Bree, Quinn, the flash, the thunder, all of it.

I have no idea where the bullet Bree fires lands as she staggers backward. With each step, it's uncertain if she'll remain upright. All this occurs in a second or two, stretching out into infinity, a timeless sequence that will stay with me forever.

I'm expecting Quinn to collapse to the ground, mortally wounded. I imagine the painting dropping with him, but he stands tall. Bree's shot miraculously went off target as she lost balance. She clutches her head, dropping the gun in a daze as she stumbles closer to the cliff's edge. But why? What happened to her?

It's then I see something my brain can't quite process. Rodrigo steps out from the shadows. His presence is so unexpected I don't recognize him at first. Despite the poor lighting, I see his face is bruised and bloodied. His clothes are soaked, covered in filth, as though he's been crawling through mud. He's standing behind Quinn, not looking at me, focused on Bree as he holds his arm cocked, readying to throw.

He propels himself forward in a perfect pitcher's motion. He opens his hand. I realize now what struck Bree. A rock the size of a fist careens through the air, riding on a wind current that dramatically increases its velocity. Bree's chaotic movements make her an impossible target, but it doesn't matter that Rodrigo's second throw misses the mark. His first effort has already saved Quinn's life.

But who will save Bree's? She's about to tumble over the cliff. I sprint after her, using the soggy terrain like a springboard to propel myself forward. My mind races to calculate the distance, anxiety mounting as I sense I won't reach her in time. So I dive, skidding across the wet ground, my arms fully extended.

Bree, off-kilter, finally loses her balance. One foot remains on the ground, while the other goes over the cliff. She falls onto her stomach, fingers clawing at the earth in a futile effort to halt her slide. At the last conceivable moment, she latches onto a thorny bush growing near the edge, but the branches snap under her weight and momentum.

That second or two proves significant. It buys me just enough time to seize hold of Bree's right hand an instant before she goes over. Her skin is cold, and the dampness makes it hard to get a firm grip. Fear stretches Bree's eyes wide. Almost instantly, a searing pain tears through my shoulder as it strains against her weight.

Her body is more than halfway over the cliff, gravity working against us. Bree drags me across the slick grass as she descends. If I don't let go, both of us will tumble down. But I can't bring myself to loosen my hold. My lungs are filling with water. Bree's fingers are burrowing into my skin, desperately trying to hold on. I'm still sliding forward, and Bree is about to take me with her.

I plant my toes into the ground, but the tips of my shoes merely scrape away the grass. I'm only a few feet from the precipice. There's no stopping us now. A scream surges in my throat as dirt splatters into my eyes. With each heaving breath, I try to fuel my muscles, but it's useless. For every inch I glide over the ground, Bree sinks that much lower.

Rodrigo and Quinn are both too far away to help.

Let go! screams a voice in my head. *Just let go!*

But I won't do it. The echoes of my mother's passing still haunt my dreams. I can't endure another untimely death.

My resolve firm, I thrust my leg sideways and, by the grace of God, it snags the base of a nearby thorny bush like the one Bree had used to arrest her slide. We're suspended for a moment. I can see Bree's face, and she can see mine. My foothold on the bush bramble is tenuous at best. Bree senses us slipping. She knows what's coming next. Sorrow floods her eyes. My chest wants to explode from the strain.

Let go! Let go! screams that voice, but I only tighten my grip. My foot, however, slips another inch. One more like that, and we'll both be done for.

Suddenly Bree's expression softens. A peaceful acceptance replaces her terror.

"Charley . . . I'm sorry for everything," she shouts. "Be good to yourself." She releases her grasp, her hand becoming limp in mine.

I can't hold on. A second later, the fire in my shoulder goes out. The strain on my arm is no more. My forward momentum comes to an abrupt halt. I hear nothing but the wind, waves, and rain. There's no scream, no cry for help. I scramble to the cliff's edge, daring to look, clutching the ground to keep from being blown over. I peer into the gloom, but all I see is darkness below.

No rocks. No water. No Bree.

Chapter 59

Rodrigo and Quinn rush over as I get to my knees. Each holds one of my arms, helping me to my feet. I sink into Rodrigo's embrace. The wind threatens to push us to our graves, so we back away from the drop-off, lowering our heads to shield our eyes from the pelting rain. We take shelter under the overhang of the gazebo.

"Your face," I say to Rodrigo, seeing up close that it's covered in bruises and cuts. "What happened to you?"

"I got into a car accident leaving here," he says. "I rolled over just down the road, and my door got pressed up against a tree. I was knocked out for a while, I don't even know how long. When I came to, I realized the electrical system fritzed out, and I couldn't unlock the doors or open the windows—and I had no cell service either. I was literally trapped inside my own goddamn car!"

I wonder if the crash occurred near the same spot where Samuel had lost his life, but now isn't the time to get Rodrigo up to speed.

"How did you get out?" Quinn asks.

"I was completely out of it, just dozing off and on . . . I probably have a concussion. Then around hour eight, I was like, 'Oh shit, *nobody* is coming.' I managed to pull the back seats down. Crawled into the trunk, found a tire iron, and used that to smash a window. Looks like my timing was good. I got back here just in time to save your ass. I saw Bree with a gun, ready to fire . . . so I picked up a rock and threw it as hard as I could."

"Who knew you getting bullied as a kid would one day save Quinn's life?" I say with amazement.

Quinn looks at me, confused, but Rodrigo explains.

"I was picked on a lot growing up, so I took out my frustrations by throwing rocks at glass bottles. I got so good at it I became a star pitcher on my school's baseball team."

"Lucky strike for me," says Quinn, astonished. He's still holding the painting. "Now she's gone, and good riddance."

But I don't feel that way. I know she's done terrible, unforgivable things. She betrayed my trust and murdered two people—maybe more, if Faith succumbs to her injuries. But still, my heart has a place for Bree, compassion that won't fade no matter what she's done.

Rodrigo knows nothing about what's happened here, and there's no time to explain.

"Listen, Faith and Iris are both shot. They're inside," I say. "We've got to get them help, but we don't have working cell phones."

As I make this announcement, I'm stunned to see strobe lights illuminating our parking lot with bursts of blue and red. Rodrigo, Quinn, and I run toward the lights and come upon a sea of emergency vehicles—police, fire trucks, ambulances, and pickups from the locals who volunteer as emergency responders. Somehow they've already moved the fallen tree blocking the driveway. I have no idea who called 911 or how, but I've never been more grateful to see the cops.

I dash over to a nearby paramedic, telling him where to find Faith and Iris. One EMT stays behind to look Rodrigo over while the other three follow Quinn and me into the hotel. I'm an absolute disaster. The mud is drying on my skin. My hair is layered with what feels like clay, and my whole body stings from at least a hundred scrapes and bruises.

But it's Faith and Iris I'm most worried about. It's a whirlwind inside as police and firefighters storm the hotel. They've come from multiple counties because Jonesport has a small emergency response team. Either way, these are clearly professionals.

In no time, Faith and Iris are being whisked away on gurneys. I get a thumbs-up from the EMTs working on Iris, a good sign that she'll survive, but there's no reassurance from the woman wheeling Faith out of the hotel. Vicki's off in a corner, talking with Quinn and

Officer Dan Brennan, the bearded cop who came to the hotel after Todd died. Was that just last night? Hard to wrap my mind around it all. No doubt, these have been the craziest two days of my life.

Before I get a chance to tell Officer Brennan about Bree, I feel a tap on my shoulder. Turning, I face Oliver. I'm happy to see him, just to know he's all right.

His pleading eyes break my heart. I may have siphoned some of his premonition talents, for I correctly guess what he's come to ask.

"Are you going to tell them what my mom did?" he wants to know.

"Your mom? You mean Hope?" I say, brushing muddy hair away from my face, dripping water all over George's expensive carpet. But what do I care? I'm not the maid anymore.

Oliver nods. "She's not a bad person."

He's a tall, gangly teen, a bit of an oddball who talks in rhyme, but all I see now is a hurt and vulnerable kid. "Sometimes good people make bad choices. They get lost along the way." I'm thinking about my mother. And Bree. "But, Ollie, it's important that we tell the truth. We have to."

He nods, though it's difficult to gauge how much he truly understands. I'm curious about something, though, so I ask Oliver because he's been inside the entire time. "Do you know who called for help? My phone still doesn't have service."

Oliver points to himself.

"Your phone works?" I recheck mine. Even though it's wet, it works, but without cell service.

Oliver says, "I looked around the office for keys to let my mom out of your room, but I couldn't find them. But I did find an old router in the back of a cabinet. It took a bit, but I got it up and running. Then I connected my phone to the Wi-Fi and used that to make the call."

In a rush of gratitude I pull Oliver into a big hug. The poor thing goes completely rigid, like I'm the first person to hug him besides his moms. We break apart, and there's an awkward moment that I end with another question. "Did you *see* any of this, Oliver?"

He shakes his head. "No. I was hiding. We're taught in school to hide when we see or hear a gun."

My heart snaps for all he's gone through. Poor kid—all kids, in a way, I suppose. But that's not the question I was asking. "No, did you *see* it," I repeat. "In your mind—you know, your gift. Did it show you what was going to happen?"

Oliver looks momentarily baffled before breaking into a slight grin. "Oh, that . . . you mean my *psychic powers*?" He pauses and looks around. "I don't have supernatural abilities, Charley. And I didn't write that lipstick poem prophecy, either. I just saw the door to Aunt Iris's room was open, so I went in looking for her, and she showed up while I was holding the lipstick tube. I had just picked it up off the floor."

"Yeah, I know you didn't write it," I say. "Bree did. But how did you know all the things your mom mentioned—about your grandmother dying and the tarot cards, all that?"

He smiles at me as though the answer should be obvious. "I've never talked to a spirit," he says. "I'm just quiet and overhear it."

Despite all the messed-up shit that's gone down, I somehow find a fraction of a smile. "You little bastard," I say. "You're just playing everyone? You're nothing but a wicked good eavesdropper, is that it?"

He shrugs, but I can tell he's proud of himself. "Nobody ever really notices me, so I just sort of hang around—and, well, people aren't very careful with their words. They like to talk, and I like to listen."

My slip of a smile widens into a full grin, remembering all the times he seemed to appear out of nowhere. "Yeah, I get that. But what about the tarot? That felt pretty authentic."

He shrugs again. "Maybe some sixth sense was at work, because those cards were weirdly accurate. It freaked me out a little, to be honest, but I swear to you, I just picked them randomly. I don't have any special talent. I just play along because it makes my mom happy. I do it for her." As he says this, all the weight and worry return to his eyes.

"It'll be okay, Ollie," I assure him. "Different, but okay."

"Yeah." He stuffs his hands into his pants pockets and takes a step back. "I guess I should find out how my mom's doing. The medic said she'd be okay, but I'm worried."

I put my hand on his bony shoulder before he gets too far away.

"She's going to be fine." I offer this assessment with confidence I've no business projecting.

He turns to go, but I call for him. He glances back at me, sadness lingering.

"I see you," I say to him. "You're a great kid, Oliver, a bit different, but great. If you ever need anything—"

He interrupts. "Yeah, I know where to find you."

He trudges off, and I work my way over to Vicki and Officer Brennan. Quinn's gone off, maybe to look after Ollie, so we talk for a time, the three of us. I tell them everything that happened outside. Even with the thick beard covering much of his face, I can see Brennan's gone pale. Two bodies lie at the base of Gull Hill, assuming the sea hasn't taken them both.

"Serves her right, that wretched woman," Vicki says, not a whiff of empathy to be found.

"Your sister?" I say.

"Oh, whatever." Vicki brushes me off. "My whole family is a nightmare. Why should she be any different? But Bree—if that's even her real name—got what she deserved. And as for you, Charley, I don't know where we left off. I fired you, hired you, fired you again—but if you want to stay here, you've got a lifetime job. You helped save our lives. Okay, you harbored the woman who wanted to kill us, but I think you more than made up for it."

Brennan sends a team of police to search Bree's room and another to organize what I suspect is a recovery mission to retrieve the two bodies from the base of Gull Hill. Hope is no longer in my bedroom. The police have her in handcuffs, sitting in the alcove. Quinn has whisked Oliver off to the kitchen so he doesn't have to see his mother taken into custody. I get permission to bring Hope some tea, which she accepts, awkwardly holding the mug in her manacled hands. A cop hovers nearby, making sure everything is okay.

Hope is surprisingly upbeat. "Thanks for this, Charley," she says. "How's my Ollie doing?"

Better than Faith, I think, but I don't want to be the one to tell her that her wife's been shot. "Oliver's fine," I say. "He's worried about you, is all."

"I'll be fine," Hope says. "Everyone has to face the consequences of their actions. I'm no exception. I don't expect the average person to understand what I did. But I'm not worried. This life is just a phase in a much grander plan. Whatever the law decides, I know my soul will eventually face the cosmic jury, and there, I'm confident I'll be cleared of all charges."

Before I can suggest that Hope might have a few bats flying around in her belfry—something my nana was fond of saying—I hear someone call my name.

"Charley?"

I stand up, nervous.

Officer Brennan approaches hesitantly. He's holding an envelope in his gloved hands.

"Yeah? What's up?" I ask with trepidation.

"We found a letter addressed to you in Bree's suitcase. I have permission to open it here, and I want you with us when you read it."

A letter? From Bree? A note from the grave. I'm thinking about what she promised, how she told me she had taken care of me. *Does this letter explain what she meant?* I follow Officer Brennan out of the room, knowing only one thing for certain: this family isn't done dishing out surprises.

Dear Charley,

If you're reading this letter, it means things didn't go according to plan. But I've done my best to seek justice. Either the police found this note or my lawyer managed to get it to you. It doesn't matter, because if it's in your hands, it means I probably didn't make it. And that's okay. I'm not like Hope. I don't think I'm in a better place. I think I'm just not here anymore.

But you still are, and you have a lot of life to live. I don't have anybody, Charley. You're the closest thing to a sister I've ever had, and I barely know you. I don't want you to struggle like I did, so I'm leaving you, as my parting gift from this world, something that will change your life. I knew the moment I asked you to take me in that I was putting you in danger of losing your job and perhaps even more. I decided to set up an insurance policy of sorts. In the event of my death, my attorney will get in touch with you to make it official, but here goes:

   This letter serves as my last will and testament. I, Bree Ashley Griffin (that's my legal name), do hereby bequeath to Charley Kelley, one painting by Andrew Wyeth, purchased with a receipt at an estate sale from a willing seller who clearly didn't know the value of what she had in her possession, which was later willed to me by George Bishop.

   It is now yours, Charley. Sell it. Start a new life. Do some good in this world. Hell knows it sure could use it.

   And Charley, there's something else. Everything that happened at the Precipice took tremendous preparation and research, including research on you. You need to know something important about Janice and Guiding Way—the place where your nana lives. On the back page of this letter is a detailed report on my findings. I'm sorry to be the bearer of bad news, but I trust you'll know what to do. The money from the painting should help.

Your friend forever,

Bree

Epilogue

The Calm

Monday after the storm

I enter Janice's office, not bothering with a courtesy knock. I don't know if my calm exterior is a self-defense mechanism or self-delusion, but whatever is keeping me from falling apart, I'm grateful for the help. Confrontation isn't my strong suit, but this is something I have to do for myself.

Janice looks up from her desk when I enter. Her face brightens with a big toothy smile that I'd love to wipe away with my knuckles, but I won't resort to physical violence. She steps out from behind her desk, revealing a flowing ankle-length hippie-like skirt that I could imagine Hope wearing. But clothes don't make the person—actions do; I know this now. I know all about Janice's actions and the impact they've had on me, thanks to Bree's phony boyfriend, Jake, the private investigator. It was Jake, working at Bree's request, who found out everything he could about the people in my life, including Janice.

"Charley—Charley!" Janice exclaims, sounding all worried.

I let her pull me into a hug, but I keep my arms dangling limply at my sides. We break apart, but Janice continues holding on to my shoulders. She's yet to notice the folder I hold in my right hand. I brought it for her, and it's hers to keep. I have a copy in my room at the hotel, and Officer Dan Brennan also has one.

"I've been calling and calling," Janice says, her voice still alarmed. "I've been worried sick about you. Are you okay? I even sent Steve to the hotel to check on you."

I know Janice sent her husband over, but I had Rodrigo run interference. I wasn't ready to see him or Janice until I could understand what Jake uncovered. Now that I do, I'm all revved up and raring to go.

I toss the folder onto her desk. It lands with a thump.

Turns out, Jake is good at his job and he dug up a lot of dirt on Janice and Guiding Way. Apparently, she and Steve are already on the FBI's radar. He couldn't get all the details, but he found out enough to know an arrest was coming soon, so I'm not blowing up an investigation. Jake was kind enough to email me his findings, and his report was lengthy.

My eyes are dark and gloomy, in contrast to the bright blue skies now that Larry has passed. On my way here, I even saw a deer nibbling on the sedge grass. From the outside, it appears everything is back to normal—but it's not normal, not by a long shot.

Janice turns around. "What's going on? What's this?" she asks, pointing to the folder on her desk.

"Nana's entire bill is covered by Medicaid," I tell her. "All the money I give you—all the rent increases you keep tacking on—that's bonus money for you, Janice. That's money that goes right into your personal bank account."

She is about to go into denial mode—I can tell by the look of horror on her face, and her head bobbing side to side as if to say no—but I hold up my hand to stop her.

"And that's just part of your scam," I say. "But it's the part that's hurt me the most. However, as you'll see in that folder, there's an investigation into you because you're also billing for services and supplies you don't provide. It's all detailed in the report I just provided."

Janice looks at me the way one might at a ghost, with utter disbelief. When she finally moves again, she opens the folder and starts perusing the pages, carefully examining the contents.

I take grim satisfaction watching the color drain from her face.

"Feel free to toss the pages into the trash, burn them, whatever you like," I say. "The FBI is on top of it, and now the local police also have a copy. I'm sure they're eager to talk with you."

I've never seen someone grovel with their eyes, but there's a first for everything.

"Charley, please—please," Janice says, gripping my arm tightly. "You don't understand—we couldn't make the business work. We did all this for the greater good. You *must* believe me . . . without us, there'd be no place for these people to go. We had to stay open, for their sake."

Her act is so good she almost convinces me she's telling the truth. But Jake made it clear: The stolen money wasn't being put back into the business.

"Tell that to the police, Janice," I say. "I'm going to go visit my nana."

Some things change—like my opinion of Janice and Steve—but some, like the potpourri and musty magazine smell of Nana's apartment, don't. And this visit won't change anything, either. As always, I will leave here brokenhearted, but that doesn't stop me from coming.

No surprise, I find Nana sitting in her favorite blue recliner by the window. She puts down her knitting when she sees me enter. I pull over a chair so I can be close to her. She has no idea what's happened to me, no clue that I almost died. She doesn't know anything about the events at the Precipice; she doesn't even know who I am. But I know her, and I am so unbelievably happy to see her that my eyes instantly mist over.

"It's finally stopped raining," she says. Her voice is so soft and fragile that each word feels precious to me. I've no idea who she thinks I am right now—the help, for sure, but I could be any number of people who work here. Eventually, though, I'll become my mother, and at some point, she'll ask me if I'm going to the bowling alley tonight.

"The storm was really scary," I say. "I'm glad you're okay." I take hold of her hand. Her skin is rough and dry, covered in age spots, and the bones are brittle and worn. Yet her strength flows into me. Waves of memories surge through my body like an electric current.

The storms of my life have come and gone, but Nana's love has never wavered, not for a minute.

"It was so frightening here." She says it as if the anxiety from the hurricane still lingers. "And I was so worried about you, Charley."

"No, Nana," I respond like a reflex. "It's me . . . it's Char—"

And then I catch myself before I can finish saying my name. I'm leaning forward in my chair, thinking I must have misheard her. "You know me?" I ask, bewildered, holding her gaze. Her eyes are the clearest I've ever seen, like two pristine pools of water that appear bottomless.

"Of course, Charley," she says, squeezing my hand tightly. "You're my sweet granddaughter."

My throat instantly closes up. Tears blur my vision. My heart is soaring now like it's caught a breeze. I cup Nana's hand in mine. I can't look away from her. I'm scared to speak, don't even want to blink, because I don't want to do or say anything that might break this spell.

"You know me," I say again, amazed. "You know my name."

"Yes, Charley. Of course I do."

Somehow I manage to get out the words obscured by a sob. "I miss you, Nana," I say. My voice is so shaky from the rush of emotion. It's no use; I can't keep the tears from falling. Nana pulls a hand free and, with her delicate fingers, gently wipes them off my cheeks.

"There, there, sweetheart," she says, peering at me with such tenderness that it's almost too much to bear. "It's okay. I'm here . . . I'm well. And it's so good to see you. Thank you for coming to check on me. I appreciate it. And tell me, how's your job? I worry about you, you know, living at that big hotel all by yourself. And you look thin. Are you eating enough?"

I laugh as I swallow another sob. Of course she's worried about my health and weight. That's Nana for you. She's always wanted to feed me. But how does she remember where I work? I've talked about the Precipice plenty of times, but I didn't think she took any of it in. Where did this recollection come from? I don't linger on the thought. I can't waste a single second of this. I don't know how much time we'll have together.

For a moment, though, I've lost my voice . . . my words . . . my way.

I'm completely disoriented, yet I've never felt more grounded and present. This moment feels like my first breath of air, or maybe my last. I didn't know how much I needed this: to be seen, heard, and remembered. With everything that's happened, I've forgotten what matters most. There's nothing like a warm embrace, a gentle touch, and caring words. But remembering my name? How can something so simple mean absolutely everything to me?

"How did you manage in the storm?" Nana asks. "It was the worst I can remember. They had us huddled in the cafeteria for a time. Was the hotel damaged?"

I won't tell her about Bree or the Bishops because that would only add to her stress. I won't say anything about Janice, either, though another pang of worry hits me hard. At least Officer Brennan assured me nobody living here would be left homeless, Nana included. But still, there are so many unknowns.

"The hotel is fine," I say. "Rodrigo and I made sure to board up the windows."

She looks at me like a proud parent. "You're very responsible," she declares, pulling her lip tight, and I think she's on the verge of crying now, too. Her eyes glisten with moisture, but no tears fall. She knows that our time is short.

"I'm so proud of you, Charley," she tells me in a whisper, as if her feelings have overwhelmed her. "I don't say that enough. You haven't had it easy, but you always pull through. You're a survivor, Charley. You've had a lot to deal with and at such a young age. And I feel I've let you down. I know I haven't been there for you like I should have . . . It's just been hard for me. But please, please know I love you so, so much, Charley. And I am deeply impressed by the person you've become." She closes her eyes tight, but tears leak out anyway.

I'm crying like a river, and I don't care. I'm holding Nana's hands, studying her face through my blurred vision, trying to memorize every wrinkle, the shape of her slender nose, the thin line of her lips, the delicate curve of her chin.

"You have nothing to apologize for," I reassure her, feeling rushed and pressured to say everything I need to tell her while I still have the chance. "Nobody has been there for me like you have . . . nobody. I couldn't have done this without you, Nana. You're all I have. I just need you to be okay."

"Oh, Charley," Nana says, brushing away my worry with the sweetness of her voice. "You're so much stronger than you know. And I will always, always be with you. Here." She reaches forward and touches my head with the tip of her finger. "And here." Now she touches my heart.

A sob bursts from my lips. My cheeks are hot from the outpouring of tears.

"I love you so much," I say, with a sputtering gasp.

"I love you, too, Charley," she tells me.

We lean into each other, falling into an embrace from our respective chairs. Her grip is firm as her hands gently caress my back.

But then she stops. Her hold lessens. For a moment, I won't let go, even though she's not exactly hugging me anymore. Eventually, we break apart. I'm watching her closely, forcing myself not to look away. And I see it happen. It's like a cloud moving across the moon, dampening its glow. Something crosses Nana's face, and little by little, I can almost see the awareness leaving her body. Her eyes, so clear and pure only moments ago, gloss over as if an opaque film has been pulled down in front of them, the color shifting from blue to gray. Her smile slips away like the last rays of summertime. I watch as her expression alters, her face strained from confusion, but just for a moment.

In a blink, she looks at me with love in her eyes again. But it's a different kind of love. The kind a mother has for a daughter who might not be eager to follow the rules of the house.

"Are you still going to the bowling alley tonight, Mary Beth?" she asks tenderly. "You know I expect you home before midnight."

I close my eyes, clench my jaw, trying not to fall apart. I manage, by God's grace, to find that hidden strength Nana insists I possess, and I hold it all together, despite feeling like a shattered shell.

"Yeah, I'm still going," I say as I take hold of her frail hands again. "But I promise, I promise, I'll be home on time."

"I'm counting on you, Mary Beth, to do the right thing here."

Nana pats my hand in appreciation. I flash on a memory of Bree, desperately clinging to my hand, before resigning herself to her fate, releasing her hold as she falls into the raging sea.

"I'll do my best," I say, trying not to let the waves of guilt crush me.

Ten months later

Sun streaks in through the sheer curtains of Nana's apartment. It's a hot July afternoon, but the air-conditioning makes the room where we're knitting feel cool and comfortable.

"Would you like some more iced tea, Nana?" I ask, rising from the couch.

"Thank you, Mary Beth. That would be nice, sweetheart."

She hasn't recognized me as Charley since that one time after the storm, but I don't let it bother me. Being together is what counts.

Rodrigo sets his knitting needles down on the coffee table. "I'll get it," he says. "This basket loop stitch has got *me* loopy. I need a break."

He heads off to the kitchenette before I get the chance, unable to stop working, even on his day off. He has a new job as the general manager of Guiding Way. Yeah, that's right. Rodrigo pretty much runs the place now.

As for Janice, she's somewhere awaiting a court appearance. After she was arrested, the Bishops stepped in to help. They bought Guiding Way, installing Rodrigo as the head honcho and his mother as director of community activities. No maid duty for her anymore.

He returns with the iced tea, which he places on the table before Nana, putting an arm around her. "Here you go, love," he says. "Extra sweet, just like you."

He goes back to his knitting. A moment later, he groans in frustration. "You're more annoying than Charley," he says to his loop stitch, and I burst out laughing.

"Well, you're more annoying than the Bumble profiles you keep sending me."

Nana reaches across the table and snatches the yarn out of Rodrigo's hands. "You're both annoying," she says sternly and starts fixing Rodrigo's mistakes.

"Those are fine men I'm sending your way," he tells me on the sly.

I send him a look of utter disbelief. "You mean Beer Belly Billy, who bragged about his day drinking? No thank you!"

Rodrigo's sneer is meant to be playful. "I know they aren't the same as Pretty Boy Quinn, whom you've been pining after, but the pickings are slimmer up here in Maine. What's the latest on Lover Boy, anyway?"

"We haven't texted in a couple of months," I tell him, wishing there wasn't a pang in my heart. "The long distance is just too much for me. Besides, I'm starting classes at the College of the Atlantic in a couple months. I'll be too busy to date."

"There's *always* time to date." Rodrigo winks at me, not letting it go. Now that he has a boyfriend, a cute paramedic who treated him on the scene that night at the Precipice, he suddenly has all the answers to my love life.

He can try all he wants, but my focus is elsewhere. If all goes according to plan, I'll be a social worker in four years, focusing on geriatrics. No more maid duty for me, either. Maybe I'll minor in library sciences because I'll never lose my love for books, but it's important for me to help people like my nana. Thanks to the Bishop sisters, my college tuition is fully paid for. The same goes for Nana's assisted living expenses.

Obviously, I couldn't accept the painting. It was never rightfully Bree's to give, not after murdering George Bishop. But the sisters felt indebted to me and have done a lot to set things right. They sold the painting at auction and used the money to buy Guiding Way and fund my college education. I've got a nice little nest egg, too. I'm renting a tiny house just outside town, four hundred fifty square feet that feels palatial after my oversize closet at the Precipice. I'll be all right.

Turns out, Vicki and her sisters aren't all bad. After their youthful crime came to light, the trio received nothing more than community service hours. They were so grateful that it opened hidden chambers in their hearts. They became far more generous with the community, and with me.

Involuntary manslaughter. It's a weighty charge. But the length of
time and the fact that they were all minors when it occurred helped
them receive a very light sentence. And let's be honest, their status in
the town didn't hurt. They have money to throw around, and they're
throwing it. It's dramatically changed the perception of the Bishops in
Jonesport, that's for sure.

My phone dings with a text message. I look. *Speak of the devil.*

"Are you the one who's psychic?" I tease Rodrigo with an Oliver
reference before showing him my phone and the text from Quinn:

Hey, wanna meet up?

His message makes my heart skip.
I quickly respond:

> Yeah, that would be nice,
> but you're kinda far away,
> remember?

Quinn:

I was far away. I decided to visit
the lovely town of Jonesport
again. I was hoping for a sunset
walk with a beautiful young
woman. Can you set me up?

He throws in a wink emoji for good measure. My hands suddenly
feel a little shaky.

Sunset can't come fast enough. We don't set a meeting place, but
I know exactly where he'll be. I see him standing at the edge of Gull
Hill, his handsome frame silhouetted by the fading light of the setting sun. Across the horizon, colorful bands of yellow, orange, and red
stretch out along a perfectly calm sea. It's as if Larry's wrath had never
been, as if no storms could form again under such perfect conditions.

As I get closer, he turns to me. His face breaks into a wide grin, golden light glistening off his tousled curls.

The look in his eyes captivates me. I try to speak, feeling awkward, but he wraps his arms around me in a big hug, banishing my discomfort.

"I've missed you," he whispers in my ear, pulling me in tighter.

"It's so good to see you," I say, and I mean it. His embrace is warm and inviting, like there's nowhere I'd rather be in the world. Rodrigo was right. As much as I've denied it, part of me has been waiting for Quinn, holding every online profile to an unattainable standard.

"I can't believe you're here," I say, gently pulling back, my hand resting for a moment on his chest. "I'm sorry I've been out of touch. After everything we went through, it was all too much to process. And it was hard to know that your life was somewhere else, not with me. I felt like I was staying close to someone who'd never really be here. I know that might sound silly . . ." I trail off, then continue in a lighter tone. "What's the latest with your family? I assume everyone is keeping it interesting."

Of the three surviving sisters, Faith's recovery has been the longest, but she's done remarkably well, even without Hope's herbal remedies.

Quinn places his hands on the repaired fence, leaning over it to peer down below. I don't join him. I can't bring myself to see the place where Bree fell to her death. I revisit that enough in my dreams. Catching the look in Quinn's eyes, I suspect he struggles with the same.

"Hope and Faith are getting a divorce," he tells me.

No shocker there. "Is she still in prison?"

"Yeah, we're not posting her bond. She's crazy. We're pretty much done with her. Oliver's working with a therapist these days. He's taking some space from Hope while he tries to process what happened. Probably for the best."

"How's that kid doing?" I ask.

"He's the same—rhyming, weird, love him. Glad I'm alive to be here for him, that's for sure. And I guess I'm still processing things myself. I never thought I'd have two moms telling me what to do with my life. But honestly, we're working it out. Iris and Vicki have patched things up, and I don't have it in me to stay angry at them both."

"Some people don't have parents at all," I say, hoping he doesn't think I'm making it about myself.

"Exactly," he responds, easing my worry. "I'm trying to focus on love and acceptance. I'm lucky to have a family that loves me, and I need to accept them for who they are, mistakes and all."

"Are you going to sing 'What the world needs now is love, sweet love'?" I ask, hoping my teasing comes across as caring.

"Nah, I have a philosophy degree, not one in musical theater. I'm going to pontificate without hurting your eardrums," he jokes back.

"Thanks for that," I say with a smile.

We move away from the fencing, slowly strolling the edge of the property, my mind flashing back on so many memories, all the events that transpired. A weight settles in my chest, a burrowing sadness knowing this moment with Quinn will be as fleeting as all the others.

"How long *are* you visiting for?" I dare to ask.

"Visiting?" Quinn replies, a sly smile playing on his lips. "I've finished school, and as expected, there aren't a lot of career opportunities for philosophers. So I figured I'd come back here and work for my family."

"Wait. What do you mean?" I ask.

Quinn stops walking. He stands tall and proud. "You're looking at the new general manager of the Precipice." His eyes light up as he takes hold of my hand. "We still haven't found a long-term replacement for Olga, so my first order of business is to hire a full-time cook."

"Don't look at me," I say with a laugh. "I burn everything, even eggs."

"Sort of had a different role in mind for you, something not work-related." His smile entices me. "Not to be presumptuous, but I was hoping you'd still want—how did you say it? For me to *really be here*."

For a moment, Quinn actually looks a little uncertain of himself. His eyes cast downward, awaiting my response.

I squeeze his hand a little tighter. "Are you asking me to delete my dating apps? That's a pretty tall order."

"I'm hopeful," he says, eyes brightening.

"I think I can make that happen." I give him a big smile that says it all.

He leans in to kiss me, sealing the deal.

Above us, seagulls glide on a steady summer breeze. Salt air bathes our bodies in its refreshing warmth. The ocean laps gently against the shore. For the first time, the future feels full of possibilities.

I can't wait to see what happens next.

Acknowledgments

Being a fiction writer means having the creative license to make up what you need. When you don't know something or need to tweak geographical details, you can invent as the story requires. After all, it is fiction. However, I pride myself on infusing my books with kernels of truth—insights into the human psyche to which we can all relate. To that end, I must clarify: the Precipice Hotel does not exist in Jonesport, Maine. Jonesport is real—you can find it on the map—but the hotel isn't there.

Similarly, while Gull Hill plays a pivotal role in the novel, it is partially invented. There is a real Gull Hill, but it is located in Provincetown, Massachusetts, not Maine. The fictitious Precipice Hotel is based on an actual hotel in Provincetown named Land's End. If you book a stay there, you'll recognize the aesthetics and some room names and understand the inspiration.

While the characters in the novel came from my imagination, there are real people I must thank for their invaluable contributions to this work. I'll start with the incredible team at St. Martin's Press: Jen, Brent, Erica, Katie, and Christina. Behind this formidable group are many others in advertising, sales, production, and art design. Thank you all for your combined efforts and talent.

I'm forever grateful to my agents, Meg and Rebecca, at the illustrious JRA for helping me navigate a career filled with more twists than any of my novels. To my support team at home: Judy, Sue, Benjamin, and Sophie—thank you for keeping me grounded.

Last, there is Kathleen, to whom I could dedicate every book. She has devoted her time and talent to making invaluable contributions to the plot and character development while assisting with editing, revisions, and more. She is truly my partner in crime.

And to whoever is reading this (and with a nod to Oliver): If you saw your family's foibles reflected in this story, take it with a grain of salt—it's just an allegory.

Yours in gratitude,

—Jamie Day

About the Author

JAMIE DAY lives in one of those picture-perfect, coastal New England towns you see in the movies. And just like the movies, Jamie has two children and an adorable dog to fawn over. When not writing or reading, Jamie enjoys yoga, the ocean, cooking, and long walks on the beach with the dog, or the kids, or sometimes both.